THE VEIL TRAP

Nanna Nuts, Mr Milly, Moggins and Me

By

S. J. Simpson

RAG TREE PRESS
ISBN-13: 978-1-5272-6192-1

To Dreams.

ACKNOWLEDGMENTS

To my family. To my wife Nic, thanks for the support and putting up with the hours of silence from the other end of the sofa.

Thanks Mum, Dad, Tim and Sarah, for their encouragement and support.

And thanks to anyone, especially Mr. Wright, who put up with my ramblings.

CHAPTER 1

Summer Calls

Five minutes, just five minutes to go. Then I'd be free for the summer; like racehorses in the starting stalls; loaded and ready to go. The end of the school term beckoned: but time dragged its heels.

I'm sure the teachers did it on purpose; drawing the tedious, of tediousness out. The bell almost audible before the current had travelled the cable's length. Toying with our over-eagerness, the last few ticks of the clock meandered; all eyes were on the black needle hands of our nine-till-three keeper. Then the tension broke, releasing us from its hold, ringing out louder than any other day of the year. The gates sprung open, and we were off!

Papers tossed into the air; chairs turned over, as a chorus of elated, giddy nonsense engulfed the corridors. Soon a tsunami of joy poured out of the school gates. My head, overrun with a ten-year-old boy's stuff. A flash of my coming summer hurtled across my mind's eye; climbing trees, sliding in mud, rope swings, hide and seek, bedroom dens, garage meetings, spooky stories, and no school! No school! Moggins! Mr Milly! And Nanna's! Summer stay.

Weeks of running wild and exploring were all I'd thought about for months. Pesky school would be long gone; locked away at the back of my mind. I'd better things to think about than algebra and punctuation. I was a champion daydreamer, the things I could conjure up in that 'thick head', as Mr Prompton would say. were 'quite astounding'.

I headed over to the bike shed, accompanied by my best pals Eddy Jugg and Jimmy Moller. We had almost made it to the school gates, ready to do the alternative school run one last time.

'Well, least we won't get called out on Monday,' said Jimmy.

'Nar, but I bet that old moaner Harding will try and dob us in,' added Eddy.

'Best make the most of those jumps then!' I replied, getting ready to push off just as a bellowing voice squashed the elated playground chatter.

'Nuts, Moller, Jugg.' Our expressions sullenly mirrored each other, as we turned slowly towards the source of our arrest.

The school's head, Mr Johnstick, stood hands on hips, his shadow stretching across the playground towards us. He was followed by his ferrety sidekick Ms Pew, or 'Ms Spew' as we'd say. Mr Johnstick was a large, tall man, his comb-over hair forever flopping into his eyes.

'Why the dickens doesn't he cut that lot off?' said Mollers under his breath.

'What's that, boy!' snapped the head, clearly out of earshot.

'I swear he can lip read!' whispered Jugg. Mr Johnstick strode over, while Ms Pew trotted to keep up.

'Something to say, Nuts?' he barked while holding out three envelopes. 'Take one each, make sure it gets to your parents,' he said, smirking, 'because, next year! You'll be in different classes... after this year's pitiful performance we've got to do something!' he added smugly. Ms Pew scrunched her face with delight.

'Really! That's so not fair! It's always us getting picked on!' I complained.

'Too much looking out the window! Too much chatting! And don't get me started on those tussles with the Bunch brothers!' he replied.

'But! But!' stuttered Jugg.

'No! No! No! If your parents disagree they can see me next term! Now push off! Oh... And have a wonderful summer, won't you?' said Johnstick sarcastically.

We all moaned under our breath, deflatedly crossing the invisible line of freedom that the rusted green gates represented.

'What a pile a' crap!' cursed Jimmy, his head and shoulders slumped over his BMX handlebars. But I wasn't going to let that crabby grump ruin my summer.

'Come on... Come on, lads! Stupid! Floppy! Haired! Plonker!' I shouted at the top of my voice. Both lads chuckled; big beaming smiles washed over their sullen brows.

'Yeah, sod him!' said Moller.

So we pedalled and pushed hard – skating and flying over the most extreme trail home we could find. We were wild and free, and our home town made a perfect playground for aspiring stunt riders. The old folks' bungalow complex was the best! Packed full of small steps and grassy humps, which on paper, sounds like an insurance claim waiting to happen, but great fun for us and a regular fixture on our trail home. Filling the air with wails and yelps of delight, we quickly shook the shadow Johnstick had cast upon us. Reaching Blunts Lane, Moller peeled off.

'Have a great summer. See you soon, Pete!' he shouted.

Jugg shot down the wooded pass onto Chaps Street.

'See you, mate! Have a good one!' he hollered, disappearing down the narrow passage.

Then it was just me. I scooted on home upon my trusty steed. The heavily modified two-wheeled ride was a terror to the old folks as it ran silent, and could easily catch them off guard as I carved on and off the pathway. I'd had a few good telling-offs about this, so tried to give them a wide berth, but today I'd thrown caution to the wind.

Darting underneath the crab apple trees, jumping off the kerb and onto the next, I'm sure a few shaken heads came my way, but I was so excited, I couldn't wait to get home and on my way to Nanna's.

For the last few years, I'd been packed off to stay with Nanna, who lived on the edge of a beautiful rugged moorland. I say 'packed off' in the nicest possible way, not to give the impression of neglect or unwantedness. The world being as busy as it is left my lovely parents without a moment to spare. They knew how much I loved to go, which made it easier. I constantly nagged about it; we always had such adventures up there. Mum and Dad would often be away working, doing their bit for the new age hippy movement, so it was the best option really.

Swinging hard on my right leg, I pushed on towards home. Usually, I'd find need to take a break by now, for the incline normally sapped my energy but not today. As I reached the top of our drive, I could see Dad's camper van. The tailgate was open, and he was pottering around looking bemused like he'd just placed something down and now couldn't find it. He turned and greeted me with a beaming smile. Taking one push, I glided down the drive straight into his arms. Dad rubbed the back of my head and gave me a bear-like cuddle.

'Good day?' he said.

'The best, well, apart from Christmas,' I replied.

'Good lad… Anything to show me? School phoned,' he said, ruffling my hair.

'Hhhmmmm yeah,' I said, handing him the envelope which he opened and quickly scanned over its contents. Dad let out a sigh.

'That Johnstick… Eeerr, well what can I say? Look, you're a good lad, I know… we know, just toe the line a little more, will you? It's just easier on everybody,' said Dad, his hands on my shoulders.

I nodded in response. My parents were the last people I'd want to let down.

'But eh, don't lose that spirit of yours, and your imagination is amazing. It's just a balance son… we will figure it out together. Now get your stuff sorted, Mum's packed all the essentials, just get the stuff you want to take,' said Dad.

I headed down the drive and round the back of the house, saying 'hi' to Mrs Summerdale as she quietly pruned her roses. She was one of the more normal neighbours and a fixture of our street for as long as I could remember. She'd always tell me how much I loved my red wellies when I was little, much like a grandparent would.

I did love my home. It wasn't big or grand or anything like that, but it was my sanctuary, where I was free to think and play how I liked, well, within reason. I did have to tone it down from time to time. I was out a lot, and if I wasn't skateboarding down the drive, sat in a cardboard box, I could be found playing 'Match of the Day' against our metal garage door, much to the annoyance of the peaceful street's inhabitants. I didn't mean to be irritating; I just got carried away, thank God my parents understood.

Our back garden was mostly paved except for a small lawn at the bottom; behind it stood a stone wall, the remnant of the farmer's field that used to occupy this area. You could see down the line of gardens at least three houses. The fences were pretty low, making rescue missions for wayward footballs a doddle. I'm sure Mum and Dad would much prefer me to knock on their doors, but I was usually in and out under cover of dusk.

The garage had a gap between itself and the neighbours. Often I had to squeeze in to retrieve a skyward punt. The entrance was hidden round the back of the pebble-dashed structure, and in summer the shrubs and bushes completely disguised the Gap. I didn't like going in there; I had to force myself, reluctantly pushing the foliage aside. Holding myself firm, I'd shuffle in.

At first, entering the Gap was scary. Cobwebs lined the wall, and God forbid I'd meet a wasp or daddy longlegs in such a confined space. With my arms pinned to my side, defending myself from such critters wasn't an option, as I was only able to move along the wall sideways. I've come out with many a graze from a panicked exit. Never after dusk would I venture in. It was way too creepy; my already overactive imagination needed no more help.

Mrs Monkwit was our other neighbour, nothing like the lovely serene Mrs Summerdale. Mrs Monkwit is totally batty, nice enough but batty. I'm sure she is building an army of crazed cockatiels. I've never seen a bunch of more berserk, unhinged, winged peckers.

Often, we'd have to venture into the aviary, when Mrs Monkwit was on holiday.

It was a frightening experience, flapping, crapping, birds, all around us; fingers hidden tight in a fist, just hoping to God they didn't see my nose as food. Dad got bitten by one once, sinking its razor-sharp beak into his thumb. 'You're a pretty one,' were the words Dad uttered, just before it attacked. It wouldn't let go either, and Dad furiously shook it trying to release the winged devil. Blood and feathers were everywhere.

Mrs Monkwit's battiness continues with the constant refusal to acknowledge that our dog, 'Milly', is female. This has become a running joke amongst us. Insisting on calling the beautiful, ever so female Milly 'boy, here boy, good boy', etc… Even though she is quite clearly missing some vital assets. Like she is clearly not a mister! Well, I found this rather funny and have been using Mr Milly ever since.

She is strong and calm; wolf-like in appearance but with these tufty, bushy back legs, that almost look like she has fur-rimmed boots on. Mr Milly had come from a rescue home; we couldn't believe somebody could let such a beautiful dog go. However, she found her way there, it was her way to us, and we loved her very much. A family's best friend, protector, and confidant; I could share all my worries with her; she would take my knots and unravel them without saying a word. Only with a look, that meant, 'I know, it's going to be OK.'

Mr Milly wasn't the only pet we had. There was Moggins, my pirate cat. If he could tell us a story, it would be of sailing the high seas; of battling huge monsters of the deep, all while hiding, a deep-seated aversion to any form of the blue stuff. With one ear bent down and the other slightly torn, he certainly looked the part. The truth is, his rugged look came mostly from run-ins with the crazed cockatiels next door. He might be a little responsible for the birds' behaviour, as he did get into the aviary once, which resulted in a timely pet shop visit to replenish the population. He is brave and stupid but always knows when I need some company, and regularly curls up beside me at bedtime.

Moggins, like most cats, always disliked trips, especially ones that involved being bundled into his mobile prison. But never when we were off to Nanna's. I always puzzled over this. How did Moggins know? This wouldn't end with a thermometer stuffed where things should solely exit from. He always strolled into his padded cell with an air of confidence when we were off to Nanna's.

For years my dad had worked as an engineer; he was a fountain of knowledge. Any homework about anything, he had an answer. With a bit of rummaging around in his head, he would always pull out a series of related facts. I was always astounded, just where did he keep these facts?

He is also extremely handy, constantly knackling and fixing, creating little oddities to make life easier. Dad is a great listener too, always available to soak up any worries I might have. He could be stern when I needed it, and I feared the 'have I got green in my eye?' question, for I didn't understand it. Whatever answer I gave was always the wrong one, I'd have to figure that one out. But all in all, he fills the role of father and dad admirably. I love his reasoning when Mum or I, or anyone really was het up; he would create this balanced view, giving it back to you in a way that made sense. I always came away feeling better about things.

Mum was Dad's rock. They were inseparable, standing together as two figures that cast only one shadow. Yes, they nagged and nibbled at each other, but their underlying bond was unbreakable. Soulmates, you might say. Mum is always smiling, always looking tip-top, even five minutes after getting up, lippy on, hair done, ready for the day. She is the mother bear that looks after us all; gentle and strong, silent and caring, always letting the other speak, ever having an ear for your problems and cuddles to soothe a worried mind or an aching heart.

Mum and Dad had set up their own business a few years ago. They ran classes and workshops for the hippy-dippy type. I didn't really get it, but it all sounded very good, and I was proud that they were helping people, although I didn't understand how. The downside was, this new business consumed a lot of their time. I'd often have to go along, waiting in the van or hanging around some village centre, or hotel conference room. I'd much prefer to be at home and playing. I could see why they were doing it, but sometimes I'd wish they had the normal nine-to-five thing, as most weekends and holidays were filled with it.

When they could, they'd take me to Nanna's, that's my favourite place to be, it's where my dad grew up, and I love it. It's a home from home, and I felt close to my parents there, even when they were away.

Mum called out from the back door, 'Petey!'

I followed her soft northern tones and was greeted by her staple beaming smile.

'School's out! You all ready for Nanna's?' she said, pulling me in for one of her magic cuddles while kissing the top of my head. 'Sort the stuff you want to take, we've packed all the essentials, just look out the fun stuff,' she said.

I squeezed her tight and ran upstairs to gather my supplies, mentally logging the items I'd most need.

My scooter, obviously, how else will I get about? And I've got to keep practising those tail whips.

My book of gruesome tales. I'd just started reading this, and I've got to say, it had captured my imagination a treat.

Bug catcher, BB gun and catapult, football and whistle rocket ball, eeeeerrrr what else? Oh yeah, my action figures. That should do it, I thought.

I also grabbed my blanket and Blue the teddy, hiding them at the bottom of my bag, feeling I was getting a tad old for them now. We all sat down and had a bite to eat before setting off. Dad liked to do this in an effort to miss the traffic, more times than not though, it was just as bad, much to his frustration.

Soon we were all loaded into Dad's beloved camper van; Moggins was in his cage on the far seat, and Mr Milly was next to me. The drive was around two hours to Nanna's. Suddenly I felt snoozy. Plumping my pillow against the window I watched the countryside pass by. Daydreaming of the adventures to come, I started to fall into one of those really annoying head-jerking car sleeps.

The radio faded, and the chat of my parents travelled further away. My eyelids brought down the curtain on the real world. After the initial darkness of sleep, I surfaced into a different world.

Awakening in bed, startled and panicked, *Blue!* I thought. *Where's Blue?*

I searched the bedroom with anxious desperation, but he couldn't be found. Suddenly a chill blew past my side and ruffled the curtains.

'Outside, look outside,' whispered a voice in my ear.

Creeping towards the BMX-patterned curtains, I paused and then flung them wide open, wincing, not daring to fully open my eyes. The garden was a patchwork of shadows, as the night sky lay a few shades off pitch black. Bright moonlight shone upon any reflective surface, allowing me to peer into the still of night.

Blue lay lifeless, face down on the lawn as if he had once possessed it. I couldn't leave him out there, all alone.

I must get him, I thought.

Just before I turned from the window, Blue was dragged behind the garage in a slow slithering motion.

'Blue!' I shouted.

Putting fear aside, I raced down the stairs, banging and bumping through the now seemingly booby-trapped house.

The back door was wide open, gently swaying as if recovering from a great force passing. Blue was nowhere to be seen. The overhanging trees created a mouth of tarish welcome, beckoning me to come forth.

'Closer,' the wind whispered.

I edged forward, scanning the surroundings, feeling danger could reveal itself at any moment. Making it to the end of the patio, I stood ready to look round the back of the garage.

Forcing myself, pushing fear to the back of my screaming emotions, I sucked in a deep breath and looked, only to see his legs disappearing through the muddy bushes, into the Gap. Blue had gone now, to the one place I really hated.

'In here,' the voice said, slyly leading me on.

I couldn't bear the thought of my Blue, being in there alone. Suddenly an unexpected emotion grew from within, rising from my core into my throat; anger overtook fear. Now I felt cross. I was brave and forcefully pushed the bushes back, entering the Gap. My jolt of bravery soon dipped, on realising I would have to go further to retrieve my friend.

With my arms pinned by my side, I shuffled in. Cobwebs brushed against my head; the stones of the garage wall rubbed and scratched my back, but I still edged my way to the now-abandoned Blue, laying at the end of the passage. Finally reaching him, I rolled his limp body up the pebble wall and managed to take a solid hold of him. My sense of relief was short-lived.

I could feel it; it was here! Behind me. The sound of bushes being moved aside ran a chill down my spine, as it made its entrance into the Gap. I had nowhere to go, nowhere to hide, and no way out! Still, it came.

What is it? What can I do? I thought.

Panicked, I called out, but only silence followed. I slowly turned my head toward the entrance of the Gap; it was there, lurking in the darkness before my eyes. I couldn't see it, but a deathly chill in the air preceded its arrival. Plucking up my courage, I called out, strained and desperate.

'What are you?! What do you want?!'

The air fell still, then a cold, callous voice hissed and teased, 'Darkness, your light.'

A hand reached in, ready to pull the prevailing horror through; mottled skin, dirty long pointed nails, red ivy veins curled round the arm, disappearing into the cave of a black sack sleeve. Panic had hold of me; a python of intoxicating fear was around my neck; at any moment, it could reveal itself fully. I stood pinned and motionless; waiting, watching, clinging on to Blue.

Now the tension neared explosive heights. Something, just something had to give. Then as if my prayers were answered, something did. I could hear a screeching car making its way up the street, its engine getting louder and louder, closer and closer. The hooded fiend now filled the Gap, both hands ready to pull itself in. I looked right and left, the revving engine growing ever louder. The grey mottled hands finally pulled its animator into view. I gasped, as a cruel deathly hood towered over me. Its jagged mouth salivating, and hypnotic eyes swirling round and round.

The fiend moved like it was half solid and half mist, not bound by form, only what it chose to be. I scrunched my eyes in shock, and tucked my head into my neck, awaiting the impending smothering attack. Just as it lurched forward and was practically upon me, the car screeched into view.

With a savage handbrake turn, the back end swung round. The car rocked to a stop at the top of the drive. The headlights flicked to full beam and shone through the Gap's boarded end, piercing the ghoul. It hissed backwards, the light now accompanied by the sound of the horn, long hard beeps, broke the trap's silence. They grew louder and louder, the headlights filling the night air. Everything now drifting away, becoming lighter, and the noise louder. With a jolt and a slip of my hand, my head jerked, and I was awake again.

The low afternoon sun streamed in through the van's window. Dad was pressing hard on the horn. We were stuck in a line of traffic; he was cursing the stupidity of the apparently 'blind' driver.

'Oh, back with us then?' said Mum, warmly.

I smiled and pulled my pillow back into place, tucked Blue into my stomach and pondered on the dream.

What would the ghoul have done? I wondered.

I often had dreams of the same kind, but the Gap had been a recent unwanted visitor to my after-dark escapades.

We made it to Nanna's village in just shy of two hours, still with ample daylight left. Dad always slowed down to a crawl through the village, as they both loved a nosey at any changes.

'Ooowwee, I don't like the look of that,' muttered Mum, as she pointed at the land for sale sign.

'Pub looks quiet,' commented Dad.

They always frowned upon any changes; suppose they just liked it the way it was, and I did too. Chattersley existed in its own little bubble of serenity. The days seemed longer, the sun shone brighter, and everyone, well, just seemed to smile more; if that's what living in the country did for you then sign me up.

Nanna lived just outside the village, on the edge of the moorland; it was a beautiful place, full of adventure and secrets. Rolling hills and valleys, hidden woods, rivers, and brooks. I was born here but moved away with my parents at an early age, it always felt like home, and I couldn't wait for my visits. I guess my roots run deep here. Mr Milly had perked up as if she knew we were close, and Moggins let out an annoyed, 'Mmmeeawww.'

I thought, *Bet that's cat for, 'I need a pee.'*

Dad turned left, off the main road and onto Smythe Lane.

CHAPTER 2

Ivy Gate

Nanna's cottage was nestled amongst her ever-increasing menagerie of trees, bushes, flowers and herbs. She was always growing something new while tending to her old friends. Bird tables, feeders and wind chimes adorned the driveway and gardens. The cottage had only one floor, well hidden behind her wall of greenery. It could hardly be seen from the lane, only a small entrance barely wide enough for a car was visible. An iron gate in need of a new latch swung gently back and forth, a faded wooden plaque announced 'Ivy Gate'. At the end of the drive sat a large garage full of old farming and gardening equipment, to the left was a field she rented from the neighbouring farm. Nanna grew strawberries, peas, potatoes and cabbages which I loved to help pick but not eat, well, except the red gems. She also had a chicken coop, home to Flashy the cockerel and his many lady friends.

Ivy Gate was joined to another cottage, the old major and his dog Maggot lived there. They kept each other company, the nearest house being Smythe Farm around half a mile down the lane. To the right of the drive was the kitchen entrance; a small window looked in over the sink. If she hadn't heard the car coming she'd be found pottering away singing to herself, usually covered in flour. But today as soon as the car's nose lined up the driveway she was there waving. Tea towel in hand: stolen away from her baking. Wearing her usual apron and a big beaming smile, glasses hung around her neck; a robin in her pocket, a mouse in her hair. Well, I made that last bit up, but that's how I saw my lovely nan, she was magic.

I squeezed out of the car, trying not to bump the door on the sidewall. Mr Milly was almost out before me, just as excited to be here. As I unbolted Moggins' cage, he burst out and disappeared into the nearest dark bush.

Greeted with big hugs and laughter, the kettle was on the hob waiting for us, cakes were laid out on the folding kitchen table, and the peace of the countryside quietly descended upon us. The subtle tick of the cuckoo clock played like a metronome to the sound of old friends reunited. I ventured outside away from the grown-up chat. Moggins was off hunting, resurrecting the predator within him, it was as if he was on safari at Nanna's, skulking in the long grass or diving off tree branches: with a clatter and a bang. The suspecting birds were never in any real danger, he never caught anything, but full marks for trying. Moggins loved playing and enjoyed the freedom we all valued up here. The evening began to close in; Dad made a call on the fading light and said, 'We better be making tracks if we're going to get to the conference on time.'

Mum nodded. 'Yes, OK, where's my boy?'

I heard her call out from the half-open kitchen door; my heart sank a little because I knew they would be off now. I did miss them. They would return on the odd weekends during the school holidays and would phone every day. We had made plans for a week camping, but I wouldn't hold my breath, they were very busy. I did love my time with Nanna, I was in good hands. We said our goodbyes, and I got the usual: 'Try to keep clean, don't eat too many sweets, don't be cheeky and please flush the toilet, no surprises for Nanna now!' instructed Mum.

'Mum!' I groaned, knowing I was guilty of occasionally being engrossed in my thoughts, to the point where I'd get in trouble for being forgetful or just not listening. 'A daydreamer, dozy zonk, sleepyhead, half a job Bob,' were just a few of my pseudonyms. We stood on the drive illuminated by the van's lights, casting long shadows on to the weathered green garage door. Dad gingerly reversed down the drive onto the lane, we watched them off, the van's engine getting quieter. I waited and waited thinking he'd forgotten, then just after the corn mill he tooted his horn twice like he always did. I sighed and my shoulders sunk; Nanna leant in and put her arm around me.

'Come on, dear, let's go inside. Fancy a game of cards? Oh, and I've got some of those coconut mushroom sweets,' she said with a wink and a smile.

That night we sat at the kitchen table playing cards, the room dimly lit from the lamp on the dresser. The curtains and blinds were still open; Nanna didn't see the need to keep the night out. 'Nobody around here to be peeping in,' she'd say.

I had my hot chocolate, and when my eyelids could no longer carry the day's weight, I said my goodnights and lumbered off to bed. Mr Milly followed; she curled up on the patterned rug next to the bed. Moggins made a grand entry jumping onto my lap, purring his way towards my face, coming in for one last fuss before we all settled down. Nanna came to tuck me in.

'Night dear, sweet dreams,' she said, flicking the light off, leaving the door slightly ajar, making sure a slight glow filtered in from the hall. I closed my eyes, my heart warm and mind full of all the exciting possibilities that tomorrow could bring. Possibilities that were jumping and shouting for my attention. *There's enough time for all of them,* I thought, gently pushing those excited butterflies to one side as I drifted off to sleep.

The night gave way to a beautiful day; birds chirped merrily outside my bedroom window. Mr Milly had already left my side. Moggins raised his heavy head as if to say, 'Just five more minutes.' I slipped out from beneath the covers, trying not to disturb him, and followed the sound of a playful song being hummed and whistled, finding at its end Nanna. She was in the front room polishing ornaments on the mantle. I loved her little tunes, they were never recognisable, and never repeated twice; like a burst of sunshine brought to life through the vocal cords, conducting her wipes, buffs and sweeps into something that looked less like work and more like fun.

'Morning sleepyhead,' beamed Nanna with a big broad smile. 'Did you sleep well?' she asked.

'Brilliant,' I replied while still stretching off the morning blur.

'What're your plans then, mister? What do you fancy doing today? It's a beautiful day outside, I suppose you'll be off down the farm to play with your mates.' I nodded and smiled; she knew me all too well. 'They've been asking for you, can't wait for you to come to visit. Ah, they're good lads, you know,' she said affectionately. 'Right, come on, let's get you fed and watered and ready for the day,' she said, putting her hands around my head and planting a big kiss upon my forehead. 'Tea? Toast?' she said, not really asking, for she knew I loved her homemade bread, especially toasted with lashings of butter and jam, and a nice cup of milky tea to wash it all down. I couldn't think of a better way to start the day.

CHAPTER 3

Ronnie and Buster

I must have set the record for teeth brushing, hair combing and getting dressed, ending up resembling something that looked sort of cared for. Nanna cast me a tut as I hurriedly shoved on my trainers and headed for the door.

'You be careful, come back when you're hungry,' called Nanna as I leapt over the row of trimmed bushes lining the drive wall.

Mr Milly was hot on my tail, bounding along like I'd got a ball or some treats in my pocket, which I didn't. We were both equally excited, for endless days of playing and adventuring lay before us. My mind free from any cares and worries. Mr Milly didn't need a lead, well, up at Nanna's at least. She was a very obedient dog, displaying almost human characteristics at times; empathising without words, while giving me that look, like when I'd been grounded, that said, 'I know your pain.' She'd sigh and puff along with my sorrow, but likewise when I was up Mr Milly would be bouncing off the ceiling with joyful exuberance. Today was one of those days.

The side door of the garage, much in need of some TLC, creaked as I opened it. All the smaller gardening tools were stored here, as 'Dolly', her beloved vintage run-around took up most of the room in the main garage. Through cobweb-lined windows, the side room looked over a small field that she rented from the Smythe family. Beyond the chicken coop and compost heap various vegetables grew. I think she had cabbages in this time, they were green anyway, that's about all I knew. Now, if I'd have spotted a glint of red hiding amongst their leafy disguise, I would have been out there like a shot; I loved strawberries. I squinted but couldn't see any. *Uhhh, cabbages,* I thought, picking my scooter up.

We made our way down the drive and onto the lane. Some maintenance had recently been carried out due to a burst water pipe, the result being a slight bump in the road's surface, perfect for some air. The lane was on a slight decline, and I gathered speed quickly. Mr Milly easily kept up though.

'Come on, girl, faster,' I said, pushing harder and harder until I'd reached my maximum velocity.

The smooth bump in the lane approached. Like a readymade ramp, I hit it hard and jumped, lifting the whole scooter up with me. Mr Milly rocketed into the air too, mimicking my move. I landed with a slight squirm from the back end, but all was well, as I glided my way down to Smythe Farm.

I left Mr Milly at the yard gate so as not to disturb any of the farm animals.

'You wait here, girl, I won't be long,' I said.

Her head tilted to one side as if to say, 'OK, but don't forget me.' I chapped on the kitchen door, and Mrs Smythe greeted me with a warm welcome.

'Ah… Pete, nice to see you… the boys will be so pleased you're here, they haven't stopped going on at me. They're off down the woods playing. Well, that's where they said they'd be, the little buggers,' she chuckled and ruffled my hair.

Thanking her, I set off to find them. Snickets Wood was on Smythe farmland, providing the perfect place for us to go wild; its thick canopy shielded the sun, making an ideal setting for the games we liked to play, which usually ended up with us scaring the pants off each other. We would sit and tell stories, making the scariest ones we could. All the time watching each other's faces, mouths open, wondering whether to disbelieve or not. I loved it, I loved playing with our imaginations, the unreal and unbelievable always fascinated me, to a point where you might say I was a little obsessed.

My trusty steed wasn't much use down Snickets, so I decided to leave it at the farm. I walked Mr Milly through the deserted yard, keeping a keen eye out for those marauding geese. My courageous canine companion seemed slightly freaked out by the toddling, flapping menaces. Maybe she'd had a flashback to Mrs Monkwit's aviary misadventure. Making it through unscathed, we picked up the trail leading down to the old coach path, its dusty twin tracks only kept visible by Mr Smythe's passing tractors. Fern and heather lined the way, with a mixture of greens and deep purple flourishes. The foliage grew denser as the path descended into Snickets Wood, swallowing the Old Coach House, now barely visible, as nature slowly year by year claimed it back, sinking into the background as forgotten memories do.

On entering the woods, all was quiet. I stood still for a second scanning for a sign of the boys, but heard nothing, until a raucous sound pierced the silence.

'Aaaahhhhhhh! You idiot! Aaahhhhhh! Not with that!' I heard what sounded like Ronnie crying out.

We rushed through the woody undergrowth; darting, jumping, and leaping. Reaching the top of an embankment, we looked down into a hollow, and there they were. Ronnie and Buster, my pals.

The scene that greeted me could only be described as brotherly love gone wrong. Ronnie, the older brother, was being beaten by his younger but sturdier brother Buster. Holding a leafy branch in his hand, he was gleefully bashing it against a prone Ronnie who painfully shouted, 'Get them off! Get them off!'

It appeared they had disturbed an ants' nest while wrestling and Buster was gladly beating them off his brother's back. Buster looked up and saw me and Mr Milly stood above them; he dropped the branch and rushed over. Ronnie gathered himself off the floor and was hot on his tail.

'Yyyyeeeeaahhhh!' they both shouted.

We were all so glad to see each other. Ronnie jumped on my back, and Buster took us both down with a rugby tackle, leaving us squirming and giggling in a pile, with Mr Milly licking our faces trying to get in on the action.

'Wait till we tell you what's been going on!' said Buster, trying to fight off the advancing affections of Mr Milly.

'Yeah, you won't believe it,' added Ronnie.

The squirming stopped, and Milly sat back. The brothers straightened themselves out like they'd something important to say.

'What... What's gone on?' I asked.

My imagination sparked, firing its engines into life.

'What!?' I quizzed, tugging on Ronnie's T-shirt. 'Tell us?' I said with playful annoyance.

'Well, you know all those stories we make up, like Smelly Cheese Fang the vampire, and the Ghoulies of Chattersley lavs,' said Ronnie. We all chuckled, remembering our stupid tales.

'Ghoulies!' laughed Buster.

Tears rolled down our cheeks as a slight chuckle had now escalated to full-on belly laughs; it didn't help either when Buster let out the breeze from his cooked breakfast.

'Ooh Buster, you dirtbag!' shouted Ronnie, offended by his odour.

We rolled around holding our stomachs, laughing so hard I started to cough and thought I might see my toast and jam again. Then Buster spluttered, 'There's a big black thingy on the loose.' Our laughs increased. 'Scoffed Mrs Flowers' chickens!' We all howled.

'What!' I said. 'Like a big cat!?' The laughs mellowed as a seriousness came about the conversation.

'Dad thinks it's a panther that's been let loose,' explained Buster.

'Yeah, he let off a few rounds at it the other day, it was freaking the cattle out,' added Ronnie.

'Really!!' I exclaimed. 'Wow!'

'The weird thing was, it just disappeared. Well, that's what I heard Dad saying. "Into the stone wall, it went," he said!' enthused Buster.

This breaking news flabbergasted me, a real-life mystery on our doorstep.

'It ate old Flowers' chickens?' I asked.

'Yeah… well, something made a bloody mess of them, and she said to Mum that it bust a hole straight through the chicken coop as big as Nell Popoff!' answered Ronnie.

Nell was a big fella, he helped on the farm. Buster always said how he'd once punched their Bull 'Limo' in an attempt to control him.

'Now your average fox couldn't do that! Could it!' piped Buster.

'We need to investigate this!' I said, bursting with excitement.

'Yeah, course we do!' replied Ronnie.

'Let's show him,' said Buster, bouncing around.

The boys led me into the darkest part of the wood, where an old oak tree hung split in two like King Kong had ripped it apart. We used to bounce on it as it formed a bridge across to its neighbouring siblings. We had tried to snap it off, but it was ages old and tough as iron, now we just played pirates on it. The public footpath ran through the centre of Snickets, and many ramblers passed this way, but no one knew it like us. Buster pointed down at the side of the path where the undergrowth was thick, the path was elevated here, and we had to jump down four or five feet.

'Look! Look what we've made,' said Ronnie. They pushed back a hanging clump of branches entwined with ivy and exposed an entrance to a den.

'Wooow, that's amazing,' I said.

'You haven't seen the best bit,' Buster beamed.

Inside the den, there was a slit around head height. This viewed directly onto the path, so you could see up, and down the trail. You could see anyone coming, and the best part was, they couldn't see you.

'Here, look,' said Buster, handing me a piece of rope. 'Now pull,' he instructed. I yanked hard, and a well-hidden trip wire snapped up across the path.

'We've had so much fun tripping up those ramblers,' laughed Ronnie. 'That one with the flask! It went everywhere! You peed yourself you laughed that hard,' laughed Ronnie.

'Shut it! No, I didn't!' snapped Buster, slightly embarrassed.

I could see what the boys were thinking, this was a perfect lookout for the mystery predator. They had wooden crates to sit on, comics to read, and a few conkers strung up to play with when things got dull. Empty crisp packets lay on the floor along with spent drink cans.

'Been down here much?' I joked. They'd obviously made themselves at home.

'It's great, no one moans at us,' replied Buster.

'Well, we will need some provisions then, let's get stocked up and meet back here,' I suggested.

'OK, yeah, be back here in an hour,' agreed Ronnie.

We were about to leave the den when Buster grabbed my arm. 'Wait, listen, it's them again,' he said.

'Who?' I asked.

'Cradlick and his cronies, they've been ripping the place up on those bikes, listen!' added Ronnie.

'Dad hates them!' scorned Buster.

I could now clearly hear the rattle of the scramblers coming closer, they didn't half make a racket, like massive angry bees buzzing their way through the woods. We peered through the slit; they were coming our way. Buster had hold of the trip rope.

'No, Buster!' shouted Ronnie as he pulled Buster's hand away. 'You'll bloody kill them! Or really piss them off! Then we're dead!'

Buster, the younger but definitely more gung-ho, retracted his hand and tutted disappointedly.

'Look, here they come!' I said as the bikes came into view.

We all ducked down in our perfect spying spot. Three bikes spun past kicking up dust and dirt, filling the den. We all coughed and spluttered, shielding our faces from any larger debris. The engines cut out dead and we could hear them laughing and jesting at their own raucous anti-social behaviour. When the air cleared, we peeked through the slit and could see them around fifty yards away.

'That's Cradlick, the one with the blond hair,' said Ronnie.

He had a girl on the back of his bike, the others rode alone. They all dismounted; the girl had a rucksack which she opened and passed around some cans of beer.

'They think they're so hard,' smote Buster, his aversion seeping from every pore. I wondered if they had wronged him before, for his dislike was not shy.

'That's Rosy Saddler too, tut-tut, drinking! Her dad would kill her if he knew she was hanging with them losers,' said Ronnie.

I didn't know them, and I'd heard people moan about the Cradlicks, I suppose they were the rotten apple in Chattersley's otherwise pristine fruit bowl.

'Yeah, and the two thickos, strong in the arm but thick in the head!' sniggered Buster, pulling a stupid dumb face.

'What's she doing with them? She's too good for that Cradlick,' he criticised.

'Ooowwweee, sounds like someone's got a crush,' jibbed Ronnie.

'No! No! Well, she is,' said Buster, his affection for Rosy showing as his cheeks coloured up.

'She used to babysit us… when we were babies!!' sniped Ronnie, gurning at his brother.

Buster just shook his head. 'Shut it,' he replied.

I agreed with Buster. I'd seen her about over the years and with her long dark hair and radiant complexion, she certainly seemed a good catch, well, as far as my pre-teen hormones could tell. I thought, well, if anyone could set Cradlick right, she could, with her soft tones and caring nature. But as for now, they all looked to be balancing on that tightrope of acceptability, and the unruliness of late teens bored with country life. Well, that's how I saw it, but what did I know? I was ten and loved this place with a passion. I couldn't imagine ever getting bored with it.

We watched them for a while, Buster scoffing and pulling faces while making two-fingered gestures through the slit. Ronnie kept telling him to keep his voice down and stop poking his stubby digits out. They were smoking too, music now blaring from a stereo one thicko had produced from his backpack.

'What a load of crap,' spouted Buster.

'Ha! Only because you like old lady music,' laughed Ronnie.

'No! No, that's rubbish, and it's not old lady music! It's classic,' answered Buster, defending himself.

I quite liked what they were playing, it was edgy and raw, they all had that rocky alternative appearance, giving the impression they didn't care how they looked, but just enough to present themselves differently from the regular crowd. Just as I was getting into their tunes, they stopped the player and looked our way.

'Ssshhh, I heard something. Who's there! Better not be those dick kids! Running around like Peter Pan! Better not be spying on us!'

shouted Cradlick. Hearing him loud and clear, we squatted down quickly.

'Crap! I don't fancy getting pummelled,' whispered Ronnie. Mr Milly let out a low growl in our defence. I ruffled her head, pulling her in close.

'It's nothing, Shaun,' said Rosy.

They carried on talking and drinking, we rose up and peeked again, then the mood really took a dive. The temperature suddenly dropped, frosting our breath. I rubbed my arms and looked at the brothers.

'What's this about? It's freezing,' I juddered.

'Me too,' stuttered Ronnie.

The grass at the side of the path crystallised. We watched as it crept up on the unsuspecting rabble. The air was different, like there was something there but not there, shimmering and moving like the heat haze of a summer's road, but it wasn't warm, it was deathly cold. Upon reaching the party, the rabble felt its presence.

'Wow, that's chilled,' said one of the thickos as he swigged from a can.

Rosy was the sensible one; immediately spooked, she looked down the path and dropped her drink.

'We've got to go Shaun, this is wrong, something's wrong! This is bad!' she said, panicked.

Shaun rubbed her jacket and stared down the path. The shimmer was on him, he looked distorted to me as if we were viewing him through frosted glass. The others were clear, but his image wasn't. Cradlick froze for a moment, Rosy tugging at him.

'Come on, Shaun! Let's go!' she now shouted.

The other two straddled their metal steeds and cranked them into life. Shaun soon followed as they raced off away from the chill. Thraped rattling engines filled the air, soon accompanied by their rebellious howls, as they tore up the countryside again.

I watched the shimmer glide off into the woods, plants and undergrowth now thawing as the temperature returned to normal.

'That was weird,' said Ronnie.

'Bloody freezing,' said Buster.

Something was off. We examined the path, picking up their empty cans, and nothing seemed unusual now. We walked back out of the woods, chatting away with various crazy theories, trying to resolve the peculiar event.

I bade Ronnie and Buster a short goodbye as they peeled off the coach path into the yard. The twin tracks merged into a single trail from here on, running parallel with the back of Ivy Gate. I made the last stretch outwardly silent, but with a hell of an internal racket going on; my imagination was having a party over the strange event we had just witnessed. Mr Milly sniffed the long grass minding her own business, never letting me get even a few feet away. I sensed this for I never had to call her once, she was keeping me close.

It was only half a mile or so before the path opened into a field at the back of Nanna's cottage; lined on three sides with thick fir and pine trees, it created a large enclosed space. Mr Milly paused, her gaze lingering a fraction too long upon the far bank. Now whether or not it was my imagination, something pulled at my worry strings; a sinking thump in my stomach hit me like I'd forgotten something important. I placed my hand on the back gate and looked across the field, its edges dark and secret, void of any friendship today. Was my leafy playground hiding something?

Mr Milly held a predatory stance, our gazes locked on the treeline. She squinted and focused intently. I thought, *Bet you're thinking the same thing girl, I know you're in there, I know you're watching.*

Her head suddenly jerked following a startled hare bolting from the undergrowth. My heart jumped, releasing me from my gaze.

'Come on girl,' I called and closed the gate behind me.

Nanna, extremely surprised to see me back so soon, was having a cuppa with the Major who had just popped round. His trusty companion Maggot; a small and tufty Jack Russell, bounced and yapped his way over to greet us. He was a mischievous little fellow, and we would often hear the Major calling him in that very stern military tone, 'Maggot!! Maggot!! Not in my shoe, Maggot!' That was the sort of thing we would hear through the walls. It did make me and Nanna chuckle. I swear he had named him so, as a way to stir up the old fuddies as he called them at the pop-in club, even though I would class him as a fuddie himself. He would often share a twinkling wink as he rasped off another Maggot-related insult.

The Major, Mr Robert Mayne to be precise, or Bob to Nanna, was a character indeed, with his taught posture and flung-back shoulders, topped with a thick groomed moustache twiddled at the ends. He was always immaculately presented, clean and crisp usually in some tweed suit. The only raggedy, dirty thing about him was his throaty tone; battered and stretched from all those years yelling at lacklustre privates. I imagined his vocal cords resembled something like a rusty, worn engine wrapped in barbed wire and running on glass shards. He would always clear his throat before speaking, like turning the ignition of an old v8 over, he would then continue with varying levels of pitch ranging from a mumble to shouting certain words. It was all very engaging, keeping us on the edge of our seats, never knowing when the next usually inappropriate word would blast out of his mouth.

He was a decorated soldier, Special Forces by all accounts, but he never went on about his days in the military. I gather it had left a heavy imprint on his mind and heart. He and Nanna were good pals and welcome company for each other. The Major called Nanna 'Lizzy' which I never heard anyone else call her. They went back a long way, and it was clear they were dear to each other, both losing their life partners before I was born; they'd stuck together and looked out for each other.

'How's it going young Pete?' asked the Major.

'Good thanks, just back to get some supplies, we're going to stalk that big cat!' I replied excitedly, filling him in on our afternoon plans.

'Oh, you've heard then?' asked Nanna suspiciously.

'Yeah, Ronnie and Buster said,' I confirmed.

'Well just be careful, it will probably be more scared of you lot!' she chuckled, obviously half believing the story, as she didn't seem too concerned over my plans to hunt the mysterious predator. At that moment, the cuckoo clock above the kitchen table did something strange, it made a click sound and the mechanism wound. Nanna stopped and looked over her half-rimmed spectacles, the Major glancing too, and now I was drawn in. We all stood and looked at those miniature doors waiting. It wasn't upon the hour, the clock wasn't set to chime.

'That's odd,' the Major said.

'Odd indeed,' added Nanna. The mechanism then activated, and the tiny little rosewood bird popped out. Nanna stood for a second then asked, 'Well, what have you got to say?'

We all actually waited, considering a response was possible from the little static bird.

'Nothing then,' said Nanna, laughing.

The bird turned, retracting back into the clock. She shared a look with the Major, like a coded message had just passed between them. Something was going on, well, in the adult realm anyway.

I gathered some crisps and cartons of orange juice while Nanna knocked up some cheese sandwiches which I stuffed into my rucksack.

'Now you be careful, you hear any funny business, and you run, run home!' Nanna's tone had taken a slightly more serious turn.

'Mr Milly, you look after him, OK!' she said.

Mr Milly let out an obedient growly yelp as if she understood.

'Be back for six, I will have tea on.' She planted a kiss on my cheek and patted my shoulder.

'Bye Pete, see you later,' said the Major as I went on my way.

CHAPTER 4

The Stakeout

We arrived back at the den; Buster and Ronnie were already inside and could be heard shuffling about, having a brotherly argument over who ate the last cookie. I walked on the path and looked down the slit into their hiding place.

'Ooiieeee! You lot need to be quieter if we're going to catch a glimpse of it!' I jibbed, slinging my bag down into the den. 'Nanna's done some sandwiches. Tuck in,' I added. They thanked me and began rummaging through the rucksack.

'Ooohh, I love these little beauties,' said Ronnie, holding the bag of midget iced cakes up.

'Right then, let's get settled in, we could be in for a long wait,' I barked in a serious but playful way. This whole thing had got my mind buzzing; my excitement was obvious and maybe spilt out as being a little bossy at times. This was serious stuff. Well, to me anyway. This was a chance to be involved in a real mystery. The lurking presence was out there, I could feel it, something was in the air, and it wasn't anything I'd felt before; there was a shadow over Snickets, and we were going to find out exactly what it was.

'Shall we take turns to be lookout then?' suggested Buster. We swapped lookout every fifteen minutes or so, while the resting two played conkers or read a comic, trying not to make too much noise. Mr Milly curled up, now and again lifting her head to see what was going on. I gathered this must be rather boring for her, she didn't understand what we were doing; I bet she thought, *What's happened to this lot? We used to play pirates and hide and seek, running wild through the woods and fields, now look at them, quietly sat in a den.*

We sat for all of two hours before the boredom set in. Buster was the first to let out a long discontented sigh expressing his lack of interest.

'It's never just going to come strolling past, is it!' he complained.

Ronnie and I both looked in silent agreement, and then I answered, 'Yeah, suppose there's no harm in having a look round the woods for signs is there?' They both approved. Mr Milly agreed as she perked up, ready for some exploring.

We set off into the woods, starting our mission by quietly observing the surroundings.

'Ssshhhhh, did you hear that?' said Ronnie. We all stopped and froze; a wry smile rose from a look of concentration as he forced a trump out.

'Ooohhh, Ronnie,' laughed Buster.

'Smells as bad as you do,' jested Ronnie.

'Right then, come here!' said Buster, trying to grab his older brother. They both bolted and shot off into the undergrowth chasing, screaming and laughing with boyish play. Mr Milly looked for permission. I nodded, and she too darted off jumping and barking; so much for our stealthy operation.

I followed on, disillusioned with our vain attempt at a stakeout. The next few days went much the same kind of way, only the staking out got less and less and 'walk the plank' and 'swing for your life' became favourites for us all. We were pirates on the high sea, Captain McBadpants and his two trusty sea dogs, Barrel and Dangle. We would blindfold each other and see who could walk nearest to the end of the old split tree. We did lots of falling off into the shark-infested waters scrambling back on board and hiding out in the den which doubled as the ship's hull. Through all the time we spent in Snickets we never got a glimpse of anything else strange, but that feeling of being watched never left me from the first day I sensed it.

On the fourth day we stumbled across something truly grim, it turned our stomachs upside down. The smell, a vicious aroma which violated our senses. For a moment, Buster nearly got the blame. Suddenly it became clear to us all that there was a rotting animal corpse close by. We followed the stench into some thick bracken; the sound of buzzing flies intensified as I pushed the bush aside to find a heap of browny-black fur lying lifeless in a muddy pool. A collar and a metal chain told of its domestic keeping.

'That's Ripper!' shouted Ronnie.

'Meanest dog I've ever seen,' chipped in Buster. 'Mum said he'd gone missing. Saddler always kept him chained up, but he got out one night last week, snapped the chain clean out the wall!' Buster continued.

'They reckon he'd gone bonkers and wasn't fit to be around folk,' added Ronnie. I snapped a long branch off a bush to use as a prodder so as not to get too close. 'Swear he had about six sets of teeth,' embellished Ronnie.

'Wonder what happened to him then,' I muttered to myself, poking the carcass with the branch trying to gain a better look.

'What if he got spooked by the devil dog? What if he went crackers and broke free!' exclaimed Ronnie.

We all peered in closer, trying to get a better look.

'Uuuhhh, that stinks,' complained Buster, holding his nose.

The dog looked to have suffered an injury to its neck; a mattered ruddy mess leaked into the puddle. I slowly dipped the end of the stick into the tar-like concoction probing for clues, suddenly it fizzed and hissed and began crawling up the stick, burning the wood and emitting a foul green gas.

'What the hell!' I said, startled. The branch disintegrated by the second, the gas cloud growing larger! I was confused; Ronnie and Buster were on their knees coughing.

'Put it down!! Let it go!' shouted Ronnie through his hands, I dropped the branch inches before it reached me. I pulled the boys up, dragging them out of the toxic mist. We fell back and watched in bewilderment: the thick mossy green vapour licked out into the air looking for something to smother, but we were out of its reach now, and it soon retreated to the rotting corpse.

'Well, that's just about the weirdest thing I've ever seen,' said Buster, tucking into a chocolate bar he'd found in one of his pockets.

Ronnie just looked at him in disgust. 'Really! Now!' he said in sarcastic amazement.

'What!' replied Buster with his mouth full.

'I really can't think of a worse time to be eating!' barked Ronnie.

'Sorrryyyy!' replied an insulted Buster.

Mr Milly was very uneasy and constantly emitted a low whining whimper, nudging her head under my armpit in a suggestive 'hurry up' way.

'Come on, let's get out of here,' I said.

'We best tell Dad we've found Ripper,' said Ronnie.

'And that funny acidy stuff, it could be a chemical leak or something,' added Buster.

Yes, it was all extremely strange, but could it still be explained? Could Ripper have stumbled across some toxic liquid dumped in the woods? An acid that could eat through wood like that could certainly polish off flesh and bone, but then again how come the rest of the dog was still intact? The whole thing just wasn't sitting right, in the pit of my stomach a burning ball spun, fear and worry gathered momentum. The cloudy mist felt alive, it seemed organic and predatory, and the scene had all the hallmarks of a trap.

I went back with Ronnie and Buster and explained to Mr Smythe what we had encountered. To our surprise Mr Smythe said only yesterday he'd found a sheep in the same way, but didn't mention gas or acid, just a blackish tar on the wound.

The following day we showed him the location, and he dragged the dog out. I stressed to be careful after what we saw, but the pool which burnt and ate my branch yesterday lay passively still, with no reaction, having no story or mystery to tell us today. Mr Smythe wrapped old Ripper in a black plastic sheet and hauled him onto the trailer, ready for his last journey home.

After the rattly twang of the two-stroke engine faded, I turned to

Ronnie and Buster. 'You saw that yesterday, didn't you?' I questioned them and myself.

'Yeah, yeah, really weird,' Buster replied.

It frustrated and befuddled me. The afternoon sun passed behind the scattered clouds casting grey-tinted shadows along the wood's floor; they stretched out to me, filling my imagination, answering my musing most peculiarly. From behind the creaking trees and rustling leaves, from underneath the tweets of passing birds and shuffles of burrowing creatures came a different noise.

It surfaced only briefly for a few seconds, our ears instantly drawn to the foreign sound; we hunted the airwaves trying to pin it down. We didn't have to wait long before it loosed, fully exposing itself. Shock gripped us; the noise rose as if coming from the crypt of all things dead, none of us had ever heard such a sound. Just as a laugh can send good vibrations, this unknown sound flooded the wood with a cruel dominance, a howling roar with grinding crushing undertones. A noise that spoke power and doom invaded our leafy playground. At that moment, just about every creature in the wood, including ourselves, stopped breathing, trying to take it in, trying to rationalise the sensations that were drowning our nervous systems.

'What the…?' said Buster, open-mouthed.

'That's it, that's got to be it. Oh my god!' I said, excited and panicked at the same time.

We all looked at each other, looking for a prompt as what to do next. Then Ronnie said, 'Den!'

We didn't hang about, bolting off through the undergrowth, throwing caution to the wind, not caring for foot placement as they sank into the unknown ground beneath. The roaring howl seemed to be echoing from all sides of the wood sounding closer all the time.

We approached the hideout from the rear, avoiding any open areas as much as we could. Buster held the roughly thatched door as we bundled in. We paused for a minute, letting our heavy breathing settle. All I could hear was my heart and lungs pounding, full of adrenaline.

'Right, let's sit a bit and get our breath before we do the watch thing again,' I said, panting. The first watch was crowded as our three heads battled for the best view.

'I thought we were taking turns?' quizzed Ronnie, slightly annoyed.

'Yeah well… we don't want to miss anything do we?' I replied. Ronnie just tutted, not impressed by the lack of confidence I had in his lookout skills. After about ten minutes we resumed the rotation; Ronnie and I sat while Buster stood watch. As time passed, my heart began to deflate. The reason in the mystery rose to the surface, floating around on top of my thoughts. Buster then broke the ponderous silence we had slipped into.

'Sssshhhh, something's coming,' he hissed. We jumped up and peered through the slit. 'Up there by that ivy-covered tree on the right, I swear I saw something,' he added.

'Where? Where?' asked Ronnie, finding it hard to contain his excitement.

'It's gone in those bushes now, it was black, shaggy and big!' said Buster.

'Bloody hell, are you sure?' I questioned, feeling my heart rate hasten.

'Positive,' clarified Buster.

We watched the bushes and trees for any sign of movement; it was around one hundred yards away from our beady eyes, squinting hard, did something move or not? It was difficult to tell. The scene was silent as if the birds had stopped being birds, the breeze was non-existent, and there were no sounds to say civilisation was near. Suddenly we all felt very alone. Mr Milly had risen from her curled position and was by my side; she brushed her head into my thigh in a settling way. Buster turned away from the slit.

'Maybe it was nothing just a boar or something?' he queried his early statement now. Shrugging his shoulders, he sat down on a wooden crate and started to flick through the comic nearest to him, letting out a big deflated sigh. 'We've spent ages in here now, shall we—'

Buster's sentence was interrupted by that sound, only much closer, we could hear every detail now; starting as a low crackling rumble it then broke into a guttural howling roar.

None of us spoke; we just shared our shocked expressions. Ronnie ducked down from the slit as we all tucked in beneath the embankment. 'It's only flaming coming!' Ronnie stuttered, fear visible in his face. Again the sound rang through the woods; imagine a lion, bear and wolf all in one, but an octave or two lower, with this metallic crackling as if the vocal cords themselves were made up of shredded steel gears.

'Did you see it?! Did you?!' I questioned.

Ronnie nodded, tears filling his eyes. 'Red eyes! It's only got flaming red eyes!' he said, trembling.

Mr Milly let out a controlled growl. I pulled her back, knowing what she thought; to be able to protect us, she needed to see the threat, but I didn't want her to go so restrained her. She felt my need and remained with us. The sound grew closer, now I could hear it breathing, sniffing and snorting the air. The beast wheezed but didn't sound weak for a moment, like a massively powerful engine on tick-over; it coughed and spluttered, trying to contain its energy that was just waiting to be unleashed. Silent it certainly wasn't and wouldn't be winning any prizes in the stealth category, but it scored top marks for scaring the life out of three young boys. I hadn't even seen it yet, but we knew it was here and getting closer.

It brought with it a taste in the air. If death had a taste this was it, rotting flesh like the truck that picked up roadkill and dead animal stock, but this was thicker and alive. I could hear the flies that accompanied the stench, their buzzing and humming growing ever closer; I feared that the Hound was now outside the slit. Buster whimpered and looked at me for comfort, but I had none to give, we were all in the same boat feeling powerless and trapped.

'We've got to go, we've got to run!' whispered a panicked, desperate Ronnie as he made a move, but I pulled him back. Our slight scuffle silenced the patrolling animal. *It's heard us*, I thought.

Now it called for calm and quiet so it could home in on our location; its snout poked into the slit right above our heads. I pulled my feet in and the boys did the same. Some kind of black liquid dropped from its jowls, hitting the ground with a fizz, bubbling as acid would. Its wheezing whirring lungs took a deep breath then snorted the air out and blew a cloud of dust into the den. The beast probed our hiding place knowing we were in there but its eyes fooled its other senses. We held tight; soon the black, raggy snout retracted and moved away from the den.

Still, like statues, we sat until it let out another roar from the depths of its rotten rusting lungs. We jumped in synchronicity, our ears working overtime trying to place its movements, not daring to move from our hiding place, not daring to look. To our relief we could hear the cracking of branches and trampling of bushes as it made its way into the wood's undergrowth, gathering speed as the rhythm of its heavy pounding feet thumped quicker until it was away. For a few moments we sat quietly scanning the airwaves; the birds came back to life, and the breeze gently blew away its presence. I summoned up the courage to look out of the slit. Ronnie and Buster looked worried. Buster made a grimacing look, as if to say, 'Don't look,' but I had to. My head slowly rose up until my eyes were level with the path; there wasn't any sign of the beast now. I looked up and down the path and into the woods as far as I could see, then ducked back down.

'Right, I think it's gone,' I said.

'Are you sure?' bleated Buster, his courage drained.

'I'm pretty sure. We should go now,' I replied with optimism.

'Yeah, let's make a run for it then,' added Ronnie. We all nodded in agreement.

I held up the makeshift door, quickly scanning the surrounding area.

'Right, coast clear.' I nodded to the boys. Mr Milly slunk in by my side ready for instruction. 'Right, after three. Three, two, one, go!' I commanded through clasped lips. We quietly but swiftly picked our way back through the woods, sticking to the side of the paths. My heart was in my mouth most of the time. After all, it was still out there. What was it? Would it have eaten us? These were questions that now firmly had the top spot in my eager, overactive imagination.

I couldn't make sense of the whole thing, it felt surreal like a dream, all I knew was I needed to get back to Nanna quick. We made it to the edge of Snickets; Buster stopped and rubbed his side, trying to ease a stitch. We all took a minute's rest, filling our lungs with the fresh air. The old coach path now ascended in front of us, and the farm was around half a mile away. Relief passed over us, and we relaxed slightly. To our horror this was short-lived, as another bone-chattering howl rose from the depths of the wood. Our eyes pinged open with shock. Buster was off without a word; Ronnie glanced at me. 'Come on! Come on!' he said with increasing panic in his voice, but for whatever reason, I stood for a second casting my eyes upon the far treebank. Beyond the grazing fields of the Smythes' farm, the trees rustled, and then in an explosion of leaves and branches, the black terror broke through the wood's secret canvas. Bold as brass in plain view it stood, still a good half a mile or so away but I could see its raggy tar-mane and the flicker of electric red eyes which were now tracking Buster and Ronnie running up the hill. It didn't move but then we locked eyes, and its intent focused upon me, Mr Milly pulled at my sleeve and beckoned me to run and follow my two mates who were now screaming at the top of their voices.

'Dad! Dad!' they yelled.

The Hound stood, looking, waiting, gauging. It paced forward a few steps and then stood again, measuring with deadly accuracy. *Could it reach me before the farm?* I thought. Then *bang*, like a shot of adrenaline had been pumped into my arms and legs all other functions could wait. I sprang forward like a greyhound, driving my arms and knees high, covering the ground like never before, Mr Milly always by my side, not ever leaving me even though she was as fast as a train. I glanced sideways only to see the Hound accelerating at tremendous speed, hunkered down, not leaping or galloping like a horse would do; instead it steamed towards me like a tank. The sheep parted in their frantic, panicked mess. I was close now, a hundred yards or so; the gate was visible, Ronnie and Buster were hanging over it shouting.

'It's coming! Run, Pete! Run!' Their voices faded and a state of concentration fell over me, all I could hear was my breath and my shoes as they flicked tiny puffs of sandy smoke off the dirt track. *Pick them up! Pick them up!* I thought.

Now another sound crept in, a heavy pounding beat thumping towards me. *I'm not going to make it,* I thought as the shadow loomed into view. Fifty yards now and I was stumbling, my concentration lost, fear ruling my senses; the black mass lurched into the air attempting to jump the wall between us. Just at the last minute, just when I'd almost given up, exhausted and out of time, a crack echoed off and the Hound fell behind the wall.

Mr Smythe stood at the gate, his smoking shotgun in hand. 'Pete! Get back here quick!' He beckoned me over behind the gate. I scrambled my way to safety huddling behind Mr Smythe. He's a tough, brave fella, and I instantly felt protected. He loaded another two cartridges into the barrel.

'Go on, Dad, finish it off!' said Buster, jeering his father on with newfound confidence.

'Yeah, blast its balls off, Dad!' added Ronnie. He moved forward slowly and closed the gate behind him.

'You stay there boys,' he commanded with an air of authority. With the gun raised and stretched out in front of him, he approached the wall.

'He won't miss, he's a crack shot,' bragged Buster as the tension grew. We all stopped breathing for a moment waiting in nervous anticipation.

Mr Smythe reached the wall and peeped over gingerly at first, then stuck his head right over, looking this way and that. He turned back, looking puzzled. 'It's gone!' he shouted, bewildered. What Mr Smythe had expected to find was completely different from what he did.

'Nothing! It's gone,' he repeated, musing over the events that had just passed. He removed his flat cap and scratched his head with a confused look all over his flushed face. He muttered to himself and I caught what I thought was him questioning how much whiskey he'd had last night. His concern evidently showed with the realisation he might be letting off shots to dispatch a figment of his imagination.

The shots had stolen the afternoon's peace and our shouting had brought Nanna, and the Major followed closely by Maggot down onto the coach track. 'What's all the commotion?' asked an alarmed Nanna. We bleated and spat out our disjointed tale of the black horror that had stalked us. 'And it just disappeared?' she said with a *poof* action, half-smiling, peering over her glasses.

'Yeah, nothing but that smell, like fireworks or matches,' explained Mr Smythe.

'Right,' pondered Nanna. She walked over to the wall and peered over. 'Yes it does, doesn't it? Smells like sulphur. Big black dog, cat thing you say? Hhhmmmm? Most peculiar.' She stood and puzzled over the conundrum then broke free of its hold. 'Come on then, boys, back to mine, tea and biscuits, and you can tell me everything that happened. Let's try to make some sense of it all,' she said optimistically, enthused by the mystery. She patted Mr Smythe on his tall shoulders and said in a more serious tone, 'You alright, Ned? Don't worry; we will get to the bottom of it.'

The Major followed Mr Smythe into the yard, saying, 'A little pick-me-up, Ned?' as he pulled his leather-wrapped hip flask from his inside pocket and gestured in a drinking motion.

'I need something, I'd say,' replied Mr Smythe.

The sky blackened as if affected by the mood, and a low rumble of thunder echoed in the distance. The rain then followed; heavy mortar balls of water bounced off the ground. Myself, Ronnie and Buster ran back up the path to Nanna's with her coat over our heads. We told her everything, all about the den and the creature we had encountered. I explained in as many details as possible, she never seemed fazed or disbelieving; she never challenged or made fun of our story as some adults would do. She didn't play it down either, nor promote or encourage any fear in our tale. 'It's nothing to be scared of,' she kept saying. I found this slightly annoying and frustrating considering she hadn't seen the thing and hadn't a clue how bloody scared we all were. In the end, I started to think my imagination had wanted this mystery to be true so badly that I'd turned this wild cat into an acid-slobbering, four-legged death machine.

We all began to calm down and pick more realistic and reasonable explanations. Mr Smythe turned up just after dark with a now wobbling Major. 'Just had a few tots with me, good man,' he slurred. Maggot yelped at him. 'Yes! Yes! Maggot, let's get you home for dinner then,' he barked. The Major said his goodbyes and made his way back home but not before Maggot had tripped him up. We saw the Major's silhouette dive then spring back up with a flurry of abuse aimed at his pint-sized companion.

Mr Smythe seemed much more composed. 'I gather Bob did most of the drinking,' Nanna joked.

'Arr, he is a good old boy. Listen, Nanna, I've been thinking, that smell, well… that could have been the different cartridges I was using, and if it was a cat, well, they're fast as lightning, it could have taken off down that wall and out of sight before I got there.' Mr Smythe took a breath and waited for Nanna's agreeing response.

'Indeed it could, my dear,' she said with a warm smile, 'indeed it could.' She paused, pondering while looking strangely again at the clock, then levered herself out of the high-backed chair. 'Right then, boys, off back with your dad now.' She gave Ronnie and Buster a warm cuddle and showed them to the door.

'See you tomorrow, Pete,' said Ronnie.

Mr Smythe interrupted my reply. 'Eeerr, I think you lot should stay out of the woods for now, just until I've checked it out.' Buster and Ronnie sighed, but I felt a slight relief.

'Good idea, Ned,' replied Nanna. 'They can find something else to do, can't they?' she said, pulling me in with a smile.

We went back into the warmly lit kitchen. Nanna's house just seemed to wrap its arms around you; it was cosy and above all, felt safe. The curtains and blind remained open, illuminating the edges of night, the fire crackled away, and I had a milky tea in hand while Nanna quietly turned the pages of her novel, all to the quiet tick-tock of the cuckoo clock. 'You have yourself a nice warm bath tonight, dear, wash away all those worries, I'll run it in a moment,' said Nanna, looking up from her book. I nodded and smiled. I was feeling quite dozy now; today's excitement had taken its toll.

A gentle pat of rain began to run down the window. I loved the rain, especially when we were all inside and snug. My ears homed in on the hypnotic tip-tap upon the glass, a natural metronome slowly putting me to sleep, just the tapping and the crackle of the fire, my feet warm and toasty, today's fears and worries drifting away. *Aah,* I thought and sank deeper into the chair. Then as if a black thunderbolt had broken the atmosphere, calling out from the murk of the night, my memories, my fear and worries came rushing back. I stood bolt upright with a thumping beat upon my stomach! There it was, that sound, in the far-off distance; it let out a gut-wrenching, distorted, howling roar, echoing and rippling through the airwaves, a chorus of nightmares making its way to all who could hear. I jerked up from my slouched position, gripping the sides of the chair, spilling my tea. 'That's it! That's it, Nanna!!' I spluttered, shaken from my comfy retreat.

Nanna slammed her paper down, swiped the glasses from her face and clutched them roughly with frustration. For a moment I thought her irritation was aimed at me, thinking she was going to tell me to stop this nonsense, saying, 'It's nothing but a loose dog!' But she didn't, she gathered her coat and umbrella and slid into her wellies. 'Right, I won't be long, back in a jiffy, drop the latch behind me,' she said sternly. Before I could get my words out the door closed in front of me. I locked it and quickly moved over to the window just catching a glimpse before the night swallowed her.

Mr Milly was on high alert, her paws on the window sill, ears pricked back, watching, anticipating. 'It's all right, girl, Nanna knows what she's doing,' I said, trying to comfort myself and her at the same time. Somehow though I knew she would be OK. We waited minutes which seemed like hours then the steely silence broke with a flurry of sound and light. First that howl rang high and loud, more aggressive than before. It was soon followed by a huge crack as a shard of lightning or something with a violet hue shot up to meet the sky. It was followed by what I can only explain as a sweeping wave of calm that flooded through everything, permeating our cores, a wave of invisible love embracing my very essence.

The light show faded, and the howls stopped. I looked intently out of the window; the rain was coming down harder, and I found it difficult to see through the fogged glass pane. I scrunched my face up to the window trying to catch sight of Nanna, only I was greeted with more than a glimpse, as her face and hands appeared from nowhere inches from mine. I jumped back. 'Bleeding hell!' I shouted.

'It's OK, sorted now. Let me in, dear,' she chirped. I lifted the latch, and she returned just as she'd gone only wetter. She took her coat off and placed the brolly back, only the handle looked slightly charred now.

'Did you see it, Nanna? Did you!?' I badgered.

'Oh, that thing! Just a little nuisance that I shooed away,' she said.

'What about the light? What was that?' I asked.

'Yes, pretty wasn't it? You don't have to worry, it's gone now,' she puffed and laughed, humming a happy little tune to herself.

'Weren't you scared, Nanna?' I questioned.

'Oh no, not me, dear,' she beamed with a glint in her eye.

'Did you get a good look then?' I continued with my interrogation, not satisfied with the answers Nanna was supplying.

'Well,' she sighed as if she had to give me something, 'it was all too dark to see, but it did make a terrible racket, I just told it to stop it, and go back from where it came,' she added, poking her tongue to the inside of her mouth, rolling a little white lie around. 'And it did! So enough now,' she said firmly while coming across the room to hug me. 'Now bed, I will come and read you a story.' She gave me her trademark kiss on the forehead followed by a ruffle of my hair. I went off to bed, satisfied it was going to be OK, even though I didn't understand how or why.

The following morning I awoke saved again from the Gap's clutches this time by the abrasive lick of Moggins' wet tongue. Both grateful and slightly annoyed I rose from my bed to a bleak, drizzly day.

The cottage was warm and toasty, the fragrance of home cooking acting as a comfort blanket wrapping itself around me. I entered the kitchen and greeted Nanna. 'Morning, dear, did you sleep well?' she said.

'OK, I guess,' I replied, still sleepy-eyed. We shared one of those comfy silences as she went about her baking preparations. I sat on the heater by the window where I'd watched her last night. I mused over the cuckoo clock silently. Nanna always paid particular attention to the little wooden bird when it burst through those miniature doors; she glanced over her half-rimmed spectacles a little longer than what you'd expect, and a slight moment between them attracted the attention of my imagination. *What if the little bird's real? What if it's been turned to wood by some crazy enchanted worm that took vengeance for the bird's buffet feast on its family after a particular heavy downfall? What if the bird could talk?* Nar, I thought, shaking my head, and carried on picking the paint from the electric heater I was sat on, looking out the window for Mr Vole to pop out. I'd become increasingly concerned about voles since I learned in one of my more informative school classes that hawks can see ultraviolet, making Mr Vole's pee extremely easy to spot from its bird's-eye vantage point. It's like holding a great big neon sign, saying, 'Look down, Mr Hawky, here are your appetisers.' *Bless the little vole; I hope he has emptied his bladder before he ventures out today.*

Nanna was at the sink washing up when she leant forward and wiped the condensation from the window. She leaned closer, looking down the drive. 'Looks like your mates are coming up, oh, and Mrs Smythe too,' informed Nanna. She opened the door and greeted them.

'We're not stopping, just popped in to say I'm off to see my mother and the boys are coming for a few days too. Pete's welcome to come if he wants?' asked Mrs Smythe. Ronnie and Buster were both holding their hands clasped in anticipation, muttering pleases under their breath.

Nanna looked over. 'You can if you want,' she said.

I wanted to, but also I didn't want to be away from Nanna or Mr Milly and Moggins. I felt the need to be here more than ever, so I declined to the sound of Ronnie and Buster's disappointed sighs.

'No problem, just thought we'd ask,' said Mrs Smythe.

'Well, thank you, and please send my regards to your mum. I will have to visit soon,' replied Nanna. The boys trudged off back down the lane, the dreary day befitting of their mood.

The next few days were uneventful. The weather returned to summer holiday expectations, Nanna encouraged me to go out and enjoy the countryside, but I was hesitant. I was missing my playmates, but it was the shadow cast upon my mind that waned my adventurous enthusiasm. I couldn't shake that feeling, when I went out to the back gate and entered the field it was still there, that watched feeling. I hadn't gone into Snickets yet. Nanna suggested a stroll through the woods one particularly fine day; my stomach flipped a little, but I accepted her offer all the same. As we passed Smythe's Farm Ned shouted from the yard, 'Nice day for it!' No mention of any ill goings-on, he whistled a happy tune while hammering the case of a tractor engine. With a deep breath we entered the woods and headed for the den.

Nanna blew any fear or doubt away, her presence pure and strong shining through the insecurities and paranoia I had attracted; it was all good, all hunky-dory when Nanna was around. She was magic, she was amazing. *I wish I could be more like her,* I thought. With my thoughts relieved and confidence growing, I felt more at ease in the woods.

The following day I ventured out on my own and lay with Mr Milly in the grass just before the wood's entrance, the late afternoon sun warming my face. I stroked my beloved friend as my head slowly settled into a spot ideal for a nap; my eyelids grew heavy and were illuminated orange and red as I looked into them. Again, the curtains drew on this reality and opened to the influence of my mind and what secrets it held, it wasn't the Gap this time, it was just where I was, just as if I was watching myself and Mr Milly curled up dozing in the afternoon summer sun.

A sepia tint filled the scene, calmness ruled my senses, but something hovered out of view. A cold breeze quickly picked up from over the moor, bringing a mass of sullen clouds. They filled the sky, turning everything a shade darker until the sun was devoured. Hurtling backwards, forever moving, unsettled, angry and frustrated, searching, scanning and sowing their murky will into all. The ground beside me creaked and groaned, expelling a foul burst of air before the surface ruptured, spiralling a twisted silver tree upwards. Within its finger-like branches sat the cuckoo clock from Nanna's kitchen, its dial spinning backwards, the little bird played in reverse. I watched feeling winter's chill creep upon me. The woods reached out, their leaves blown away exposing a line of skeletal tree profiles superimposed upon the dusk background. The darkness took form and searched for me. I had a light shining from my heart high into the sky, a pillar of pureness that the shadow wanted to smite, extinguishing its source. It hated the light and wanted to corrupt, deceive, decay and destroy the lighthouse in the night.

Mr Milly's white coat turned to a shaggy black mess; I shouted and shouted, 'Wake up! Wake up!' I cried, knowing it was taking me. I closed my eyes and imagined myself back in my body. 'Awake! Awake!' I called. In a flash I was sucked back into my body and out of the dream. I sat startled, the scene had changed; the wind was up, the light was fading, and that presence was lurking again as if I had brought it back from the dream.

I gathered myself and backed away from the woods, turning to begin our ascent; it took everything not to look back. I was both intrigued and scared of what I might see. Gripped again by my curiosity. Twisting my senses just like the Hound did. I should have turned on my heels, I stood motionless. Should I look? Should I? It's as if I had to face up to something, a foe unknown to me but somehow I did know, we were connected, it knew me, and I it.

Mr Milly had trotted on and was sniffing in the long grass. She suddenly turned her ears pricked staring at me, rolling out a low rumbling growl that quickly escalated into a snarly snapping bark, her reaction confirming my fears. I turned slowly, realising the threat she perceived was coming from behind me. Sparks were flying in my head. What was it? I spun around and at first saw nothing. I squinted, trying to home in, sensing the vista had more to show. My eyes fell out of focus; the air in front wasn't behaving as I'd expect. A slight shimmer could be seen, an outline of an invisible cloak tattered and torn blew in the breeze moving closer and closer.

Mr Milly was now at my side, my jumper in her mouth, tugging, begging me to go. Almost hypnotised, I couldn't budge; my eyes had become fixated upon its centre. Two swirling discs had become visible, still shimmering, not fully clear, but its effects were paralysing. 'Let me in, let me in,' came a frosty whisper. Struggling to break free, magnetised by the unnatural presence that unfolded before me, my fear slightly suppressed by the multitude of questions now jockeying for position, all the what-ifs had suddenly become undeniably real!

Mr Milly finally pulled me onto my back foot, we turned together and ran like the wind, hurtling along the old coach track. I took a glance back but couldn't pick anything out. We made it back to

Nanna's leaping over the back gate and bundled through the kitchen door. 'Nanna!? Nanna!' I called out. She rushed through to see what the commotion was.

'What on earth is going on!' she exclaimed. I struggled to catch my breath. 'It's OK, Pete, it's OK, let it out, now come on, you're safe here. Now tell me, what's all this about?' said Nanna calmly.

So I explained in detail; she didn't seem the slightest bit disbelieving or overwhelmed or well, anything, just notably calm and understanding, listening to my ramblings with a nod and sighs of agreement.

'What's going on, Nanna? There's weird stuff happening all the time, that Hound thing, the dead dog and the green mist and now this. I know something's out there, and it's bad!' When I had expired my last spluttered sentence, she sat back gently and began to speak.

'Hhhhmmm,' she pondered. I could tell she wanted to tell me but didn't quite know how or if she should.

Nanna took a breath and continued. 'I thought it was a just a little nuisance, but it appears to be more, my dear. There's more to this world, much more; hidden in our subconscious are the keys to doors of remembrance. We are designed to put these odd experiences to the very back of our mind then eventually forget where they are, to the point where we will question whether it was actually a real experience or something we read or saw on TV, all the time echoing through our eternal being that it's not real, but my dear, it is! We aren't supposed to remember or question its authenticity.' Nanna didn't mince her words and always talked to me like an adult whether I understood her ramblings or not.

'So that Hound, and that ghostly thing just then! They're real! Really real!' I questioned, still none the wiser.

'Really, real,' confirmed Nanna.

'What do you mean? I don't understand.' I was bamboozled, my head was spinning. I needed answers, ones I could understand. I felt sweaty and anxious.

'Here, my dear,' said Nanna, passing me a drink. 'I will try to explain, my dear, but I'm afraid this may take a little time to digest, and once you know and understand there's no forgetting, life will be different, are you OK with that? Trust me, am I scared of anything?' she said.

Knowing Nanna was right, I took a swig and pinned my ears back as she continued. 'There is more to this story than words on a page when you read a book. What's going on in your head? Are you not seeing those people, those places in your head? Is the story not playing a movie inside your mind? You are creating, my dear, not physically but energetically. There is a world beyond human perception, beyond sight and sound, but it's there nevertheless.'

'How do you know, Nanna?' I asked.

'Because I've opened to it. Once people drag their heads out of the doldrums of life, of the inane cycles of just being, you start to think about our place, what are we doing here? I was shown a secret a long time ago, a way to tune in and enter this other world where the unbelievable exists.' Nanna paused and took a bite of biscuit, giving me time to take it in.

'How? How? What is it? What's this other world?' I badgered her for more information, now becoming excited at the very idea of this reality.

'It's a place like this but so much more, a place of dreams that are and are not to be. All paths are open, all possibilities possible, nothing is set in stone, all is moulded at the will of our minds. Every idea, every daydream every nightmare and every fear,' said Nanna, smiling a little, knowing my anxieties had been overtaken by enthusiasm.

I sat wide-eyed and silent, trying to take all this in. Nanna could tell by the lack of response and the glaze upon my face that she may have actually blown my mind.

'I don't mean to scare you, dear. Let me put it like this. Before anything is made, it exists as thought energy. With enough concentrated energy this thought can burst into reality as an idea; this idea is then built upon with willing hands and minds. This is how great accomplishments are achieved. Everything is energy, even a simple thought, so beware of your thoughts, be a master of them, for they can betray you and present your greatest fear at your door. Think good, and you will attract and create good, think negative bad thoughts, and it will attract like. This is a place of dreams that will and won't come true, a place where everything is alive in every possible way. All options are open, all possibilities possible before our human minds have got in the way of our wildest imaginations. Once you open your eyes to this universe you can never close them to it, it's like waking and remembering all you always knew. When you sleep tonight call upon your truth, your love and power, ask to be reminded what you have forgotten, and tomorrow we shall take a walk in a different world. Don't be scared, my dear, most fears come from the unknown and you're about to unravel the unknown and fear itself,' said Nanna, always maintaining a half-smile upon her face.

'So the beast and that... that other thing, what are they?' I questioned, finding it difficult to describe the latter in words.

'Yes, yes, a Sulphur Hound and a Veil Lurker, both most unpleasant to come across,' she said, shaking her head as if to lose the images within. 'Things will make more sense in the morning, my dear, we will be ready to talk properly then, trust me,' comforted Nanna. She stood and walked across to the kitchen dresser. 'I've got something that will help you, something to keep with you.' She rummaged around in a bowl of crystals sitting on the top of the dresser. Nanna was most fond of her multi-coloured stones as I saw them, but they had a deeper meaning and purpose.

'Ah-ha,' she said, plucking a smallish black cube from the rainbow rubble. 'This one, here, take it, get to know it, put it under your pillow, keep it with you.' Nanna passed me the stone which I examined closer; it was solid black inset with white flecks.

I held it for a moment, and instantly it drew me in, my hand started to get warmer, and a spinning motion started as if an invisible wheel circled it. 'Wow, it's doing stuff,' I exclaimed.

'Oohhh, you're ready then, it's communicating, activating with your energy. It's a good match for you, I'm glad,' she said, sitting on the arm of the chair. Nanna grasped my hands together and looked into my eyes. 'Dear boy, you are the light in the night, the gap in the clouds and the sun that shines down, you have nothing to fear, you are stronger than you could imagine, I will guide you and be beside you.' With that she kissed me on the head and said, 'Come on, let's get you and your friend off to bed now.' She walked me through to my bedroom and tucked me in. 'Remember, just ask to recall all that's been forgotten, repeat it as you go to sleep and see what happens. Sleep tight, see you in the morning,' she whispered.

'Night, Nanna, love you,' I replied. She blew a kiss and mouthed her affection back. Mr Milly came in beside me while Moggins curled up by my feet.

Closing my eyes, asking to be reminded, I repeated the words again and again. The blackness I stared upon looked back at me. Stars shone like tiny pinpricks in my mind, a slight pressure in my forehead rose, and my eyes wanted to look inside me. The stars moved faster and faster, closer and closer, forming a tunnel in front of me which I flowed down, finally opening into an expanse, a plane of eternity where my body was forgotten. I was everything and nothing all questions were answered without saying a word, without having a question. My soul remembered as I fell into a deep, warm sleep.

The next morning I awoke early feeling normal as usual, not like I'd expected to feel. I lifted my hands above me and examined them. *Nothing different there,* I thought. I carried on the examination in front of the mirror, pulling my mouth apart, tongue, teeth, eyes all looked the same. I thought something might have changed because I remembered the starlit tunnel before sleep and the pressure I'd felt on my brow. I gazed into the mirror as I do, lost in my contemplation, that's when I noticed something, a slight haze of yellow around my head, but as soon as I became aware it disappeared, I couldn't look directly at it. 'Hmmm, very strange,' I mused.

The kettle's whistle called me into the kitchen where Nanna was sat at the table. 'Morning, dear, anything to tell me?' she quizzed. I explained what I'd experienced, and she nodded. 'Good, good, now we can start to unravel, can't we?' On that note she looked up at the cuckoo clock and said nothing, the clock wasn't due to chime.

'What you doing, Nanna?' I said, bemused.

'Waiting for the news,' she answered.

'But the paper's in front of you,' I reasoned.

'Not that news,' she replied.

She looked back at the clock and then opened up today's free local paper, pushed her spectacles into place and began reading the headlines, letting out a large sigh. News of award-winning marrows and perfectly crafted cakes couldn't hold her attention long; the paper was soon folded and sat back in place. She gazed again at the clock. 'Come on then,' she said in a frustrated tone, then almost willed on by her focus the gears of the clock cranked round, and the mechanism sprung into life. It wasn't on the hour, it was showing 8.13, what a strange time to chime. *Must be broken,* I thought. Then the little rosewood bird popped through the tiny doors.

Nanna looked up. 'Well what's all these shadowy goings-on then? Even the boys down the lane have had a whiff of it,' she said, seemingly quizzing the clock, well, to be more precise the bird that was now centre stage.

'Who you talking to?' I asked. Then most extraordinarily the miniature bird fluttered into life, as if woken from a spell. Its tiny wings flapped, the grains of wood streaked around its now malleable shape. *A real wooden bird!* I thought to myself, mouth wide open in disbelief. Looking properly flummoxed I said again under my breath, 'A real wooden bird!' Repeating it to myself didn't make any more sense of it, but after recent events, I wasn't really surprised.

The bird buzzed round the room dipping and diving, enjoying its freedom from the clock, whizzing round the ceiling light, round and round quicker and quicker, finally flinging off, hurtling across the room inches from the dresser top. Finally, it stopped dead, suspended in the air gently hovering, its wings beating in a blur. I watched in amazement as the little miracle gently descended to the arm of the chair I was sat in. Two tiny black dots looked upon me; it radiated kindness and was the most beautiful thing I'd ever seen, I just wanted to scoop it up and hold it in my hands.

The bird chirped in a way I'd never heard, an orchestra of brass bells and chimes that tinkled away, laced with the pureness of a crystal glass ringing and echoing throughout the room. It was heaven to my ears; the bird stopped its happy melody and turned its head to look at Nanna. 'She says hello,' said Nanna.

'You can talk to her?' I asked.

'Yes, my dear, and you will hear her too, but for now, I will translate,' said Nanna. The bird looked back at me and began chiming and ringing, then stopped. 'She is very happy you know now, and she is very pleased to meet you,' translated Nanna. 'Yes, yes, OK,' grumbled Nanna. The bird sang on and on as if telling me her life story. 'OK, *OK*, I will give him the short version,' interrupted Nanna. 'Right, this little miniature miracle is my direct dial to the Veil and all things beyond,' stated Nanna. The bird chimed away again, and through the delicate tones I heard three letters strung together.

'W…I…T?' I quietly repeated.

'Ah, that's great,' said Nanna. The bird was overjoyed by this; it fluttered off around the room again in a flurry of 'loop the loops'.

'Wit,' I repeated.

'Yes indeed, Wit, or wooden tit,' smirked Nanna.

'So, what is she?' I asked.

'Well let's start with what she does first, what she is will become clear as time goes on, dear.' Nanna paused for a moment while Wit settled on the table in front of her. 'Wit is my insider, she knows what's going on with the weird stuff, as you say; she lets me know what's afoot around here and I don't just mean the local gossip. Right then, what's all this shadiness then?' asked Nanna. Now the bird's chimes and rings were different, with lower notes, her brightness dulled. I knew it wasn't going to be good news.

Nanna sat back and sighed. 'There's an imbalance, the Veil thins, shadowy fingers are spreading into the third reality.' I looked confused. 'Our reality,' Nanna continued. 'Like sickened ivy, it yearns to choke the good! And blight the light!' said Nanna.

'Well, that doesn't sound good at all, what's the Veil? What's this power?' I asked.

'It's an invisible barrier between this and that world; when the Veil is thin both realities can mix, that explains the strange things you've encountered, doesn't it?' said Nanna.

She went onto describe Wit as an oracle, who telepathically communicates with her: conveying feedback on the vibrational state, of this and that dimension.

Wit places pictures in Nanna's mind's eye, telling her when the frequencies are out of pitch, in particular when the pull of the dark and light are unbalanced, helping Nanna make more sense of the situation. Kind of like a serious game of charades.

Nanna sat back and puzzled; one arm of her spectacles in the corner of her mouth, she mused over the incoming information.

'So how many dimensions are there? How do you get into them? How do you know?' my flurry of question stirred Nanna from her contemplation.

'Well, do you know, I think we'd be better showing you. Come on, grab your shoes and put a jumper on,' said Nanna enthusiastically.

We gathered ourselves and headed for the back gate; the air was cool today, and the sun was slow to warm the dewy grass. Walking along the trail towards the old coach path we paused to look upon Snickets and the surrounding fields. 'It's pretty, innit, Nanna?' I said, taking in a deep breath of fresh country air.

'It is, my dear, and it's about to get a whole lot more,' said Nanna, winking. She then grabbed my hand. 'Close your eyes, think of your feet as roots travelling deep into the earth, now think of a beam of light coming from the centre of all there is, through your head and into the ground,' she said in a calm, soothing voice. 'Do you feel it?' she added, and to my surprise I did, I felt a surge run through me, tingles and currents of energy activating all around my body.

'Yes, I do,' I replied.

'Now open your eyes,' Nanna asked.

The sight that unfolded was something else, coupled with an exhilarating rushing sensation, my senses were overloading. I was still stood on the old coach track, still in our world, but somewhere else at the same time. Everything was enhanced, everything was alive; the grass, the trees and flowers. Their beauty accentuated by an accompaniment of gentle coloured mists that sparkled and danced around them.

Blues, golds and yellows decorated Nanna, twinkling like a galaxy of stars. Mr Milly was shimmering ice white, proud and good. Nanna held her hand out and in a tiny explosion of glitter Wit appeared. She fluttered off and buzzed around us; there was a beautiful orchestra of the most delicate sounds I had ever heard. If love had a sound this was it, a warm swell expanded from my navel and enveloped me from head to toe, feeling like Christmas morning and all my birthdays wrapped in one.

I looked at my spectrum of colours, it was like an oil painting; the shades weren't as fluid and seemed less vibrant than Nanna's. I could see what looked like a miniature storm deep within the varied colours that surrounded my physical body. 'That's your aura, your energy that can tell you a lot if you can access it,' said Nanna, watching me examine myself.

'How do I do this…? All the time?' I replied, mesmerised by the living art that engulfed me.

'It's in every moment, all of this, always,' she said, opening her arms in a welcoming gesture to the energies around. 'You just have to tune in, my dear, we are tuned in now. Just like when a radio switches to a different station, so can we,' explained Nanna. 'Our limited senses won't allow us to see, feel or hear everything, it's been locked away, like a secret level in a game where you get all the powers,' said Nanna, leaning in with a gleeful grin.

Everything here seemed to reveal its true identity. What we saw every day was such a small part of the picture, even the sun appeared different, appearing much closer – it was purple and looked like some kind of portal. 'Wow,' I said, my eyes trying to take in the surreal sight before me. I gazed upon the woods and thoughts of the Sulphur Hound, and the Veil Lurker popped into my head. My aura instantly responded to these thoughts; the colours changed as if a brush stroke passed through them, a dark purple smudge appeared and swirled seemingly gathering momentum.

The woods now had eyes, deep in the shadows, they looked out, blinking between piercing stares. The trees creaked and bent out of shape, the whole scene dimmed. 'Eeeer, now then, you need to watch that!' grumbled Nanna.

'What? What's happening?' I replied, confused.

'Remember to be master of your thoughts, or they will betray you, bringing your worst fear to your door,' said Nanna while grabbing my hand. 'Take a deep breath, suck in all the good, all the love, all the hope and joy you can, all the memories that touched your soul and lifted your spirits bring them all together now in one place, in your heart, breathe them in, feel them,' instructed Nanna. We did this together, holding our breath for a moment where time seemed to stop. 'Now let it out, let it blow away all the negative worries, all the troubles and concerns. Let it melt them away,' said Nanna. We both blew out together and opened our eyes. A dome of translucent energy spread out in all directions, it felt the same as I experienced the night Nanna went out into the rain and dealt with the Hound. The wave lifted everything it touched with the most gentle healing wind, illuminating all with a warm golden glow.

The dome expanded to the treeline and devoured the makings of my negative residual thought energy. It was no match for all the good we had to give, the trees blew as if shaking off a cold standing tall again, relinquishing their stoop. The sky brightened, and the scene returned to as before. 'Right we should talk, uuurrrmmm, about those, errr, things… when we aren't tuned in, my dear. You will learn to control it, don't worry,' comforted Nanna.

Wit chirped again and landed on her shoulder. Nanna leant her ear to the tiny bird and closed her eyes. Now I could see the pictures too, similar to an old slideshow, the images faded and monochrome physically projected in Nanna's aura, it was amazing to see. I saw a place, a village sunken in a bog, people with wretched pained expressions upon their faces clutching and stretching out for help, red eyes in the dark and rivers of light contaminated by tar that flowed into them, then in quick succession as if our presence had been detected, the Hound's grizzly face and swirling eyes of the Lurker. Just before Nanna could pull the plug, there was another, a woman in the shadows, her menace filling the air. 'Enough now!' exclaimed Nanna, pulling her head upright and opening her eyes. Wit disappeared in a puff of glitter, and the Veil rose, tuning us back into our reality.

'Who was that? Where was that village? It looked awful, Nanna,' I asked, concerned.

'A pain,' she replied, 'only a niggle though, and that place, that was Blackend, not a very nice place, but everything has a balance, and that's where the negative is drawn to,' she added. 'I will explain it all later, that's enough for now, let it all soak in,' said Nanna.

I couldn't even begin to make sense of the wondrous world I had just been opened to. Nanna seemed so in tune, so in control, while I felt like a bull in a china shop with my rampaging imagination. Now I was aware of my reckless thoughts, I would try to curb them and think with discretion.

We stood together, looking at the surroundings. Nanna turned and stared over the treeline towards the moor; she rubbed her chin and touched her cheek in a thoughtful pondering manner. 'Is it there, Nanna? That place, is it on the moor?' I asked.

'Yes, my dear, out of sight but not out of mind,' she said, gazing at the horizon. 'Let's fill you in over a cuppa, shall we?' she said, smiling.

My world had just been turned upside down, I had been given the key to those locked doors at the back of my mind. I had so many questions bubbling up inside me, excitement and fear playing a delicate balancing act. Was that lump in my stomach butterflies of excitement or wasps of worry? I couldn't decide.

CHAPTER 5

The Light Shedder

B ack at Ivy Gate, Nanna put the kettle on and then rummaged around in the back of the kitchen dresser.

'I know you're in here,' she muttered, then with a victorious clutch she emerged from the cupboard holding a key. Its handle a copper spiral with small gemstones placed within its pattern, it glistened and shone in the sunlight.

'Be a love and pull the curtains, draw the blind too will you?' asked Nanna.

I found this request slightly odd as she always kept them open even at night, but I did as she asked, my anticipation building as to what the key was for.

Nanna sat at the kitchen table, pulling the chair up close. She positioned the key in front of her and placed both hands face down either side. By now, I could tell what she was doing. Nanna closed her eyes. A look of concentration spread softly over her face. I could see a shimmer around her as a golden trail of light shone upwards from the wooden table's surface. Tiny rays piercing from within multiplied, and glided around, making a keyhole.

'Right then,' she said, opening her eyes and picking the key up. Inserting it into the table, she turned it clockwise, making a clunking sound as if opening the door of a heavily secured safe. When the noise stopped, the golden rays disappeared, revealing a wooden door hinged to the table's surface.

Nanna pulled on the handle, the door opened, expelling a blast of air and dust. She coughed and wafted it away then peered inside.

'This should shine some light on things,' she said, plunging her hands deep into the table. My head followed her action, and just like a great magician, the underside remained the same, no false boxes or mirrored panels.

I moved behind Nanna, standing so I could see into the opening. What I saw was rows of books. Nanna scanned over the shelves' contents at will until she paused upon a large old book. It had a dark purple cover bound in a leather strap. She leaned in further and pulled the book from the opening, placing it on the table. She wiped it and blew the dust off. Golden inscriptions, symbols and shapes adorned its cover. These made no sense to me, but it all looked very mysterious and quite important.

'Is that Santa's naughty book?' I smirked, trying to lighten the mood, more for my sake than Nanna's.

'Ha! And would your name be in it?' she responded, squinting at me knowingly before opening the book. For a moment I thought it could have been; my memories cast back to our cover-up of Moggins' marauding massacre in Mrs Monkwit's aviary, oh, and that broken school window, oh, and the flaming dog poo trick.

'No, it's not!' tutted Nanna, breaking me from my self-indulgent imagination. She beckoned me over. 'Come on, pull a chair up,' she said.

We sat at the table. The room was lit with a diffused orange glow as the curtains attempted in vain to shut the sun out. Nanna opened the book, my eyes tracking her every movement, the tension growing as I couldn't wait to see what it would expose. What secrets was I going to learn; what mysteries were to be unravelled?

Nanna passed the book.

'Open it,' she said. I unclipped the leather strap; it creaked with an age-old yawn. I looked at the first pages and then back at Nanna, and then to the book again.

'Is it a trick? Why are the pages blank?' I quizzed.

'But they are not. The answers are written on them, just ask the question,' said Nanna. 'It will explain what you need to know and how you can best understand it. Focus your intent upon the page and see,' she instructed.

I peered at the book with a barrage of questions buzzing around my head. Images started to appear and lines of text streaked across the page. But before I could make head or tail of them, they disappeared, and more illustrations and diagrams appeared over them.

'Calm your mind, my dear,' said Nanna as she held my hand, immediately slowing my thoughts. The page wiped clean, and then a clear picture became visible. Spread over the two pages in front of me was a map with arrows and text describing the different places I could see; Ivy Gate, the village, Smythe's farm, Snickets, the moor and that place, Blackend.

Lines intersected here and there, some were white and others black. As it drew my attention to these features, the image morphed, rearranging itself to show me what I wanted to know. If I kept my thoughts true and clear, it worked brilliantly.

'Wow, this is amazing!' I gasped. I was in awe of this voodoo technology. The white lines stood out now as my curiosities focused upon them. They crossed under Nanna's cottage and then raced off in all directions. The lines were thicker as they left the intersection, gradually thinning the further out they got.

'That's source energy, like the veins of Mother Earth. Where they cross is a concentrated seat of power. The white is the light that will see us through the night,' chirped Nanna in a merry little tune.

'Fear is the dark knocking at the door!' I said, reading the words as they appeared in front of me.

The picture changed again, now zooming out, showing Blackend equally matching Ivy Gate. An array of inky lines crossing at its centre where a dark whirlpool slowly rotated anticlockwise. When the two contrasting energies met, there was conflict. The black veins wrapped around the pure white stems which flickered and turned a shade darker, gradually becoming its opposite.

'Is this what's happening? Is it spreading?' I quizzed worriedly.

'Hmm, it appears there is an imbalance, it seems Blackend stirs again,' answered Nanna, her chirpiness now culled. 'This is my patch, and I've kept watch for longer than you know, my dear,' she said, a sternness now present in her mellow tones.

The map disappeared, and the page sat quietly, not responding to my questions. I gave Nanna a puzzled look. Mr Milly moved closer and tucked in by my side; she made an uneasy whimper which I had now come to recognise as a sign of impending doom.

A shadow spread across the ceiling, the lights flickered and flashed on and off. The cutlery drawer opened and slammed shut, a wind had gathered momentum from nowhere and began swirling around the room. The book bounced, flicking the pages back and forth. I stood up and pushed my chair back, not knowing what to do but needing to be away from the book. Nanna didn't move, seeming intrigued but not worried.

'Do something, Nanna! Do something!' I shouted.

Silence fell, and darkness filled the room. A low bellow sounding like a detuned bagpipe trying to speak crept up my spine; its freezing presence iced the mirror above the dresser. I stood still, not knowing what would happen next. The book suddenly flung itself open. Images of the Hound and the Lurker and other demonic horrors flashed faster and faster until the page bled and tar ran on to the table. It was all getting a little out of control.

I looked at Nanna. She saw the playful curiosity within me had withered, and I was now fearful. My pale shocked face pleaded with her to do something.

Is this a test? Is it? I thought, not knowing anymore, I couldn't tell, I was so confused. At that point, Nanna raised her hands into the air and slammed them down.

'Enough!' she commanded.

The whole room shook as she trembled with power; a power laced with a protective anger. The book slammed shut and was sucked back into the table. The door following suit bashed against the wooden surface, throwing the key into the air which Nanna caught and placed in her pocket.

The room returned to normal, Mr Milly rubbed her nose into my thigh. Nanna came over, pulling me into a secure cuddle, rubbing the back of my head.

'Sorry, my dear, too much too soon,' she said, placing an invisible plaster over my grazed emotions.

I couldn't help feeling that my curiosity and fear might compromise Nanna's position. I had never seen her react like that, it almost scared me more that the intruding nightmare.

'Nothing to fear but fear itself,' whispered Nanna into my ear.

Her energy spread over the whole room, and a blanket of protection fell over us. Again I felt like it would be all right, Nanna would make it so.

'Now let's get those blinds up and curtains open,' she chirped. 'Biscuits, anyone?' she said, looking at Mr Milly and me.

The sun streamed in, we sat quietly and munched on Nanna's home-cooked shortbread. Mr Milly chased the remains of the biscuit around the carpet trying to get every last scrap.

'Whatever you want to know, I can tell you the good old-fashioned way. No Veil or magic books, just a plain old tale, OK?' she said, pausing for my response. I nodded sheepishly, understanding there was no going back, I knew things now, and they needed explaining. I needed to understand my part in this.

'No Veil then?' I replied meekly.

'No dear, not until you want to,' comforted Nanna. I pulled my feet up onto the chair and snuggled into its arm.

'Go on then, tell me. What's Blackend?' I asked.

Nanna paused, pondering how best to say this without promoting fear.

'Bleak and black, with no end to the hopelessness. A place that's gone so far down the wrong path it doesn't know how to return. Where all your hopes and dreams are sucked from your soul and burnt in a flame of jealousy.' She stopped and took a breath.

'Bloody hell, steady on! I thought we were taking it easy?!' I bleated. 'Wow, certainly not Butlin's then!' I added. Nanna held her breath and puffed out her cheeks childishly. She smirked, and we both let out a burst of laughter.

'Well, I've never sugar-coated things, have I? A spade's a spade,' said Nanna.

'How did it get like that?' I asked. Nanna began to tell the story of Blackend.

'Well many years ago, when belief in the powers and dimensions were more freely thought of, when myths and legends lurked on the moors, a group of settlers were led away from the small community which we now call Chattersley. Conned with a crooked promise; lured from the protective seat of power that emanates from this area to a darker way. A way that professed them a deeper connection to the mystic powers of the Veil.

'A sage named ShawlInka led them. She was a traveller of dimensions; of time and space. Some say she was a witch; a demon in human skin; a shapeshifter; a being of great power; a being that can bring the creations of the Veil into our reality. Whether these people followed her through fear or through deluded ego, I do not know, but they were corrupted, and they followed her to live beyond the safety of their homestead.

'They set up a new commune on Sackhole Moor, communication all but ceased. ShawlInka cut them off from their light and opened them up to the dark. Dubbed 'Blackend' by the locals, for it was said a swirling cloud never moved from over the area. People stayed away for fear of red-eyed wolves. The moor madness spread wide and far, and the place soon became a source of foreboding tales spreading its vibration, just as she intended. No one knows where the people of Blackend went or what happened to them. The village remains, but there is no sign of life. Rumour said ShawlInka took them to the lower astral, where she bled the goodness and light out of those poor wretched souls, creating a negative gateway that's been present ever since.

'No one goes there now, apart from warriors of light trying to heal the land. In all my years at Ivy Gate, Blackend's influence has never stretched this far. Hope, courage and goodness need to push back and stop its spread. It looks like we might have to pay a visit but not before you, my darling, have a lesson or two in minding your mind. A mind like yours, with that overactive imagination, could be a death sentence or a saviour. Let's make it the latter, shall we?'

Nanna smiled, looking pleased with my reaction to the story.

'See, that's not too bad, is it?' she said.

'It sounds bleeding horrid!' I said, spitting my drink out.

'But you're OK with it? You can handle this, can't you my dear? You'll feel better when you know what you can do,' she said convincingly.

'What I can do!?' I asked.

'It's more like what can't you do. I've seen your strength, you were born for this, you came back for this, to discover and remember all that's lost and forgotten. To be a tool for the light. Let me show you, my dear,' requested Nanna. I paused, uncertain of what this entailed.

'Whoa! I was born for this? Born for what?' I asked, growing more perplexed.

'Sorry, dear, I do get carried away. I've... we've walked this path before, many times, waiting for, shall we say the ripe conditions,' explained Nanna.

It seemed I was being dragged into something I had no knowledge of. A situation beyond earthly perceptions. But it was clear Nanna knew all about this hidden world, and her over-boiling enthusiasm for the new recruit couldn't be hidden. I was in now, and these things were happening whether I liked it or not. Nanna's words were slowly rebuilding my pluck and confidence.

'If you can just begin to see, your courage and faith will grow,' added Nanna.

'OK... OK, show me how,' I said, gently putting my trust in her.

'Right, no time like the present, let's see what's in that squiffy mind of yours,' said Nanna.

'What! Now... right now!' I exclaimed, thinking I might have the grace of time to digest the situation.

'Yes, I promise. You will feel better. The more you know, the more control you will have, come...' Nanna held out her hand.

We set off to the field at the back of Ivy Gate. By now it was early evening, the sky was scarlet with oranges and pinks twirled and laced through the clouds. The birds chirped as they settled, calling out to each other, probably saying, 'Night... great day flying around, same again tomorrow, let's try to drop one on the old Major's head,' followed by a chorus of chirped laughter that filled the tree rafters. I usually loved this time of day, as a stillness would fall upon my world, the day almost done and my bed beckoning, but not today. My senses were pumped up, and my lovely bed was nowhere in sight. Well, not until Nanna had finished with me.

CHAPTER 6

The Training Grounds

Nanna led us into the fallow field, surveying the sky and surrounding treelines. When satisfied the spot was right she stopped.

'Right, this will do. Next to me, dear, please. Fall in, Mr Milly,' she chirped, tapping her side. We stood facing the far end of the field. Lined up like frontline soldiers; bound by more than family ties, there were secrets now that lined the twisted path we followed.

'What we doing?' I quizzed. Nanna reached over and held my hand; I placed mine on Mr Milly who looked for Moggins, but he was being as cattish as ever, no doubt off pleasing himself doing as he wished, probably curled up by the kitchen radiator.

Wit had joined us, bursting into reality in a sparkling eruption of glitter. The tiny bird hovered above us, her presence confirming that my world was transforming, the barrier between this and that reality becoming more flexible and permeable, one frequency seeping into the other. Wit perched on Nanna's shoulder as she began to speak.

'Same again, dear, like on the coach track, but try to imagine the two different frequencies, try to see you slipping between them, right then? Ready?' I nodded. 'Good. Feel your feet sink into the earth like roots of light, see those roots burrow deep into the core of the earth, grounding you with the vibration of the great mother. Breath the light up, bring it into you.'

I did what Nanna said. Time seemed to stand still, my feet tingled and heartbeat slowed, the doors to my imagination were all but shut, nothing distracting me, nothing calling for my attention.

'Now connect to the power above, the stars, the sky, and the source of all,' continued Nanna.

I imagined a beam of sunlight powering down from the heavens; it touched the top of my head and joined with the power from below. At that moment, a switch flicked, and my world changed! Like a waterfall, a rippling curtain washed away the disguise and revealed the truth. Allowing me a glimpse behind the scenes of life, cleaning away the distortions placed upon our reality, our world. Everything looked the same but wasn't, we were still here in the field at the back of Ivy Gate. The birds still chirped with their dusky chatter, as the orange glow of Nanna's kitchen flooded out of the windows, illuminating the surrounding area.

I looked at Nanna and Mr Milly, they were surrounded by a colourful haze of blues and greens, sparkling tubes of glittering particles flowed around them. Everything seemed so much more alive, the grass and even the air looked to be breathing. I was humbled by the beauty and imagined that if every human could see the world this way, we would be much more considerate of our actions upon others and our surroundings. Even making a footprint in a flowery meadow would seem like a crime. I didn't understand why this beautiful world was hidden from us, I got the distinct impression this was the first of many great reveals. How deep did these secrets go? Eagerly I awaited Nanna's instructions.

'Now… all is good, yes?' asked Nanna.

I nodded, but something else caught my eye. In the bushes at the edge of the field, I could see two boys hiding, they were chuckling, pushing and shoving each other playfully. Dressed in what looked like raggy foliage, one wore round welding goggles pushed onto his forehead, the other a patch with a hole cut out to see through. The mysterious spectators looked like they had ringside seats for whatever was about to proceed. I squinted with curiosity. Nanna turned and glanced; she shrugged and puffed with a snort of contempt.

'The Rag Tree boys,' she said but gave no further explanation for the strange onlookers. Nanna continued, 'Now see the treeline at the far end of the field, focus your intent and energy on it,' she instructed.

The field was lined by pine and fir trees making a thick, dense wall to project on, the dark green foliage concealing what lies within and any mysteries it may hold. I gazed softly, unintentionally loosening the grip on my imagination. It quietly snuck in and walked me down the path of murky possibilities. Then before my eyes, before I'd had time to adjust my daydreaming a mist seeped out from the wood; it laid a blanket of disguise across its length. Already a tone had been set, my intent was beginning to create. My mind tried to reason and read between the lines, but I had already pre-empted what lies within the smoky wall.

Nanna took a sideward glance and raised an eyebrow, not saying a word, just letting the events unfold. A darker patch appeared in the mist, the shape morphed, rose and fell, undecided upon itself.

Lingering on the edge of creation, all the time my untamed mind questioning all the possibilities, then it broke free in a guttural roar.

'Watch it,' Nanna snapped. I tried to control my thoughts, but it was too late, it thumped down on two front legs, its matted mane and black diamond teeth now visible. The electric flicker of its eyes pierced through the fog; we could all now clearly see what had birthed into reality.

'Oh no,' I muttered. From my right side I could feel and see light emanating from Mr Milly. I turned to see her doubled in size, my mouth wide open again in wonder at my canine companion. She was majestic, shimmering ice white with dazzling blue streaks running through her coat. Her claws and teeth were razor-sharp diamonds and a fierceness I'd never felt before sparked within her ready to counter whatever creation lurched from the dark corners of the night.

'Peter! Enough now! Mind those thoughts. Make them clear, not runaways,' barked Nanna.

I jumped back into my skin after Nanna's harsh tongue had whipped me from my mindless creation. I gained control, cleared my mind of all things sulphur and hound-ish, the shadow slowly shrunk back into the mist.

'Good boy! Now we don't want any unnecessary conflict, do we Mr Milly?' Nanna's tone had softened considerably.

Mr Milly looked at me as if to say, 'Well I wouldn't have minded a go at vanquishing that foul beast.' Her fierceness dissipated as she returned to her normal form. The shadow shrunk and stopped around the size of a deer, gently emerging from the mist, nibbling the lush grass under its nose.

'Now that's much better, but any thoughts of that ghastly Sulphur Hou—' said Nanna.

Before she could finish her sentence, her praise collapsed. The deer's head snapped back with a god awful crack. The legs dislocated, the skin split and the eyes popped out. The Hound burst from the remains of the deer like it had been beneath the sea for a thousand years. It gasped and gargled, then, it focused its deathly attack on me and lurched forward.

Mr Milly fearlessly raged back into her majestic form, filling the air with the essence of bravery and courage. She dropped back onto her hind legs, ready to launch her assault on the Hound now approaching at breakneck speed. It was all happening way too fast. I couldn't focus my intent, I could see this turning out rather badly and the fact I was thinking that wasn't helping the situation.

Nanna stepped forward. She shimmered and glowed, she didn't look like Nanna, she was younger but not young, yet not old. Her hair hung loose like time itself had unravelled it. A purple cloak sat upon her shoulders with elegant gold symbols woven in it.

She was beautiful. Hold on, that's Nanna, right? She was the mother in every way – protecting, comforting, nurturing, strong and silent. She held her hand out in a stop motion while tilting her head forward, her eyes closed, gaining focus and then *bang!*

A wall of air, light and love rose up in front of us and accelerated to meet the dark intent that grew larger by the second. The wall overtook the eager Mr Milly and pushed on. The two forces collided; the Hound was left as nothing, the very essence of it was stripped, peeling its shadow away and dissolving it. The lifeless creation crashed to the floor and quickly dissolved into ash before our eyes.

The mist dispersed giving way to a single lone figure. The ghostly grey outline walked towards the edge of the mist. Slim and feminine, it carried a threat cool and calmly, not like the slavering, pain-lusting

Hound that came before. Nanna squinted at the image, and then it was gone, breaking into swirling particles like a flock of birds leaving a nested tree, the scene came quickly to rest, and all was quiet again.

'Well that was unexpected,' said Nanna, now back in her normal day wear.

'Did I make that? Was it a real Sulphur Hound?' I asked.

Nanna peered over her spectacles at me.

'Did it look real?' she asked. I nodded in response. 'Well then, as real as Mr Milly at the side of you, the difference is you made it, so you have some control over it, like when it changed into the deer... and then back again! A Hound made from a dark creator will not bend to your will,' she added.

'The figure in the fog?' I asked inquisitively. It was obviously at the back of Nanna's mind too, that's why it was projected onto the mist. Who or what was it?

'Nothing to worry about, dear,' she replied. Nanna was herself again, and Mr Milly had returned to her normal size. The rustling bushes at the edge of the field now captured our attention.

'What now?' puffed Nanna tiredly. The Rag Tree boys were still there. A blend of dimensions was occurring; we were disconnected from the full creative power of the Veil, but Wit and now the boys had filtered into my reality. They were laughing, pushing and play fighting, not giving a care to the fact we were all watching them now re-enacting the previous events which they seemed very excited about.

'Pow! Take that, you foul dog smell!' said one boy as he lifted some dubious-looking mud on a stick and pushed it toward the other's face.

'Aaawww! Death bum dirt in the face, nooo!' They collapsed on the floor in fits of belly laughter, still pulling and pawing at each other like puppies playing.

'Boys,' called Nanna. Still rolling round in the dirt, their heads turned our way. 'I've someone for you to meet,' she said. They stopped their racket for a moment and staggered to their feet, drunk on silly games, stumbling and bumbling towards us in that kind of stupid walk your parents would hate, tripping each other up with every step.

'Oooiii! Ouch! Stop it, ha-ha!' Their mischievous chuckle came closer.

CHAPTER 7

The Rag Tree Boys

'Well, that caught you by surprise, didn't it?' laughed the boy with goggles while releasing a well-aimed tap to his companion's groin.

'Ooowww,' he whined, doubling up on the floor. Nanna passed me a contemptuous look, tutting and throwing her head back in dismay.

'And we thought you were a handful,' she said with a raised eyebrow.

'These little roughyins are the Rag Tree Boys, Ikol,' she said, pointing at the boy on the floor with the holey patch, who gave me the thumbs up. 'And Okol,' pointing at the other boy proudly standing beside his fallen mate. His goggles pushed onto his mucky brow, and two grubby hands pulled down on a pair of tattered braces, which barely looked to be holding his leafy shorts up.

'Please to meet you,' beamed Okol. 'We've seen you playing in the woods.'

'Yeah, you and the other two. We like your games, especially swing for your life, that's a gooden,' said Ikol brushing himself down then giving Okol a scare as he feigned an attack.

'Swing for your what!?' exclaimed Nanna, appearing overly concerned by our boyish games, even though she had just introduced me to a world of unimaginable danger.

'See, old black smelly breath is back, he's not been around for a long time!' said Okol.

'Yeah, big slobbery chops,' said Ikol, gesturing with his hands against his mouth. I loved how they played the Sulphur Hound down. They weren't scared or bothered by its presence.

'Do you reckon we could ride it?' said Ikol.

'Bet I'd ride it longer,' replied Okol boastfully, engaging again in their natural state, rolling around nipping, slapping, laughing and ribbing each other. It was uninhibited boyish play and appeared that's all they had to do.

They argued on, but without malice. It was brotherly banter, the type only best friends could have. Showing no fear for what they had just witnessed, it was all a game to them. We watched as they frolicked on.

'Who are they, Nanna? Where do they come from?' I asked.

'The Rag Tree Boys are the embodiment of childhood spirit; mischievous, daring, and very excitable.' She nodded to them on the floor. 'Created from the energies of children's play; your games in the woods, or in the garden, the garage, the attic, in the playground or in the trees. The real play starts in your mind; existing on the other side of life as wonderful, glorious, excitable, mischievous energy. Never interrupted by tea times, school bells or homework, they do what they want when they want,' explained Nanna.

'Where do they live?' I asked.

'The Great Rag Tree in Snickets,' said Nanna.

'I've never seen it,' I replied, slightly puzzled.

'You will now, my dear,' said Nanna knowingly.

The boys stopped mid-grapple, their seemingly uninterested ears half-listening to our conversation.

'Come! We will show you!' shouted Ikol excitedly.

'Yes! Yes! Come with us, we will see him back safe, Nanna,' said Okol. Nanna paused and looked at the reddening evening sky.

'Do you want to, dear?' she asked. I nodded to which the boys started a hoedown, dancing, spinning around and around, slapping their legs with joy.

'Well, OK. But not for long, just show him quickly,' she said.

'Thanks, Nanna,' I beamed.

So I followed Ikol and Okol down the old coach track and into Snickets. Mr Milly as ever was by my side. We followed the path for a while, past the Smythes' den, then we took a track I'd never seen before.

It veered off towards Pikes Cut. The trees hung low, and I'm sure if it wasn't for my escort, things could have turned a tad sinister.

'Grumpy old trees this lot,' joked Okol, slapping a stick across one. It groaned, and they both laughed. A different tree soon became visible, one I hadn't noticed before. Standing in a clearing was a huge trunk as wide as a corn silo, its roots standing proud upon the wood floor, boastfully showing its age, towering high into the canopy much taller than its surrounding siblings. What first looked like brightly coloured ribbons hung from the ancient branches. On closer inspection they were shown to be a menagerie of children's playthings; lost kites and football scarves, mittens, balloons – some popped, others not, jam jars stuffed with toy cars and action figures, tin-can wind chimes, milk bottles with glowing lights, it was like the lost property of childhood souls.

A ladder rose up from the base. Coloured paint was splattered over it, like a rebellious rainbow not conforming to its arc. I climbed, following Ikol and Okol staring open-mouthed at the wonderful, beautiful mess.

'Come on,' shouted Ikol, halfway up the ladder.

'You can always find us here now,' added Okol.

Ikol pushed up a trap door, slamming it back against the plank floor. We surfaced upon a wooden deck, my eyes adjusting to the horde of scattered objects strewn across its surface. A chaotic collage of the ultimate boys' den greeted me; wooden swords, shields, catapults; pots with slits carved in them, doubling as helmets; comics books, board games; whittled figures, some looking like dragons and others miniature versions of themselves. Underneath all this littered mess were blasts of colours shining through from chalk pictures and scribbled comments, which at a glance looked like funny jibes at each other.

I reached out with a wondrous gaze for a jar containing a toy tractor, just like one I had had years ago.

'We collect all this, so its spirit never gets lost, be a shame for all that nice playing to be wasted. All these things are filled with the excitement they gave those little squidgers, so we keeps them alive here in the Rag Tree,' he said.

'But… not many kids play out here? And there's so much stuff?' I quizzed gazing at the laden branches of the great tree.

'Yeah, things work a bit different this side. We are here… we are there,' played Ikol.

'We are, every-bloody-where,' sniggered Okol. 'But this is our source, our home… do you like it?' asked Okol proudly.

'It's… it's… amazing!' I gushed.

'Probably some of your old gear here,' said Ikol, reaching into a bucket and plucking out an object, which he tossed towards me. 'Catch,' he called, his tongue smugly half licking the side of his mouth. I caught the object now clearly not a boy's toy, but a very girly pony with rainbows down the side.

'That's yours, innit?' They both chuckled.

'Yeah sure,' I replied sarcastically, feeling more comfortable by the minute with my newfound mates. I was starting to understand who and what the Rag Tree Boys were.

On the platform, the treehouse seemed much bigger than below. I peered down and called to Mr Milly.

'I won't be long, girl, you just sit awhile.' She whimpered and moaned dissatisfied, but nevertheless settled down under the great tree. I felt a tad guilty in that I presumed she had thought there was some good playing to be had.

The platform had buckets hinged on the outer railings, some full with rainwater collected from a system of half-hollowed logs. I gathered they didn't serve a practical purpose and were for tipping on unsuspecting victims below.

'We keeps trying to get those ramblers, some feels it, some don't,' informed Ikol.

'Depends how sensitive they are, or how thin the Veil is,' added Okol.

I noticed a load of conkers were strung up from the lower branches. One, in particular, stood out. It was pinned to a board with the words 'Earth Cracker' scribbled underneath.

'Like Thor's hammer, that,' said Ikol, laughing.

'Crack the ground right open it will,' said Okol proudly. I laughed, but they stopped.

'No, really, that little conker's got all the best hopes and wishes of any kid that ever played conkers. For it to be the bestest, strongest, hardest conker ever. To obliterate all the others in the schoolyard and become a childhood legend,' said Ikol.

I walked over to the conker and examined it; threaded on a metal chain, it was probably the largest conker I'd ever seen, but, *Crack the ground open? Hhhmmm,* I thought. Even though I'd been opened up to the seemingly unbelievable, my mind constantly tried to reel me in, battling my imagination and the boundaries of reality. I had just seen my dog and Nanna transform into majestic version of themselves to fend off some being created from the darkness of my thoughts. So why couldn't it crack the earth open?

'Cos anything can be real here,' spoke Okol, as if answering my very thoughts. Ikol and Okol both sat down and started whittling wooden figures with flint knives they had crafted.

'Have a look around,' said Ikol.

As I wandered off, I could hear their bickering starting again, jibing each other about the figures they were making. Apparently, they were of each other, and they weren't being too kind about bodily proportions.

The platform had a large open area with a table in the centre, it was made of an old tree trunk sat on six smaller logs. The trunk had been carved, so the top was flat; seats shaped like wooden mushrooms were scattered around it; plates and cups lay upon its surface and at the centre was a hole, which aligned with a hole in the floor below. I gathered this was their version of rubbish disposal.

I could just see them after eating whatever they ate, shoving it all down the hole without a care in the world. I wondered what on earth was down there and what horrendous stench it must create. Sniffing the air, I peered over the table to satisfy my curiosity. I wasn't disappointed as a potent whiff seized my nose, causing me to clutch it, thus cutting off the foul stench.

'Poouurr,' I spluttered. The boys erupted in a chorus of jeers and laughter.

'Ha-ha, that will teach you,' said Okol.

'I dare you to smell it again,' said Ikol. I released my fingers and delicately sniffed again, feeling some peer pressure from the boys.

'It's gone? It smells of jam and toast now?' I said, bemused.

'Well isn't that a surprise?' winked Okol.

I wasn't getting this game at all. Was it because that's what I expected and that's what I created? I certainly felt I had a lot to learn. My eyes roamed around the boys' home and were drawn to the structure that surrounded the Great Rag Tree.

It was a cabin with windows and a door. The door was draped in one of those colourful fly curtains. The windows had no glass, only curtains, which danced gently in the evening breeze. A warm glow emanated from inside.

I pushed the fly drape to one side and entered the heart of the boys' layer. Again the size of the room belittled its outward appearance, it stretched around the massive diameter of the grand old tree. I counted six beds arranged in a circular pattern pointing out from the trunk; the covers were a patchwork of other blankets and clothes. Toys and games were strewn across the floor; it was messy, but at the same time not, it was a perfect picture of a playful boys' room.

Glowing jam jars hung from the roof, filled with an array of toys which somehow were radiating a warm, caring light. It had a feeling of my bedroom, a feeling every kid should have about their home, their safe place.

Splitting the circle of beds was a large wardrobe. Now, I did think this was slightly out of place. Surely this was a parent's addition, for it stifled the boys' unruly flow.

'Are there more of you?' I called to the boys outside. Ikol replied, already by my side as if predicting my question. He spoke right into my ear, making me jump.

'Four others. We are the oldest, little scamps they are. They'll be off making mischief in the woods. How do you like it then?' he answered.

'It's amazing. I love it, it's the best place ever,' I gushed.

'Well, we like it,' added Ikol.

'What's the wardrobe for? Your school clothes?' I jested.

'Ha-ha, yeah, school. Let me show you,' said Ikol.

He walked over and flung the wardrobe doors open, exposing a spiralling staircase that rose up inside the Rag Tree.

'Wow! I thought it was a little out of place,' I said, continually surprised by what was presented to me. Things were and weren't as they seemed.

'Come, I will show you,' said Ikol.

I followed him up the central staircase trying not to look up as the treads were narrow and different heights; some sloping this way, some that. I could see the evening light shining down upon us as we climbed, Ikol skipping and humming a happy tune while I picked my way carefully. He reached the top and called me on.

'Come on, slow coach, it's as hard as you make it, remember?'

At that moment, I stopped and thought. I imagined the staircase; safe with big wide treads and no chance of falling off. Without any further ado the stairs creaked and shifted and lo and behold, became what I'd seen in my mind's eye.

That's better, I thought.

'Yeah, that's the way!' shouted Ikol.

I playfully skipped my way to the top to meet my new friend. He greeted me with a broad smile and led my eye with his arm as he rotated around, showing me the view.

'That's not bad, is it? Best view in the Veil,' he said. Again, I was stunned by what met me.

All I could manage was a drawn-out, 'Wwwooooowww.'

We were high above Snickets on a wide balcony that circled underneath the umbrella-shaped canopy of the ancient tree. I knew this tree was not visible in my reality, but it was real and alive and part of me now. I started to wonder, what was my reality? Feeling the limitations placed upon us as humans; restricted to our 3D world. I could see Nanna's cottage, its roof just peeking out behind the treeline. The village lights twinkled, and I could see the cars trundling about. Mr Smythe's tractor was in the field heading back to the yard. The sky was now blood red, and the last of the woodland birds made their way home while their siblings chattered, waiting expectantly for their return.

The breeze dropped to a baby's breath. Nothing seemed wrong with the world, everything felt in hand, peaceful, serene, real and surreal at the same time. The first stars could faintly be seen making their nightly appearance. At that moment, harmony was prevailing.

Miniaturised, life felt much less serious from up here. Even the Sulphur Hound and the Veil's shadowy threat seemed petty. Well, that was all it needed, my thoughts grazed upon the surface of the night gently blowing into its ear, awakening its lurking secrets.

Ikol drew a long breath, ready to cast his voice out to his siblings but held it at its peak. His attention pulled down to the wood's canopy where the trees rustled and clattered below, like a pack of marauding wolves were rampaging through the undergrowth. I couldn't see what was creating the racket, but I could hear voices shouting. I found it hard to tell whether they wailed in pain or excitement. They grew louder, screaming and yelling, rushing towards the Great Rag Tree. Okol now came bounding up the staircase to meet us.

'Any sign of the rest?' he questioned.

'I think we've got trouble,' replied Ikol. They both peered over the balcony's railing; the trees were swaying, and a troop of agitated young voices could now be heard.

'Go on! Run, faster, you twerp!' came one voice, then a squeaky voice replied.

'Shut it! My legs are smaller than yours.' This back-and-forth banter continued towards the Rag Tree. Ikol locked eyes with his brother.

'What they done now!?' he said.

They both turned and hurtled down the staircase. I followed with less recklessness; they jumped whole sections finally rolling out through the cabin door and onto the deck just in time to see what all the commotion was about. Four raggy-looking boys burst out of the bushes.

'Choc! Let! Bot! El!' cried Ikol in a commanding manner.

'Come on, lads! get a move on!' shouted Okol at the motley crew. The smallest boy was lagging behind, his little legs struggling to keep up.

'Wait, you morons!' he yelled. They all made it to the base of the tree. Okol undid the latch on the trap door and beckoned them up.

'Quick! Quick! What's up?' he asked, concerned by their rattled behaviour.

'Woohoo, it's a Lurker!' shouted the smallest and last boy up the ladder.

'That's Choc, don't be fooled by his size,' said Ikol. Okol shut the door and drew the bolt. They all gathered at the platform railings.

'Are you sure? A Lurker?' questioned Ikol.

'Oh yeah,' replied Choc, rubbing his hands enthusiastically as if they had goaded it into hounding them.

'It's coming! Chased us all the way from Spitting Bridge,' he said, eyes glowing with thrill and chest heavy with breath.

'A Lurker?' I asked.

'I think you've had a run-in before, the frost that shimmers in the woods?' said Okol.

'Oh,' I replied, thinking the action was done for the day.

The other boys gave me a smile and a squint of uncertainty. Not overly bothered by their new visitor, they looked out into the woods.

'Sssshhhhhh,' hissed Okol, 'look,' pointing to the rhododendrons that lined Rag Tree's perimeter.

A silence preceded its arrival. Anticipation, curiosity and fear gathered in my throat. I felt it, I knew its vibration, it was a frequency I had felt before. That day in the den when it shrouded Cradlick and again on the old coach path, I knew it, and it knew me. Now though it didn't hide, uncloaked and fully visible in all its glorious misery it moved into view.

'Lurker, told ya,' said Choc, rubbing his hands in delight. It pulsed in and out of form, from a gritty cloud of wispy fingers to a solid tar spectral shape; a cold light was emanating through two cut-out eyes, like in a cheap Halloween costume. They moved in a spiral helter-skelter motion, round and round down and down they went.

I was already drawn into the Lurker's presence, finding it hard to free my thoughts. A bolt of concern shot through my mind as they surged back. 'Mr Milly!' I shouted, then turned to Ikol. 'She's still down there!' I said, panicked. I looked over and underneath the deck to see her. She was already puffed up, ready to go.

'Here, grab a weapon,' said Okol, looking at the array of wooden toys lying about.

'But they're toys!' I exclaimed, thinking, *What on earth are they going to do against the Lurker?*

Okol reached down for a sword while locking eyes with me. 'Toys! Haven't you learnt anything yet?' He smiled, grasping it with his scruffy hand. Then in one move, he swung the wooden blade into the air while saying, 'Sun Slasher.' The harmless toy burst into life, turning into a magnificent sword; long with a shallow curve, it shone gold like the sun. He swished a few practice slashes, leaving solid swoosh marks in the air as arcs of sunlight that gently faded.

Okol looked proudly upon his creation, but this quickly changed to dissatisfaction. He released the sword, returning it to a harmless wooden toy before hitting the deck.

'Nar,' he said, muttering to himself while rummaging around for another.

All the other Rag Tree Boys were doing the same thing, seemingly not panicked by the Lurker's nearing presence.

'Bone Bender! Brain Basher?! Ballbreaker!!' said Ikol to a chorus of smutty laughter. They didn't seem to be taking this seriously at all, as the Lurker slowly moved into the clearing.

From the ground, the platform must have looked like a disco, with all the multi-coloured lights flashing and flooding the night air. I couldn't wait for them to do something. My beloved Mr Milly was down there all alone! Although I was quite sure she would be a formidable opponent, I couldn't leave her.

I scrambled down the ladder and stood next to my glistening majestic companion. I could feel her power and strength; electricity flowing through her coat, diamond claws and teeth shining bright. She shielded me, bowed her head and let out a snarl that said, 'Come closer at your peril,' while the disco still continued above.

'Death Pea Shooter!'

'Shield of Reflect!'

'Bum Stinger!' They were still laughing.

'Come on!! Come on! Stop messing!' I shouted up to them. I think the distress in my voice pricked their conscience and reminded them of Nanna's words – 'Look after him.' The laughing stopped.

'Make your flaming mind up,' I heard Ikol say in a clenched voice.

'Come on!' I screamed up again. Okol flew over the deck railings and landed by my side, handing me the Earth Cracker.

'Here, take it, make it real,' he said.

The other boys soon followed and gathered at the bottom of the tree. Their smug playful looks now replaced by steely glistening eyes and clenched teeth, all our focus centred upon the approaching enemy.

Against the blood-red sky, it moved into the clearing, trailing with it a shroud of misery. The plants wilted in its presence, and the leaves on the floor scrunched up, crystallising from the chill it brought. Our breath misted, and my skin pimpled. The Rag Tree Boys paused, looking equally fearless and unmatched for this foe. With an array of shining, glowing weapons and armour, they sized up the approaching intruder. 'After three, boys! On my count!' said Ikol through gritted teeth 'One… Two…'

He never got to three as the smallest and seemingly least fearful boy broke rank. Choc rushed forward brandishing a hammer which minutes ago was a mere child's toy. Now it shone bright and was the length of his torso; blue flames licked up and down the handle.

'Knock its block off!!' he screamed furiously, not befitting a child of his size or age. His swooshing of the great hammer was a sight to behold.

The others and Mr Milly were only a stride behind. The Lurker stretched its tar-like tentacles forth trying to trap anyone that strayed near its grasp; green fish-shaped arrows hurtled ahead of the pack fired by Ikol's bone bow. They fizzed past the Lurker; one made it home, finding its target and piercing a hole of light straight through its midnight structure.

Mr Milly had launched herself over the boys and landed squarely in front of the dark foe. The attack now centred upon my canine friend, she lunged forward, swiping with her diamond claws, shredding and tearing the Lurker. Light poured into the wound. Mr Milly gathered herself for another strike, but the Lurker in its anger lashed out with devilish speed. Two tarred snakeheads shot forward, one attaching round her neck and the other her front leg. She was immobilised, and the power flickered within her. Choc swung but missed with his hammer; now on his knees in front of the enemy he looked up and for a second linked eyes with the foul presence. He was drawn instantly into a hypnotic gaze, the spiralling black and white eyes sucking him deeper into a comatose state. Bot and Let were fighting off the other arms of darkness; suddenly they appeared swamped. I looked down at the Earth Cracker in my hand.

'Come on! Come on!' I shouted, shaking it, hoping something would happen. Mr Milly was trapped, and the boys were on their back foot. A wave of anger rose within me; images of what I wanted to do to that thing started flicking across my mind's eye.

Smash it! Crack it! Punch its flaming lights out! I thought.

Clenching my grip around the chain, it flickered from a conker to an ancient ball of black tourmaline, flecks of sparkling ice within, its chain made from the bones of gods surrounded by glistening purple energy. It did indeed live up to its name.

Looking up at the raging battle, my courage floundered, and the Earth Cracker became a conker once again.

'Come on, come on!' I said under my breath.

This time I grasped the chain harder and summoned the courage that the boys displayed. Suddenly I felt a great pulse race through my body and down into my arm. The weapon ignited into life, whispering to me, 'Swing, swing away.' Letting out a roar, I hurtled toward the battle.

Choc was still in a trance; Mr Milly tied up in the Lurker's tar arms; Bot and Let were warding off the attacking tentacles. Only Ikol and Okol looked to be holding ground. As I approached, the Lurker's focus centred upon me, it was trying to drain the courage out of my soul. Stumbling, I fell onto one knee, again looking at the ground and the now normal conker. It wanted me to give up.

'You're finished!' I muttered with bite, springing back to my feet, leaping into the air. The Earth Cracker once more courageously charged, burst into life. Swinging it high above my head, I brought the weapon down at the base of the Lurker. The Earth Cracker made a deep, low boom, shaking the ground. We all paused, trying to steady our feet; the soil split and tore apart like the mouth of a mountain opening to speak after a million years. As the crack widened it filled with a ferocious light, piercing through the Lurker, cutting the ghostly structure with pure white laser beams; punching holes clean through its distorted skin. The Lurker fizzed and steamed as it was drawn into the crack.

To our horror, while Mr Milly was now clear of the Lurker's grasp, Choc wasn't, he was still hypnotised, ambling forward following the Lurker to its fate.

'Choc!' they all cried in a panicked chorus.

Ikol's eyes scouted the surroundings. Thinking quickly, he pulled a piece of rope down from the tree. He closed his eyes and then snapped it into life. Ikol looked down at the now golden rope proclaiming it, 'Saving String.' He flung the golden whip round his head, gathering enough speed to reach Choc. Loosening the whip at the extent of its rotation, it shot out towards him. Reaching its target with only seconds to spare the golden rope wrapped itself around Choc's waist, just as his first foot stepped over the crack.

The Saving String instantly broke Choc's trance and sat the youngest Rag Tree Boy on his rear while the Lurker was dissolved into the mouth of light. The opening closed upon itself, and the drama was silenced. The boys dropped their weapons and rushed over to Choc. Ikol patted me on the back as he passed by, Mr Milly rubbed up against my leg, and the Earth Cracker was a conker again. The light was all but gone and the day was done.

The boys trudged back towards the tree; Bot and Let had their arms around little Choc.

'Stupid spinny eyes,' he muttered.

'Make a helmet next time, an anti-spinny one, that would do it,' said El, bolstering his sibling's confidence.

Choc looked up and smiled, stroking his chin. 'Anti-spinny thing, yeah,' he said, his thoughts already leaving the fight behind.

Okol stood over the seam the Earth Cracker had left. 'Told ya, split the ground right open,' he said, smiling at me.

'We better get you back now,' said Ikol.

'Or Nanna won't be thanking us,' chirped Okol.

I waved a weary goodbye as the other boys made their way up the ladder. Okol saw Mr Milly and me back to Nanna's. There was a subdued silence within the conversation; we were all a bit shaken by today's events, I sensed even the Rag Tree Boys were uneasy about the whole thing. On returning to Ivy Gate, Nanna sat me down with a hot chocolate.

'Well haven't you been busy today?' she said, peering over her glasses, holding my eye then puffing out a laugh like she does. I looked up and smiled, trying to break my vacant stare, for I was lost in all that happened today.

The Hound on the field; defeated by Nanna who was and wasn't Nanna; a magic invisible tree home to the craziest tribe of fearless roughyins I'd ever met; then an epic battle against the soul-sucking Veil Lurker.

What a day indeed, I thought as a visual accompaniment of today's events flittered in and out of my mind, bringing a host of new questions and things to ponder over.

'What's the Lurker's deal then, Nanna?' I asked.

She cleared her throat. 'Well,' she said, moving to the high-back chair near the window. She took a breath. I could tell a long description was coming. I sat back and pricked my ears ready to catch what I could. Nanna began.

'A Veil Lurker, an entity that exists where the curtain between dimensions is at its thinnest. The Lurker looks for a way into our realm where the light energy has dulled, and the black tide ebbs onto serenity's white beaches. In such places it can manifest gaining power and form, it can take over your thoughts, becoming the shadow controlling you. Only light can dissolve its influence.

'They have no place amongst harmony; no place in a happy home; no place in good and true people. You, my dear, are innocent; a beacon in the dark night; a lighthouse in the midnight void. They are attracted to you, they want to subdue your light, your goodness.

'They can control the slightest situations in our lives, but as long as you know they are at work you can protect yourself and those you love. Look for the signs; ringing in your ear; a chill on your cheek; a sudden onset of irritability or thought patterns that are spiralling out of control. Stop and check, enter the Veil, you can clearly see who has been touched once in that realm. The mark of the Lurker will be visible in their aura as a squid-like organism wrapped around the person's energy centre,' explained Nanna.

'Wow, so I can see it?' I asked.

'Oh yes, just like we looked upon our energies, you will see where the mark is.' Nanna continued. 'Their presence, along with the Hound, is a sign that all is not as well as it should be. The tables have turned in their favour; these are tools of the dark, of the negative, both with different purposes. The Sulphur Hound with its gruesome matted mane, its bone-shaking roar and imposing stature are made for one thing, to create fear the old-fashioned way, through outright terror; through myth and tales of what lurks on the moor. People talk and pass on these stories, spreading angst and worry, making the Hound more real, more powerful, thus spreading its territory.

'The Veil Lurker is different, its weapon is stealth. Don't get me wrong, to see a Lurker in all its nightmarish glory isn't to be taken lightly.'

'You can say that again,' I spluttered.

'I know, my dear, but that's not what it does best. What it excels at is infiltrating society. When the Veil allows it to reach a community, it will touch people, finding a way in through life's traumas. It can manifest as addiction or depression, causing friction in the home and amongst loved ones. Ultimately though it is looking for that one person, that spirit that has been broken by loss or misfortune. These people are on the edge and capable of carrying out terrible acts with the Lurker's influence, so terrible that it will leave an emotional scar, a rip in the very fabric of time and space, connecting this dimension with lower ones, where the ill and negative seek to spread forth and contaminate.'

'Can these rips be closed?' I asked.

'Yes, my dear, they can, but people need to be aware that this is what's happening. We live in a world of nonbelievers. Unfortunately, they accept things as fate, or just bad luck, when actually in most cases the Lurker's touch has given their misfortune a helping hand. The rips can be healed. If a source like Blackend is cleared, then it will have a massive effect for miles and miles, all smaller rips and contaminations will be healed,' explained Nanna, then took a sip of her tea.

'So this is all her fault,' I said agitatedly.

She pondered. 'Yes, well, look at her as a… as a… regional sales manager. Yes, a sales manager, trying to push and peddle the wares of Evil R Us.' Nanna chuckled. 'And this is the area she covers. Her sales reps, the Hound and Lurker and I guess other such foul creations are an extension of her tough selling tactics. You will buy fear, they say. And what do we say?' I looked at Nanna, confused. '"Not today! Shove off," we say!' laughed Nanna. 'We don't need or want it, so why buy into it? If nobody did then it wouldn't exist, their business is fear,' explained Nanna.

'So are there more like her?' I asked.

'Oh yes, and more like you and me, and the Rag Tree Boys, it's incredible really,' she said.

'So who's in charge of ShawlInka? Who's the big boss?' I quizzed.

'Let's not worry about that yet, it's a story as old as time itself,' she said.

After I'd finished my hot chocolate, Nanna ran me a warm foamy bath, where I continued to puzzle over the day's events. I knew I had just scratched the surface, and my internal remembrance would hopefully fill in the pieces. This was a new logic to me, different to everything we as humans are taught. This is knowing without knowing anything, questions not answered with diagrams and words but instead with feeling and frequencies, simpler and innately more complex.

This dark threat worried me, but hope and pride occupied the same space, for twice we had battled them, and twice the light shone through. I held onto that thought as I settled down for bed.

CHAPTER 8

Chattersley's Charms

The following morning I awoke from a deep slumber. My dreams didn't seem so crazy now. Dreams of monsters and wild children that rule the woods, of invisible energies, of a conker that opened the ground up before my eyes. As I lay there staring at the ceiling, I thought with a flip in my stomach, half excitement half nerves, *It's real: all of it's real, unbelievably, undeniably real.* I had seen it, touched it, and felt it. I was changed but no different, more knowledgeable yet still naïve. I was a child and an eternal being, both brave and scared, lost and found. I was everything all at once, I'd found a reset button, a skeleton key to my truth. Speaking from a ten-year-old boy's point of view it was awesome!!!

I clambered out of the heavy bedspread, weighted down with Nanna's knitted blanket. She worried about me being warm enough in the night, so I ended up entombed in a snuggly den. Already the promise of a fine day filtered through the thin curtains.

Mr Milly and Moggins had made an early start; I grabbed my dressing gown and headed into the empty kitchen. The kettle had just boiled, and toast made from Nanna's homemade bread was piled up on the pull-out table. The clock chimed and Wit did the circuit through the tiny doors. I paused and waited for it all to be a dream. The miniature wooden bird rolled round with no sign of anything magic until she was just about to disappear back into the wooden house. My heart rose into my mouth as Wit chimed, 'Good morning!' in her angelic way; she accompanied this with a puff of golden glitter and released her static form with a fluid nod. A sense of relief spread through me as if I'd woke from a nightmare to find it was only a dream; it was the same only I had woken to a dream.

The back door was slightly open, and I could hear laughing from the front garden. Gingerly I hopped over the gravel path and onto the cool dewy lawn.

'Good girl, and again,' I heard Nanna say. I rounded the corner out of the shade and into the full morning sun, squinting and shielding my vision.

Mr Milly looked obsessively at the ball in Nanna's hand; she was laughing and Mr Milly barking. It was such a pure and simple scene; you could see why people might not want to know what's happening behind life's curtains. Sun out, bright blue skies and my loveliest friends in the world laughing and playing, how could anything be wrong when life could be like this?

Once we'd had breakfast, and I was dressed and ready, Nanna gave me a list of bits and bobs to fetch from the village.

'I think your mates are back now, I saw their car drive past this morning,' she said.

'That's great! I'll see if they want to come,' I excitedly replied. Although I felt the weight of a secret, one that if I could share, would sound crazy. I longed to tell them about the Rag Tree Boys and the fight with the Lurker, about Wit and the beauty of this other reality only a thought away. Still, the possibilities of the day seemed endless, and I was happy to do normal stuff with my normal mates. Deep down I was grateful for their lack of knowledge, the break from all the crazy goings-on is what I needed, yet I could still feel it, a tidal wave on my shoulder ready to engulf me at any moment.

I fetched my trusty scooter from the garage and glided down the drive avoiding the patches in need of repair. Swinging a right out of Ivy Gate and onto the tarmac lane, pushing and swiping with my engine leg, I gathered speed until almost upon the hump. I quickly boarded the deck, tucked in and sprung into the air pulling the bars with me.

'Whhhoooaaaa!!' I yelled. That was the highest yet. My metal steed took me the rest of the way to Smythe's Farm, no pushing necessary; I glided effortlessly down the shallow hill, the only breeze in the air made by myself.

Approaching the farmyard, I could hear Ronnie and Buster's voices coming from the barn. They were good brothers. Yes, they ribbed and teased each other, but they were the best of friends, much like the Rag Tree Boys. It's a good job they got on because there weren't many other kids around here. I think that's why they liked me coming to stay at Nanna's so much.

Aware that their voices had taken on the tone of an argument, I listened in.

'I can't find it.'

'Well, you dropped it.'

'Oh, shut it! If we don't find it, we're in for a right rollicking.'

Even amid trouble, there was an air of comradery about them, I doubt either would drop the other in it; they appeared to have lost the tractor key in the hay.

'You tell her.'

'You dropped it! You tell.'

'Look we'll both go, OK.'

It seemed Mrs Smythe was the one to fear.

'Alright,' I said, loud enough for them to hear above their squabbled panic.

'Oh, hi Pete,' said Ronnie.

'No, we've lost the tractor key,' said Buster.

I offered to help; we hurriedly searched through the mass of hay, but it was literally like finding a needle in a haystack. We plonked ourselves on a bale after fifteen minutes of energetic rummaging. The brothers looked thoroughly fed-up, heads in hands, sighing deeply. I joined them, taking a deep breath and without realising could feel my energy connecting to the Veil.

I wonder… I thought, concentrating and focusing above and below. Suddenly as in the field last night, a ripple descended, and all things hidden from our limited senses were exposed. I could see an upset stomach brewing in Buster after overeating last night; I could see the glow of two rats buried deep within the warm hay. Ronnie and Buster's energy were very similar: a bluey-green haze, I would say a gentle energy. Apart from the slightly darker patch in Buster's stomach I could also see the key still glowing from being held in Ronnie's hand, it was only feet from where we had been searching. I plunged my hand into the bale and hay presto, I retrieved the key.

'Woooow, how did you?' said Buster, open-mouthed.

'Yyyeeaaahhh!' shouted Ronnie in relief.

The brothers were so thankful and relieved; they quickly headed into the kitchen to put the key safely back in its place.

'Now the drama's over, what do you fancy doing?' said Ronnie.

'Village? I've got a list of stuff to get for Nanna,' I replied.

'Does that include sweets?' said Buster.

We all smiled and nodded. The boys picked up their bikes from the lean-to by the farmhouse, and we headed back up the lane.

My swinging leg had to work considerably harder this time, no massive air off the hump, only managing to squeeze a few inches in. As we approached Nanna's cottage, we could see the old Major flapping around in his garden. He was bent over chasing what looked like a stick of rhubarb.

'Maggot! Maggot!!' he rasped, demanding that his furry companion drop the rhubarb: of course, the little dog was hidden from our view, we found this quite amusing. I never tired of hearing the Major call his dog the way he did, his contempt and frustration for his uncontrollable pal was clear and provided a constant source of amusement.

We all chuckled and headed off down the main road. It was a good twenty minutes or so, maybe longer at our lethargic daydreaming pace. It just felt like one of those days, for talking complete rubbish and quizzing the oddities of the world.

'I wonder. What's the biggest banana in the world?' said Ronnie with a glazed expression, his question half interrupted by a pause as his front wheel twitched sharply left to avoid a large pothole.

'You,' Buster replied.

'Me?' replied a confused Ronnie.

'Well you're the biggest narna I know.' They both laughed.

'Been down the woods since?' asked Buster.

'Yeah… not been in the Den though,' I coyly answered.

'No sign of the beast then?' asked Ronnie. Last night's memories flashed over my mind's eye, the field and Hound, the Rag Tree and the Lurker, I was bursting to tell them but couldn't and if I could, where would I start? I settled for an unconvincing underwhelmed answer.

'Err… no.'

'It was black as tar, like a bear and a lion and its red eyes… and… and its acid dribbles!' said Ronnie.

'Oh my god, yeah, its eyes,' added Buster.

'It was real, wasn't it?' quizzed Ronnie.

'It must have been, we both saw it,' replied Buster.

'But it can't just have disappeared, can it?' questioned Ronnie.

'We should set a trap,' suggested Buster.

'Yes. Yes, bet it's just a big black cat loose on the moor,' said Ronnie. Their fearless attitude reminded me of the Rag Tree Boys; now they wanted to trap it! They were proper lads, full of adventure and daring, just my cup of tea.

Ronnie continued, 'Tom Sadler said his cattle had been attacked, same as Dad said, so it must be still out there.'

'Did you hear that howl again the other night? We saw some really weird lights coming from the field,' added Buster.

'I'd tell Nanna to watch her hens,' said Ronnie.

But I knew the Sulphur Hound wasn't after mere chickens but the very light of our souls; it would feast on our flesh, but it was the fear in us it craved. I thought that might be a little heavy to throw into the conversation as we sauntered on for a while, pondering deeply, Buster soon lightened the mood.

'Do you think we will ever run out of bogies?' he said, picking his nose.

'I don't: why does our dog's farts smell like burnt rubber?' he continued, examining his finger.

'Or hot cheese,' piped Ronnie.

The mood remained light-hearted as we entered Chattersley. It was a small village with a handful of shops, a post office, convenience store, video rental place behind the handy supplies shop, and a few crafty-type shops which seemed to be the standard for such a picturesque village setting. The Inn on the Moor stood behind the village green looking both inviting and foreboding, whispering with an alluring slur to passers-by to call in.

Next to the Inn on the Moor was the butcher's and then my favourite shop in the village, the sweet shop. It sat on the corner of Chapel Street, perfectly placed for the small school just around the corner. I'm sure many screaming children were dragged past it, come home time. It was one of those old-fashioned ones, all the jars lined up like a confectionary front line battling the war against fluoride and dental hygiene. The sweets were weighed and served in white paper bags just right for a small child to hold. The proprietor, Mrs Totts, was one of Nanna's acquaintances, having the typical sunny disposition most Chattersley folks had. She was a pleasant, kind lady. I believe this to be a sincere kindness, and not just because we were good customers.

We eyed up the treats before us; Buster was practically dribbling at the thought of that extra-large gobstopper. Ronnie went for a mix, and I just loved the sherbet. American Cream Soda was my current favourite, along with some strawberry laces to dip in. Mrs Totts usually chatted about the weather or what games we were playing, but today her topic of conversation was different.

'Eeeaar boys… weren't it you that saw that thing in the woods? Talk's all round the village. You be careful down Snickets, won't you? Be home before it gets dark, something doesn't sit right with me. Mrs Flowers losing her chickens, Tom Saddler's dog, mind you he had gone bonkers, your dad's sheep, and it just disappeared under his nose, dint it?? Anyway, you lot be careful, keep an extra eye out.'

And breathe, I thought as Mrs Totts gasped for breath ready to start again.

'OK, Mrs Totts,' we chimed together, stopping her next harmless rant. She didn't seem bothered by the discussion, just passing the gossip on, getting verification from our nods that the tale had substance. Still, she was warm and kind and even though she was profiting out of rotting teeth and kids' hyperactivity, we thought she was alright. We said our goodbyes and made our way outside.

'Ooohh tell your nanna I've got those coconut mushrooms back in!' she shouted as the door swung shut. The convenience store was next on the list, so we crossed the green and made for the bench opposite, Buster already not able to speak as the huge gobstopper had quite literally done its job, although it didn't stop him trying to talk dribbling nonsense.

The sun shone down as we perched on the wooden bench, happily swinging our legs, not talking, just communicating with satisfying grunts and lip-smacking. The convenience store was small but packed with just about everything you could imagine.

'If it's in a can or packet, it's in there,' said Ronnie.

'Dad hates it, nothing fresh, not like it used to be,' pitched in Buster, taking his stopper out momentarily, checking what colour it was. I had to listen to Nanna and the Major harping on about its contents, how things were much better in the good old days and how overpriced and under-nourishing the products had become since it was taken over by the increasingly popular mini-market franchise company.

CHAPTER 9

Cradlick

We sat on the bench for a while, minding our own business, swinging our legs happily, passing comment here and there, watching the Chatlins go about their daily errands. Buster and Ronnie seemed quite up to scratch on the local gossip and were filling me in on all kinds of juicy titbits. Our heads were synchronised, from left to right, and right to left, we watched the approaching villagers coming and going with an occasional nod. Then through the general peace and quiet that accompanied the errand runners came something different.

A young man approached. I thought I recognised him from the woods that day; his appearance was shielded by a black hoodie casting a shadow over his face, only his blond hair poking out verified his identity. I thought he was rather cool. A silver key chain hung from his jeans; his head was down as he approached.

Buster muttered under his breath, 'Cradlick,' and both himself and Ronnie dipped their heads in the opposite direction hoping he wouldn't see them. Buster cast insults under his breath. 'Loser, fagger, thicko,' he muttered.

Ronnie looked his younger brother side on and said through clenched teeth, 'Pack it in, he will bray us.'

Buster defiantly looked up. 'I don't care!' he said louder than Ronnie liked. 'Dad's always telling him to get off our land. He rips up the crops on that bike,' continued Buster. By association the boys felt he would have it in for them.

The strange thing was, and everyone seemed to ignore it, was the small elderly woman by his side. Even Cradlick appeared to be doing his best with his head down, hood up and earphones in. She was desperately trying to get his attention; almost shouting in despair as she trotted alongside him trying to keep up with his purposeful march, but he was oblivious. I was fixated on the peculiar event. While Buster and Ronnie did everything not to look, I stared until our eyes met, and when close enough he snapped viciously at me.

'What!' he snarled.

Giving me no time to respond nor wanting or caring about one either, he just glared. He was pale almost with a greyish tinge; beads of sweat were on his head like he was sickening for something. Still, he paid no attention to the lady, who was now pleading with the young, seemingly troubled man.

'Please, Shaun, listen to me please,' said the elderly lady. 'Snap out of it, it's not you, don't do it, please. You're a good boy, my boy, it's them, not you,' the lady pleaded.

Cradlick looked like he had the weight of the world on his shoulders. He came across visibly stressed, and the old lady was clearly disturbed too. They hurried into the shop.

'Why didn't he listen to her?' I questioned.

'To who?' said Buster and Ronnie with a bewildered look upon their faces.

I relinquished my position on the bench and curiously edged towards the shop's entrance. I looked in through the door. Down the aisle I could see Cradlick waiting in line looking very agitated; he was having trouble standing still, fidgeting, looking nervous and unhinged. The woman was still by his side trying to get his attention, then it clicked! She reached for his arm, but it passed straight through her grasp. I gasped! *The Veil,* I thought. *She's in the Veil.* Was she dead? I didn't know, I didn't understand it enough yet, but I knew I could see her and they couldn't.

I focused, and the picture became clearer. The old lady now recognised that I could see her. The minute her grasp failed she turned and looked at me. She knew, and I knew we shared something.

'Help me!' she pleaded. 'Help me stop him.'

Cradlick's aura was dark; he carried the mark of a Lurker, a storm was building within him. The malignant presence grew and pushed on with its intent; he was at breaking point, shoving the man in front aside while drawing a knife from his pocket that he'd been grasping all along, his knuckles white, drained from blood as he squeezed the weapon. Cradlick now focused on the shop keeper who had stepped back and was slowly raising his hands in a surrendering way.

'Shaun! Shaun! Whoa! Come, what's all this about,' said the shop keeper. He clearly knew Shaun and that his actions were out of character.

'Just open the till and give me what you've got, now!' barked Cradlick at the shop keeper, his attempt to calm the situation frustrating him more. He continued and tried again to turn the situation around.

'Come on, let's talk this out. No need for this now, is there?' replied the shop keeper.

'No! No.' Cradlick rubbed his brow with the back of his hand as if he had a headache or he was trying to clear the negative thoughts that had become intruders in his mind.

'No!!!' Raising his voice and lacing it with violence, he then followed with a quieter stuttering voice. 'They need it, they want it.' Like he was justifying his actions to himself.

The shop keeper, seeing Cradlick was not of sane mind shrugged his shoulders at the other customer who had been pushed aside. I could see him gently inching his way closer to the exit. Unfortunately, his skills of aversion were questionable. As he backed into a display of stacked crisps and dips that were on offer, the noise making Cradlick spin round.

'You!!! Stay,' he spat forcefully at the petrified man whose fight-or-flight instincts kicked in, sending him crashing into the stand, scattering its contents down the aisle like bowling pins. He continued slipping and skipping his way out of the door, pushing me back as he made his clumsy escape. Once outside, he headed for bright red phone box across the village green. The woman was now so distraught she was weeping as if all was lost. I took a step into the shop. I didn't know what I would do, but my intuition gently poked me in. Buster was now on my shoulder, trying to get a peek.

'What you doing!' came a worried voice from behind me.

'It's OK, I'm just looking,' I replied.

'Well, this is close enough for me. Don't go any closer, Pete,' said Buster.

I took another step in and quickly scurried down the far aisle.

'Pete! Don't go!' stressed Buster, Ronnie now peering in too. 'Come back… let's go… come on,' they both strained.

'It's OK, don't worry,' I said, trying to shush them down.

Making my way down the aisle, half crouched trying to make as little noise as possible, I thought of the Rag Tree Boys and how they could turn anything into a glorious weapon, how I made the conker glitch into life and brought it down at the Lurker's feet.

I can help, I can help, was the message looped in my head. I got to the end of the aisle and took a look round the corner. I could see Cradlick's back and the actual point where the Lurker had attached its poison; it was on the centre of his torso with oily, slimy tentacles wrapped around his heart. I looked back down the aisle trying to think of something I could use to eliminate the Lurker's touch. *Hhrmm,* I pondered. Then in the cleaning products section, a pink rubber glove hung half out of a basket. *Well, needs must,* I thought. *Not my colour but let's see.* I put the glove on, trying not to make the obligatory *snap* sound.

I moved forward, adoring a fetching pink glove. Kneeling behind the towering display of baked beans I paused, placing all my energy into the glove. I closed my eyes and opened then hoping to see my majestic creation but no, not a flicker. *Come on! Come on!* I thought time was running out, the voices were getting louder, and the situation was going to end badly if I didn't do something. Closing my eyes again I thought of the Earth Cracker. The memory ran through my body; I could feel the energy running down my spine, into my arm and, yes, into the glove.

I slowly opened my eyes, not daring to look. From the glow, it was evident that a transformation had taken place. The glove now pulsed with a glittering pink light, highlighted with a pure white haze, and in the centre a crystal blue whirlpool of diamond light, a tornado of goodness in my hand! Seeing an opportunity, I emerged from behind the stack of beans, half squatting, slowly gently rising into an upright stance.

Cradlick's back still faced me, I was only feet away from him. I had to touch the infected area with the glove and was getting closer by the second, then disaster fell! The rounded mirror behind the counter had given my not-so-stealth-like intentions away. Cradlick glimpsed up and caught my reflection, spinning round like a caged tiger that had just been poked in the rear.

'Watch it!! Just back off, little'n, you don't want to get involved!' snarled Cradlick. The focus was on me now. Cradlick's irritation spiralled, his eyes now split between the shop keeper and me. I raised my hands in the air, one sheathed in the pink glove which to everyone else was just that! A pink rubber glove. But in my vision, it was a beaming, glorious, magnetic vortex, and was having an effect on the Lurker's touch from four feet away. I could see it twitching, particles were breaking off its black tar centre, they floated towards the glove, turning ashen the closer they got, then *whoosh,* they were sucked in at lightning speed. I had to get closer to free him; the shop keeper's eyes widened as he locked on and saw the glove, at first I thought, *Can he? Can he really see it?!* But no, he couldn't.

'You little thieving rat! You going to pay for that!!' It seemed the shop keeper's tolerance for petty theft was zero; he was even more rattled by my 'borrowing' of the glove than Cradlick holding the shop up, probably because Cradlick hadn't taken anything yet, never mind his intent to harm.

'No, no, you don't understand,' I said sheepishly, realising exactly how it looked.

I tried to think of a sensible answer as to why I was creeping around wearing one pink rubber glove. 'I was just trying it on... for... for... errrrrr, my nan?' I was relatively pleased with my answer, but my smile turned into a grimace as I tried to judge how successful the lie had been. The shop keeper didn't buy it; he raised his voice, ignoring the Cradlick situation.

'You put it back! Put it back now!' he shouted. Cradlick winced as if his head was pounding with all the aggro.

He turned, telling the shop keeper to, 'Shut it!' This was it, I grabbed my opportunity, lunging forward, attempting to place my hand on his back, but Cradlick was quick and edgy, twisting his torso back towards me, aiming his knife toward my body. As I entered his space we clashed, both of us committed in our actions now. On paper, it looked bad for either side. I could just see the headlines, 'child killed and troubled youth sentenced to prison'. With only inches to spare I planted the glove on his chest, feeling the knifepoint press against my stomach.

Cradlick collapsed to his knees; the knife clanged upon the floor as he released his grip. The glove sucked the Lurker's touch clean out of his aura along with some other minor patches of possible addiction. It cleaned him; he was reborn, free from any dark energy that had hitched a ride upon his dissident ways. Colour came back to his open-mouthed face like he had woken from a dream.

'What did you do?' he said.

'Yeah, what did you do? Is that some new Kung Fu?' said the puzzled shop keeper.

The old lady crouched by Cradlick's side trying to hold his hand. She couldn't so she reached out to me and touched my arm and rubbed it gently.

'Thank you, my dear, thank you. You have a special gift, they're going to need you,' she said ominously, then faded into a mist blowing a kiss as she went. The shop keeper came round from behind the counter and put his arm on the broken boy's shoulders.

'You stupid boy, what was all that about?' Cradlick looked up, bewildered. A tear ran down his cheek. We could all hear the police sirens in the distance. 'Quick! Get him in the back,' instructed the shop keeper.

We all helped him through to the back room and sat him on a chair. 'Look, I know that's not you, I know you've been having a rough time with your nan passing,' he sympathised with Cradlick, tapping his chin in a playful, fatherly way. 'Come on, we can sort this out,' said the shop keeper. There was definitely a connection or history between the two. While Cradlick composed himself the shop keeper thinking out loud said, 'The tape,' having a eureka moment. He dashed over to the CCTV console and hit the stop button then rewound it. As he did we could see the events that just passed played back in high speed. What's more, I could see the elements in the Veil, the sparkling glove with its vortex sucking the badness in, I could see the old lady, I could see it all on the TV!

Cradlick still in a daze looked at the screen then looked at me with puzzlement upon his face.

'What?' he stuttered. 'What was that? Nan?' he blinked, questioning his own eyes, but before he could query any more the tape was wound back past the incident, the record button firmly pressed, and the evidence was erased.

'That should do it. I'll sort it with the old bill. Here, where's that knife? I will lose it somewhere,' questioned the shop keeper.

'He dropped it out there,' I answered. Cradlick nodded and

pointed out toward the shop counter.

He returned with the knife and shoved it under some crisp boxes stacked in the corner.

'Right, when the coppers get here I will say it was all a misunderstanding and the fellow that phoned didn't get the full picture. No problems, right?' he said. We both nodded. He buzzed around anxiously waiting for the police to arrive.

'Do you know him?' I asked.

'Vanishall's all right,' replied Cradlick, watching him through the door hurriedly picking up any sign of disturbance.

Mr Vanishall was short and sturdily built, his rounded belly poking out between a brown three-quarter smock. He had a thick neck, and his white hair had almost given up residence only leaving two wispy side skirts around a ball-shaped head. He walked with a slight limp; I wondered why. An old war wound? Or tripped over a wayward can of beans? Both images played out in my head. He had a kind face, his vocal tone was quite elevated for a burly man, he was energetic and bounced around like a rubber ball. Whether this was his natural state of being I couldn't tell, I didn't know him that well. Nanna talked kindly of him, and the Major would puff on his pipe, saying, 'Well Jim was a boy, you know. He could handle himself.' I gathered from this comment he knew how to fight. Maybe he was a rogue as a youngster, and he empathised with Cradlick. That's why he was going out of his way to protect the troubled youth.

What a good, kind person, I thought.

Cradlick stared at me, still in shock. He leaned over. 'What was in your hand? What was that black stuff coming off me?' he said through pursed lips then withdrew from my space.

Taken aback, I paused with my response. 'Eeeerrr, I don't know, what thing? What black stuff? I didn't see that, must be the shock, you mustn't be feeling well,' I bluffed badly.

He gazed into my eyes with a mad, silent look. 'Yeah… OK… I'm not myself, been feeling strange,' he said, relieving my eyes from his stare. He looked at his hands for comfort, rubbing his thumb into the opposite palm while he mulled over what had just happened.

When the police arrived the man outside had briefly filled in the attending officer, but Mr Vanishall tamed the story down to a stressed and emotional young man who had not long lost his nan and needed a break. The officer was all too happy to leave it at that, the lure of an easy life levering his judgement. He had a stern chat with Cradlick, but that was it.

I guess he was known to the local constabulary for other minor misdemeanours, I don't think he was a bad lad. I know the Cradlick name took a lot of the rap round here and were the first to be called when any wrongdoings surfaced in the village. The officer, known now to us as PC Newley, stayed quite a while, soon forgetting the alleged disturbance and moving on to general village chit-chat.

The conversation turned to Mrs Flowers' chickens.

'You're Nanna's lad, aren't you?' I nodded. 'Those your mates outside?' asked PC Newley with a nod to the open door. I looked out and smirked as they were playing dead arms on the bench.

'Yeah,' I said.

'You lot saw it, dint you?' he quizzed. I nodded. He turned to Mr Vanishall and continued, 'Arrr, strange business, we've had big cats on moor before like this, exotic pets gotten loose,' informed PC Newley.

'Or let loose. They want locking up anyway, letting a dangerous animal out like that,' added Mr Vanishall.

'Well we've got extra hands coming in to keep an eye on things, probably end up trapping it. Either way, it will more than likely end up dead, unless it's already fled the area,' said Newley. His radio beeped, interrupting their conversation.

We listened intently to the incoming call, trying to make sense of the broken police code. PC Newley finished the call. 'Well, speak of the devil, sighting out on Holme Road.' He gathered himself together, finishing off his tea. He wasn't in any real hurry and tootled about in a carefree manner. I guess this was as hardcore as country crime gets.

I hoped he didn't run into the Sulphur Hound, for I was sure chickens were just the appetisers and sooner or later it would work its way up the food chain. I knew Nanna had vanquished it, but for good? I didn't know, could there be more? I wanted to tell PC Newley to be careful, I wanted to warn him of the potential danger he might find himself in, but I couldn't, the words stalled in my throat and at the risk of sounding insane I held them in, but my face leaked concern.

'You all right, son? You look a bit peaky,' said the concerned officer.

'I'm fine,' I said, clearing my voice.

We all left the shop together, the air now thick with the promise of another mystery. Newley offered us a lift back. By now we had whiled away most the day in the village, and the light was fading. Nanna must be wondering where we were, so I didn't hesitate to accept the officer's kind gesture. We clambered into the back of the police van like a right motley crew. Cradlick was dropped off first.

The van stopped just outside the village at the end of a lane that led up to his house. I could see broken farm machinery and tatty caravans strewed around the grounds. Two dog kennels were perched on raised embankments either side of the lane. As the van pulled up their excited inhabitants burst forth barking and slavering; thankfully they were secured on metal chains. It looked a bit grim and I felt a little sorry for him. PC Newley rounded the rear of the van, opening the door to let Cradlick out.

'Now then, Shaun,' he paused, looking down at his feet then back up to link eyes, 'bit of advice. Talk things out first, don't let stuff build up, no one wants to see you go the way your brothers went. There are plenty of good folk around here, plenty that will listen. Mr Vanishall, now I think he did you a big favour today. Don't let people down, stay on that straight and narrow, and you will be fine. Where you working these days, anyway?' questioned Newley.

Cradlick paused, not expecting to be answering questions about work. 'Gunwin's Chickens,' he replied.

'Ah well, at least it's summat,' replied Newley sympathetically. I gathered by his response that it wasn't a place you would aspire to work at. Cradlick exited the van, turning to look at the three of us bundled in with our bikes and scooter. He focused upon my face.

'Thanks for...?' He paused. 'Well, just thanks anyway,' he said with a slight smile emerging. His face had softened, and a sincerity poured from his eyes and heart. I knew, he knew I'd helped him, he didn't understand how, just that I had.

'That's OK,' I replied quietly.

'Right boys, let's get you home!' chirped Newley. He slammed the door, and I watched Cradlick trudge up the lane as the van moved away.

'Bloody hell, Pete, how did you get involved in that?' burst Buster. Obviously he had been holding himself together while in Cradlick's presence.

'Shhhhh,' I said, and nodded my head back toward Newley.

'Ooops.' Buster cupped his mouth.

'He's all right really, isn't he?' said Ronnie.

'Hhhmm, suppose, still not good enough for Rosy Saddler,' replied Buster, smiling and giving his brother an elbow in the side. We all chuckled and the mood lifted.

We headed off back out of the village towards Ivy Gate. The street lights had just hummed into life, and a light drizzle patted the side window of the van as we trundled our way home. I stared at the silhouetted passing countryside. Ronnie and Buster's bickering grew fainter as I mulled over everything that was happening; this strange new world was unravelling itself at an alarming pace.

PC Newley stopped at the bottom of Nanna's drive.

'I'll see you in. Won't be a moment, lads; stay here,' he said to Buster and Ronnie. I grabbed my scooter, said my goodbyes and headed towards the soothing glow of Nanna's cottage. She was already at the kitchen window, and when she opened the door Mr Milly shot out and clambered all over us. PC Newley was doing this awkward dance as Mr Milly pawed in a sensitive area. 'OK, OK, get down now. Aren't you lovely? No, no not there!' he said, protecting himself. She settled down and came by my side. 'Evening, Mrs Nuts, nothing to worry about, lads were caught up in a misunderstanding in the village, thought I'd drop them back as it was getting late,' said Newley.

'Well, I was getting a little concerned, thought I might have to send my little bird out to find you,' she said with a wink; at which we shared a smile. It was lost on PC Newley though. 'Thanks, Officer,' said Nanna.

'Right then, off to find this panther or whatever it is,' he half-laughed.

'Oh, it's been seen again?' questioned Nanna.

'Ar, apparently on Holme Road, better get going and check it out,' he said meekly, shrugging his shoulders.

'You take care, Officer,' said Nanna. I could feel it in her voice as if she was throwing protective energy at him. He smiled and waved goodbye.

'Don't forget Buster and Ronnie!' I shouted.

'Oh, oh no, yes,' he said like he clearly had. I could just imagine them two in the back of the van all night.

Nanna placed her arm around as we walked up the drive. I looked up to her face lit from the glow of the kitchen light.

'I like him, he's a nice man. He will be OK, won't he?' I said, concerned.

'I'm sure he will,' she said, but I wasn't convinced. After tea, I got changed into my pyjamas, and we gathered around the kitchen table. The Major and Maggot had joined us for a game of cards.

'Maggot! Pulled up my rhubarb today,' he blurted. Me and Nanna jumped as he shattered the silence of our studious concentration. Nanna smirked, and we carried on. The Major didn't need a flow of conversation, he just let out random lines from his internal storyboard, usually with no warning. 'Cat's crapped again! Huge mess! Yours!' he barked, not looking up.

We both looked at Moggins who paused his grooming as if he

knew. His look said, 'Yes I do, and I will continue to do so, thank you.'

I couldn't stop thinking of PC Newley out there alone. I was worried for him. I know he is a copper, and they're the ones supposed to protect us all, but this was different; no sirens, truncheon or handcuffs would help him against the Hound. I hoped to God it wasn't still roaming around. Nanna looked at me and then the clock; it cranked into life and Wit made a rotation, stopping for a moment, the tiny bird not giving her secret away while we had company or so I thought.

'News then!?' snapped the Major. I looked at Nanna and the Major, shocked.

'Do you, do you eeerrr?' I couldn't find the words without giving something away.

'A little,' he said, his voice softening as if dropping an act.

'Yes, he knows a little,' Nanna replied.

'Enough to know summat's up,' added the Major, placing his cards down.

'We should go, best check on him,' said Nanna.

'Newley?' I asked. She nodded in response. We gathered our things, the Major fumbled around putting his coat on, Nanna put her wellies and mac on. They both looked a right pair. *Fuddery OAPs* to the rescue, I thought, giggling inside. I was glad this was far from the truth.

CHAPTER 10

PC Newley

The rain was now coming down in buckets, and a faint rumble of thunder threatened in the distance. Nanna opened the kitchen door and popped her umbrella up.

'I'll get old Dolly out,' she said. That was her pet name for the car. Dolly was rarely used, spending most of her time tucked away in the garage. I think she was the only car Nanna had ever had, and somehow it complimented her personality; plain and simple; reliable and a little quirky. Nanna turned the engine over a couple of times before it wheezed into life sounding like a big lawnmower rattling and knocking. As the revs settled the engine had this melodic rhythm to it; happily singing away, elated to be hitting the road again. Nanna locked the garage up, leaving Dolly running.

'Come on then,' she said, waving at us to get in. Me and Mr Milly bundled into the back; the Major lowered himself into the front while holding the door frame, letting out a moaning sigh as he plonked himself in position.

'Flaming knees,' he grumbled. 'In, Maggot! In! I'm getting soaked,' he snapped. Maggot responded and jumped onto his lap, showing an equal dislike for the rain. Nanna joined us, shutting out the heavy downpour. The screen fogged up with the sudden rise of temperature, she attempted to clear her view with a handkerchief which was usually stuffed up her sleeve.

'Right, let's go and find him,' she said, flicking the lights onto the full beam. She dipped the throttle and shifted into gear with a crunch.

'Steady, old girl,' said the Major.

'It's been a while,' winced Nanna as we exited the drive onto the lane.

Nanna turned left, heading away from the village out towards the moor. The wipers were going like the clappers but still couldn't clear the torrent of rain hitting the screen. There were no street lamps out here, and the night had a lonely darkness to it. Nanna squinted, clearly struggling to see her way.

'No rush, take it easy,' said the Major. I didn't know quite what to say; how much did the Major know about the Veil? Should I just ramble on with my seemingly insane questions about Lurkers, Hounds and ancient mystics selling fear to humanity? Not to mention the Rag Tree Boys and Mr Milly's majestic alter self.

Then the Major, being more sympathetic to the situation than I realised, cleared the air.

'I lost my wife, you know, before you were born, my lad,' he said, half turning his head, making it clear he was talking to me.

'Oh, I'm sorry,' not knowing what to say really.

'Your nanna helped me, helped me see death for what it is,' he continued.

'Oh… and what's that?' I delicately questioned.

'Not the end,' he replied, 'that's all I needed to know, that's it's not finished or lost.' He paused. 'So I've seen a bit, know a bit, enough to make me a believer that truth is stranger than fiction,' he said.

'You're right there,' I piped.

'Right,' nodded the Major. 'Been in the army, seen things no man should see, done things no man should do, fighting someone else's war, not our war, not our fight. Anyway, Nanna helped me get rid of those gremlins. Well, most of them, hey, Maggot,' he rasped, stroking his furry friend.

I felt for the Major, his voice held the accounts of emotional battles won and lost, but his eyes twinkled with hope. I'm glad he had Nanna; otherwise, I feel it could have been a different story. We paused at the crossroad.

'Where did he say, Pete? Holme Road?' asked Nanna.

'Yes, I'm sure that's what he said,' I replied. Nanna continued straight over. We'd been travelling fifteen minutes or so now; the signposts were pointing toward the Moor parking area, and the Foxes Den free house.

'Good pint in there,' commented the Major. 'I could murder one now,' he said cheekily.

'Robert Mayne!' tutted Nanna, more at his choice of words considering the current situation. He let out a low, broken chuckle like Santa with a cold. The car slowed as we approached a right turn.

'Holme Road,' said Nanna. I think we all gulped a little as we headed down the single-lane road with no sign of anyone or anything. We reached the end where the road exited onto a gravel parking area popular with ramblers. Nanna rounded the car park; her headlights shone upon the police van.

'Oh,' she said. The van was in front of a cattle gate, beyond was a gravel track lined with fir trees. Nanna pulled up next to the van.

'Right, I will have a look, you lot stay here,' she said.

'Not on your Nelly, old girl,' commanded the Major. She sighed and puffed as she does.

'Come on then, but you stay with Mr Milly and Maggot,' she said, turning to me.

'OK,' I said, equally relieved and scared. Nanna locked the door; she knocked on the window signalling to wind it down, I did so.

'Be a love, put the headlights on, don't want to be breaking our necks in the dark do we?' she said with a wink. I loved Nanna's concern for such an eventuality, knowing how fearless she really was.

I watched them holding each other up, doddering towards the cattle gate, huddled underneath Nanna's umbrella looking more like they were returning from a boozy night out than a search and rescue mission. Their shadows stretched down the potholed lane, watching with bated breath; they rounded the corner and disappeared behind the thick blanket of trees. I was alone now, well, void of human companions; still, my beloved Mr Milly and tufty scrappy Maggot were here to protect me. With heightened senses, I awaited their return.

I desperately wanted to see them come back into view, having found PC Newley safe and well. I kept that thought in my head giving it energy. I thought, *Well, at least I haven't heard that howl.* I pondered how far Blackend was from here. Without realising, my wondering had cast a line out into the deep, dark, night; it was listening and waiting, and it murmured back.

The rain pelted down on the roof of Dolly like BB shots bouncing off a tin sheet. We were steaming up again, so I wiped the windows. The gravel parking area from what I could see was strewn with potholes, and undulations that were filling if not already full with rainwater. I had an image in my head, of a clip I'd seen on TV where someone fell into a puddle; they only suspected it to be shallow but ended up to their neck in it! I laughed then but not tonight.

I gazed upon a large puddle directly ahead. Illuminated by the car's headlights, it had a glossy, black, oily texture to its surface and was around a metre or so wide. It looked fairly deep. I thought, amongst the splashing of the pounding rain I saw something else; a shape broke the surface only for a second. I couldn't tell what it was so moved forward between the two front seats to get a better view. Mr Milly licked my cheek, and I turned to stroke her, then again out of the corner of my eye, I saw a ripple. I thought, *What's in that puddle?* Well that's all it needed, without realising my mind had spiralled down into a barrage of negatively themed questions.

'Oh no,' I groused and watched through squinted eyes as first, an oily hand reached out of its embryonic stew, taking grip upon the gravel surface, pulling hard, bringing forward another arm which both together dragged forth a featureless head.

At this point I panicked and looked to get out of the car. Mr Milly whined, and Maggot was barking and bouncing up and down on the front seat. 'Oh my god! Oh my god!' I spluttered, as I got hold of the door handle. I felt trapped, but where could I go? 'Nanna, Nanna come back,' I wined. The oily ghoul was half out of the puddle. I looked out of the side window, and to my horror, there were more, seeping, crawling and slithering from other such pools. I couldn't go anywhere, Dolly was surrounded, and then things got really bad as the lights flickered. 'Oh no, stay on! Stay on!' I pleaded, but my wishes fell upon deaf ears; they clicked on and off as if sending out a last SOS then died.

The rain halted, not wanting to detract any suspense from the dreadful scene about to be played out. I could hear now, I could hear the moans all around us, getting closer. I huddled, thinking, *Shall I go into the Veil? I can be strong there,* but I was confused because like the Hound these entities were in our reality, or were they? I just didn't know! I rocked back and forth, wishing the Rag Tree Boys were here, but would they be any good on this side of the Veil? I was so mixed up. Through the moans, I heard another noise. Placing my focus upon the sound, I could distinguish footsteps coming across the gravel. I kept quiet, not knowing if this was another messenger from the negative crevices of my mind. They got closer, and the moans subsided, a heavy bang came on the roof, and I nearly jumped out of my skin. I could see the fluorescent colouring of a police jacket next to the window and with much relief, the face of PC Newley pressed against the fogged glass looking truly sodden.

'You OK?' he said through the window. 'Where's your nanna?' he questioned.

'Looking for you,' I replied, reaching over to release the lock. PC Newley opened the door and put his head in.

'What you doing out here then, lad?' he questioned, surprised to see anyone out here in this weather and at this time.

'Err, looking for you?' I stuttered.

'For me? Why?' he quizzed, looking perplexed.

At that moment the brief relief of PC Newley's presence faded, and my eyes were drawn to the ground near his legs. It shined as black as night and wormed towards his foot; he saw the fear in my face and quickly looked down just as a glove of darkness grabbed his calf. He looked back at me, terror and disbelief in his eyes. I held out my hand for him to grab but he floundered, not knowing what to do; he tried to push them off but to no avail.

Mr Milly was snarling, her lips curled up repulsed by the oily fiend. PC Newley was dragged to his knees, the hands were all around him now, clambering, pulling him into their mire.

'No… Noooo!' He let out a truly spine-chilling call. I grabbed his hand.

'No! No! You can't take him. No! No! He's good!' I screamed, feeling my anger grow and the paramount disgust I had for the shadow-dwelling presence. The light in the car grew, a seam opened, and blinding light splintered through.

I was hanging on to him with everything I'd got. Dolly buckled, and the back end sank – we were all going down! But I wasn't letting go, the anger grew and grew, the seam of light shone upon my arm, a shape took form, moulding to my will, manifesting as a glass-plated gauntlet that hung suspended in the air. PC Newley in shock and amazement shouted out again, 'Help! Help!'

'Aaaarrrrrrrrgghhhhhh, he's ours!!' I cried out with a rage I'd never displayed before as the gauntlet snapped to my arm illuminated with heavenly light; I knew this was my courage, my pride, my goodness. I remembered what Nanna said and pulled in as much as I could; all the hopes and dreams I could gather in ten seconds, then I pushed them down my arm. The gauntlet shone brighter and grew larger, the hands screeched and retched as we both struggled to keep hold.

Seconds felt like minutes, my strength wavered, the victim within me, raising its ugly head. With one last pull my grasp failed and PC Newley disappeared into the puddle.

'No!' I cried out. The seam disappeared, and the gauntlet was gone. The threat still lingered as the car's suspension sunk deeper into the pool. 'Nanna!!' I wailed out into the night, tears streaming down my face. Suddenly the headlights flickered back on, and the radio sparked into life, playing an odd but happy little tune. Nanna was right there, in front of the car while the Major stood behind the cattle gate. She approached the puddle crouching at its side; the oily hands searched, licking and feeling for prey.

'Nanna don't!' I shouted. She just looked and waved her arm in a 'calm down' movement. I was worried; it took PC Newley, it could take her too. She looked upon the septic pool, then sunk her hand beneath its surface, as if she was fishing around for some lost keys. I had images of her being dragged in too, and my panic escalated. Nanna's hand pulled, yanking on something, for a moment I didn't know how this was going to go until she rose to her feet dragging a ghoulish, horrid mess out of its hiding place. She looked upon it as a dirty, filthy rag that was fit for nothing but the tip. Nanna then spread it out on the gravel.

All the other hands stopped moving, now they waited. Nanna walked round the black shape, totally in control. She pulled it up into the air, holding it out in front of her, hanging like an old grotty trench coat. I could feel the energy gathering.

'Bring him back!' she scolded, sinking her fist into the fiend. She then opened her hand to release a light which expanded within it, spreading and eating its way outwards. The oily fiend laughed and cackled hideously. 'Bring him back!' she repeated, turning the light up in a clockwise motion causing the shape to screech as if it was being erased from existence, then just before it expelled a different voice came forward.

'Come and get him,' it said in a creaking deathly threat. The oily ghoul burst into a million stars and floated off towards the heavens, the other hands disappeared, and the puddles were now full of nothing more than rainwater. I ran from the car and into Nanna's arms.

'Nanna! Nanna! They took him! They took him!' I sobbed into her coat.

'I know, I know, my dear,' she whispered. The Major had made his way over to us and placed his hand on my shoulder, silently offering his support.

'Well, this won't do will it?' he said, looking at Nanna.

'No, it won't,' she replied, squeezing me extra tight, then at arm's length she held me so I could see her face. She crouched so our eyes were on the same level and wiped my tears away. 'We can get him back,' she said, her face pouring out empathy for me.

'But how? I don't get it,' I spluttered through my sobs. 'I don't understand, how they can take him?' I questioned juddering my words out.

'The same way you brought that armour to life, you did that! I saw it; you brought that from the dimension of instant creation into our world! Now… that's power, my dear. See the Veil as a curtain that's closed; so far we have been poking our heads through a little and having a look round. We can step further, but there are less of us on this side. If we step fully through the curtain, there is nothing left of us in this reality… only our residual energy, and when this disappears we have lost our connection to this realm,' explained Nanna.

'How long have we got to get him back?' I asked.

'It depends how strong the light within him is. He's a good, true fella, so we have a good chance, but we need to prepare. We will have to go to her, we will have to face everything she has!' said Nanna, her voice growing increasingly stern. 'You have no idea how strong the light is within you. This whole thing looks like a trap, and not for PC Newley, but you! And do you know why? Because she is scared! Yes, the fear-peddling Sales Manager of the year is fearful of you! That's how powerful you can and will be!' Nanna stood back, finishing her sentence in a flurry of hand gestures dashing and crossing the air. I could see the passion rising, her belief, her belief in me, I could feel it, I knew it.

'We will get him back, won't we Nanna?' I said, stern and brave.

'Yes we will,' she replied, pulling me into a tight cuddle again.

'Right, all that sounds well and good. Now I need a drink. Foxes Den?' said the Major, rocking on his heels. We both looked at him as if really.

'What now? Come on, Bob!' said Nanna.

'Well… it'll steady the nerves,' he replied. Nanna tutted and looked at me; I nodded.

'It's OK,' I said.

'Just one,' said Nanna strictly. We all clambered back into Dolly and set off back down the road, the orange glow of the pub being the only lights for miles, a welcome sight for weary travellers. We pulled into the sparsely occupied car park.

'Wait here, girl,' I said, giving Mr Milly a rub behind the ear. Maggot was already out of the car following the Major.

'No you don't, little bugger,' he sniggered, picking Maggot up and placing him back in Dolly. We entered the Foxes Den; the landlady greeted the Major with a wide smile.

'Hello Bob, usual?' she asked.

'Ar and a Coke, and whatever Liz wants,' he replied.

'An orange juice, thanks,' said Nanna.

We found the snug empty to the Major's delight. The fire was roaring, and the red velour seating and dim lighting welcomed us in. I could see why the Major liked this place; it was very cosy, like a pirate's den I thought. The Major cradled his beer, took a sip then spoke.

'What's to do then?' he said in a rather composed manner, not his usual fits and starts of blurting language. 'People will find out he is missing, you know,' he said, hushing his voice.

'Yes they will, and so he is. Who would ever believe what happened? And if they did, what exactly are they going to do about it?' replied Nanna. 'Let people think what they will, we went looking for him because my grandson has an overactive imagination, he was worried about stories of a loose panther in the area and to ease his mind we went to find PC Newley. We came across his van at the parking area and assumed he was out looking on the moor, and that's all there is to it,' said Nanna.

My heart was heavy with thoughts of poor Newley, my mind flicking over images of his terrified face as his hand slipped from mine. What horror befell him in the depths of the dark abyss? Nanna's eyes turned on me.

'Watch it, dear, stewing about it won't help,' she said. I felt for his family and thoughts of my dad being in the same situation flicked over my mind.

'Does he have kids?' I asked.

'I believe so,' said the Major in a sombre tone.

'We've got to do something, Nanna,' I pleaded, pulling on her sleeve.

She cupped my hand and said, 'We will tomorrow, we shall make the necessary preparations.'

'Well, I'm ready! Show me, I can learn,' I asked, pleading now with a reason firmly placed upon my very essence. Knowing how wrong this was, and that I could help make it right, tonight a new vigour and purpose was born within me. My worries and fear had taken a backseat for now.

'OK, OK,' said Nanna, hushing me down. 'We will sort it, starting tomorrow, now let's finish our drinks and get home,' she added. We all sat for a few minutes quietly reflecting on our own versions of today's events. I gazed into the fire, its dancing flames hypnotising me into a warm vacant state.

Nanna and the Major were chatting quietly, their voices drifting into the background. My vision blurred and the edges softened until the only thing in focus was the orange-yellow flames licking up the fireplace. A shadow loomed into view, coming towards the table. I assumed it was the landlady collecting glasses for I wasn't alarmed or concerned about the approaching figure, then from nowhere came a great clatter.

My daze was sharply broken, as a heavy iron ring, with more keys than I could count attached to it, slammed upon the table. A grubby hand held the ring: mucky and brown with dirty yellow fingernails. I followed the hand up to a wet and grimy black coat sleeve, and then further to a white shirt collar that wasn't so white and resembled a blacksmith's rag. The coat was open, presenting a pinstripe waistcoat yet the pinstripes were lost in the garment's sootiness. A watch was neatly tucked into its breast pocket, and a large rusty chain sat upon his chest: somewhat similar to mayor's adornments, but this looked like it had been lost at sea and was rusted and tarnished.

His other hand held a chunky ringed chain attached to the most miserable dog I'd ever seen, it was a lurcher I think, from what I could make out, but again it looked like it had just bathed in a pigsty. Finally, I raised my head and looked upon the man's face, a stunted top hat inset with two crows feathers perched upon an old weathered face. Straggly greasy hair poked from the velvet rim and hung limply, framing his oval face in a most unappealing way. His eyes were small and squinty, and although his overall appearance was of a market trader from hell, a threatening air he did not carry. A smile broke, exposing a set of unkempt yellow teeth with dark clefts where some were missing; we all paused, looking at the strange man, waiting for him to speak.

'Can we help you?' said Nanna firmly, getting in there first.

'No dogs in here, pal,' said the Major. He always used pal when dealing with door-to-door salespeople, I found it very contradictory and confusing because he obviously didn't like the person. *Why call them pal, then?* I thought. The stranger's smile broadened; he swallowed, pulling at his collar.

'I'm parched, this seat taken?' he said, his croaky voice genuinely sounding dry. Nanna and the Major made some grumbling noises, but the man didn't wait for a response, he pulled the stool out and sat down.

'We are just going,' said Nanna, quite annoyed by the man's blatant bolshiness.

'Well that's alright, but you might want to listen to what I've got to say first,' he croaked again tugging his collar. 'Be a good chap,' he nodded to the Major and then glanced over to the empty bar. The Major glared back and looked at Nanna; silently they agreed.

Nanna nodded, and the Major stood up and went to the bar. 'You lost something tonight, that's not good for me,' he said with beads of sweat now forming on his brow, the cosy fire making the man uncomfortable. We shared a perplexed look. The Major plonked a pint of bitter down in a very uncaring way; it sploshed and some spilt on the table. 'Tar,' said the stranger, taking two or three long gulps. He placed the glass down forcefully, wiped his mouth on his dirty sleeve then spoke. 'I do apologise. Let me introduce myself, my name is…' He hesitated, reaching inside his coat pocket, pulling a business card out. His squint suggested he couldn't read the text. 'Bloody pixie writing,' he cursed. The stranger rummaged around again and retrieved a pair of glasses that he then perched upon his stubby nose and tried again to read the card.

'My name is…? Grevling Dier?' His pitch peaked towards the end, not sounding too convinced, like it was the first time he'd heard it. 'Well, that's what they've called me this time, well I'm,' he looked at the card again, 'Grevling Dier, loss adjuster for third to fourth.'

'What does that mean?' asked the Major sharply.

'Well I gather from tonight's events you know, don't you?' he asked with a nod. We all looked at each other, not really knowing what he meant. He nodded at me, I looked at Nanna, she nodded at me and I nodded back, the Major nodded at Nanna and then she nodded back, we were all nodding in agreement but to what?

'The copper! Kevin Newley!' he barked under his breath. We all nodded in unison now. 'See, people pass over, that's the cycle, but not normally like this. I keep count on who's coming and going, now I've got a problem. He's gone over, and he wasn't supposed to. How he got there ain't none of my business, and it would make my life a whole lot easier if he'd come back. I've got to clean this up now, that's why I'm here,' said Grevling Dier.

Nanna took a sip and placed her glass down gently. 'We fully intend to get him back,' she said.

'Well don't take too long, because every day that passes a bit of Mr Newley will be erased,' said Mr Dier. By now, I was bursting with questions and plucked up the courage to ask the strange man.

'Erased?' I said.

'Erased!' he replied, taking another big gulp, finishing his pint off in record time. 'Gone for good, everything he did, everyone he ever met, everything has to be removed, like he was never here. Right bleeding pain in the arse, that's why I suggest you get a move on and get him back. I don't know what that entails: well I know that moody mare Inka's involved and, I've seen you pair sticking your heads through the Veil. I see it all, you know. Anyway I will be here until the job is done, either way, I won't be far away, and I will be staying close.' Grevling Dier finished his sentence and stood up with a groan. 'I hate this dimension, so bloody heavy,' he moaned. 'Right, be seeing you, thanks for the drink,' he said, nodding to the Major. He bowed to Nanna and backed away, making his way to the exit looking like a proper scratty street urchin.

'Well that was interesting,' said Nanna.

'Indeed,' added the Major.

'Who is he?' I said, picking up the card he left. 'Grevling Dier, loss adjuster third to fourth, what's that mean?' I queried.

'His name changes, for he doesn't have a true physical form, he is a manifestation of the situation he is sent to resolve, and since these events are smothered in evil doings, his image resembles so,' answered Nanna.

'So he's not a bad man?' I asked.

'I believe not, I believe he is impartial, and his only concern is to keep the records straight. He is above the squabbles and part of a higher system that governs the laws of dimensions,' she added.

'Oh,' I replied, not really knowing what to do with that information; again this world and its rules changed at a rapid rate, I was just hanging on trying to keep up. I was intrigued by Mr Dier, I wanted to know more, I wanted to know about the system and why there was one. Nanna placed her hand over mine.

'Yes, he can tell you a lot, my dear, he is a good source for he is impartial. Or is he? Remember, he is part of the system. You need to work out these answers for yourself,' said Nanna, again spookily answering my very thoughts. 'Right, let's make a move. Thanks to Mr Dier, Mr Mayne got another pint in,' joked Nanna as the Major wiped the beery froth from his bristly moustache.

'Home, James,' he spouted, clearing his throat: the cheery landlady bade us farewell as he placed his empties on the bar.

We emerged from the cosy pub, into the still calm of the night, the orange radiance of the pub eaten by the relentless tide of the nocturnal cycle.

'Ha! What those two up to!?' chuckled the Major, pointing at fogged-up Dolly: the car was rocking, and the fleeting image of Maggot could be seen bouncing around on the front seat, Mr Milly letting out little playful yelps, trying not to get drawn into the tufty little dog's mischievous games.

They were both glad of our return, greeting us with plenty of face licking. Nanna turned Dolly over, and we were soon off on our way home. I was perched between the two seats feeling a need to be close to my adult guardians. Dolly's headlights illuminated the grass verge and stone walls that guided our way. I looked into the night, still on edge. Nanna was chatting, making plans for tomorrow.

'We need those ingredients, dear,' she said. I was in a daze again and didn't respond straight away, so she turned slightly, taking her eye off the road. 'Petey, dear,' she continued. Her eye had strayed long enough not to notice the figure quickly loom into view.

'Nanna, watch it!' I shouted. In quick reply, she pulled the wheel to the right, and we missed the wandering figure.

I stared out of the window as we passed, and then out of the rear window saw that it was, in fact, Mr Dier. He waved before disappearing into the night. Now there was someone I wasn't worried about. I felt his ease with the solitude of the dark; it didn't matter to him, he was beyond the fear and joy that this plane of existence emitted. I found some security in knowing that there were powers above this game of light and shadow. 'That's him, Nanna... Mr Dier,' I said excitedly.

'So it is,' replied Nanna.

'Nearly a grave end for Mr Dier,' chuckled the Major, his poor attempt at humour amusing him while Nanna tutted.

'I weren't that close. He didn't look worried, did he, dear?' She looked in the mirror this time and engaged my eye for a second.

'No, no he didn't, Nanna,' I replied, amused by our similar train of thought.

We arrived home with no further incidents. The Major and Maggot came in for a while and had a nightcap before making their short journey next-door.

'Where's Moggins, Nanna? I haven't seen him all day,' I said, concerned.

'Do the whistle, he'll come,' she said. I stuck my head out of the back door and attempted Dad's whistle. He did it for all the cats we'd had, it was a chirpy little tune. I'd love to know where it came from; it always seemed to work, well, when he did it anyway. I blasted away between pursed lips and cast my own, disjointed version out into the night. Ten attempts later and nothing; I was starting to get worried for my feline friend.

'He's not coming,' I said, disheartened.

'Let's try together,' said Nanna, coming to the door. She whistled, and I joined in my pitch homing in on hers. I could feel it, how Nanna put her intentions into everything she did. How it manifested into our reality, it was literally like throwing a line out to him and patting him on the shoulder, saying, 'Come home.' Our joint whistles echoed into the night.

'Sssshhh, listen,' said Nanna. 'Sounds like the approach of a very clumsy cat,' she added, with the sound of rustling bushes and an elevated 'meeeooowwss' rising out of the night. Sure enough, my lovely pirate cat emerged from the foliage onto the drive. He headed straight for me. I scooped him up and took him inside. With everything that had gone on today, I was happy to be with my favourite friends tonight.

CHAPTER 11

Crystal Cooking

I woke the following morning having paid another unwanted visit to the Gap. Something felt different though; my awareness was subtly bubbling under the blanket of the dream scene. It didn't scare me as much this time; my recent altercations with the very real monsters lurking just beyond our perception had put the Gap into perspective. I woke thinking, *It's my blinking mind, I should be able to control what goes on in it.*

The cottage had a chill to it this morning. I parted the curtains to a foggy, dreary day. I couldn't make the road out clearly as the fog wisped and twisted in an eerie dance. My thoughts soon turned to PC Newley, accompanied by a heavy ache in my stomach. I got washed and dressed and found Nanna in the kitchen; she was peering out the kitchen window through a swipe she had made in the condensation.

'Where are you?' she muttered to herself, so engrossed in her snooping she hadn't noticed me enter the room.

'Who?' I replied.

She turned with a smile. 'Aahh, you're up. Tea? Toast?' she asked.

'Err no, not today, I'm not hungry,' I replied, subdued.

'Newley?' she asked. I nodded.

Nanna came over cupped my face as she does, held my eye and said, 'It will be OK, you know.'

'I feel sick, like I've lost something,' I replied.

'That's empathy, darling; you're a caring soul,' comforted Nanna.

I had never had this feeling so intensely before, a sickly in-trouble kind of dread. I couldn't stop thinking about the people that were missing him, the ones on the phone to the police station questioning why their husband or son hadn't come home, and the worst one was the kids waking up asking, 'Where's Daddy?'

'Will you get these from the village, dear?' asked Nanna, handing me a list. 'Most of it's from Maggie's, she knows what we need,' added Nanna.

'OK, yeah,' I replied.

'Take Mr Milly, the walk will do you both good,' she said. I called her, and she came bounding in from a very out-of-character lie in. I clipped the lead onto her, thinking about Nanna's near miss with Mr Dier last night.

'Who were you looking for?' I asked, returning to my original question.

'Oh… your interesting friend,' she replied, peering back out of the window.

'Mr Dier?' I asked, my elevated voice highlighting some interest.

'Indeed, I don't think you'll have to go far to find him,' said Nanna knowingly. She pulled herself away from snooping and gave me a big hug, placing a twenty-pound note in my hand. 'That should be enough, be careful now and don't be too long,' she said.

I left the cottage and ventured into the cloudy atmosphere. Nanna was waving and smiling from the window without an apparent care in the world. She ruled her thoughts with an iron fist, the human mind with all its brilliance was a maze of traps. Nanna was master of them, and I wanted to be too.

It must have been a good five degrees cooler today than the staple twenty-ish of British summertime. Most people grumbled about our weather, talking fondly of their childhoods when the summers were warmer and brighter. My summers were just fine. I think grownups filter out those rainy, cloudy days while looking back through a nostalgic tint.

The cloudy vapours swirled and twisted around me; it truly was a pea-souper. Mr Milly wasn't fazed, her dog senses ranked smell and hearing before sight anyway. The lane was quiet; no sounds of anything, no cars, no birds chirping, it was an eerie day indeed. I looked right down the lane towards Smythe Farm. I, too, was snooping for Mr Dier. I thought about calling for Ronnie and Buster but decided not to as my heavy heart would be difficult to hide and they would surely smell a rat. What could I tell them? I wasn't in the mood for making porkies up. I was afraid my weariness would blurt out the truth, not caring of repercussion.

We sauntered to the end of the lane and followed the main road to the village. The fog sat densely upon the approaching outline of Chattersley and not one vehicle passed us in the half-hour trek. We drew near the convenience store, where Mr Vanishall was renewing his offers board. Emerging from the fog like two apparitions, Mr Vanishall did not sense our presence until we were on his shoulder and I spoke.

'Morning Mr Vanishall,' I said.

'Bleeding rabbits!!' he mildly cursed, jumping up from his crouched position, grabbing his back sharply. His face winced and instantly reddened. 'Ah! Me back,' he puffed. 'Whistle next time, will you!' he said, his wince softening into a smile. 'What you up to? No mates today?' he asked.

'No, just me and Mr Milly, I'm getting some bits for Nanna,' I replied, showing him the list.

'Well come on in, let's get you sorted, This fog's terrible, innit?' he replied.

'Oh no it's, it's stuff from Maggie's,' I said, feeling bad he had got the wrong end of the stick and feeling somewhat obliged now to make a small purchase from his shop.

'Ah, Maggie's, she's started selling all those funky candles and crystals, all that hippy stuff, they say she's got healing hands,' he said, winking.

'Maybe she'd give your back a look,' I replied, my tongue pressed against the side of my mouth.

'Hey, you cheeky goat! Ha, yes, maybe she could.' He chuckled at our amusing conversation while grabbing his back and puffing with pain.

'Everything alright after yesterday?' I asked, halting the laughter.

'Yes, yes, Shaun's OK, he's been in today and apologised, said he hasn't felt right for a while, but since yesterday his head is much clearer. I do feel for the lad, you know, tough growing up in that family,' answered Mr Vanishall. 'And err, PC, err? What's his name? the copper that came out. PC? I can't flaming remember, bloody old age,' he said with a strained, confused look upon his face.

'Newley, PC Newley,' I said.

'Newley? Nar that doesn't sound right. Newley?' he said, rubbing his chin and looking at the floor. It was apparent that the removal of PC Newley's existence had begun. Mr Vanishall was desperately searching his mind for a memory of him, but it skulked out of sight, then he shouted out, 'Newley, yes, Newley! Of course! Hope the young lad's all right, he went off looking for that big cat, dint he?' said Mr Vanishall excitedly.

'Yes, yes! Newley,' I replied, overwhelmed that he had found a way back to his remembrance.

'Your nanna's into all that?' he asked.

'Into what?' I replied, somewhat confused at the conversation's sudden turn.

'Maggie's stuff, crystals and meditation,' he said, accentuating the word meditation by placing his hands at the side of his head, fingers in an 'OK' shape mimicking the stereotypical mudra used.

'Yes, she is,' I replied.

'Ah, I had a feeling she was, bet you are too. Anyway happy shopping, say hello to your nan,' said Mr Vanishall saying his goodbyes as another potential shopper loomed out of the fog.

Maggie's shop, recently renamed Crystal Videos, was at the other end of the village, past the Inn on the Moore and hidden round the back of Porter's Pet Supplies. It now doubled as holistic retail and a video rental service. I know this was a weird combination but in small villages like this people dabbled and diversified their trades to survive.

The pet shop was also a hardware store, selling all manner of tools; there were bags of hay and rabbit food outside along with sacks of chopped wood. A lot of ramblers passed through Chattersley, and the pet shop provided ample supplies for would-be adventurers. We snuck down the side of the pet store, passing through a mossy green gate. I tied Mr Milly to a fence post and gave her a rub behind the ear; she made a little whine in response and pawed the air saying in doggy language, 'Hurry up.'

I turned the handle and pushed the door open. The old-fashioned bell chimed and announced my arrival. The shop was empty; a smoky, incense-infused mist sat in the air. The counter was immediately on my left, the likes of which you would find in a hotel where the receptionist could hide behind the raised front. In this case, it was Rosy Saddler that was skulking out of sight; head buried deep in a glossy magazine, her long dark hair straight as an arrow, gently tucked behind her ear. She chewed slowly on some gum and pawed over the collage of pictures splattered upon the pages. I could tell just from a glimpse it was one of those trashy celebrity magazines. On top of the counter was a display with birthstone bracelets and necklaces; a box of tarot cards propped a sign up next to the newest big film release, it said: 'Clairvoyant readings available enquire within.'

With my presence so far ignored, I cleared my throat, indirectly announcing myself. This was greeted with a sullen sigh. Rosy's head slowly rotated towards me; at the last minute her eyes rolled round, breaking free from the page's hold. When they settled upon me, it was with a look of utter contempt. *How dare I interrupt her?* they said silently. I felt the colour flood to my cheeks. Words babbled around in my head, sounding utterly stupid. *What's happening? How could she do this?* I thought, I'd battled Hounds and a Lurker, so how could this girl make me feel like a squirming little worm? She didn't look like an agent of ill; her clear cream complexion, blushed cheeks, and deep brown eyes weren't features I'd associate with a dark enchanter, but she was undoubtedly emitting something that had my senses and emotions confused. I cleared my throat again and fumbled with my list.

'Eeerrr is Maggie... Is Maggie...' I croaked through a suddenly choked throat. My tongue felt swollen, and mouth was dry as a bone.

'Is! Maggie! What!' snapped Rosy. *Geeze,* I thought. *Give me a break.* Wasn't she supposed to be nice? Buster couldn't speak highly enough of her. *It must be hanging around with Cradlick and his mates,* I thought. Her head rolled back to the pull of the magazine.

'She's giving a reading in the back, you can wait,' she said, her tone softening. Extending her left arm, she waved towards the shelves of rentals. 'Have a look,' she said. I gladly took the offer up and quickly moved from her space.

Past the counter were rows of shelves stacked with every kind of film you could imagine. Tilted mirrors were fitted beneath the ceiling so you could always be seen, even when you might reach for that inappropriate video. I'd been caught before; egged on by Buster and Ronnie.

'Go on, go on, pick it up,' they'd say, pointing at the big-busted lady on the top shelf. I'd reach up only to lock eyes with Maggie or whoever was manning the till.

'Boys!' she would say in a disapproving tone. This would be enough to have us scarper with an age-appropriate rental, even though Nanna didn't own a video player; the Smythe boys did and we often piled down theirs for a movie night when I was staying.

I wandered around and perused the film selection, occasionally glancing up, watching Rosy in the mirror. I don't know why. But, I was drawn to do so. I loved a good movie and just looking at the cover art sent my mind spiralling into a fantasy frolic.

'I must mind my mind,' I muttered, picking up a copy of one particular film that caught my eye – 'Wings and Wheels'. It appeared to be a race between a car and a plane. *Hmmm, one to avoid,* I thought, placing it back. Then another drew my attention. I glanced up to the top shelf, my image reflected back from the tilted mirrors. 'Midnight's Call'. The pale-faces, red eyes and blood tipped fangs mesmerised me. 'Wow, this looks great,' I said under my breath, forgetting for a moment that whatever was in this film wouldn't come anywhere near to what's actually out there. My brain continually struggled with what's real and not, it so easily wanted to flick back to a not-knowing status.

Soon I got a sharp reminder of this other world. As I stood on tiptoes reaching up for the video's box, my eyes focused on the cover; drawing it toward me, my immediate surroundings fell into this soft, dimmed peripheral focus, and without realising the colour of my aura became visible in the mirror, an aqua green haze materialised around my body. I had the cover of the film in one hand, still focusing on it but at the same time using my unfocused vision I could see the hidden. I looked at both, caught in a daze. I paused and shifted my full focus upon the energy surrounding me, that's when I saw something else, a shadowy figure lurking behind the shelves, watching me watch myself. I didn't feel threatened, but I couldn't tell if it was part of ShawlInka's crew or not; it didn't feel malevolent, if anything I got this overwhelming feeling of loss. As soon as I acknowledged its presence it disappeared like a shadow does when the sun plays host to it no longer, streaking across the aisle through the wall. It was followed by a gush of air. The shop door blew open, clanging the bell as if a herd of buffalo had just passed; the back door slammed against its hinges, and a woman's voice shrieked out in shocked surprise. I spun round to check, but the room was empty, the feeling was gone, and my aura had faded out of tune.

I looked back up at the mirror. Rosy was looking at my reflection, her mouth open. She got up to close the door. Maggie came through with another woman who was clearly in bits.

'It's OK love, that's an extremely positive response,' said Maggie, trying to comfort her.

'Positive! It knocked the table over,' the lady said. She couldn't wait to get out as Maggie tried to walk by her side amidst the narrow aisles offering encouraging support, not wanting the customer to be put off from returning. She left in a flurry of mad chatter, the door slammed shut, and the bell rang over the silent room.

'Well, that's just great!' despaired Maggie. 'If they aren't talking, they're running through the place. It won't be long before that's round the moor. Consistency! A steady flow, is that too much to ask!' complained Maggie, looking up to the ceiling with her hands held out.

'That's never happened before,' said Rosy.

'No, no, it wasn't the norm, did you see anything?' she asked.

'No, but I think he might have,' replied Rosy, pointing at me. Maggie turned, a smile emerging from her troubled face.

'Petey love, how are you dear? Come here, give us a hug,' she said, making her way over to me. She greeted me very much like Nanna. 'Gosh, you're getting big,' she added.

'Oooh! You're Pete, Ronnie and Buster's friend?' asked Rosy.

'Yeah,' I replied.

'You were in the shop with Shaun, he's been talking about you,' she said. Her look changed towards me, as if I'd been upgraded from a worm to a mouse. She appeared to have time for me now.

'Yeah, it was all a misunderstanding,' I said nervously; it was a touchy subject, and I still didn't know what I could say about it.

'Hhhhmmm… Well, Shaun said you're a gooden, special he said,' commended Rosy.

I blushed and looked at the floor. 'Nar, it was nothing really,' I said timidly.

'Yes, I've heard you're in the thick of it lately, aren't you, young man? First that cat at the Smythes' farm then the kerfuffle in the shop!' said Maggie.

She was Nanna's friend but felt more like family. I didn't see her that often but I always got a warm, toasty feeling from her. She was younger than Nanna, I'd say about fortyish, I always thought how similar they were; they even looked alike, just Maggie was a younger version. Her hair was darker with a slight curl, she had a gypsy look, her skin always had a year-round glow, she smelt of lavender perfume, and her bright red lipstick would always leave my cheek marked.

'Did you… did you see anything?' asked Maggie.

'Well, he looked like he'd seen a ghost,' smirked Rosy.

'Short, skinny, old fella, with a walking stick? Or a redhead in Victorian dress?' asked Maggie, very matter-of-fact. No? Hmmm, let me think. Well, I have got a two o'clock reading, they could be gathering for that,' she muttered more to herself than me.

'No, I didn't, I didn't see anything,' I replied.

'Your face said different,' poked Rosy.

Maggie held my hand and said, 'You're with friends, my dear.' She nodded and stared deep into my eyes, knowing I knew more. 'Anyway, what you out for in this murky weather?' she asked.

'Nanna sent me to get these,' I replied, handing her the list. She put on her glasses and looked over it.

'Yep, yep,' she said, doing a mental stock check, then she paused and bit her lip, musing over what the list meant to her. 'Everything all right? Nanna OK?' she asked, concerned.

'Errr yeah, fine,' I replied, caught off guard.

'Right, well you tell Nanna I'm here if she needs my help,' said Maggie. I nodded. 'I won't be a minute, I will just get this from the back,' she said, leaving me and Rosy alone.

'I've seen stuff, you know,' said Rosy.

'Seen what?' I asked.

'Ghosts... Don't you believe?' she asked, pawing at my affections. I felt she was fishing for information, and I was bursting inside to share my incredible adventures with someone. I'm sure it had nothing to do with wanting to impress an older girl as I hadn't wanted to before.

'In the shop, Shaun says you did something to him,' she added. Rosy approached; I began sweating as she stood close. 'What do you know?' she said, swaying playfully. She ruffled my hair in a sisterly way and looked into my eyes as if trying to suck my thoughts through them. Maggie's footsteps broke the tension; Rosy stepped away and sat behind the counter, soon engrossed again in the glossy magazine.

'Right, this should do it,' said Maggie, handing me a box full of bits. She pointed at the different items. 'Copper wire, quartz, resin, brass shavings, tourmaline, amethyst. Hmm, I think that's it.' I handed Maggie the twenty-pound note.

'Is that enough?' I asked.

She cupped my hand. 'It's fine, love, it's on the house,' she said, smiling.

'Oh, thanks,' I replied. 'I'd better be getting back now,' I said. Maggie showed me to the door. 'Bye,' I said over my shoulder.

'See ya,' said Rosy, not lifting her head.

Mr Milly had waited patiently. Maggie came out and gave her a good fuss.

'Anything I can do!' she shouted as we left the ginnel.

I thought on the way back how we were all on different levels of understanding; obviously, Maggie had knowledge and believed deeply in different realities, but I don't think she had experienced the full emersion of the Veil. I saw her as a listener, decoding the white noise of the realms out of sight. I didn't know what to make of Rosy, I was weirdly fascinated by her and left feeling quite opaque in her company, but she had listened to Shaun and believed him! I hoped one day she would believe my crazy stories too.

With our box of bits, we headed back out into the murk. It hadn't cleared any and was swirling around ready to swallow us up. The fog had a deadening quality to it, eating up any natural reverb. Mr Milly was on alert, her ears pricked slightly, twitching to any sound that made it through the curtain of mist. We passed through the village not seeing another soul; the road up to Nanna's was quiet at the best of times. With no street lamps and the nearest neighbours being the Smythes, it could be a lonely journey and today more so.

Somewhere around the halfway mark the fog got really dense. Chattersley nor Nanna's could be seen, only the road and the stone walls either side. Things started to get weird; Mr Milly became disoriented, pulling the other way back to the village then across the road, then the other way. She whimpered, and I could sense her frustration. I was lost too now – which way was it to Nanna's? This sounds silly because it was one or the other, but I felt stuck and turned this way and that looking for a sign, twirling round. The fog seemed thicker and was closing in. Lost in a cloud feeling dizzy and sick, I could hear whispering in the wind, round and round, quicker and quicker into a blur I descended.

The box fell out of my hands as I struggled to remain balanced; the whispers became louder until a voice broke through.

'Make you heave, that will,' it said, laced with gravel. I stopped abruptly, bent over with my hands placed upon my knees. Staring at the spinning floor, my balance eventually returned, and the road surface came back into focus. Slowly I looked up towards the voice and saw Grevling Dier emerge from the mist. Behind him was a shack made from corrugated metal; a wood fire burned from a barrel outside. He rolled up a smoke, his dirty digits poking out from black tatty fingerless gloves. Dier's dog came over and licked my face. Mr Milly whined and pawed the air, gesturing a pleasant greeting to the scraggy lurcher. 'What were you thinking? Spinning round and round, did you want to see your dinner?' said Grevling.

'I haven't had any yet,' I snapped, rising to my full stature while holding my sickly stomach. 'Where am I?' I asked.

'Lost, aren't you? Looking for me, you need to get lost first,' he said, winking. He turned his back, puffing on his stubby roll-up, and wandered inside the shack beckoning me to follow. I glanced around trying to get my bearings; I was still on the road, but my immediate surroundings were cocooned in an ivy wall of fog, and the shack certainly wasn't there on the way down to the village.

I tugged on Mr Milly's lead and followed Mr Dier, pushing the planked wooden door open and entering his domain. It was dark; lit only by the glow of fire burning from a strange black globe; it sat on a bed of pebbles rotating anticlockwise, flames licked up and around its form accumulating in a plume of oranges, reds and purples. I'd never seen anything like it.

Mr Dier walked over to a makeshift table, documents and books spread across it. He pulled up a chair and began sifting through the mound of papers. I moved closer to get a better look.

'Crappy business, this, don't get yourself caught that side,' he muttered, picking a scrap of paper and throwing it on the fire. The flames leapt higher and changed colours; a short scene comparable to a TV soap played within them. One of the faces was PC Newley – it flickered then disappeared.

'What was that?' I asked.

'Interaction with the gas man Friday of last week, gone now,' he informed. 'See how flaming annoying this is, every conversation, every meeting, every moment that's been recorded by anyone has to go. Bloody pain,' he moaned. 'I could chuck it all on now, but rules are rules,' he said, continuing to fling scraps of paper at the hungry fire. I walked over to the ball mesmerised by the images it devoured from time.

'Now you've been told, don't play with fire… Well don't play with that, it will suck you into the never,' he chuckled, finding himself amusing.

'Why can't you… just not erase this stuff?' I asked.

'Cant! Can't! Because the system would go up its own arse, it would only take one to be free.' He cleared his throat, trying to cover his last words.

'Free? Free from what?' I quizzed.

'Flaming questions, that's what! You should just get on with it and get him back! I'm dragging my feet here for you lot, I'd rather it be settled that way than the other,' he grumbled.

'What other way?' I pushed.

'Recalibration of the soul, not a nice procedure,' he replied, turning the pages of a childhood scrapbook. He plucked a picture from the page; it was of a young Newley, happy and smiling with his parents on a sunny beach. He looked around my age. Dier played with it between his fingers, rotating it this way and that; he was about to release it to the fire when I stopped him.

'No… please,' I begged, the very thought of my most precious days being erased twanged my heartstrings with an unforgiving hand. Mr Dier looked at me and placed it back.

'OK, kid, I'll give you as much time as I can, but I'm watched and audited too you know, so make it happen soon,' he said sternly, now sitting upright, searching the inside of his jacket from which he pulled out a pocket watch. It was ivory white – when he flicked the case open it revealed a featureless face as if it looked into the depths of deep, dark space itself.

Mr Dier looked intently upon the timepiece as he grasped it between his grubby mitts. Out of the miniature abyss materialised two white clock handles. He pushed them round and nodded in acceptance; flipped the lid back and leaned forward, handing me the watch. 'That should help, it will show you what you need to see, when time's up, it's up,' he said, locking eyes with me, conveying his message loud and clear. He then carried on scouring the table and with his head down and pointed to the door, 'We both have work to do,' he said.

I took my leave, glancing round the strange room one last time.

The road was still surrounded in fog, but Mr Milly had her bearings now and pulled me forward. I trusted the old girl and let her take me home to Nanna. Finally, I got a glimpse of Ivy Gate and looked back at the shack, but it was gone. Chattersley Church steeple poked out from the silvery blanket as the surreal faded away and gave way to a more normal scene.

Nanna's lights were on early today but gave little warmth to the misty, isolated feel. She was in the front room for a change watching snooker, I sat on the couch next to her.

'Get everything, did you?' she said, not relinquishing her gaze from the TV.

'Yeah I think so, Maggie sorted it, no charge either,' I replied, passing her the note back.

'Ah, bless her soul,' said Nanna, smiling. 'Anything else happen, did it?' she quizzed like she knew something had.

'I saw Mr Dier,' I replied.

'Did you now? Thought you might bump into him, and what did Mr Dier have to say?' asked Nanna. By her tone I sensed something resembling distrust or dislike, it was only slight but nevertheless I sensed it.

'He gave me this,' I said, producing the pocket watch and handing it to Nanna. She flicked the case open, scrutinising it.

'Hhhmmm, so that's how long he's got, that's generous of him,' she said sarcastically. 'You know this doesn't belong in this realm,' she said, looking deep into my eyes. 'Beware, they know not everyone has the energy to carry this in physicality,' said Nanna, warning me.

'Who knows and about what?' I questioned, slightly disturbed now.

'Your awakening hasn't gone unnoticed, the crows have left the tree,' she said, a shadow creeping in on our conversation, 'but you're not fully awake yet. This is a vulnerable time, we need to be vigilant and not make rash decisions,' she said.

'But we are still going to get PC Newley back, aren't we?' I asked, concerned that Nanna thought it was too dangerous.

'Preparation, preparation, preparation,' she said, tapping my head then pointing at the box, smiling. Together we examined the contents.

'What's it all for?' I asked.

'Cooking,' she said, smirking.

'Cooking! Cooking what?' I asked.

'No time like the present, hey? Come on, we'll have to do it in the potting shed,' said Nanna, flicking the TV off.

'Now?' I grumbled, feeling I'd only just sat down.

'Yes, come-come,' she said, opening the door and gesturing with her head for me to get a move on. 'Bring the bits,' she said. I sloped on through the house following Nanna's purposeful stride.

'Why in the shed?' I asked, putting my shoes back on.

'Terrible smell, dear, best out there,' she said, puffing and wafting with her hand.

We entered the potting shed through the adjacent door to the garage. We called it a shed, but it was part of the same building, just accessible through an internal and external door. 'Leave it open, dear, let the fumes out,' said Nanna, waving her hand at the door. 'Put that brick there,' she said, pointing at an old breeze block. The potting shed had a window that looked out onto the chicken coop and the fields beyond; it was mouldy, fusty and damp. Grey cobwebs clung to the rotten frame. Flashy the cockerel was out strutting his stuff, and I thanked our lucky stars the Sulphur Hound hadn't sniffed them out. 'Pure of thought,' said Nanna, policing my musing as we stared out of the window.

'How do you do that?' I asked.

'I can sense every minute change in your energy field, my dear, and for this procedure, we need the highest, purest thoughts, OK dear,' she said.

Nanna arranged the items on the dusty bench. 'Hmm, this won't do,' she said, brushing it clean. 'Right, first we take the copper and cut it to a special length, called a lost cubit,' she said, placing a wooden stick on the bench. 'This is one I made earlier,' she said, laughing.

'Why this length?' I asked.

'Frequencies. Different lengths, different frequencies. We want this one, an ancient frequency of power, again not passed through to the base population. Now when we do this keep your thoughts as positive as you can; bring that Christmas morning feeling into your heart or whatever makes it swell. Feel the warmth spread, keep that feeling and push it out, into the work you're doing, dear,' she said.

'Ahh,' I said, gathering my thoughts. Funnily enough, Christmas morning got sidestepped by Rosy Saddler poking her face in. *Oh well,* I thought. *Whatever works.* I pushed the swell from my heart down my arms and into my hands while I cut the copper wire.

'That's it, use it all, dear, we want as many as we can get,' said Nanna.

Next, we curled the wire into a spiral shape using a jig Nanna had made; the spiral was reflective of sacred geometry. Nanna explained that the length coupled with this shape intensified the frequencies and added a particular tone to its vibration. Next she took a few crystals and broke them into smaller fragments. 'Right, now we are set. Get the moulds, dear,' she said, pointing at the rubber tray indented with circular impressions. Nanna then placed quartz fragments in the bottom of the first mould, on top of that she sat the copper spiral and then more crystal fragments. 'Right, now do the same, keeping those thoughts pure. Pour your goodness into each one,' she instructed.

When all the impressions were filled, she cracked the resin open and mixed it. 'This is the smelly bit. Hold your nose if you need, dear,' she said. Nanna donned a pair of fetching rubber gloves and did the resin bit as it was toxic but one set, is fine. It apparently bound the ingredients together, creating a pressure on the crystals, squeezing their structure. I didn't understand how they worked but I had total confidence in Nanna and trusted that these little concoctions would be vital to our cause.

When all the moulds were complete, she snapped the gloves off and tossed them onto the bench. 'Right, that's done, they will be ready tomorrow,' she said.

'Tomorrow!?' I said, pulling the pocket watch out and dangling it in a tick-tock motion.

'Yes dear, I do understand, but above all we must be ready, trust me,' she comforted. I nodded and flicked the watch open. It wasn't like a typical clock, it was set out in days, in fact, the whole dial was a week, and as the needle moved round, it left the face behind it white. As I studied the watch, I felt something in my hand pulse. 'A timepiece, is it?' said Nanna cryptically.

'What do you mean?' I asked. 'Why can't you tell me? It's obvious you think there's something amiss with Mr Dier,' I said, frustrated.

'Oh, my dear, I'm sorry, I can't tell you everything, you must find certain things out yourself. Certain things can't be told because it's different for everyone. Perspective is a funny thing; everyone has a different view of this world, this realm, and it's the same of all other realities, it's a big old confusing, complicated game,' sighed Nanna. 'Come on in, I'll get tea on now,' she said, gently placing her arm around my shoulder.

Over tea Nanna explained a little more about Mr Dier's place in things, well, 'from her view'. She kept emphasising this bigger picture and a system much like our governments that set rules and policy's for the many dimensions beyond our perception, rules that aren't written on paper, you can't find books and study them, they are inherently woven into the fabric of universal knowledge.

'You know that feeling you have? That feeling of knowing all, where no questions need to be asked or answered. If you give yourself to that energy, you become the rules. When the ego and lower-dimensional mind runs the show, you are playing a different game, one that can be bent by shadow,' she informed. 'Egos are easily bought by the temptation of power over others. This is a very unevolved way of thinking and humanity will forever war and be manipulated to the will of the ill-minded if they continue to think this way,' said Nanna.

'But if more people knew about the Veil and truth behind death and dimensions they maybe wouldn't think that way. And they wouldn't fight, and maybe we could stop all this,' I said.

Nanna looked over her spectacles. 'Eureka! And what's stopping this flow of knowledge? Why is it hidden?' she asked, peering intently at me, sensing a breakthrough in understanding.

'Because... Because they don't want us to stop fighting?' I

suggested. Nanna slammed her hand on the table; she then placed it over mine and looked hard upon my withering naivety.

'And does that sit well with you? Feel… feel where it lies within you. Where in your body right now is that answer?' she asked. I closed my eyes and scanned my subtle energies.

'I feel a burning in my stomach but also a swell in my heart,' I said. Nanna nodded. I knew I was right. 'But why would they want to do that?' I asked.

'I've been around a long, long time, dear, seen many things, played many roles and I'm only just beginning to unravel the countless layers of this great deception,' she said. 'Mr Dier is fulfilling a role. He has never been born into a human life on earth, he has no reason to question the cycle, to him it's a school,' explained Nanna.

'A school?' I asked.

'Indeed, they would peddle this as the hardest school in this cycle of creation, a place where only the most advanced souls would choose to come,' said Nanna.

'Why come? To learn what?' I quizzed.

'To climb the evolutional ladder quicker, to gain access to higher dimensions, the ultimate goal being one again with everything, having not one form but being in every form, being part of every single atom in creation, being the creator,' she said, taking a breath. Again her enthusiasm poured out over the subject. I guess it had been a while since Nanna had anyone to muse over these subjects with so deeply.

Nanna continued, 'So as I see it, Mr Dier is in control of a cycle that will keep the souls in a system of perpetual reincarnation.'

'So they never get out?' I asked.

'That's correct, they will keep the soul coming back with this and that lesson to learn, and yes, the soul is gaining experience from these incarnations, but they are in effect trapped here unless they remember. Remembrance is the key. Even when they are on the other side, they aren't allowed full access to their knowledge, they are kept in a semi-dumbed-down state. The soul is so relieved that there is actually something after death, they don't question it any further. Some souls can be fooled into this state for many, many cycles,' explained Nanna.

'Why? I don't understand why,' I asked. Nanna moved in closer.

'We are in a battle, heaven and hell, light and dark, good and evil, it's been raging for millions of years and earth is the last stronghold of the dark. The bravest, strongest souls have chosen to incarnate into this prison system, knowing full well that it's a trap, knowing that they will become fodder for the fear machine, knowing they will suffer at the hands and minds of the corrupt. They will die many times, in the hope that one time they will remember, and when we all do the game is up; it will be like a chain reaction, a domino effect sweeping the globe, driving the dark anomaly into oblivion,' she said, sitting back, satisfied that she had presented the information suitably.

'Wow… OK, that sounds nuts,' I said.

'Ha, nuts indeed,' laughed Nanna. 'I've always said the truth is stranger than fiction. Light will prevail, my dear,' said Nanna.

'Am I one – one of the brave ones?' I asked.

'Ooohh! You are! You're a dare-devilling warrior of space and time, here to stick your boot up fear's backside,' chuckled Nanna. My serious look melted, and I joined in too.

'So, Mr Dier? I still don't get it?' I asked again.

'Hhhmmm, how can I put it? We are all privy to certain

knowledge; his perspective is different. He sees his role as an important part of helping souls along their evolutional path,' she said.

'So, he thinks he is doing a good job?' I asked.

'Yes, yes, I believe he does,' answered Nanna. That was enough for me at this time, I was relatively happy with the way things were being explained. I was creating an imaginary mind map, Dad used them all the time, it helped him connect information together when he was trying to make sense of something.

Still, I had a bucketload of questions, in particular about the Veil. 'Am I still visible here, when I'm there?' I asked Nanna who had now moved over to the sink where she was washing the dishes up.

'Well it depends on the strength of the energy in that area, like around here you can go by will, and you will disappear. Hhhhmmm… how can I explain it better?' she mused.

'In the shop, I was still here, but when I was with the Rag Tree Boys would I have disappeared?' I asked.

'Right… well… in the shop because you were predominantly in this realm, yes, you physically stayed in this realm, but your senses saw into the Veil. When you were with the Rag Tree Boys I would say you mostly disappeared into the Veil because you were predominantly surrounded by that dimension and its vibration. It's like a universal law – like attracts like, dear. Some places where the power is weak, we have to make a portal where we can step through into the Veil,' answered Nanna.

'Oh! How do we do that?' I asked.

'Sealing stones, dear, like the ones we've just made in the potting shed.' She turned and winked. 'Told you, all is in hand,' she said, smiling. 'They do other stuff too, but we shall deal with that tomorrow,' said Nanna.

That night I went to bed full of mixed thoughts. I felt some pieces of the puzzle were aligning while others looked like they'd never fit. Mr Milly curled up next to me. I wondered what she thought of it all. I bet she didn't overthink it, and it was just what it was. Moggins was nowhere to be seen as he hadn't responded to our call tonight; he must be off doing his own thing. I wish sometimes I could be a fly on his collar, I do love his feline independence but sometimes wish he was more reliable like Mr Milly.

Nanna's warm milk eased me into soft, welcome sleep. My body was glad for the time out, hopping dimensions and carrying weighty secrets were more exhausting than simple boys' play. Mr Dier and the watch mulled around and then floated off, the Gap teased menacingly in the background but was pushed aside by the Rag Tree and its crazy inhabitants, Rosy Saddler and Maggie flickered and faded, finally Nanna and the stones we made today took seat in my dream theatre ready to see me off till the curtains closed.

Hours passed peacefully; my body fully relaxed and beginning to recharge, but this wasn't to continue. A tapping and scratching noise roused my brain waves from delta back into beta. I lifted my head and squinted, trying to clear my sleepy eyes, the streak of light from the landing cutting through the darkness seeing my focus quickly return. The noise sounded like a twig or branch on the window. I was hesitant of opening the curtains as I knew there were no trees close enough to cause this, but still, it tapped and scratched.

I had to check I was awake. Was this another Gappish dream only at Nanna's? I called Mr Milly under my breath, trying not to wake Nanna.

'Milly... Mills,' I said to my sleeping companion. I ruffled her neck, and she soon came round and moved to my side. Feeling equipped to investigate further now, I approached the window. With my arm outstretched I pulled the curtain slightly back. Once my feeble wince relaxed I could see nothing sinister, so I pulled the curtain further, still nothing. 'Hhhmmm, strange,' I said, looking down at Mr Milly. She looked back with a, 'Can I go back to sleep now?' face. I had one last look, drawing the curtain further, confident it wouldn't reveal anything nasty. As the curtain reached its full extension, my action committed, a shape flashed into the corner of my vision; my heart jumped, and I sprung back, dropping the curtain, letting it fall halfway back across the window. 'Bloody hell! I'm fed up with this!' I muttered, quickly flung from the comfort of sleep into a fight-or-flight adrenaline rush that I'd imagine you would encounter on the harsh African savannah.

The tapping and scratching escalated, then a noise like a siren began to wind up. 'Mmmmmmeeeooooowwww.'

It sounded like… 'Moggins!' I said, hopefully curious, and began approaching the window again. The shape entered my side vision the meeoowwws increased and my fears were laid to rest as I saw Moggins hanging from the window frame. His ample body, impressively long, stretched out, filling the full height of the window. A look on his face expressed immediate failure due to the fact he couldn't hold on much longer, and he was right as he plummeted to the ground with a thump.

I quickly opened the window; sticking my head out to see him gathering himself together. 'Come on, Moggins,' I laughed, my furry friend dissolving the preceding tension. He made a quick purr sound and readied himself to jump. I moved away from the window as he scrambled onto the ledge and thudded down onto the floor, his tail high in the air as he rubbed against my leg, proud his plan had paid off. I bent down and stroked my pirate cat; he seemed happy to be indoors.

I shut the window and pulled the curtains, thinking, *What a fuss,* glad it was nothing untoward. With my back still turned Moggins emitted a different sound; he hissed and spat. I spun around thinking it was a cat-dog thing, but it wasn't.

Moggins glared into the crevices of my unlit room. Mr Milly focused too upon the same spot, her hackles showing. Their intent focused upon the wardrobe sat in the far corner. Down its side was a narrow space; this was the darkest part of the room. I stared upon the black space.

'Who's there?' I called.

Mr Dier's watch started to tremble; it moved as if by an invisible hand, scraping the bedside table's surface. The catch slowly flipped back, and the case flung open, casting out a pulse of energy through the air. Again my heart was thumping like a sledgehammer. I backed towards the window. The wardrobe rocked slightly, enough to set the alarm bells ringing in my head. The shadow grew and spread across the floor and ceiling. Mr Milly's low growl rolled out, while Moggins was spitting and hissing. 'Who are you?' I pleaded for an answer. The black shape moved forward, a shadow within a shadow now extended what resembled an arm. It reached out.

I began drawing on my power, quickly pulling up energy and channelling it into the stars. A brilliant white seam split the darkness like a knife; my courage stopped its retreat and began bolstering my offensive manoeuvres. Ikol shot into my mind, and I suddenly imagined a weapon of light. I imagined wielding it in my hand, a blade of such brightness such pureness no evil, no creature of the night could refuse its smite. I closed my eyes and *bang*, like a flash I felt it in my hand, its power flooding through my senses. Opening my eyes I looked in awe upon the blade which I quickly pointed at the shadow. It didn't cower or seethe as I thought. I doubted for a moment my creation; re-summoning my courage, I stepped forward.

The dark shadow did too, and we met only feet away. My blade shining bright, casting a light onto the wraith's arm, its face remaining hidden in gloom, the hand gestured and slipped back into the unrecognisable shape.

'Go! Go on! Leave!' I seethed, both angry and frustrated. I paused, waiting for it to respect my command. It slowly retreated soon followed by a quiet sobbing that emanated from the side of the wardrobe; a forlorn rejected cry saturated with grief and vulnerability filled the room, mauling my empathy's struggle into submission.

I lowered the blade, and it faded from creation. Slowly I crept towards the sobbing, my courage holding firm. I reached the wardrobe and peered down the side, the crying now sounding more like a child's. 'Who's there?' I asked. The sobbing suddenly stopped. 'Who's there?' I asked again. Not being able to make anything out, I stuck my head in further. I did think, *Why the hell didn't I just turn the light on?* I was about to do so when it rushed forward as if the narrow space was a long corridor leading far back. Footsteps running hard and fast accelerated towards me, gathering a gush of freezing wind with them. In a flash, two hands grabbed my shoulders, a grey moonlit face bursting into my field of view. I pulled back, but it had me.

'Nighlight!' It said, its breath visibly chilling the air. 'Nighlight!' it repeated, holding my gaze. I squirmed, but we were locked together. Its face began to look familiar, through the distorted illusion I could see someone I knew.

'Newley... Newley!' I called, his eyes lonely and spent. Newley was an echo of his earthly self.

'Be warned, it won't be me!' he repeated long and slow with purpose. A loud slam came from the corridor behind him, the sound of a heavy metal door being unbarred and the rattle of iron keys disturbed Newley. He looked back in fear. 'Tick tock,' he said as his image was sucked back into the corridor where it faded into nothing. The light flicked on suddenly, and I jumped again.

'What on earth is going on, dear?' said Nanna.

'Newley! He was here! He was here, by the wardrobe!' I spluttered.

Nanna pulled me into her arms and stroked my head. 'It will be OK,' she said.

'We need to help him!' I pleaded.

'And so we will,' said Nanna. She wandered over to the bedside table and picked the pocket watch up. She examined it, flicking the case open then shut. She closed her eyes and took a deep breath; Nanna's earthly form glistened ever so slightly, a golden hue sparkling with tiny diamond specks surrounding her outline.

The watch quivered in her hand as if a struggle was taking place. The ivory timepiece would not give up its secrets without a fight. Nanna frowned and her look of concentration intensified. After a brief exchange she yielded with a disappointed gasp.

'What, Nanna?' I asked.

'Hhhhmmm, not sure,' she pondered, removing her glasses and placing the arm in the side of her mouth. 'Did he say anything?' she asked.

'Nih… nigh… light… or something like that,' I replied.

'The Nighlight,' said Nanna.

'Yes, that's it… that's what he said… What does it mean?' I asked.

'The Nighlight, a mysterious place indeed; where souls are prepared for earth's frequencies. I believe it serves other functions too, where the soul is really wiped clean,' replied Nanna.

'What, everything!?' I quizzed.

'Not just one life, all lives, all gone. The soul won't remember anything while it remains within the invisible walls of this re-incarnation prison. They are then ripe to do the bidding of the negative, easily manipulated, bought by the power of the ego and driven by material lust, its connection to any inner guidance and past knowledge is all but lost. This is the ill's best opportunity to corrupt a soul and integrate it into the carousel of darkness and fear,' said Nanna.

'I saw a corridor, and heard keys and a door slam,' I said.

'Sounds like you saw Newley in the lower levels of the Nighlight. I have never been down there or well, from what I can remember, but I've heard it's grim, a manifestation of the collective vibration emitted by the souls waiting for their turn. The atmosphere is one of ominous doom!' she said. I instantly pictured a high tower, its top shrouded in stormy clouds, lightning flickering at its core, its walls made from grey slate with narrow slits like archers' windows placed in no particular pattern. I could feel it's chill and the despair in the air.

This was worse than our perception of death. I felt the pain of the awakened souls; they've waited many lifetimes to finally remember their path. Now caught, they awaited the erasing of their purpose, their essence.

'I don't get it. Why are we allowed to cross the Veil? Dier knows that we do, doesn't he?' I asked.

'Indeed he does; there are players and watchers, dear. Imagine football. We are team light and the petty nuisances we are encountering are team dark, the game is away at Negative United, they own the stadium, the pitch and the sky we play under, the game is always away, and always at their ground. The crowd are the population watching this age-old battle play out, cheering and jeering like at a pantomime. Dier is a referee making sure the right amount of players are on the pitch, watching no one creeps on making the play uneven because it has to seem fair. Now this game has to keep the population enthralled, it's a balance – we are the glimmer of hope, we are what keeps the people coming back, not suspecting the game is always fixed in favour of the negative. They want it to look like we could win. Now… without the light people would be desensitised to fear and that's all they would know, they would become numb to it and fear would become a castrated emotion. People would stop coming to the game. Fear needs light to keep it alive,' said Nanna, pausing, letting it all sink in. 'Are you getting this?' she said.

'I think so… Because we can be happy and feel love it makes fear more powerful?' I suggested, sort of making sense of it.

'Yes, yes! And that's how they want it to be, we have to experience love and happiness to know what the opposite is, making this world and mix of extreme emotions and vibrations where the very highest and the very lowest can be achieved. It shouldn't be like this. If the earth were free, humanity would learn quicker from its mistakes, it would be allowed to shake off the evil that's shackled our evolution,' added Nanna. I shrugged, letting out a yawn.

'Oh… sorry, it's a bit heavy for two in the morning,' I said.

Nanna laughed, 'So it is,' ruffling my hair. 'Bless you, I have trouble making sense of it too,' she said, tucking me in. 'Let's put this in the kitchen out of the way,' she said, picking up the pocket watch. I nodded, thinking that was for the best.

I soon settled back into a deep slumber. At least Moggins was in, that was one less thing to worry about; he was curled up between my legs, purring away. I thumbed the stone Nanna gave me; it eased my thoughts, smoothing out the wrinkles, leaving no place for dark thoughts to hide.

The following morning brought a sunnier outlook, the curtains letting through the diffused early rays filling the room with a yellow tint. The first thing on my mind was the watch and how long was left. I threw the bed covers off and went to retrieve it. Nanna had placed it in the singing bowl, full of the crystals she used for clearing negative energies.

I picked it up and flicked the case open; the black dial was showing two days gone – we were on the third. Each segment had a day and night subsection. I hadn't actually seen the dial move yet, so I couldn't gauge it accurately, I just thought we would need to be at Blackend with at least one day to go. I placed it back where it was, and looked for Nanna. Mr Milly trundled through sitting at the door, pawing the air to be let out. Moggins soon came looking for his morning fill.

'Nanna,' I called out and opened the door for Mills. Hearing a rattling coming from the garage, Nanna soon appeared with the box from yesterday. She waved and stroked Mr Milly who was caught between relieving herself and pawing good morning.

'Morning... I've made a start. I was up early,' she beamed, making her way over to me with her trademark swaying walk. 'Come, come, spread the cloth on the table,' she bossed with a smile. I did as she asked before she plonked the box down. 'Right, I've popped them out of the mould and made some adjustments,' she said proudly, picking one of the sealing stones up. 'Aren't they pretty? Look! …Best batch I've done. That's because you helped.' She winked. 'Now this one I've put a hole through, I've got some leather laces we can use,' she said, rummaging through the top drawer. 'Got it,' she said, clutching a piece of black leather cord, which she threaded through and tied in an adjustable knot. Nanna held it up; the sun shining through the sealing stone cast a kaleidoscope of shimmering colours upon the far wall.

The clock chimed and Wit rolled round, shaking off her illusion, bursting into flight with her happy, angelic chimes filling the room. She buzzed around the sealing stone that Nanna was holding up giving it her blessing. 'P… e… t… e… y,' she tweeted again, and again, each letter echoing golden bells and seashells.

Nanna puffed and laughed at Wit. 'Well she seems impressed,' she said, beckoning me forward. Wit flitted her wings at lightning speed, hovering above my head then gently descending until she sat upon my shoulder, her exquisite chirps enchanting my ear and warming my heart. She was the epitome of everything good, transforming my feelings and lifting my spirits. Nanna placed the sealing stone round my neck; it lay upon my chest, having weight unbefitting to its size and a pulling force like it was magnetised. I could feel its power, but I had no idea what we were going to use them for yet.

'That's it, it may feel a little funny until it's synced with your vibration, dear,' said Nanna, proudly observing her creation.

'What do they do, Nanna?' I asked.

'Well, I've been planting and dropping these little beauties for years,' she said.

177

'Planting?' I quizzed.

'I say planting, they don't grow, dear. Well, not at least physically, but they spread their energy, a good way to purify a negative area… They are like a… Like an amplifier,' she said.

'Aahhh,' I said, rotating the stone in my hand watching the crystals catch the light. It certainly was a pretty little thing.

'We'll go later dear, at dusk,' said Nanna, now busying herself dusting.

'Go where?' I asked.

'Into the field, more training, best at dusk, we will get a better effect… You go play if you like. Everything's in hand, dear,' she said.

'Oh, Ok… What about the watch? Aren't we running out of time?' I asked.

'It's fine, all is in hand… Go on, go play, forget about this for a few hours,' she said.

'OK, I think I'll call for Ronnie and Buster,' I said.

'Good. Not before some breakfast, though. Come on, let's get you sorted,' chirped Nanna.

CHAPTER 12

Hide and Seek

O nce fed and watered, I grabbed my neglected scooter and made my way down to the Smythes' farm. Mr Milly was by my side as we turned onto the lane. I dropped my head and dug deep, pushing with long hard leg sweeps. There was no wind, and the sun was still low shining directly into my eyes. My other senses checked in and allowed me to push on, gathering speed. I approached the hump in record speed and was just about to launch when Mr Milly let out a sharp warning bark. I quickly looked up to see a figure silhouetted against the blinding sun.

'Watch it!' called the voice. I squirmed and ditched my steed, placing my hands out to stop my fall. I tumbled hard into the grass verge where I came to an abrupt stop; my palms grazed and burning hot; one knee heavily grass-stained, the other slightly torn.

'Great,' I sighed, somewhat deflated. Mr Milly was slobbering over my face, checking I was OK. The figure stood looking down at me, the sun hiding their features; shielding my eyes I looked up, squinting.

'Didn't you see me?' came a soft female voice. I recognised it instantly, then came the fragrance of summer flowers as she knelt down, out of the morning sun. Rosy held out her hand.

'I guess not... Sorry,' I said as she helped me to my feet.

'Let's have a look... You wanna get those cleaned?' she said, sincerely concerned about my slight injury.

'Err... I'm OK, I'll wash them later,' I replied.

'Boys hey, always pretending to be tough,' she said, ruffling my hair as Nanna does. 'Is your head that full of mystery, you can't see what's in front of you?' she teased. 'I still want to know what Peter Nuts knows,' she said. I just looked at the floor, embarrassed, not knowing what to say. 'Shaun won't stop going on about what he saw,' she paused and lingered, but I wasn't giving anything away, 'and you found Ripper didn't you?' she said.

'Yeah in the woods,' I replied, nodding.

'Strange times... Well I better be going, or Maggie will be moaning. You watch out, look up once in a while,' she said cryptically. Rosy gave a little wave and turned to make her way to the end of the lane. I didn't know what she pursued so intently, but she certainly showed an interest in what she thought I knew. Intrigued by her curiosity, I gathered myself, picking up my scooter; now with a few extra scrapes. I meandered the rest of the way with my confidence squashed.

Mr Smythe was in the yard, his head buried under the lid of a tractor. His farmhand Nell Popoff, somewhat of a local character, was dipping the throttle while Mr Smythe waved his free hand.

'Shut it off, shut it off!' he called over the chunky thumping engine. He looked up and shouted over the yard, 'Morning Pete, they're in the pig shed!' I waved a thank-you and made my way to the boys, soon picking out their bickering over the general farmyard noises.

'I think Porkster is fatter than Mince,' said one voice.

'Nar, nar! Mince is the king, look how big his belly is,' argued the other. I entered the pig shed to find Ronnie and Buster hanging over the sty railings while pointing at its inhabitants. The smell was powerful and soon washed away the remnants of Rosy's summer scent. 'I think it's you! You're the fattest pig,' said Ronnie, glancing sideways, waiting for Buster's reaction who returned the look while holding it together, then like lightning Buster grabbed the back of his brother's trousers and hoiked his already tilted body over the railing and into the pen.

'Ooooiiii! Get off!' yelled Ronnie as he plunged headfirst into the pigs' sty.

'Ha, you deserved that… I might be a bit on the sturdy side, but I'm strong with it!' he said, flexing his ample upper arms. Ronnie, spurred on by Porkster's interest clambered to his feet, his retaliation diffused seeing me standing at the door of the shed, my hands holding the bubbling laughter in.

'Pete,' he said with delight. Buster turned too, greeting me with a beaming smile. Ronnie climbed over the rail, slapping his brother on the head as he went.

'How was your gran's?' I asked.

'OK… glad to be back though, what you been doing?' asked Ronnie.

'Err… not much… this and that… err, doing stuff for Nanna,' I replied shiftily. The boys knew me well, and I felt I hadn't dodged the question sufficiently.

'This and that?' poked Buster.

'Well I'm glad, you can do your adventuring with us,' said Ronnie.

'How about we go down Snickets?' said Buster.

'Yeah, walk the plank or hide and seek!' said Ronnie excitedly.

'Dad says it's been quiet down there, no sign of the beast,' added Buster.

'Sounds good,' I said, agreeing with a nod. Mr Milly, feeling left out, poked her head through my legs to the boys' delight; they fussed her and ran outside, getting her to jump up on their chests.

'Here girl, jump! Jump!' called Ronnie. Our visit certainly seemed to have revved the boys into action, they were like two rubber balls ready to bounce off anything they touched. The farm dogs Dot and Silver sat under the yard wall looking on with jealous eyes. The boys didn't have the same relationship with them, as Mr Smythe was quite strict about them being working dogs. I'm sure they would have loved to join in; I felt a little sorry for them. Buster, being the more sympathetic type, rubbed them both behind the ears as we passed.

'Where you off, lads?' asked Mr Smythe.

'Snickets,' replied Ronnie. Mr Smythe and Nell shared a look.

'You be taking care. I'll be in the low field, just shout if you need me,' he said in his thick Irish accent.

'OK... Go on,' said Mr Smythe, taking his hat off and returning to the mechanical issue before them.

We left the yard and headed down the old coach track. I was finding it increasingly difficult to keep my secret and very nearly blurted it out a few times; the Lurker and Newley were right there on the tip of my tongue desperately seeking new ears.

'Beat you there!' called Ronnie as he rushed off in front soon followed by the rest of us. We hurtled down the track kicking the dust up beneath our feet. Ronnie reached Snicket's entrance first.

'Yay! I won!' he shouted, rotating round in a victory stance.

We paused at the wood's entrance for a second, with myself attempting to ease a stitch. A shared thought passed between us and I felt the frequency in the air blip. Nanna's sealing stone drooped down, hanging outside my T-shirt, and Buster quickly spotted it.

'Wow, what's that!' he said.

'Oh… Oh, this… Nanna made it,' I replied, not realising the stone was showing.

'Cool, what's it for?' asked Ronnie.

'Err it's a birthstone thing, you know, Nanna's into that stuff,' I replied.

'Well I like it,' said Buster.

'Me too,' added Ronnie.

Now that the boys had drawn my attention to the stone, I could feel its energy around us; a golden presence radiated subtly between sight and sound. Buster then took up the gauntlet and set off racing through the woods.

'First one to the Den!' he shouted, leaving us in his trail. We chased him down, but he was quite speedy for as he says, 'a sturdier build'. As we rushed through Snickets I thought I saw something, running with us from tree to tree, parallel to our route; it was in the corner of my eye on the edge of peripheral vision. Again, like before I turned my head to focus, but whatever I saw was gone. I carried on running, but my attention was drawn now to the other side. Something was mirroring us seemingly on either side around fifty yards or so into the dense wood.

We arrived at the Den in a sweaty mess, crashing through the bodged thatch door in a last-ditch attempt to claim victory. Buster was having none of it and held his arms out, securing the win.

'Winner!' he said proudly. 'I'm quite nippy aren't I?' he said, vulnerably looking for a kind response, which he wouldn't find from Ronnie.

'You are, you left us for dead,' I commended; Ronnie just scoffed, not having time to rub any insecurities his younger brother may have.

'Anyway… fancy "Back t' Base"?' asked Ronnie.

'Yeah! Come on, I'll be on,' said Buster excitedly.

'Split tree to Fern Hollow,' stated Ronnie, marking the boundaries of our game.

Snickets was massive by our gauge and to use the whole woods would be a fruitless exercise in seeking.

'Mills, you help Buster,' I said. She just responded with a sideways look but understood my request. As soon as Buster's eyes were shut, me and Ronnie scarpered, tearing through the undergrowth making a hell of a racket. I soon found a spot and ducked down behind a fallen tree trunk; it was hollowed out, making a perfect home for small woodland creatures. I could still hear Ronnie searching for a spot. The noise soon stopped, and I assumed he had found an acceptable hiding place. The woods fell quiet, my thumping heart slowly decreasing as I got my breath back. Now this game was a bit different to hide and seek. Yes, we hid, but we also had to get back to the Den without being tagged. Buster could use any means to tag us, it didn't have to be his hands. Usually a ball would do but to add a little extra spice we would often use a catapult and conkers. No one wanted to get hit by these little beauties so we would play more cautiously, only making a run for it when we were sure.

Peeking over the log, through the woody vegetation I could just see the top of the Den, I thought what a good job they'd done when a twig snapped behind me. I froze, clearly feeling a presence moving on my position. I stared forward, quickly trying to think as my steadying heart was shoved back into top gear. It was behind me, I knew something was about, I knew I had to turn; I did so like pulling a plaster off my fear. Spinning around, I pushed myself up against the log and scanned the area but nothing revealed itself to me.

'Idiot,' I said, sighing, feeling a little silly. Out of nowhere two hands grabbed my shoulders, and a grubby face with what looked like stubby horns slid alongside me.

'Boo,' it said.

I quickly realised it was Okol with his aviator goggles sat upon his forehead. I thankfully sank down in relief.

'Bloody hell, I thought you were about,' I said gladly.

'Can we play?' he asked.

'Oh… err… I don't know? Can you? I'm playing with Ronnie and Buster,' I said, a little confused as to how this would work.

'Well, we could have a little fun with them, couldn't we?' he smiled.

'Will they see you?' I asked.

'If you want,' replied Okol. 'That amulet's helping, it makes it easier for us to flit between,' he said, pointing at the stone around my neck.

'Right, OK then… I'm not sure how, though?' I queried the proposed play.

'Don't worry, it's just larking about,' said Okol. With that, he whistled with his fingers, and it rang out through the woods. I saw the other boys emerging from their scattered hiding places, camouflaged brilliantly by their grubby complexion and leafy, raggy clothes. I wondered what Ronnie and Buster would make of them and how this was going to go down.

'Coming!' called Buster. All eyes were on him and Mr Milly as they exited the Den. He turned to survey the area, his arm outstretched, pulling back on a catapult.

'Oh no,' I said.

'What's up?' said Okol, his eyes gleaming bright.

'Buster's got the crappypult… RUN!!' I shouted, leaping to my feet. What happened next was pure hysteria. Ronnie jumped and ran, Buster chased us down, and just to confuse matters six other strange scraggy-looking boys raced around screaming, 'Crappypult! Run! Run!' Both Ronnie and Buster stopped for a moment, their mouths wide open watching the Rag Tree Boys hurtle round. Choc broke the ice first; he screeched to a halt before Buster, only measuring just above Buster's waist, his big brown eyes and chubby cheeks easing Buster's worries.

'Come on then, Busty! Catch me if you can,' said Choc, sticking his tongue out. Ronnie let his barrier down at Choc's teasing taunt.

'Busty!' he said, doubling over. 'Busty!' Buster glared at Ronnie and let a smile out at Choc. He pulled back on the catapult.

'Aaahhhhh! Busty's coming! Run! Run!!!' yelled Choc, and the hysteria escalated further. It was total mayhem, screaming, shouting, conkers flying through the air. In the end, nobody knew who they were running from or who they were chasing.

'Aahhhhhhh! Run!' I shouted as Choc and El came bursting through a bush covered in leaves and muck. Okol placed his goggles carefully in position, twiddling an imaginary knob at the side which instantly turned solid. He clicked it this way and that, adjusting them, scanning the area. He called instructions to himself, logging his actions.

'Commander Okol searching for scallies, engaging heat and movement detector.' He then made a machine sound as the goggles powered up. We ran and screamed, jumped, tripped and fell, we hid in ditches and up trees, under bushes and behind logs. I don't think we'd ever had as much fun. Buster and Ronnie were red and sweaty; Buster's hair stuck to his forehead and Ronnie's cheeks were fit to burst; both breathing heavily but showing no signs of stopping.

'Pirates on the brig!' shouted Buster, holding his hand to the sky.

Everyone paused then shouted, 'Yeeeaaahhhh!' filling the woods with an echoing raucousness that I'd never heard rivalled. Buster raced off towards the split tree closely followed by the urchins of the woods. Bot and Let were playing sword fighting, their imaginary weapons halfway between the two realities. The more the boys got into the game, the more their opaque creations illuminated and solidified, the blades actually making a swooshing noise that could be heard amongst Snicket's earthy sounds.

Buster and Ronnie hadn't noticed anything yet, being so caught up in the hysterical play. The marauding gang approached the tree; Buster and Ronnie jumped onto their imaginary pirate ship and turned to brandish make-believe cutlasses.

'Stop right there, aaaarrrrrggghhhh! We are the crew of Captain McBandpants!' shouted Ronnie, his face turning from exhilarated joy to disbelief as he observed the approaching gang. At that moment, the secret had leaked.

Ikol, Okol, Choc, Let, Bot and El came to a standstill. I could now see what bewildered the Smythe boys. From the corner of my eye a glow enveloped the party; yellows, oranges, reds and greens filled the air. I turned slowly to see them adorned in every aspect of their imagination. It was a sight to behold, and Buster and Ronnie's faces said it all, their mouths wide open, slowly lowering their invisible weapons in disbelief. The Rag Tree Boys looked upon themselves, Choc looked up at me, his big brown eyes peering through his horned helmet.

'Spinny hat thingy,' he said, shrugging his shoulders, making a circular motion with his hands and wobbling. I nodded, smiling.

'Yeah, anti-spinny hat.' There was a pause; nobody knew what to say. I opened my mouth not knowing what would come out. 'Err... I... this... is the... Rag,' I eked out an introduction when a voice came calling through the woods.

'Lads!! Ronnie!! Buster!!' called a strong male voice. It was Nell, the farmhand. Buster and Ronnie turned to see him trudging down the path; when they turned back all that was left of the Rag Tree Boys was the rustle of bushes. I glimpsed Okol behind a tree; he winked and waved, still visible to me. I discreetly gestured and then turned back to my mystified friends. They jumped down off the split tree.

'What... was that?' said Buster, slapping the side of his head as if he was dreaming.

'Do you know them?' asked Ronnie.

'Hmm, sort of...' I replied.

'Did you see...? That was amazing!!!' said Ronnie, breaking their dazed confusion with excitement.

'I know, I know, I did, I did. Wow…!' said Buster. They were circling each other, too thrilled to stand still.

'You must tell us, Pete, who are they!?' asked Ronnie.

'Who's who?' said the approaching Nell, sucking hard on a cigarette. This shook the boys out of their excited state. They now stared at me, wondering what to say.

'Sssssuuusshh,' I breathed, patting my hand down. The boys responded appropriately as if we'd just spilt a drink on Mrs Smythe's new carpet and were trying to cover it up. Nell sauntered up to the split tree.

'Was that you lot? Making all that racket?' he said, blowing out a plume of smoke. He was one of those men that lived in overalls and wellies, his flat cap permanently on tilt, looking as if some small woodland animal had once inhabited it. He was most likely older than his years, a tough life broadcast through cracked and leathery hands. Once Buster told me his dad had been trapped in a cattle pen by 'Limo' the bull. Nell went in trying to distract the agitated beast and ended up chinning it. Buster said, 'Limo's legs wobbled he hit him so hard.' I gathered he wasn't someone to mess with and that he would likely plant one on you before asking why.

'What's up? Cat got your tongue…? Young Nuts… what you got to say?' He aimed the questions at me, getting nothing but ums and errs from the brothers.

'Yeah, we did get a bit excited playing pirates,' I said.

'Sounded like someone was being flaming murdered! Thought I'd better check… You know, with all this funny business going on. You ain't seen anything funny, have you?' he probed.

'No… no, nothing funny,' said Ronnie unconvincingly.

'Not a sausage,' said Buster, swinging his arms around his waist in an even more unbelievable manner. Nell squinted at them and followed the look through to me.

'Alright… Yeah… whatever you say.' He leant on the tree and dragged again on the withered white roll-up pinched between his fingers.

'I have, you know… Seen some weird stuff,' Nell said, looking at the treetops. 'Once I was down here one night, walking home, back when lambing was on, it was black as coal, no moonlight, not a breath of wind… The woods… there were something different that night, they watched me, I felt eyes in the dark. Now, nowt much fazes me, but that night I quickened my step, and then I saw it!' His focus left the treetops and found our enraptured gaze.

'What was it?' said Buster, totally sucked in. Nell flicked his ash onto the dirt.

'I don't rightly know, but it wasn't anything I'd ever seen before. White swirling circles deep within the trees, they picked me out, and I froze, I couldn't move, I felt magnetised. It floated towards me, closer and closer. I don't know what it intended, but it wasn't good. I shouted out, "Show yourself… Come on for a knock then…" although I fear my fists would have failed me. That's when I saw the boys,' said Nell.

'Boys? What boys?!' asked Ronnie.

'Well, I heard them first, whistling and calling. The wind picked up as if they were travelling on it, the trees rustled and bushes shook. I saw them, five or six young scruffy kids; one blew straight past me legs. I can see his face now, he had these funny goggles on like flying ones, he was half here, half there, not solid. He shot off into the undergrowth towards the eyes, it was then that I felt the pull break and I could move, so I did, like a shot.' Nell took another puff. 'Weird stuff, eh?' he said.

'Ghost boys,' said Buster, his eyes pinned wide open, nodding to Ronnie and me in a really, really, obvious way. 'Ghost boys.' He did it again as if we didn't already get it.

'I... Ghost boys or something like that,' said Nell, making light of it now. 'So nothing to report then? No?' he asked again.

'No, nothing like that,' I said firmly. I didn't know if we should be talking about them, and part of me wanted them to be my secret. Sounds like they'd seen off a Lurker though, and Nell got away lightly.

'Anyway, your dad wants you back where he can see you, that cat incident has got him a bit jumpy,' said Nell.

'OK,' said the brothers, clearly disappointed.

'Come on then,' said Nell, turning and ushering us on. We followed him but stayed twenty yards or so behind.

'Bloody ghost boys!' said Buster through clenched teeth, his face about ready to pop, struggling to contain his excitement.

'I knew it, I knew something was odd about them,' agreed Ronnie. We chatted all the way back, hushing our enthusiasm. 'You said you knew them!?' interrogated Ronnie.

'Well... I know of them, I've heard Nanna talk of the boys in the wood.' I wasn't particularly lying, just skirting around the truth.

I wouldn't know where to start, or how to explain the marvels that were beyond our perception. I didn't feel qualified to start filling them in on this battle of light and dark that's been raging for aeons, I could just imagine how my explanation would go.

'Right, boys, this is the deal: Earth's a prison for reincarnating souls; trapping them in a cycle of life and death. Our lovely blue planet is a sick theme park where we are made to experience fear in all its horrid glory because fear is a desirable energy, to negative beings. The wild ghost boys in the woods are real, only not in this dimension, they have never been born or died in this realm. Nanna's a time-travelling being of light: her wooden clock has a real wooden bird in it called Wit. I made a pink rubber glove come to life and sucked an insidious squid off Cradlick. Newley's been taken, he is in the Nighlight awaiting a terrible fate. The Hound is real, and the Lurker was what Nell described. And finally there's a bad lady called ShawlInka who's running the negative crew round here. OK, lads.'

It sounded crazy to me, and I was knee deep in it. For now, I went along with Buster and Ronnie's theories. I loved seeing them so enthralled by the mystery ghost boys; part of me wished I was back there with them and not further down the path of understanding.

Nell entered the yard before us. 'All right… they're here,' he called over to Mr Smythe. As we rounded the corner we saw a police officer standing with Mr Smythe, their backs towards us. I took a hard look at the policeman; from behind it could have been Newley. My heart jumped for a second at the thought that it could be him, then my stomach dropped at the thought of his poor soul trapped in the Nighlight.

It can't be, I told myself, Mr Smythe turned.

'Here they are. Thought someone had met a grizzly end down there with all that racket,' he said, holding his long arms out to embrace his sons, but my eyes were firmly fixed on the profile of the officer. Time slowed, and with each degree, his face turned towards me, my mind made a million calculations as my internal conversation argued it out. *Is it? It can't be, but it looks like him and sounds like him,* my heart leaping and sinking with each beat, then finally I was sure.

'PC… Newley?' my tone tailing off, and peaking with a high degree of uncertainty.

'Yes, son… can I help you?' he said politely. I stared and stared, my mouth open; no words came from the scrambled mess my head had become. 'Son, you OK?' he asked again.

'Pete, come here lad,' said Mr Smythe, grabbing my shoulders and lowering himself to my level. 'Tha's colours all but gone, lad, let's sit you down,' he said, rubbing my arms. They walked me over to the water trough, and I perched on the side. I blew out a deep breath as an icky feeling was rising from deep within. I glanced up and focused on PC Newley.

'You're back,' I said.

'Back? Back from where?' he answered, scrunching his face quizzically.

'You went onto the moor looking for that cat?' I said. He let out a slightly awkward laugh and moved from one foot to the next, not quite sure where to place himself.

'Oh… yeah… I found some tracks, bloody big ones, that's why I'm here, lad. I'm going round all the farms and asking them to keep an eye out for any signs, looks like it's still at large,' said Newley.

'Flaming hell! That's all we need. Summat wasn't right with that… That… well, whatever it was, it needs catching! Or a pound of lead shot in its earhole!' barked Mr Smythe. He was clearly annoyed at the seeming incompetence of the local constabulary. Newley visibly shrunk as Mr Smythe's agitated persona shadowed him.

'Yes, I understand your concern, it's under control, I will keep you posted,' he said. 'Right, must get on... be seeing you,' said Newley. I watched him return to his van; he looked the same and talked the same but somehow he was different. He could be excused not remembering the finer details of being pulled into the lower dimensions, and being banged up in a tower waiting for his soul to be wiped clean. He could be excused forgetting that. Why anyone would want that rattling round in their heads... Maybe it was the shock, maybe they removed those memories as part of maintaining the system. I wondered what Mr Dier would have to say, or whether he would be gone now.

'Ooohhhh,' I moaned, letting out a very fed-up sigh.

'What's up, Pete? You were fine five minutes ago,' said Ronnie, placing his arm around me. I smiled at him; he was a great friend, and his empathy for my deflated, sickly mood was much appreciated.

'Let's get you a drink, come on,' said Buster, not to be outdone by his brother.

'Ah, good lads, take him inside,' said Mr Smythe, patting me on the back rather heavily, not knowing his own strength. Buster got me a drink and soon I was rosy-cheeked again.

'Flaming ghost boys! And that horrible cat thing! What's going on!?' asked Buster enthusiastically. Mrs Smythe interrupted our conversation.

'Ghosts, what ghosts?' she said, her keen hearing picking the bones out of our chat from down the hall.

'Err, nothing Mum,' called Ronnie.

'Come on, let's go to the barn,' he suggested. I was itching to get back and tell Nanna about Newley's return but I didn't want to bail out on the boys and dampen the atmosphere, so we lounged on the stacked hay bales for a while, free to explore the boundaries of our imagination, the two brothers buzzing from their encounter with the Rag Tree Boys. Mine was preoccupied with how the game had changed now; *this must have made the situation easier. Surely we just had to cleanse Blackend now? I didn't have to worry about Newley's soul? Did I??* Something scratched at my relief, stalling what should have been an upbeat mood. Time passed and the purpose of the day tugged at my stomach.

'I'm going… I have to go now,' I said, much to the disapproval of Buster and Ronnie. Once the disgruntled chunter had died down they saw me off. I picked my scooter up and made the less leisurely trek back up the lane; the faithful Mr Milly trotted alongside me.

'See ya, Pete!' shouted Buster as I was halfway home. It was an odd moment, I had that feeling like when you're desperate to get a last glimpse of a loved one as they depart, when your stomach and heart aches, when you think you might not see them again. I felt that in Buster's call.

CHAPTER 13

The Training Grounds, Round Two

I ran the final stretch, ditching my scooter by the garage door, bursting into the kitchen, my chest heavy with breath.

'Newley's back!' I sputtered, barely drawing Nanna's attention from sorting the sealing stones out.

'Ah, just in time,' she chirped. 'The light will be perfect soon.'

'Nanna! Newley's back!' I repeated, frustrated at her reaction.

She turned, removing her glasses, 'Is he now?' replying with a cushioned contempt.

'I saw him at the Smythes',' I panted.

'And what do you think about that?' she asked.

'What? What do you mean?' I quizzed, getting a little tired of these games.

'How do you feel? Not your head, get the answer from your body... your energy centres,' she said.

'Well... I suppose... Not good, icky, I don't know... I don't feel relieved,' I said.

'Good, that's right, because there isn't any relief as of yet,' answered Nanna.

'But how? What's going on?' I slumped into the chair, increasingly perplexed.

'PC Newley may not be what he seems. I don't believe they would give such a bargaining chip back so easily; plus there are system rules to uphold. Whatever's going on, we will find out soon enough,' explained Nanna, not at all phased by my news. 'Let's just concentrate with what's in hand.' With that, the gears of the clock stirred into life, and the tiny hammer struck sounding the hour, the doors opened and out rolled Wit doing her thing. I never got tired of seeing her come to life; my heart glowed when she came out to play. Wit buzzed around, bells and whistles filling the room, Nanna nodding, 'Yes, yes, that's all well and good, but is it clear?' Wit chirped on. 'Right, well, that will have to do,' she said, winking.

'What will have to do?' I asked.

'It's in hand, dear, just checking the area,' she replied. Nanna placed the stones in a black velvet bag, pulling the gold cord tight. 'Right, let's go shall we?' she said, looking at Mr Milly and me.

Again we ventured out to the 'Training Grounds', as I'd come to think of them. The sun was almost gone. 'Perfect,' said Nanna, looking at the greying sky.

'For what?' I asked.

'The light show, of course. Here, take these and place them in a circular pattern around us,' she said. I started to lay the stones out like Nanna said. 'Eeerrr, no dear, further out... We don't want them getting too close, do we?' she said.

'Okay,' I said, slightly concerned. This time I placed the stones further out, around the length of Nanna's driveway from us. I made the circular pattern then I returned to her side. Nanna held out her hand, which I took; she nodded and closed her eyes, taking a deep breath.

'Right, as above is below, remember?' she instructed with a sideways glance, one eye still open. We both connected to the Veil and the ripple of full immersion fell over us.

Nanna opened her eyes and scanned the area. 'Hmm, looks clear,' she said.

'Have we disappeared from the real world?' I asked.

'What's real?' she said cryptically. 'Right, now focus on your amulet, make it the centre of your thoughts, bring your light into it,' asked Nanna. I focused hard, sensing the energy flow through my crown down into the amulet; the copper spiral glowed orange like a lightbulb filament. All the tiny crystal fragments sparkled, each giving off hundreds of laser rays; like a closed tap holding back a dam's worth of pressure, I could feel its power growing, ready to be used.

'Now, think of all the stones you've placed, feel them like the one round your neck,' asked Nanna. I tried to extend my thoughts beyond the boundaries only I had made for them. I reached out but was pulled back to the security of what I knew. 'Push... stretch... feel,' said Nanna, softly breathing out. I tried again; this time my feelings pierced what I can only describe as a bubble of consciousness. Once I passed this barrier any doubt was removed. I felt the first stone, then the second, and so on till all were in my thoughts, both individually and collectively. 'Good, now let it flow,' said Nanna. I didn't have to think twice, the amulet was eager to release its power; a surge of energy passed through my body into the amulet, shooting a beam of pure white light out. It hummed with a gentle warmth, the first sealing stone lit up with an initial burst of golden sparks then the next. Within seconds it had passed through all the stones like electricity until it completed the circuit, making a circle of light.

'Woow!' I exclaimed. Against the dusk backdrop, the neon circle was spectacular, pulsating with goodness and power. 'What can we do with them?' I asked.

'Watch,' she said, casting her gaze upon the far treeline where I had seen the Hound appear from before. She closed her eyes and fell silent. Mr Milly rose from her seated position and whined, poised ready for the next foreboding event.

'Nanna!?' I called, stress audible in my voice.

'Watch,' she replied, her eyes shut tight.

The distant trees released their static formation. A presence shrouded by the dense green camouflage created movement amongst the branches; they rustled slowly at first then more violently, the treetops swayed heavily back and forth seemingly disturbed by a great force below. *Sulphur Hounds,* I thought like one wasn't enough! What was she doing? I pondered, looking at Nanna's face. I was confident she had everything in hand, but in the same breath were speckles of doubt and raindrops of worry. *She must know what she's doing,* I thought. *She must!?*

The trees swaying slowed, settling back into formation as if the struggle had passed and the danger dispersed. I stared at the treeline and then again at Nanna, having the unnerving suspicion it hadn't even begun yet. Mr Milly's ears pricked, rotating slightly, looking for any sign of threat. She anxiously panted, her eyes busy patrolling the surroundings; she padded forward two steps, sniffed the ground then stopped, lifting her head slowly upwards, releasing an agitated growl.

'What is it, girl? What?' I asked but was quickly answered as her growl was countered with a devilish cackle; it started quiet, rising to a cruel, callous laugh. I was trying not to form an image in my head, but the words, *Witch… witch… witch,* ran riot through my thoughts, for the tones were higher than a male's and even though no words were spoken a level of intellect was present within whatever lurked in the woods.

The breathless air stirred into life as a malevolent wind came upon us. Cackles travelled on every gust, malicious words licked around us, circling in all directions with a suffocating madness.

'Little boy of light,' it creaked in my ear.

'Snuffed out,' whispered another ghoulish voice. Nanna was still silent with this slight smile upon her face. Mr Milly was glitching into her magnificent form, then the voice stopped, the wind drew back into the woods in one godly breath, holding for a second then breaking viciously in a vertical gale. Bursting through the wood's canopy, spilling forth a vast flock of large black birds. They spiralled upwards, squawking and snapping at each other, swirling as one into a tornado shape, hurtling round and round faster and faster.

'Hhhmm… Scragens,' said Nanna.

Any colour left in the sky was drained; the birds broke rank as the voice commanded, 'Crack them! Pick them! Bring me their bones!'

And so a dark tide spewed towards us, the hellish flock full of yellow pin eyes and bony beaks hurtled across the field.

'Eeerrr Nanna… Nanna!' I shouted. She opened her eyes and turned her head towards me.

'Use them… use the stones,' she said calmly. I thought this was all getting a bit ridiculous, talk about being thrown into the deep end. My amulet pulsed and was full of light; the other stones sat ready.

'What? What should I do!?' I screamed, panicked with the flock nearly upon us. Mr Milly, fearless as ever, reared up ready for battle.

'Petey... I'd do it now, love,' said Nanna, growing calmly concerned. The wind blew back my hair, and the dust off the field smothered us, the sound of beating wings and giant birds of death was only feet away as I searched every ounce of myself for courage and strength. 'Now, now! Now!!!' shouted Nanna.

Shield! A shield! I screamed inside. In a flash a dome of pure light shot up and encased us. The birds crashed against it, bursting into particles of ash and rag; one made it through and hit the ground but swiftly shook the crash landing off. We edged back against a scene of a feathered massacre outside the dome.

The bird eyed its prey. Bones showed through its coat of torn and ripped feathers, its yellow eyes focused solely on me, edging forward snapping its jagged toothy beak. I back-footed, feeling like I was in a cockfight now.

'Just focus, remember all you've done, all you can be, remember,' said Nanna. I calmed my emotions, took a breath and imagined the Earth Cracker, the glove and the blade of light I brought forth before. I could feel it coming, the charge was lit, and I was in total control now. I raised my hand; light filled the air around it bringing forth a suitable weapon to banish the aerial foe. The bird, sensing my pending attack flung itself in a last-ditch attempt, but I was ready to strike. We were about to clash in a blur of black and white when my victory was snatched clean in front of me. Mr Milly lurched into the air and took the ghoulish bird between her diamond teeth, bursting it into rag and bone; she spat it out and looked sheepishly upon us while backing away from the extinguished flying fiend.

'Mills,' I said, half disappointed and half relieved. I rubbed her ear and whispered, 'Thanks, girl.'

She moaned as if to say, 'I'm sorry, I couldn't help myself.'

Nanna tutted and rolled her eyes. 'Well, we aren't done yet,' she said, bringing our attention to the scene outside the dome. The flock was now a pile of bits, dust and ash, bones and rags piled up against the edges of the light shield, the air thick with echoes of ill intent. As the commotion settled, I peered through the opaque haze of the dome. There in the distance, just in front of the treeline were two figures, both silhouetted, their features shrouded in shadow, one taller and broader, the other was hooded and slight in comparison. I focused on the larger figure; it appeared to share the same raggy outline of the Scragens that now lay as lifeless ashy rubble.

'Who are they, Nanna?' I asked, not taking my eyes off them.

'Hhmmm, a bigger Scragen?' she said.

'And the other?' I asked.

'Not… sure… yet?' she said, pacing forward, trying to get a better look. 'They'll have to come closer,' mused Nanna. The air between us was reminiscent of bonfire night, charred with misty ash tinged with a red glow, the embers of the fallen still floating around as dust particles.

'Come on then, it's getting late!' shouted Nanna, sounding genuinely irritated. She rocked back and forth from heel to toe, hands on hips looking ready for a pantomime scrap. She turned back and faced me. 'I can't abide them, will they just get on with it!' The wind stirred again, twisting the mood; the whispers returned again, chanting under the breath of its malicious command. I couldn't work out what they were saying, but I felt it gathering momentum, the tempo quickening and the voices becoming louder and more aggressive. The taller figure strode forward then stopped, pausing for a moment before entering a crouched position, one hand planted on the floor, its head bowed. The chants suddenly ceased as if all was now ready.

I focused intently upon the squatted figure. Suddenly the silence was broken by its cloaked companion, a shriek of violence and anger tore through the air. With that, the crouched figure pushed off the ground and rocketed into the sky like an arrow of death. When it reached its maximum altitude, it opened its wings exposing its intimidating form, hanging there for a second. I gulped in anticipation of its next move. I'd hoped it would just flap its wings and bugger off, but my optimistic expectations were dashed as it began to dive towards the dome, rotating like a torpedo of doom fearlessly racing towards us.

'It won't get through, will it?' I said, panicked by the ferocity of the foe.

'That's not its plan,' said Nanna, tracking the plummeting death arrow.

Nanna was right, it missed the dome. I was relieved for a split second until it smashed into the earth, throwing up a huge impact crater. Mounds of dirt were flung high into the air as the winged attacker disappeared from sight. The sound of the explosion was replaced by a rumbling, grinding, tearing noise; the ground shook beneath us, shuddering our stance. I covered my ears; deafened by the sound. The earth bulged in the centre of the dome. 'It's coming! It's coming through!!' I shouted just seconds before the ground erupted and the winged devil burst through spewing rubble everywhere, breaching our safe haven.

A wind accompanied the intruder's arrival and blew like a hurricane, bringing us to our knees. I shielded my eyes from the debris that threatened to strike us down. Our glimmering dome of protection now looked more like a Halloween snow globe. Feathers and bones from the Scragens hurtled around at lightning speed. I dodged one then another; finally my luck ran out as a rock smacked the side of my unshielded head. I wobbled and fell on my side, my thoughts lost for a moment as my head rebooted. I lay on the floor, my vision blurred. Nanna's voice in the background called out, Mr Milly's shadow casting a protective reassurance upon my weakened state.

I was vulnerable, but at the same time lost in a conscious blip. I didn't care either, emotion was astray for those few seconds until reality kicked back in. The wind suddenly stopped, the debris suspended in the air crashed down as if by command. The winged devil's form loomed in my distorted vision. I looked across the floor and saw the dark avian figure pace forward.

Mr Milly growled; I knew she wouldn't let anything happen. Nanna came alongside and pulled me up, she was her glorious alter self again. I knew things had gotten out of hand for her to show her true essence, her power gloriously filled the air. She pulled me to my feet and cradled my head. 'Sorry, dear, these things can be… somewhat unpredictable,' she said in my ear.

As my vision cleared, I got a proper look at the creature. Tilting my head back to take in the full scale of the foe, for it towered above us all, its huge black scraggy wings folded behind now making a broad shoulder line. My gaze settled upon its head; like the smaller Scragens two yellow pin eyes glared out with precision from behind a leather and bone mask; its mouth was hidden by the large, curved, jagged beak; a plume of jet-black feathers sprouted from the edge, a befitting mane for the wicked sky dweller. Again the game paused as we all sized each other up, I hadn't a clue what I was supposed to do against this agent of evil.

My eyes were drawn to the large Scragens' intimidating sword, the handle exposed as the creature drew its heavy coat to one side. With one sudden movement the weapon was drawn with a metallic ring; the graphite-coloured blade did not shine or reflect any light off its surface. I inched back into Nanna's arms, but I couldn't get any closer than I was.

'A Bane Blade,' whispered Nanna, 'wielded by a Slaughter Hand… I wouldn't get too close,' she added.

'I wasn't planning on getting anywhere near it, thanks! You're the expert, Nanna, or whatever your name is today!' My anger sadly showed. Again I felt so much was asked of me, and I didn't feel in the slightest adequate.

Nanna gave me a look; even though her face had rolled back years, freed of the ravages of human life, she was still Nanna, more so than ever. She was mother and grandmother of us all, but I sensed her frustration, she wanted me to believe in my power and vanquish this formidable foe. Our brief distraction gave opportunity to the Slaughter Hand, spinning its sword in a blur of black flashes, arrogant of its skill and intimidating stature.

'Well, we better get to it then,' said Nanna, winking and nodding at Mr Milly who snarled and puffed up. Nanna was illuminated ready to unleash heaven's fury; the Slaughter Hand reeled onto its back foot, wings expanding, preparing to launch an attack, not put off by the majesty of its rivals.

All hell was about to break loose, when the strangest sound came into earshot. We all stopped in anticipation as it grew louder. *A siren or a plane, or a cat? A cat!* I thought.

'Mmmmmeeeeoooowwwwww,' it called. I looked up and saw the approaching shape; it passed through the perimeter of the dome and flew round the Slaughter Hand.

'Moggins…?' I said out loud.

'Ooohhh… yes… That's…? Moggins,' said Nanna, tilting her head, amused and bemused. Moggins' alter self was some sort of flying mechanical bat cat thing. A mechanism covered the top half of his torso, spreading out into wings made of plate, like the golden fish key ring I had at home. He had flying goggles on too, with miniature rockets on each wing, and red tracer beams that dotted the towering foe, now somewhat distracted by my mechanical bat cat Moggins.

My mouth was again wide open in disbelief. I wanted to laugh, but the situation stifled my brief exuberance. The Slaughter Hand flung its blade high and fast, but Moggins was just as swift. His golden armoured suit darted around evading the Hand's attacks. 'Mmeeeooww!' he screeched while letting off a dozen tiny rockets. They impacted on the foe's chest, knocking it back, but the Slaughter Hand retaliated with twice the ferocity, vaulting into the air, its frustration and anger evident. But the winged devil couldn't hit my brave, lovely Moggins.

'Go on, Moggins! Go!' I shouted, encouraging my feline friend on. Spurred on, he let out a finale of rockets, bombs, mini ninja stars and finally, when the Slaughter Hand was floored in a cloud of smoke, Moggins let off a party popper to celebrate. He hovered in triumph, the tiny jet engines perched beneath his golden wings manoeuvring to keep him stable.

'You did, you did it!' I cried. Moggins turned his little head towards me and let out a purr of acknowledgement. It was at that moment my overconfidence in victory bit back. From the cloud of dust came a speeding knife. Its aim was deadly, hitting Moggins straight between his two front legs. 'No! Moggins!' I screamed, breaking from Nanna's embrace, rushing towards my falling companion. Moggins hit the deck hard, my regard for personal safety lost as I saw his limp body recoil on impact. I was feet away when the phoenix of death rose from the smoke; the Slaughter Hand thumped to the ground, its sword held in both hands pointing down over Moggins ready to finish him off. Moggins meowed in that awful hurt way. The cackle came once again, projected from the figure in the distance; it crowed and creaked, 'Fear… is power!' seemingly satisfied with the turn of events.

'Don't touch him! Just leave him alone!' I shouted. The Hand raised its blade ready to strike. Without care, I flung myself over Moggins and winced, closing my eyes in anticipation of the final strike.

'Pete… think, think!' shouted Nanna in the background. All I could think of was protecting Moggins even if it meant my end. The Hand struck hard, and I bore the blow, but to my surprise with no pain, nor the seeping of whatever etheric substance I would be subject to losing. It did not sever my flesh or my spirit; instead, I heard a ting of something hard.

I yielded my buried head and glimpsed a piece of glinting armour on my shoulder and back. The blade of the Slaughter Hand pressed firmly upon it, but the armour would not break. *I did that… I did that!* I thought.

'That's it, Pete, use the stones again, use all their power!' shouted Nanna. I nodded and began thinking of the most magnificent warrior, one to be feared by all nightcrawlers and agents of ill, the image was clear. I could feel the immense supremacy and sovereignty this being had; it was just there, beyond sight in the realm of being and not being. My courage, my honour, my goodness ready to kick some Scragen butt. 'Use them!' shouted Nanna again.

I didn't have enough force to bring him through, so I made a decision to cut the power to the shield and channel all the stones back to my amulet. With the dome's light extinguished we were plunged into darkness. As the energy of the stones entered my amulet it sparked and set off like a firework, engulfed in a blaze of blue and purple shards of solid light forming and falling to the ground as diamonds.

The furnace of light grew and grew, its presence bubbling into reality. Armour was snapped on me from head to toe, encasing me with its spirit. Finally, he was with me.

'Rise up,' said a new voice within.

And so I did, flinging the Slaughter Hand's sword clean out of its grasp; the black foe edged back as I rose to my feet. I saw the world from inside a glass helmet. I was me, but in the same breath I wasn't; detecting the presence of all the incarnations I'd had, and now in this particular manifestation, all the warriors. Through the starlit tunnel of eternity, came all those times my soul had faced injustice; when they had looked evil in the eye with no yield to give. They were all here in me now. Suddenly the doubt and worries of what I should do were gone, replaced with a multitude of solutions for ridding any foe in my way. I didn't have to think, I knew it, it had always been here because I'd done all these things before. I was suddenly a master of war. I'd fought battles through space and time, in heaven and hell and now back on earth, where I'd been many times before, and now again I called upon him to smite the black veins of the dark.

I didn't waste any time; the Slaughter Hand was gathering itself, wings spread out wide, a Bane dagger in each hand. Hissing with fury, mad beyond sense it launched itself at me, eyes wild and fearless, fighting for something it didn't understand, driven by cruel deceptions; no empathy or compassion, just hate and anger. I stood towering above Moggins now as a huge glass-armoured warrior of light. The Slaughter Hand closed in, its fury just seconds away; eyes glowing, yellow pupils focused with evil, screeching a hellish roar it released its wrath upon me. With a calculated swift move I caught the winged demon in one hand, stopping its attack instantly like it had hit a brick wall. The Slaughter Hand recoiled like a rag doll, its feet dangling off the floor, dropping the daggers as it clutched at my hand trying to release my grip from its throat. I charged my armoured gauntlet; the deep glassy plates shone brighter and the silver-blue colour changed to sparkles of brilliant platinum. The Slaughter Hand fizzed and crackled, hissed and screamed as the light transformed its very being, destroying the dark within forever. Finally giving up and succumbing to its fate the Hand exploded, popped and banged in a glitter ball, its rags and mask dropped to the floor, their host gone for good.

I released my grip. The whispers of the Slaughter Hand's master crept back in, drawing my attention to the figure in the distance. I turned and strode out to the farthest stone. I wanted the cowardly shadow caller to see me, to see what I was capable of. We stood facing each other a hundred or so yards apart, the whispers flowed round and round. I knew they were trying to get inside my armour, but my moulded bulletproof glass suit wasn't having any of it. The pure focus of this new alter self was divinely driven, nothing would distract it.

'Show her,' my alter self said, and with that a magnificent spear made of silver, entwined with carvings down its length, formed in my right hand, its head fanned and barbed to cause maximum damage. I wrapped my fingers around it tightly, making an intuitive connection with the weapon like it was now an extension of me. A pulse of energy ran its length acknowledging our alliance. I raised the spear and brought it down on the earth sharply, causing a ripple of force to spread out towards the caster. It was accompanied by an ominous low boom and flash of light. The shadowed figure remained still, not giving away any sign of its intended path of action.

I waited a few more seconds then lunged back, pulling the spear into throwing position; with lightning speed and accuracy I launched the heavenly lance towards the foe. It was never going to miss, it had enough force and speed to knock anything into another dimension. Trailing a plume of sparks the divine weapon sought its target and was about to erase the shadow when trickery played its hand, foiling our success. The shadow was just exactly that, the spear passed through nothing, splitting twenty trees until it came to a stop. The shadow formed again and whispered eerily before it turned and blended back into the night.

With the danger gone my thoughts hastily returned to Moggins. We all gathered around my brave pirate cat; his breathing was laboured, the Bane Blade had pierced his mechanical armour and entered into the energy body of his alter self. As I knelt the warrior left, and I resumed my normal form.

'Nanna what do we do!? What do we do!?' I asked, panicked and worried by Moggins' sickened state.

'Well it's a bit like the Lurker and how it leaves its touch, but this is deeper... It's complicated, dear,' answered Nanna sympathetically.

'But he will be OK? We can fix him, right?' I said, stroking my fearless feline friend.

'Well... we can,' Nanna puffed, 'but he has to stay on this side for the wound to heal properly,' she continued.

'You mean here? Stay in the Veil?! …But he will be dead then?!' I said.

'Oh, my dear… If he comes back, the wound won't heal properly. He won't be the same cat as before, happiness would be lost to him,' said Nanna, her empathy pouring over me as she placed her arm around my shoulder and squeezed tight.

A tidal wave of sorrow surged over me, resulting in a well overdue cry. My body more than happy to release the pent up emotions, I sobbed heavily for my beautiful pirate cat. I didn't want him to have a rubbish life and felt guilty for stirring all this trouble up.

'What happens then? Can he ever come back?' I asked, tears streaming down my face. Nanna shrugged her shoulders.

'It's rarely heard of. Rules, dear,' she said sympathetically.

I stroked the little fellow. 'Sorry, Moggins, sorry,' I said. Mr Milly comforted me by licking my cheek.

'You saved him, dear… don't forget that,' said Nanna.

'Where will he go? Who will look after him?' I asked.

'We will,' called out an approaching voice. We all turned to see Ikol, Okol and Choc emerging from a small crop of bushes they'd been observing from. 'We will have him back to his adventuring ways soon enough,' said Okol.

'Yeah he can sleep on my bed,' said little Choc, still looking as grubby and mischievous as ever.

'Bless you, my dears,' said Nanna.

'Yeah, thanks,' I added, wiping the streaming tears from my eyes.

'You're getting the hand of this warrior lark, eh!' said Okol, blowing his cheeks out in admiration. I smirked a little and let their praise lift me.

'I guess. I still don't know what I'm doing really,' I replied, playing myself down.

'Nonsense! You are doing splendid,' disagreed Nanna.

'Yeah, he was great! Wwooooossshhh!!! Straight through ten trees it went!' said Choc, enthusiastically mimicking the spear I had thrown.

'See… impressive,' said Nanna, winking. Okol nudged my shoulder, sympathising with the situation.

'Right… well, that's settled then. Moggins will go for some R & R at the Rag Tree,' instructed Nanna. Mr Milly whimpered solemnly, sad to see her friend go. I tenderly picked up my dear pirate cat and handed him to Okol, stroking his head as I went.

'Don't worry, we will look after him, you know where he is,' said Okol. With that, the boys headed back down the field cradling Moggins. I'd never seen them walk more orderly, they had precious cargo and were well aware of it.

I knew Moggins was in good hands, but still, I watched with a heavy heart. I was waving goodbye to a piece of my friend for good. I turned again to Nanna and sobbed into her coat.

'It will be OK, dear… it will work out… You did great today, you know.' I wiped my running nose on my sleeve and looked upon her comforting face. 'Come on, we've seen all we need today,' said Nanna. She held my hand and counted us back to the really real as I'd become to think of it, but it was getting less really real each time I went into the Veil, more so now Moggins was on the other side. The Veil dropped. I helped Nanna collect the stones, placing them back into the velvet pouch. We made our way back across the darkened field towards the orange glow of Nanna's kitchen lights.

On our return we found the back door slightly ajar. Nanna paused. 'Funny, did we leave that open?' she mused. I shrugged in response, not being able to rightly remember.

Nanna pushed the door. 'Hello?' she called suspiciously into her own home. No unexpected presence was visible on first sight. She then pushed the door further just as a gruff voice replied.

'Good evening.' I jumped a little. Nanna tutted lovingly at my nervousness. The high-back chair facing away from us was occupied; the top of a familiar black feathered hat and the tail of a particular scraggy canine gave the uninvited visitor away.

'Mr Dier... what can we do for you?' puffed Nanna, not impressed in the slightest, his grubby digits poking out like little sausages from the tatty fingerless gloves massaging the chair arm as his face turned towards us.

'Come... we have need to talk,' he said, his gravelly voice in need of some warming up.

Again, Nanna tutted. 'Cheeky bleeder,' she cursed under her breath. She took the chair opposite, and I sat on the radiator by the window. I was extremely intrigued to find out what Mr Dier had to say about PC Newley. Both parties paused, Nanna obviously agitated by Mr Dier's long, drawn-out actions. He did seem to milk the attention and played on the anticipation of his news.

I couldn't wait any longer and without thinking blurted out, 'Newley's back.' Dier looked at me with disappointment, as if I'd stolen the words out of his mouth. He cleared his throat and began to prepare again.

'Oh, get on with it, man,' piped Nanna.

'Alright! …alright… Yes, I gather you've noticed then,' he said.

'I saw him at the farm… how can that be? I thought he was being erased?' I asked. Mr Dier looked amused and frustrated at my barrage of questions. Again, he cleared his throat.

'Well, things… hmmm… events, shall we say… have taken a turn. The order came from beyond… A suitable replacement has been found,' he replied.

'Replacement!? What does that mean?' quizzed an annoyed Nanna.

'Well it means I'm not faffing around here, going through scrapbooks anymore,' enthused Dier.

'So does he remember anything? What about the stuff I saw you throw into the flame, those memories, what about them?' I said, continuing to pursue Mr Dier. He shifted uncomfortably in the chair and removed his hat, exposing a brown crown and scraggly locks hanging like dirty curtains around his face. Dier examined his hat for a moment, trying to escape the focus placed upon him. He blew a layer of dust off the top and ran his stubby fingers down the length of a crow feather, all the time stalling his response. I began to smell a rat.

'Look… Yes, some are lost now, but all memories fade in this reality, it's designed that way. It won't make a significant impact on any party,' he snapped. We sat and pondered upon Mr Dier's news as he piped up again. 'Anyway, no need to worry… You can stop counting that clock… All the cracks have been filled, all is back to normal,' he said quite unconvincingly. Now he sounded just like a dodgy builder trying to make a quick exit before his incompetent mistakes gave him away.

'So his soul is saved?' I pressed.

'Eeeerr… Yyeessss… you could say that,' he said, weaselly rising from the chair, replacing his hat. 'I will be off then now,' he said, tugging at his dog's chain. Mr Dier shuffled to the door and tipped his hat.

'Be seeing you, Mr Dier,' said Nanna in a harsh tone that pierced straight through him.

'Err…' he cleared his throat, 'yes, be seeing you.' He avoided eye contact with Nanna but gave me a parting look, a look that could be conveyed to say many things; I saw guilt and remorse, I saw a liar with his arm twisted.

As soon as the door latched behind him, I sprung to my feet.

'What does he mean!? What replacement!?' I asked, straining my annoyance through clenched teeth. Nanna shushed me with her finger and waved me to calm down with the other hand. She went over to the window and looked for any signs of Mr Dier, then closed her eyes briefly. I guess she was scanning for his energy.

Nanna then let out a sigh. 'Right, OK, he has gone… He means not what he said,' she said cryptically.

'You mean he is lying?' I said.

'It certainly isn't the whole truth. Yes, Newley is back, but this reality is so easily manipulated.' She mused over Dier's possible motives and their potential paths of action. 'Why would they…? Hmmm.' Nanna paused in thought.

'It's not him! I tell you, it's not him!' I shouted, frustrated at the deception of Mr Dier.

'OK dear… we will figure this out together, don't worry,' she said just as the clock chimed into life and Wit rolled round, bursting through the doors in a dazzling display of aerial acrobatics, leaving a sparkling golden trail of joy behind her. Wit fluttered above me, her wings beating in a blur. She floated lightly down on to my shoulder and tucked in under my neck, letting out a few sympathetic solemn chimes for Moggins which I kindly appreciated.

Wit quickly shifted to an excited buzzing state; she had something to tell us. 'Go on, girl, show us,' said Nanna. With that, Wit began to project the familiar sepia stills into the air and my head, just like snapshots taken by a hired private eye. They were of Newley, he was preparing to do something terrible. There was an explosion; many souls floated up, a dark portal opened right in the middle of Chattersley, then a pair a weighing scales, one side black and the other white, tipped in the black's favour, and then the scales collapsed.

'Told you,' I said.

'Yes, what better place to hide an agent of ill,' agreed Nanna.

'We have to stop him, and get the real Newley back!' I pleaded. My link with Wit finished, and she fluttered over to Nanna, continuing to chirp in her ear. She paused, taking it all in, her face staving off the worry.

Nanna then replied, 'Yes dear, we must.'

That night I took many thoughts with me to bed. Suddenly the game had changed, pieces were being manoeuvred that didn't appear to obey any rules I knew of. Dier's deception puzzled me. Although I was never clear what game he was playing, now I was sure he was hiding the truth. In the backrooms of my mind was the figure at the treeline, and the warrior presence I had pulled through into reality. I wondered about the giant glass knight and thought of all the different souls I'd felt within him, wondering who they'd been and the battles they had fought. As I pondered, a metallic reverbed voice replied with an echo that travelled as far back as time itself. 'Ikron,' it said, clear and strong.

'Oh OK,' I replied. *So he has a name now,* I thought.

Images of the day floated around but never strayed far from Moggins. Finally, when my eyes could no longer resist the pull of sleep I painfully allowed my thoughts to settle on my pirate cat and how I missed him curled up next to me. My stomach burned and the knot of loss tightened. I shed a tear again, calling out to him, 'Love you, Moggs. Miss you.' I drifted off deep into the dream realm, where I was becoming more aware of my crazy muddled adventures. I emerged from the other side of sleep with a rush of energy into my brow; a tunnel opened up in front of me with a spiral of stars rotating round and round. I floated towards its end feeling distanced from my physical form, like I was spread out across the universe. A far-off prick of light became brighter, growing larger until it engulfed me.

I was suddenly at the Rag Tree. Moggins was curled up on Choc's bed, the boys were round him making a right old fuss, talking tales of bravery and marvellous mechanical bat suits. I stood with them as an invisible observer until Okol turned and smiled.

'See, anytime you want,' he said, then the others turned and smiled.

'Hi Pete,' said Choc and Bot. They waved me in closer alongside the bed. Moggins lifted his little head and purred as I stroked him; my heart glowed, elevated with our reunion. I could have stayed there forever sinking into the Rag Tree's energy, it was safe and warm and felt like home. I smiled, happiness flowing from inside. Ikol turned again, his face wearing a scrunched-up, inquisitive look. The other boys now looked too as I felt a chill upon my neck; a rush of wind vibrated my body as I was pulled back down a long corridor. I watched the Rag Tree Boys' faces accelerate away from me, or me from them.

I couldn't turn to see where I was going, hurtling backwards until the motion stopped. A room setting dropped down and slid in from either side; my familiar BMX printed curtains hung in front of me. 'The Gap,' I murmured.

'Yes, the Gap,' came Ikron's voice. I began to repeat the same steps I always did, opening the curtains with a fearful squinted grimace and watching Blue slither behind the garage. I followed like I always did; the same feelings engulfed me, fear of the unknown, of being trapped and being powerless. I crawled in knowing what was to come, my only saving grace was the thought, *What will save me this time? The honk of Dad's horn, or a sandpapery lick from Moggins or Mills?*

'No one will save you,' came Ikron's voice again.

I really felt doomed this time, proper doomed as the blotchy shadowed arms reached in, its pointed fingernails scraping down the Gap's side. I grabbed Blue and held him close; the ghoul leaned in ready to swallow, my heart thumped full of panic. I sought an escape in Blue's eyes. The shiny black button pupils reflected the moonlight; I gazed into them, images formed. I saw Moggins, I saw Nanna, I saw Mr Milly, I saw Mum and Dad. I felt if it took Blue, it would take them all. My cry of despair rang out like always, but this time Ikron joined. His cry harmonised with mine, growing louder until it pushed weakness aside and I roared, 'No…!! I am light!!' Ikron pulsed through me, down my arm and into my bear. The limp teddy twitched, his eyes flickered with lightning, the sky opened, and a pillar of cobalt light shot into his furry head. The ghoul hissed and reeled backwards. Blue grew, my hands now too small to hold him, forcing me to release my little bear, letting Ikron free within him.

The Gap, the prison of my dreams became too small and weak to hold the rapidly expanding force. Blue burst through the garage walls, knocking them flat. A cloud of dust rose up above. Blue stood tall and strong like a giant teddy gorilla; he let out an earth-shattering roar. The Gap ghoul was the one now looking cornered; it retreated into the shadow of its cloak hastily looking for an escape. This way and that it darted, but Blue wasn't going to let him go, he stomped over to the raggy dark dweller and beat down upon the ground, missing at first but then catching it and hoisting it to his eye level. He roared again and smashed it into the ground, again and again, each time the embers of wickedness leaving its host until there were none left. Blue dropped the lifeless withered bundle at his feet, and with one final show of disdain stomped and ground its remains into the earth. He snorted in triumph, a job well done. Blue raised his mitt and pointed at me with his thumb. 'Your saviour. You! Little warrior of light.'

With that the scene changed again, Blue shrank back to his normal size as Ikron withdrew to the back of my mind, the chill came once more and I rushed backwards, pulled by some invisible force. The image of the Gap laid in ruins disappeared into nothing; my anxiety had been quenched with the Gap Ghoul finally vanquished, for it had haunted me for many nights. I felt my path had always been heading this way, and the events I had recently been part of, had been a necessity for me to progress and push through my fears and worries. I hurtled backwards, passing down a starlit tunnel until finally, I came to rest in my bedroom at Nanna's. The floor came up to meet my feet and the walls and ceiling smoothly clicked into position.

Had I returned from the dream realm? Was I back? The soft glow from the hall light filtered through the crack in the door. Mr Milly lay curled up beside my bed, I could hear the gentle tick of the cuckoo clock from the kitchen, all felt well. I was just about to slide back under my covers when I heard a sobbing come again from down the side of the wardrobe. I let the bed cover go and, although my heartbeat had jumped up a few notches, I approached the noise with less caution than before. I peered down the side of the wardrobe into darkness. The sobbing sounded farther away this time; I could make out a light, far in the distance. I stepped in, taking a few cautious paces. Looking back, my bedroom was just there. I stepped in further, continually looking back, going deeper and deeper into the darkness, the bedroom now farther away but near enough if I had to get out quick.

With reality distorted and feeling ever more immersed in this game of illusions, I was confused whether this was the dream realm or a crossover with the Veil. The wall by my side changed and was now made of wet grey slate; lights were visible from chambers leading off from the main hall or tunnel I was in. On reaching the first door a heavy burgundy light shone from the metal grill two thirds up. It looked like a jail cell to me. Placing my fingers on the grill I pulled myself on to my tiptoes and looked in. There was a wooden bed with sacks on it, and small animal bones strewn across the floor. I was relieved the cell appeared unoccupied. I lowered myself and was about to remove my hand from the grill when a force came down upon my fingers, trapping them. A pair of dirty bluish fingers with sharp yellow nails clamped my hands down. A voice came from behind the door.

'Now why be leaving so… soon?' it said.

I pulled and squirmed but couldn't release my hands. I watched as a head appeared behind the grill; two bright yellow eyes peered down at me, they were large and round with pitch-black pupils. The remaining features were small in comparison, having no hair and pointy ears. Its nose was missing – only slits were visible. A small chin housed a set of spikey discoloured teeth which gated a black snaking tongue that rolled around looking hungry and happy to see me.

'Let me go,' I barked, struggling to release myself.

'All in good time… What brings a being like you here?' the creature having such a repulsive look sounded quite well-spoken.

'What are you? …Let me go!' I shouted.

'Ssuusssshhh, we don't want to bring attention to your presence here, do we?' it said, increasing the pressure upon my hands. 'You can help me… You did before, didn't you?' said the creature.

'How?! How could I?!' I barked back.

'Oh you have… but despite all your efforts, souls will be lost and end up here… waiting to be snuffed out,' it continued.

'You look like you need snuffing out!' I replied through clenched teeth.

'Oh…' It reeled back, sarcastically. 'Harsh words for one that doesn't understand,' said the creature. 'Even the ill have no use for me now… You should pity me… you freed me before… now free me again. I can help you, help you get his soul back… oh yes… I know all the tricks of the ill, so I do,' continued the creature.

I was perplexed as to how I'd helped it before. I didn't trust it for one minute, and started to feel I might need some extra help, so I began knocking on Ikron's door deep within, but I found him difficult to bring forward. There was something about the repulsive creature that didn't warrant the force of the eternal warrior. I focused hard and thought of my power; managing to squeeze out enough, I released a bolt of lightning that shot down my arm, electrifying the grill, sending the creature flying. It screeched, hitting the back wall of the cell hard then slumped into a heap on the floor. The creature whimpered and muttered to itself, but through the incoherent mumblings, something started to sound familiar.

'Who are you?' I said, quickly forgetting my recent entrapment, again pulling myself up to the grill.

It cowered in the corner cackling sarcastically at my lack of knowledge. Slowly the creature turned, illuminating its ugly features. Our eyes locked, and with my empathy detected, it snarled and quickly rushed the door in anger. I jumped back as it pressed its vampiric face at the grill spitting in disgust.

'Remember me! Remember when I go! Remember where I am!' it hissed and then disappeared from sight. The hall fell silent. I quickly looked back down the length of the corridor; my bedroom was just visible, so I decided to continue towards the sobbing. I passed a few more cell doors relinquishing the temptation to look in. Soon I reached a point where the crying became quieter if I walked further, but there wasn't a door. I looked all round the slate walls, finally homing in on a grate in the floor.

Here the weeping was much clearer, and it was now accompanied by two other voices that were being amplified by the channel underneath the floor. I pulled at the grate, wanting to get closer. It was heavy, but with some effort I got one end up and then levered the rest out, sliding it to one side. The exposed hole opened into a channel three or four feet down. I gathered it was some sort a ventilation shaft but wasn't entirely sure. Lowering myself into the confined space, I found the walls and floor were smothered in a wet residue accompanied by an aroma of tar and paraffin that swamped me, but I pushed on into the blackness before me. A faint flickering glow my only visible waypoint. Other tunnels branched off at random intervals. I focused and chuntered to myself, 'Just go straight, no turns, just straight, what are you doing…? Really, this is madness, it's a dream! A big silly dream.'

I carried on down the narrow vent, the sound of my own voice giving me some comfort. Around fifty yards in I approached a grate where I could now clearly make out three voices; a sobbing one which I presumed was Newley, a harsh ratty one that resembled fingernails dragged down a blackboard, and then there was a more familiar one, its gravelly undertones and drawn-out hesitation hid a meekness beneath its robust walls. 'Grevling Dier… What are you up to?' I said under my breath.

I peeked cautiously through the vent grate; the room was different to that of the creature I'd just encountered – the ceiling was much higher and in the centre of the floor was a wood and metal chair to which Newley was strapped. Mr Dier was sat at a bench with papers in front of him looking like the accountant for Death himself. The other figure was hooded, it slid around Newley, pawing over his pain, taking great relish in his suffering.

'No! No, no, now that's enough, Litch, your lust for these macabre practises is intolerable,' said Dier, turning toward the other figure. 'Have some control. There's procedures and policies, you know,' he snapped.

'Yes and I'm the administrator of pain,' he hissed back. 'Oh… That moment, when the soul is obliterated, all its voices crying out at once. I never… never get tired of it,' said Litch, pretending to weep while slithering around the wooden arm of Newley's chair. 'What are we waiting for anyway? Can't those righteous busybodies upstairs make their flaming minds up, instead of playing little gods…?' said Litch.

'All in good time… This is a special case,' smirked Dier.

'What's so special about this… ordinary creation?' asked Litch.

'Bait, that's what this is, hoping for a last-minute substitute they are. All in the name of balance, nothing's sacred when it comes to keeping the balance,' replied Dier.

I thought of what Nanna said about the football game, and how it's always made to look like the light has a chance, but will never win. This balance they were talking about, wasn't a fair distribution of good and evil, it was all in favour of the negative, and I was starting to see the framework that surrounded our reality was corrupt. Mr Dier just seemed to be mindlessly following procedure, and I wasn't sure at all where his soul sat in this whole thing. My focus turned to Newley; he looked drained and had become somewhat featureless, displaying a more generic human appearance, as if the character that hosted his form was somewhat departed. I wondered if he had already been exposed to the power that would ultimately take his essence. He was only just still here, and I feared we wouldn't have time to save him.

Litch playfully swung on a large paddle lever next to the chair. He laughed and poked at Newley.

'Into the meat grinder it went. Stripped bare the soul sought purpose, it sought life, so into the meat grinder it went, again and again into the meat grinder it went!' he cruelly sang with a forced baritone voice. He flung his arms open in admiration while gazing at the ceiling. My eyes followed, finding a circular rim standing proud. It looked like it could be an opening but was closed. Litch played heartlessly with Newley as they both knew what lay beyond it. I assumed it was whatever would be used to erase Newley's soul. My eyes left the circular hatch and panned back down to the scene below only to be met by a fierce, cruel gaze. I'd been spotted!

'Err, Dier… we've got a visitor,' said Litch, pointing with his stick-like finger towards me.

I gulped.

'So we have. Well go get him then,' said Dier, calmly ushering Litch on.

'Yaa ha ha, purge the vents!' he shouted, instructing unseen hands. I heard clanking and hissing and expected something suitably horrible to be heading my way. The tunnel was a tight squeeze, and I scraped my back turning. I rushed down the passage as quickly as I could in a crouched position. Something stirred behind, moans echoed down the passageway. The tar on the walls and floor looked a lot like the puddles that took Newley; it was sticky and made me feel sick to my stomach. Reaching the grate without a minute to spare, I slumped on the corridor floor, just as a rush of black and purple fire spat forth from the vent, bringing with it something else, something that wanted to take me. The tar fiends from the car park spewed forth, arms clambering out of the hole and onto the corridor, pulling their coats of foulness along. They were quick, like a river of fingers and hoods dissolving and reforming in and out of the black ooze.

I sprinted down the hall, passing the creature I'd encountered. It jeered and howled as I ran by; the whole corridor behind me was a mass of tangled arms and tar cloaks all wanting to drag me down and put me in that chair. I ran and ran; my bedroom didn't seem to get any closer, and I was without the focus needed to call Ikron. Finally I got to the end only to find a heavy door blocking the way. Through the grill, I could see my room and the glow of the hall light.

'Nanna!! Nanna!!' I screamed, turning to face the black horde. 'IKRON!!!' I shouted. They were on me. I closed my eyes as a massive blast of energy came from behind, a strong hand reached in, pulling me back as the door slammed shut, closing out the fiends. The malevolent echoes of the halls silenced as a soft, warm voice replaced the coldness of the corridor.

'It's OK, dear, I'm here.' I opened my eyes slowly to see Nanna at my bedside. She stroked my head. 'Bad dream? It's been quite a day, dear,' she said. I sat up and tried to explain what had happened.

'Was I there, Nanna?' I asked.

'Part of you… yes dear,' she said.

'Was that the Nighlight?' I asked.

'It sounds like it, dear, your heart is heavy with Moggins' suffering, and that energy carried you down the darker corridors of the dream realm,' replied Nanna.

'So are dreams real?' I asked.

'Just like the Veil, with enough energy dreams can manifest into reality. You're both sensitive to emotion and powerful with it, it's a balancing act,' she said.

'That's what they said, that's what Dier and that Litch were going on about,' I replied. Nanna kissed me goodnight, and I beckoned Mr Milly onto the bed for some added security, although there wasn't much space left once she happily accepted my offer. I slipped back to sleep keeping my thoughts as good as I could. I glided through the meadows of the beautiful Veil with Moggins as my wingman, now that's a dream I could happily repeat night after night.

I awoke with Mr Milly trapping me under the bedsheets. I was rapidly overheating and dying for a cold drink.

'Come on, girl.' I roused my canine friend, and we headed to the kitchen. Nanna was up; she nursed a steaming mug of tea while gazing out of the back window.

'Morning, dear,' she beamed. 'I trust you finished your sleep with better dreams,' she added.

'Yes, much better,' I replied, getting myself and Mr Milly some cold water. I joined Nanna in the adjacent chair.

'You did well yesterday and by all accounts in your dreams too,' she praised.

'Hhmmm, yeah, I suppose, sometimes Ikron...' I said.

'Ikron!?' interrupted Nanna.

'Yes, Ikron, the glass knight... that's his name,' I replied.

'Ahhh... Ikron,' said Nanna, clearly impressed by the link I had already established with my inner power. 'Anyway, what about Ikron, what were you about to say before I so rudely interrupted?' asked Nanna.

'Yes, I was going to say, sometimes I get the impression I shouldn't be using him, like he knows more than I understand,' I replied, thinking back to the creature in the cell.

'Well that's a certainty. Tune into his knowledge, after all it's yours too, he can help you, but not always with courage and strength,' replied Nanna.

'What are we going to do about Newley?' I asked.

'Yes, yes, we must look into what he is up to, but you... err... I'd suggest you give him a wide berth... Go see Moggins, I will look into what PC Newley is up to,' replied Nanna with an air of concern.

'OK but if my dream was anything to go by, Newley hasn't got that long left,' I said, airing my frustration.

'I don't think he will be going anywhere while the other pieces are in play, and you must remember that the dream realm is not bound by time like this reality; you could have been experiencing the past, present or future,' informed Nanna.

'Oh… OK… What pieces? Am I a piece?' I asked, thinking back to Dier's conversation with Litch. 'Is Newley Bait?' I added. Nanna sat forward, placed her mug down and cupped my hands.

'You are a bright light, brightest light for a long time, and they are aware of your awakening. They have waited for this moment like I have; you're a super striker for Light United and are capable of catching them off guard and clinching a last-minute win… Of course they don't want that, they'd rather you didn't awaken, for you will only grow brighter and stronger and be more of a problem. Once you master the Veil and your powers, they will be in real trouble. For the first time in aeons we could rid this reality of the parasitic negative for good, not to make a big deal of it!' puffed Nanna. 'We have to be vigilant, keep away from… hhmm… let's call him Ill Newley for now. We both know the soul occupying his body isn't legit, we know he has come back to do bad things. You are being ambushed on both sides of reality, and we must play a smart game, dear. Be on guard, watch your thoughts and your surroundings, read the story before it's told,' said Nanna.

I nodded and digested her words of warning. I sort of knew that's what the deal was, I'd gone through quite a lot in the last few weeks, and Nanna's straight-talking didn't stun me like it might have before. I realised there was much more at stake here, and earth, our home, our reality had been hijacked by a negative influence that had set the rules for our lives, rules that kept us locked up in fear, blinded from our true selves, our true knowledge, our eternal essence. I knew I'd played this game many times before, and now with the presence of Ikron within me, I felt the history of those conflicts echoed through time. This was the last stand of a scourge that still more than ever lusted after pain, only ever wanting to spread its poison throughout creation. These words passed over my internal movie screen as if reading a script; they were my words, and then, they weren't.

Nanna stood and brushed her apron off. 'Right, I'll get on with these then,' she said, surveying the ingredients on the table. It looked like her famous apple crumble would be making an appearance soon. After the speech she had given me words failed to come forward. I looked at her, my mouth ajar. 'Well we've got to eat! So it may as well be nice!' laughed Nanna.

'What's your other name, Nanna?' I asked, the question just popping out. 'When you're different in the Veil, what's her name?' I asked again.

'She has had many names, but I suppose the one that fits the best is Shelaya,' answered Nanna, musing over he own response.

'Why Shelaya, Nanna? What does it mean?' I asked.

'Oh it doesn't have a grand meaning, and it wasn't bestowed upon me through honour, it was the life I'd had when I first awoke on earth to my pasts and to my truth. "Shelaya, truth seer,' they called me, for it was in that incarnation I properly awoke remembering the lives I'd once had, and that was thousands of years ago,' said Nanna, fixed in a glazed stare, casting her memories far back through time.

'Wow! That's a long time,' I gasped.

'Indeed it is,' she replied, her heart dwelling for a second on something that it had once been close to.

'You OK, Nanna?' I asked.

She snapped out of her daze. 'Ooh, yes dear, right as rain, now what was I doing?' she said, carrying on about her business.

I'd soon got ready and was heading down the old coach track toward Snickets. Mr Milly sniffed at the Smythes' yard gates, expecting me to turn in. I really did want to call for Ronnie and Buster but thought it was best not to completely let them in yet. They'd played with the ghost boys, and that was enough for now. Plus, I didn't want to be answering a million questions about things that I hardly understood.

I stood halfway down the track and pulled Mr Milly in by my side.

'Right, Mills, let's go in,' I said, looking at her for reassurance. I scanned the area to see if anyone was watching and when clear I placed my hand on her head and said quietly, 'As above is below,' imagining the rush of Mother Earth's energy and the central sun colliding in my heart flooding me with truth and sovereignty. The pressure in my brow increased and my body tingled, I felt the ripple of energy flood down my entire body and I knew the Veil had dropped.

I opened my eyes to a scene of beauty; the thought of seeing Moggins and the Rag Tree Boys filled my heart with joy and excitement, this was mirrored by my surroundings. Everything was bright and sparkling, the colours of the flowers and trees were breathtakingly vivid, realer than real. Snickets held no shadow today. The daisies that lined the path lit up like tiny suns, the ivy lovingly wound its spongy emerald leaves around the tree trunks, and my favourite had to be the bluebells, they almost created a blue carpet through the wood, droplets of the ocean frozen in time, a sea of miniature barrel waves curling in upon themselves, tinkling in the most precious way as the meadow breeze gently blew through.

A haze of tranquillity infused everything. I breathed in heavy and felt it, I could taste the wood, I could feel all of it like it all came together to form one vibration; it was truly wonderful. Mr Milly sniffed and snorted through the undergrowth, puffing golden dust clouds of pollen as she rooted around. 'Oh,' I said. I hoped to God she wasn't going to do her business now! How would that work in the Veil?

Her tummy growled, and she quickly spun around, giving me a look that said, 'Stop it! I didn't need to go until you thought of it,' so I immediately took my mind off Mr Milly's business and headed to the clearing where the Rag Tree was.

Tiny whispers crept into my ear. 'This way, yeah, that's it,' they said, 'just a bit further… we can see you,' they chirped as I rounded the corner to see the Boys stood on the platform of the great tree. Waving excitedly, their faces beaming with delight, my heart swelling to another level, we all rushed to meet each other, the Rag Tree Boys finding the quickest way down to the ground. Some did it with style while Choc and El just sort of tumbled off, falling in a heap, which then turned into a wrestling match.

'And a-one and a-two and a-three,' laughed Choc, pinning the dazed El down. Ikol and Okol greeted me first, while Choc, Let, Bot and El patted and pulled at me.

'Come and see! Come and see!' said Choc, looking up at me with his adorable dirty face and big brown eyes. He raced off with his tufty mop of hair dancing in the air.

'Yeah, come on,' said Ikol. We all dashed up the ladder and ropes, seeing who could get to the platform the quickest. Everybody bundled through the cabin door but stopped abruptly as not to disturb the patient. Mr Milly was again left down below.

'We need a basket or something for Mills, don't we?' said El.

'That's a great idea,' replied Okol.

'Cool, I'm on it,' replied El, excited to be helping. Moggins was on Choc's bed; he looked fine, he was curled up having a lovely snooze.

I walked over quietly, taking care not to wake him, overjoyed that my beloved pirate cat was alive and well, albeit in another dimension, but hey, that didn't seem to matter right now.

'He will be right as rain soon,' said Ikol.

'I wanna see that mechanical bat suit again… Mmmeeeaaawwww, bang, bang, boooooommmmm!!!' shouted Choc, forgetting we were supposed to be quiet.

'Choc, sssuuusshh,' said Okol.

Choc bowed his head. 'Oh yeah, sorry,' he said with a slight smile.

We stood around Moggins when I had a feeling of déjà vu; it was just like my dream. Okol turned to me and said, 'You left in a hurry last night. Did you sort it?' I was a bit taken aback as to what he meant. Did he know about the Gap or the Nighlight?

'Errr yeah… well I think so,' I replied unclearly.

'Good… We've got your back, you know,' said Ikol, chipping in. I knew they had, there wasn't an ounce of badness in any of them, they were all so just and true, brave and honest. I loved being around them, they felt like my brothers.

'We are, you know, we are the brothers of childhoods,' said Okol, responding again to my thoughts.

I sat with Moggins for a while, the other boys leaving me alone with my feline friend. I stroked him fondly, and he purred like he always used to.

'Good Moggins, you get better quick,' I whispered. My quiet moment was disrupted by a clatter of buckets outside.

'Granny rambler alert,' called one of the boys. I left Moggins and went out to see what the commotion was all about. The boys buzzed around like worker bees tipping pots and pulling levers, releasing pales of water into the network of hollowed-out wooden channels. The water gushed down and round, dropping into buckets, their increasing weight opening more miniature dam doors until finally, the large tipper buckets fixed to the deck rails were full.

'Hurry, hurry, they're coming!' squealed Choc with excitement.

'This time! Blue rinses,' laughed Bot. The Rag Tree Boys took their positions and waited. I gathered by the military precision they executed, they had done this many times.

Sounds of play and jokes fell from the air smothered with lip-licking concentration. I admired their dedication, and surely such commitment should be worthy of a grand reward. I snuck over to the platform rails and homed in on approaching voices. Soon two figures came into view; this was the prize the boys sought so eagerly. I sounded out their description. 'Heavy hiking boots; cargo trousers tucked into thick rolled-up socks; jumpers wrapped around the waist; laminated map necklace, ambling creaking pace... They're just ramblers,' I said to Okol, who was the closest to me.

'Yeah but we've been trying to drench them for ages. Some of them can feel it, others can't, it's pot luck really,' said Okol, ready to spill the contents of the bucket on the unsuspecting walkers. The couple picked their way along the overgrown path. This was not on the ramblers' usual route, as the Rag Tree was off the beaten track. Their chat consisted of Chattersley's upcoming fete; one of the ladies clearly had stern views about who was running the beer tent.

'Well, I'll be taking my hip flask, I'm not paying those prices. I tell you, that Pat Gunwin, he's just out for himself. People just think they can come in and change everything, well it's not right,' said the one elderly lady. I was quite interested in their tittle-tattle, they spoke freely deep in the woods, where they were sure no prying ears were listening in.

I could see their auras quite clearly; the one lady that was doing all the moaning had red flecks running through hers. They swelled and glowed as she talked more heatedly of her grievances with Pat Gunwin, whose name was well and truly being dragged through the gutter of village gossip.

'Nearly... nearly... just a bit closer,' said Okol, concentrating, watching the blue rinse ramblers amble towards their trap.

'Now!' shouted Ikol, releasing his bucket. The water plummeted down to the ground, splashing just in front of the old couple. The moaning lady stopped and looked befuddled.

'It's... it's raining, did you feel any spots?' she asked her companion.

'No dear,' the other lady replied. They carried on through a barrage of water; torrents of the stuff was chucked over the deck at the poor old dears, who kept stopping and holding their hands out.

'No, no, I'm sure it's raining,' they said, and that's as much as the Rag Tree Boys got out of them today.

'Bloody useless! I thought the Veil was thinning an' all, be better going back to tripping them up,' grumbled Okol.

'Yeah, trip 'em,' jeered Choc with a wicked little smile.

'Have you ever appeared to any of them?' I asked.

'Yeah but it's never intentional, it seems to just happen, it's as much of a surprise to us as it is to them,' replied Okol.

'Yeah little Choc's nearly bust blood vessels trying to spook em,' added Bot. Choc laughed, reflectively nodding in agreement.

The boys moved away from their positions and started jibing each other, picking wooden weapons up and playing while I was caught fascinated by these two worlds, separated only by frequencies and thought. I watched the two old dears stagger off through the woods, kind of glad they didn't get a scare. When they had all but disappeared from sight, and their voices were inaudible, I was about to turn away from the woodland vista, when something else caught my eye. Deep in the thick blanket of trees, I spied another person. I squinted and made out two figures.

'What you looking at?' said Okol, now on my shoulder. 'More ramblers?' he asked.

'I don't know, somebody's out there,' I replied. 'I can't see them very well though.' Okol picked up a hollow piece of wood about the size of a rolling pin and passed it to me.

'Here, use this,' he said, winking. 'Remember we are in the Veil,' he added, nudging me.

'Oh yeah…' I replied, looking at the wooden pipe. That was all it needed; with the slightest thought the pipe morphed into a telescope.

'Nice one,' said Okol. 'Now who are they?' he asked. I squinted through my new invention, focusing upon the two figures.

'Ah… that's interesting… PC Newley and… Mr Dier… what are they doing out here?' I asked myself.

'Newley, the one who's back but isn't?' asked Okol. 'And Grevling Dier yeah… We know about him, boring old fart, too many flaming rules. He's a right stickler for them,' mouthed Ikol, clearly not in the slightest impressed by their dimensional framework and those who govern it.

'What are they doing?' I mused to myself. They were chatting;

Newley was throwing his arms around looking agitated, Mr Dier waved his hand in a calming motion while looking over his shoulder for any hidden onlookers. He reached into his inside coat pocket and pulled out a watch, like the one he had given me, and handed it to Newley. Mr Dier appeared to be instructing him on how to use it, cupping his hands around it. Newley's aura glowed yellow, images which I couldn't make out properly flickered past fast, as if his mind was unsettled. The watch emitted a ripple of energy, acknowledging activation, and a holographic picture appeared above it. Dier nodded, signalling to Newley that this was good. They chatted and looked at the watch's projection. Newley turned and pointed through the woods; Mr Dier nodded in confirmation, handing Newley a shovel that he had seemingly produced from thin air. They parted but not before I eyeballed Dier. He stopped and turned, looking in my direction. We locked eyes for a second; the corner of his mouth curled, letting a wry smile of knowing out, then he shuffled off while Newley went in the other direction.

I tracked Newley as he stayed in view. He headed to a clearing around half a mile from the Rag Tree. It was here that he stopped and paced around checking the watch's projected image. His aura was swirling yellow, now red and black crept in as a vortex of ill gathered momentum. Newley started to dig, and as he did, the ground got darker and blacker with each strike. His intention was clearly not of a wholesome nature.

'What's he looking for?' I asked Okol.

'Whatever it is, it ain't good, I'd watch him if I were you,' replied Okol.

'What about those firecrackers and bangers?' said Ikol.

'Oh yeah, there's some stuff buried round here. I bet fifty or sixty years ago after the war they stashed a load of stuff out here,' added Okol.

'Firecrackers!? Bangers!? You mean explosives from the war!?' I asked.

'Yeah, yeah, make a big bang they will,' replied Choc, not seeming too concerned.

'That's what he's up to, that's what he's going to do!' I shouted, grabbing the boys' attention. 'He's going to blow up the fete!'

Newley eventually retrieved a metal box. He smashed the lock open with the shovel blade and stashed the contents in a holdall, discarded the shovel, slung the bag over his shoulder and trekked off out of the woods.

'Who's going to question a copper?' I gasped.

'Yep, you've got to give it to them, that's a smart move,' added Ikol.

I waited until Newley was gone then said my goodbyes, my mind buzzing after witnessing Dier and his accomplice plotting in the woods. I couldn't fathom what Mr Dier was gaining from conspiring with the now Ill Newley, but I had begun to see a different side to him. He certainly didn't look to be playing a neutral part, and gave the impression his strings were well and truly being pulled. The question was, how conscious was he of the puppetry that animated him? A shadow had crept over the woods as my mind had turned from a joyous reunion with Moggins to the dark and deceitful dealings of Ill Newley and Dier. I did well to control my imagination as Mr Milly and I strode back through Snickets; foulness was only a thought away. The glorious, colourful, vibrant woodland had sickened slightly. I pushed the shadows back and thought of Ikron and the power the light has. Reaching the edge of Snickets unscathed,

I fussed Mr Milly, breathing a sigh of relief, then counted myself out of the Veil, the dimensional filter dropped, and we were fully back in our reality.

I was more aware now. Just because I couldn't see the Veil didn't mean it wasn't there, for it continually affected this reality. I knew more than ever it was the missing piece to our world. I passed the Smythe farm and headed straight back to Nanna's, itching to tell her about what I'd seen. Bustling through the kitchen door, I was greeted with an empty room.

'Nanna,' I shouted, pausing for a response. My eye caught the bowl of crystals on the sideboard. Dier's watch still sat where Nanna tossed it. I grabbed it and stuffed it in my pocket.

'Out here, dear,' called Nanna from the front garden. I found her leant over the stone wall that separated the two cottages; she was nattering to the Major, peering over as he pointed down.

'Look, bloody little ferret, he's been at me roses again,' grumbled the Major, presumably moaning about the mischievous Maggot.

'Yeah, they look done,' replied Nanna.

I walked over to the pair. 'Alright, son? Been down the woods?' asked the Major.

'Yeah,' I replied.

'No funny business I hope,' he quizzed further. 'That was some strange stuff,' he added.

'No... well, yes...' I hesitantly replied.

'It's OK, love, you're amongst friends,' comforted Nanna.

The Major cleared his throat. 'No, it's fine really, I must be getting on, be seeing you later... Boys' night, haha,' he said, winking. I looked at Nanna, bemused.

'Oh yes dear, that's right, I'm popping out tonight, spot of business to do, so the Major has kindly offered to entertain you,' replied Nanna.

'Oh, OK,' I smiled, shrugging my shoulders.

'Good lad,' said the Major, his gravelly tones strong and comforting. 'Right, I'll leave you to your chat,' he said, taking himself off. 'Maggot!!! Where are you...? Little blighter,' he shouted, rounding the corner of the cottage, leaving Nanna and me alone.

'So?' asked Nanna.

'I saw them! In the woods. He's got some explosives now!' I blurted out incoherently.

'Whoa, whoa, slow down. Now who did you see?' asked Nanna. I went on to explain about the secret meeting between Dier and Ill Newley, and how Newley had retrieved a holdall that the Rag Tree Boys thought were explosives.

'He's gunna blow summat up, isn't he!' I shouted in frustration. 'Didn't we see it? Didn't Wit show us!' I continued.

'Yes, yes dear, they are moving quickly,' mused Nanna.

'And this,' I said, pulling out the watch. 'They used this as a tracker or something.' Nanna looked at the pocket watch.

'You must remember, this is an item from the dimension of instant creation, it was never made in this world, it does not obey this reality's rules. It's not what it looks like,' said Nanna. I looked over the ivory case, opening and closing it, the face still showing the black and white dial.

'It's not a watch, is it? Is it to track me?' I asked.

Nanna shrugged, and half nodded. 'It's whatever they want it to be. Use it, change it, turn it on them,' said Nanna, cupping the watch in my hand.

I spent the rest of the afternoon sat on my bedroom floor failing to prise the secrets from Dier's pocket watch. My thoughts easily side-tracked when I tried to look inside the watch's essence. After what seemed hours, I had a eureka moment.

'Ah, the stones!?' I said, thinking out loud.

I hastily retrieved the velvet pouch from Nanna's kitchen cupboard and emptied its contents onto my bed. I placed the sealing stones in a small circle, positioning Dier's watch in the middle. 'Right then, Mills, let's see what these do,' I mused to my dozing companion. 'As above is below,' I said, doing my mental preparation for entering the Veil. The curtain dropped now quicker than ever, my bolstered belief in alternate realms obviously accelerating the process.

Next, I brought the pillar of light down into my amulet and then into the stones. They all lit up beautifully. I squinted at first, but my consciousness immediately adjusted the brightness. They hummed a delicate little tune ready to do my bidding. 'Right! Come on, Grevling Dier, let's see what you're up to,' I said, sending my intention through the stones. They vibrated slightly then each one shot out a beam of white laser light into the watch. The device pinged off the floor, repelled by the rays. My mind worked quickly as I instructed the stones to stop the watch; they held it in a tractor beam as the multidimensional timepiece flung itself around the room. The stones kept hold as if reeling in a mighty catch that was fighting for its life.

I intensified the beam's flow with thoughts of Ikron, of hope and all the moments my heart had swelled with love. 'Give it up, Dier,' I said through gritted teeth. Finally the ornate pocket watch yielded, shaking in the air, vibrating with tremendous speed, until a puff of purple oily smoke expelled from within its workings as it dropped to the floor. I cut the flow, drained from the fight. The stones gently went out, and the watch sat steaming in front of me. Once composed, I reached out and picked up Dier's secret; noting a neutral feeling instantly. I cupped the timepiece, pouring my intent into it. 'Work for me, little watch, do my bidding,' I whispered, and with that our bond was made. A pulse returned up my arms sending a warm flood of joy into my heart. *It's alive,* I thought, and the spirit or soul or whatever it was within the watch was overjoyed to be free. 'Show me in the best way you can…' I said hesitantly. 'Show me Newley. That is, Ill Newley,' I asked.

The watch glowed with a pale blue hue; an invisible magnetic force began to swirl in my hands. The latch popped and the case flung open. A holographic image projected out from the watch's face, and I could see him, I could see Ill Newley! 'Amazing,' I commented, blown away by this Veil technology. I watched him doing his rounds, nothing suspicious, just being a copper, no one suspecting him, but I knew it wasn't the real Newley and the soul that now animated him, was of a dark and murderous nature. He was full of smiles, patting kids' heads and seeing old dears over the road. So far though, I had no inkling as to the whereabouts of the explosives or what exactly he intended to do with them. The watch was giving me video stream of Ill Newley as if an invisible camera was following him. I wondered if, and what, the dark had seen of me and my exploits. I wondered if I had been spied on in such a way.

I commanded the watch more directly this time. 'Show me the bag Ill Newley dug up in the woods.' The watch responded, cutting the stream and providing me with exactly what I'd asked for. The bag lay open on a workbench, in a garage or shed. Tools were lying about, also barrels, bottles and other brewing equipment. Mum and Dad had the same stuff in our loft at home. I gathered this was Newley's home, but the bag was empty, he had already shifted the explosives! 'Show me what he did with the explosives!' I asked. The watch paused as if thinking about its response. I wondered if the information had been blocked in some way.

Then it started to stream again, showing me Ill Newley; he was at the bench, his back toward my Veil Spy. I couldn't see what he was doing with his hands, but he did hold the watch up, shaking it, seemingly frustrated. 'It's not working,' I muttered to myself. He slammed it down in anger, turning away. I caught a glimpse of the bag and bottles that were on the bench, he then looked right at the Veil Spy, peering directly into the multi-dimensional lens. My stomach turned. I gulped, feeling I'd been caught.

Ill Newley stared and shook his head, turning back to the table, grabbing the watch with both hands, wrapping it in concentration. I saw the purple pulse push down his arms, activating the device; a glow filled the room, silhouetting the rotten copper.

He laughed and began working on the explosives one at a time, each accompanied by a flash of dark light as he repeated the procedure. I tried to angle the Veil Spy better, but this time Newley spun round with a manic look on his face. His cruel essence and distorted face flooded his eyes with red and black ink, frenziedly laughing in my face, louder and louder, closer and closer, his image deforming, trapped within the projection.

The negativity grew and swelled. Mr Milly backed up away from the watch as I sat watching the monster grow. He reached out with a liquid limb; it morphed and changed, trying to find a way through the Veil Spy's lens. He pushed and groaned, finally breaking through, shooting tar cobweb strands that anchored onto the ceiling and walls, ready to pull Ill Newley's foul essence into my room.

'Stop it, stop now!!' I shouted. 'Watch, stop it! Take him back!' I screamed again, but it didn't respond. I focused hard on the stones and blocked out the deathly tide that ebbed my way 'Ikron, make him go!' I commanded and with that Ikron's metallic voice answered with a plume of white fire shooting from my amulet into the stones, finally blitzing the watch. Ill Newley's cruel essence shrieked and fizzled into nothing.

The projection stopped, and the watch snapped shut. 'Bloody hell! Nothing's ever straight forward, is it Mills?' I said, seeking comfort from my canine companion. She whimpered and yawned as if growing tired of these near-disastrous incidents. The watch steamed in front of me, Nanna popped her head round the door.

'Everything alright, dear?' she asked, squinting peculiarly at the smouldering timepiece.

'Eeerrr... yeah?' I replied.

'Good...? I'm off in a mo', I will drop you round the Major's in a minute. Get your things together,' said Nanna.

'Oh, OK. Can Mills come?' I asked.

'Err, better not, dear. Maggot can be a bit tetchy at home,' she replied.

I was ready in no time. Dolly was running outside gently warming her rattling clunky engine, Nanna locked the door. 'Now I won't be too long, you be a good lad for Bob,' she said.

'Where you going?' I asked.

She tapped her nose and said, 'Spot of business, in the village, dear.'

The Major gave me a warm welcome. I watched Nanna drive off through the small leaded window in the front door. She stopped at the end of the lane, signalled right but didn't move for a second — there was no traffic. She then turned on the left indicator and went the other way, out towards the moor.

'Where are you going, Nanna?' I said to myself.

CHAPTER 14

Night Caller

The Major's cottage was a mirror image of Nanna's; his backroom acted as the main living area, two high-back chairs faced an open fire, there was no telly – just a radio that always hummed some old tune. The kitchen was crammed into what is the pantry in Nanna's cottage and was usually home to a big pot of steaming mussels; his seafood fetish was well talked about. A door then leads from the kitchen out to the rear garden and garage. I never went in any of the other rooms, only peeking into the front room when the door was left ajar. There was a nice polished dining table and a cabinet full of trophies, photos and keepsakes. I don't think the room saw much use, the Major wasn't the kind to throw dinner parties; neglected from company, it didn't have the warmth of the backroom, which was a den of cosiness. Maggot had a soft padded bed next to the Major's chair, he always sat in the red one nearest to the back door, where he could cast an eye down the hall, unlike at Nanna's where the hall was never used as an entrance; all visitors came to the backdoor.

Maggot rarely left the Major's side; he was a loyal but a mischievous companion and definitely filled his days with many unexpected and unintended disasters. I sunk back into the chair adjacent to the Major. I loved it because I thought it almost had wings, or a cape that wrapped around the sides. When I was sat far back it created a little secret place, where I felt hidden and snug. I'd stare at the fire feeling at peace with the world; there was a picture on the mantle that always caught my eye, it showed the Major years younger, he was collecting an award in his military regalia, the inscription said for outstanding acts of bravery awarded to Sergeant Robert C. Mayne.

I always felt safe in the Major's company. We didn't chat much, I didn't feel the need to, he made me feel like family, and there was an ease in our silences. I always liked the way he called me 'our Pete' which is how Mum and Dad would refer to close family members. 'Ours' meant to me, being one of us. The Major drew the curtains as the evening ticked on. We sat in front of the fire, our feet and knees toasting, the Major reading his paper and me a comic book, my head beginning to nod as my eyelids grew heavy. I was just drifting off into an inviting snooze, my grip relaxing the book I held, when a rap came to the front door – three long, hard knocks.

Maggot was the first to respond; he sprung into life, piercing the air with his shrill scrappy barks. I jumped milliseconds after Maggot's reaction, dropping my comic book on the floor, startled by the blunt interruption of our peace. The Major folded his paper, puffing heavily on his pipe, casting a quizzical eye down the hallway.

'What the dickens! At this time!' he said while still puffing away and staring over the top of his reading glasses. He paused, contemplating not bothering. I feared for them; if it were doors sales they would probably get a right dusting down. He moaned and lifted himself out of the chair and strode toward the front door where he unlatched the bolt and chain.

Maggot stood behind him, letting out a protective growl. The Major pulled the door open already chuntering in a displeased manner. 'What's all this about then!?' he said, his sentence falling short of the finish as he was greeted with an unoccupied doorstep. 'Hello… anyone there!?' he called. 'Hello!' he shouted out into the darkness. 'Bloody kids…!!' he grumbled then slammed the door. 'I hope it's not your mates down the lane!' he said.

'What, Ronnie and Buster!!' I replied, defending my friends.

'No… You're right, can't see it being them, Ned would string 'em up,' said the Major placing his arm around me, his gravelly chuckle clearing the atmosphere. 'That Cradlick lad, he's always mooching around this way looking for trouble… could have been them larking about? That family's bad news!' said the Major as he searched for a rational answer.

'I think Shaun's a bit different, he deserves a fair chance,' I said.

'Oh! Well… if you say so, youngen,' replied the Major as he led me back down the hall, our seats awaiting our return. Maggot took his place back on his blanket, I slumped into the chair, and the Major was just lowering himself into position when… it happened again, but this time the back door. *Rap, rap, rap,* the same three long knocks rang through the cottage. He gave me a look, his patience wearing thin. 'Away with you! Go on! Off with you!' he shouted, waiting for some kind of response, having no intention to go and see who the pranksters were. I was starting to get a little freaked out now, and was doing all I could to keep my imagination in check, for it desperately wanted to take me down that dark alley.

I would have felt much better if Mr Milly was with us. Maggot was doing his best to ward the caller off, but his growls rolled out more like a cheese grater, before reaching yappy ear-piercing heights. 'Maggot! Maggot! Suusssshhh now,' said the Major, calling for quiet, trying to home in on any sounds that might give away the caller's identity. He paused, listening intently. The lights flickered, and the telephone buzzed into life for a second then stopped; he saw the panic flooding my face and gestured me to calm down, patting the air slowly, then once again it came from the front door, three long knocks. The Major stood up and came over to me, holding his arm out as shelter. I snuck in, and he whispered in my ear, 'Don't be scared, lad, I'll look after you, come on, follow me.' He led me through into the front room not bothering to flick the lights. Rustling around in his pocket, the Major produced a key. 'Right then, now we'll see, won't we?' he chuntered, unlocking a tall narrow cabinet, exposing two guns stored vertically. He pulled one out, handling it like an old friend, stroking the barrel. He cracked the loading chamber and slid two new cartridges in, then slowly clicked the barrel back into position. He turned and winked. 'Shove this up their bloody nose! Send them home with brown pants, little crappers!' The mission was on!

He crouched slightly and held the gun in both hands, ready to stick it up any unsuspecting mischief-maker's hooter. I know he was an old man, but by the way he moved and how he held himself, I imagined he would have a been a deadly foe if it came down to it. He glided through the room and into the hall, his arm searching for me behind him every few steps.

We ducked down below the front door glass, waited for a second, then rushed the door, flinging it open, bursting forth, the gun stretched out ready to capture the night caller. He aimed into the darkness flitting this way and that looking for the scurrying jokers. 'Come on, you little beggars!' he shouted into the night. His eye patrolled the area, and when he was satisfied that there was no one about the Major lowered the gun. Maggot trotted out and sniffed the flowers then proceeded to pee upon a gnome that was dressed in military gear. 'Maggot! Off! Get off! You little shhhhiii!' shouted the Major, shooing the tufty rascal off with his slipper.

We went back inside, and he shut the door, this time bolting it, and pulling the chain over. I could smell a rat; this had the hallmark of something sinister and not just kids messing about. The Major peered through the small-pained glass window, checking the area again. He turned and sighed, 'Well that should have—' The Major's sentence was cut off by the back door slamming. 'Bloody hell! The cheeky bleeders!' he cursed, assuming his offensive stance once again, the gun probing the way forward as he cautiously moved down the hall to the back room.

The door to the kitchen was closed. Maggot stood behind us emitting his ankle-biting snarl. 'You get the door and fall behind it, I'll point the shooter at them,' he whispered. I gulped and nodded. The Major moved into position, and I reluctantly took mine. With my back against the wall, I stretched over to reach the knob. 'Ready… One… Two—' The major's count was cut short as the brass handle began to turn. We both backed off, now in the hands of whatever was intent on spooking us. The Major held his hand out, signalling me towards him. I nodded and fell back with our offensive position now compromised. The brass knob reached its full rotation, pulling the latch back; the door then began to slowly creek open.

'No Nanna?' came a croaky, frail voice, wheezing with laboured breathing. The Major and I exchanged puzzled looks as a withered hand grabbed the sideboard, steadying the hooded hunched figure that now shuffled into the room. Suspicion overloaded my mind. Physically the figure appeared non-threatening, but somehow still gave me a serious reason to change my pants.

'Alright, me dear, what can we do for you?' said the Major, his tones mellowed by the presence of the frail old lady. Her face shadowed by a dark hood, only the tip of her nose, mouth and chin were visible in the flickering amber firelight. She nursed a basket that hung over her left arm covered with a white doily cloth.

Wow, that's some hairy chin, I thought. Her sharp nose curved down to meet it, giving her the stereotypical witchy look. *Nar,* I thought, *way too obvious,* and I let myself relax a tad. She shuffled closer.

'Sorry, I'm looking for Elizabeth Nuts? I'm confused. You weren't answering the door,' stuttered the old lady. My heart wavered as she struggled to get her words out; she seemed genuinely unnerved and upset. 'I let myself in, it was getting cold out,' she added, excusing her actions.

'She's not in, my dear, can I pass a message on?' said the Major.

'Well... yes, I have these herbs, you see, she asked for them,' she croaked.

'I can take them,' I offered.

'Ah... Yes, yes, you're her grandson... aren't you just the shiniest star in the sky?' she said, trailing off with a sarcastic twist. The old lady uncovered the basket to reveal an array of herbs and wildflowers. The Major placed his gun in the corner of the room, cracking the barrel for safety.

'Sorry about the gun, thought it was some ruffians playing the fool,' said the Major. The old lady tilted her head up from the basket, her smile exposing an incomplete set of crooked yellow teeth. She chuckled in a spine-chilling way, just staring blankly at us.

'Here... these are the ones,' she said, lifting a handful of black velvet stems from the basket. They were adorned with trumpet flowers covered in hundreds of tiny hairs, creating a furry look not dissimilar to mouldy, rotten fruit. I didn't trust her one bit; my inner knowledge was screaming at me. Maggot wasn't buying it either, his little growl ringing out as a warning.

She came closer; her head remained bowed until she raised her hand, brandishing the flowers bringing her face to the fore. *Bingo! Black eyes!* I thought as she came fully into view.

'Here… these are the ones,' she said again, cackling, thrusting the velvet flowers into our faces. I dodged out of the way, but the Major was dumbstruck, totally surprised by the nature of this new foe. The hag blew on the stems, covering the Major's face in a cloud of black spores, swirling around his head, searching for an opening.

'Don't breathe them in,' I called. He looked at me sideways, trying his best to hold his breath, but failed as the nauseous gas that accompanied the poisonous flora forced him to inhale. The cloud of spores shot into his mouth, eagerly accepting the Major's open invitation. Clutching his throat, he stumbled and slumped into the nearest chair, his face already ashen grey as a malevolent toxin filled his veins.

Maggot whimpered and bolted to the front door. I hesitated, not knowing what to do. I tried to focus and bring forward my power, but somehow she was stopping me. I felt her presence within my mind, her voice cackled and whispered in both realities, the room started to spin. I was about ready to pass out, when I heard Ikron.

'Run!' he said, and with that I took a sideways drunken stumble toward the front door fumbling with the latch, turning to see the old hag following me, her form now more witch than old woman. Black veins ran down her bluish, cracked skin; her eyes jet black, the yellow teeth were pointed now, caging an oily snake behind them. I knew this was her, but I didn't want to say her name, so she did it for me.

'ShawlInka! ShawlInka! Shawl… Inka!' rang through the corridors of my mind, the simplest task now taking all my concentration and effort. Finally, I unlocked the door and threw it open.

We ran out into the night, desperate to get away. 'I am the night,' came the sickly voice in the wind. It subsided from my mind the further I got from the cottage. I sprinted hard and fast down the lane onto the main road into Chattersley. I ran and ran until my heart and lungs were fit to burst, my side splitting from stitch. Eventually I stopped, gasping for air. Maggot was just behind me; he stuck close, whimpering, not understanding the level of fear he had just experienced. I took in big long breaths as soon as the stitch would let me. My lungs recovered, and breathing slowed, my mind was clear of her and the night fell silent around us, just my breath and Maggot's whimpers. I turned and looked back at the cottage and was smacked by a sudden rush of guilt and empathy.

The poor Major, I thought. I could see the lights from the hall beaming out; the door was still open. There was no sign of the old hag though. *Where was everyone when I needed them?* I thought. Was this just what she had been waiting for, to get me alone and away from Nanna? I contemplated my next move. My heart was riddled with guilt; leaving the Major like that was a cowardly move. I wasn't thinking straight, I needed to get away, and even Ikron said so.

I mulled it over in my head, trying to justify my actions when the sound of an approaching vehicle broke the quietness of the evening air. I turned to face the noise, it was coming out from Chattersley, a single bright headlight shining out against the backdrop of the village's night-time illumination. The noise grew into a twangy rattle, which I soon recognised as the raucous, detuned scramblers that Cradlick and his crew used. It ripped up the road towards me, each gear being driven hard, every rev possible being squeezed out of the engine. As it got close I waved my arms; the bike slowed and came to a halt, I could see the distinctive blond hair of Cradlick poking out of the helmet. He slipped it off and greeted me with a surprised look.

'Alright, kid… what's up? You in trouble?' he said, my face telling its own story.

'You wouldn't believe me if I told you,' I replied.

'Oh, I don't know, I've been wanting to talk to you. What you did in the shop, you did something. Didn't you? You know stuff, don't you? What's going on?' asked Cradlick. 'And whose is that dog?' he said, nodding at Maggot. 'He looks as scared as you,' he added.

'It's Maggot, the Major's, and he's in trouble!' I replied.

'Maggot!' laughed Cradlick.

'He's been poisoned!' I shouted, trying to cut through the amusement of Maggot's name.

Cradlick's laughs petered out. 'Poisoned?' he asked.

'Yes, you have to help me!' I pleaded.

'Well, I do owe you one… I think?' he replied, signalling me to hop on the back. I straddled his bike with Maggot under my arm. 'Where to?' he asked. I didn't know, my head was spinning.

Get Nanna? Or go back? I asked myself. I knew if I focused, I could protect us. I knew the Major might not have long.

'He's in the cottage next to Nanna's, there… the lights are on.' I pointed up the road. Cradlick kicked back the side stand.

'Buckle up,' he said, winking as the bike reared onto its back wheel. I struggled to hold on with Maggot taking up half my grip. We shot off up the road, our loud, boisterous steed somehow building an air of confidence within me. Cradlick parked the bike in the lane just as the cottage hall lights flickered and went out.

'Point the headlight at the door!' I instructed. Cradlick moved the bike to illuminate the entrance.

'What's going on?' he asked, looking spooked.

'Right!' I said, grabbing my amulet and focusing intensely as Nanna had taught me. The Veil dropped, and the power shone through. I glowed golden white, my heart beating fast and hard. I pulsed a ball of ivory light round us; it sparkled and gleamed. Cradlick looked at me, open-mouthed. 'You can see?' I asked.

'Ever since the shop,' he replied in awe.

'Come closer, come inside the sphere,' I said. Cradlick stepped in, looking amazed at what his brain was trying to explain.

'Think you need to fill me in,' he said, staring at the glistening ball that surrounded us. I nodded. The cottage was quiet, not a whisper nor movement, and I wasn't picking up any auras within either. We moved slowly to the door where I sent a small ball of light down the hall and into the back room; it stayed in the corner and illuminated the scene.

'No light here,' cackled the voice which sounded more annoyed now. A shadow stretched out over the back wall, shaped like a spindly tree branch with bony fingers; it snuffed the ball of light out.

'What the!' said Cradlick, as we moved down the hall. I sucked up my courage and began to bring Ikron through, dark in one corner, light in the other, with the grey face of the Major between us.

Maggot growled at the sick presence. I saw him change, his alter self, manifesting a metal jaw and snout that protruded forward from his normal tufty body. They clanked together, his yap gaining menace. I gathered my courage, Ikron just a thought away. She stood in the shadows skulking, plotting, waiting.

'Leave!' I commanded, my voice wavering. 'Leave now!' I said again, Ikron's metallic tone quickly covering any signs of weakness in my words. I began to sparkle and pulse with energy; the old crone rolled out a callous, mocking laugh.

'Leave! You will have to do better than that!' she taunted.

Right, I'll show the old bat! I thought, bringing my power into me. I could hear Ikron rushing from the corridors of eternity into me. He came, like a lightning storm raging in the heavens, thrust down to earth through a mighty spear.

'Come on! Come,' I said, my confidence bolstered now by his imminent arrival. I surrendered myself to him, dropping my guard for a split second. That's when she made her move, travelling across the room, releasing her form, appearing like a series of still photos under a strobe light. Within three frames she was on me; her hand pierced the light shield, the hag's bony fingers clutching my neck with incredible force.

'Make me!' she threatened. I gasped for breath. The light surrounding me affected her arm; particles floated off, burning in the air, transmuting the dark into light. She gazed upon this, grimacing with fury.

Maggot bravely pulled on her tattered garments but was quickly punted away with the force of a premiership footballer, hitting the wall hard with a squeal. Cradlick paused, not knowing what to do, then rushed to my aid. He came in with a right hook, but this was no bar-room brawl, and wouldn't be solved with earthly brawn. The hag blasted him back with a bolt of dark energy, sending him flying out of the front door.

'Let me go!' I spat through gritted teeth, proclaiming the victim within was present. Ikron shrunk back, and I was alone. My sphere, having little or no effect, dulled; the particles slowly floated off her arm but were of no concern to her dominating dark power. I struggled for breath and feared I wouldn't take another. She didn't say much, but I felt her disdain for me, how repulsed she was by my purity, how in her sick mind evolution of the spirit needed fear, it needed suffering and pain. Love and hope, to her were weak, only ever needed to give the dark a background to play upon. In her twisted mind was a forest of snakes and poisonous flora; it was eternally dark, it always had been. She despised me, and had waited for my awakening only to snuff my light out. I struggled one last time but to no avail.

Then through my faded vision, I caught a glimmer of hope. A sparkle of gold dust trailed over my head. I looked up and saw Wit; she flitted around and buzzed above the old hag, much to her annoyance. Wit then settled on the mantle and winked, vibrating with a tinkling angelic chorus of bells and chimes.

'Argh! That noise!' spat the hag. Then an expectant look came across her wicked face, just before all hell broke loose. Flashing colours of green, blue, yellow, orange and red came from the back garden as the windows unlocked themselves, and the curtains blew wild. A light show filled the room coupled with the sound of a very excited and angry mob. Simultaneously at the front of the cottage, I could hear Mr Milly and the motorised whirrings of Moggins mechanical bat cat suit. The back door burst open, nearly knocked off its hinges as the Rag Tree Boys fell in, their array of glowing weapons and armour ready for anything. The boys paused for a split second then broke rank, as little Choc belted out a war cry! From all directions, they attacked, bouncing and launching off walls and furniture. Thrusting, slashing and bashing with everything they had. Okol's fish arrows ricocheted around the room, while Ikol's sun sword closely shaved the witch, who despite the boys' furious assault, still held me firm, draining the life from my earthly body.

She fought the boys with her free hand, blighting them with smoky air blasts. Out of one blast came a squid-like entity that pinned Okol to the wall, while Choc's manic charge was repelled, sitting him on his backside in the smouldering fire, from which he quickly exited with a chorus of oohs and aahs, while blowing his cheeks out.

'She's a trickster!' he shouted as he quickly recovered and aimed his silver stone hammer at the hag's back, but she was quick, too quick. The room flickered with strobing light; it all seemed too easy for her. The boys moved in slow motion, and she was one step ahead of their next move. I looked at her, full of hate.

'Old! Ugly! Coward!' I squeezed out through gritted teeth. She laughed, her horrid teeth oozing a black liquid.

'Hate me! Despise me! Feeeaaar me!' she snarled, and that's when I thought, this is exactly what she wanted. I grabbed her wrist; my last thoughts weren't going to be of fear, or pain, or suffering. I can't change everything, but I can change my thoughts. So I gathered all the happiest moments I could and pushed them down my arm into hers, and that's all it needed. The hag's eyes pinged open in shock, her concentration lost for a split second. Ikol was right on it, his arcing sun sword catching her side, igniting in a rainbow of sparks. She reeled, and her grip loosened.

Then a voice boomed, 'ShawlInka!!' followed by a pulse of light; tinged with a violet edge, it blasted through everything. The boys' hair was pushed back off their faces as they struggled to stand firm. ShawlInka was catapulted back against the wall. Mr Milly and Moggins burst in following up the strike, now standing over the witch ready to finish her off. I slumped to the floor but was caught by Cradlick.

'Easy now,' he said. We both turned to see Nanna make her entrance in the timeless form I'd come to know as, 'Shelaya,' I said with the little breath that was left in me. Cradlick looked more wowed by Nanna than the events he had just witnessed. Maybe it was the pureness, and power of goodness that emanated from her that just made your face expel a soppy smile. She made your heart swell and spirits soar, raising everybody's vibration around her.

Nanna walked through into the room, patting Cradlick gently on the arm and ruffling my hair. She was a picture of goodness; her blonde hair had a slight curl as if time had unravelled each lock, laying softly on a purple velvet cape. Her face was untouched by the ravishes of life; she gazed out of silver-blue eyes, rimmed with a strong dark line, all encompassed by the most majestic, magnificent, glowing, glittering light, that was more her, than the earthly form she embodied. ShawlInka cowered and hissed in the corner, all eyes trained on her. Shelaya strode towards her, causing the witch great discomfort the closer her energy got.

'You have no place here, ShawlInka,' she said, her voice echoing through dimensions. 'I banish you, and your eyes of the night,' she commanded, her voice carrying the power of bindings and protection. ShawlInka writhed in pain, twisted by two invisible hot pokers. Shelaya repeated a third time, making her foe spit black tar onto the floor as if hit by a thundering right hook too swift for the eye to catch.

ShawlInka looked desperate now; she stared into her hand full of the oily liquid she'd expelled.

'Stop… Stop,' said the night caller, holding out her hand looking for yield. Her chest was heavy with breath, and her face drained of the evil confidence she displayed minutes before. Shelaya paused. ShawlInka started muttering to herself; to my ears it sounded like the babble of a confused old person or a defeated soldier that was traumatised and lost, but this wasn't just a weak old lady chuntering to herself, this was an agent of ill, looking for a way out. The words came together and gathered momentum, and before we knew it she was chanting under her breath, summoning back her power. Suddenly her head flicked back with a force that would have broken any human's, her eyes pitch black, rolled round in their sockets, chairs squeaked and dragged across the floor, the picture on the mantle flew across the room, hitting the opposite wall. That's when the calm, serene 'Shelaya' lost it.

'No! ShawlInka! Begone! Back to the black! Back to the black, black I send you back!' and with her power turned to ten, she unleashed a piercing light. We all shielded our eyes for it was a fierce light, one you dare not look at; it was judgment and executioner and was without empathy, it was the hammer of good, the spear of justice, everything opposite to the dark. ShawlInka screeched a wretched cry, and when the light faded, she was gone. Shelaya departed, and Nanna stood in her place.

'Some people just can't take a hint,' she said, puffing, catching her breath as she walked over to me. 'Well… you can't unsee that!' she said, patting Cradlick on his shoulder.

'The Major!' I shouted, bringing the group's attention back to the sickened war hero. Nanna quickly placed her hand over his mouth and closed her eyes; she held the position for a minute or so then moved back.

'Give him some space,' she asked. The Major began to cough; he spluttered and coughed harder and harder until he cupped his hands and produced what looked like a spikey black thistle.

'Crikey! …What on earth have I been eating?' he said. Nanna took it from him and threw it in the fire where it ignited in a short burst of licking fingers.

'You stay with us tonight,' instructed Nanna as she lifted him out of the chair. He scanned the Rag Tree Boys, scrunched up his face in a puzzled manner, paused then shook his head of the questions that were queuing up.

'What's going on, Liz? It's never been like this,' he said, too weary to be making sense of the answers he might be given. The Rag Tree Boys glitched as the Veil's influence diminished. Moggins came over for a fuss.

'He's fighting fit now,' said Okol, making his way across the room and placing his hand on my shoulder. 'Don't worry, we all know you've got it,' comforted Okol.

'Got what?' I asked, a little perplexed.

'Inside you, we all saw what you can do, just believe, it will get easier,' he replied.

I thought, *I hope it does,* because I felt pretty overwhelmed just then. I was unnerved how she apparently blocked Ikron, filling my mind with doubt, bringing the victim forward. The Rag Tree Boys left via the back door, teasing and picking at each other. Choc was still pulling at his shorts from where he'd sat in the fire.

'Stop it! It was flaming hot!' he said to El, who was making fun of his red puffed face. Moggins jumped into Ikol's arms; they hopped over the back wall into the field and disappeared with a flash of colour back into their realm. Wit buzzed over and fluttered down onto my shoulder. She chirped and twitted with tinkles and chimes.

'Was it you? Did you get them, Wit?' I asked, having a hunch the little rosewood bird had saved my bacon. Wit vibrated and let out a tiny explosion of golden dust, I gathered this was a yes as she ecstatically accepted my praise. Cradlick just looked dumbstruck, his mouth hanging open.

'Who…? What…? How is this happening…?' he mused out loud.

Nanna came over to the unexpected initiate, placing her finger under his jaw and gently pushing it shut. 'Oh, there'll be plenty more of that before we are done… And just how did you meander into this little game?' she asked, casting an eye at me.

'Errr… I don't… know… the shop… Pete took something… I saw it on the tape,' stuttered Cradlick, trying to piece it together and produce a reasonable, rational answer.

'Well I thought bugger lugs would have something to do with it,' she said, ruffling my hair. 'Well, we will just have to fill you in, the best we can, love… is your mind ready?' said Nanna.

'Errr… I think sssoo… Yes, yes,' replied Cradlick, more eager to learn than to forget.

We closed the windows and locked the cottage up, then made our way back to Ivy Gate. I volunteered my bed for the Major, Nanna got him settled and returned to the kitchen where she laid it out as plain and simple as she could for Cradlick. He sat digesting the information and the wild story he had been fed. He pushed the hair from his face, holding it back for a moment.

'So… is this all fake then?' he asked.

'No, no, not fake. Shall we say, a distortion of the truth,' replied Nanna.

'A lie then,' added Cradlick.

'Yes, yes, it is most definitely a lie; for it is not the truth… Yes, you're born, and yes, we all die… it's the bit that makes it a circle that's missing, the bit between life and death. It's a mystery, they say, left to folklore and manipulated religious texts, but it's the only real bit, where you can remember what you really are. What you saw today is the realm beyond the physical, where you might say the dead go. You saw that realm, did it look dead to you?' asked Nanna.

'It was… more alive than anything I've ever seen,' replied Cradlick, his eyes glistening with emotion. 'So Nan, is she there?' he asked.

'Oh most definitely. Your energy, vibration, frequency, cannot be destroyed; it just shifts, so if she isn't here anymore, then she is somewhere else that's for sure… You just saw one of those places. Pete's seen quite a bit lately, haven't you dear…? He's starting to get his squiffy little head round it. We will help you the best we can, but be careful what you say to people, this is the most misunderstood subject known to the human race. There are prying eyes and pricked ears, the dark tide has ebbed onto our shore, and we will have to drive it back. Keep your cards close to your heart, and stick with us, dear. Your mind is open now, best you do not forget that,' said Nanna, letting Cradlick take it all in.

'So that's her?' I asked.

'Yes dear, she must have known you were alone. Her influence grows, it's an aggressive response to your expansion,' said Nanna, straightening out the table cloth, going about her bits and bobs.

'It's me; it's all because of me!' I barked.

'Dear… It's always been coming, it would happen this way whatever route you took. You are bound to the story, the book would be incomplete without you,' said Nanna sternly.

I sort of accepted it but found it difficult to understand how my presence had poked the fiery ashes of ill into rearing its ugly head. We spent the next few hours chatting; Cradlick began to let it in, as Nanna yielded to a torrent of questions. Once he started, he was enthused and overwhelmed. I think that this world had dealt him some pretty crappy cards; he was finding some peace knowing this wasn't it, and how his life and the ones around him could have been affected by other realms. He began to realise he wasn't this loser that everyone blamed, he was a character playing a role in a game of distractions and lies.

'Well I think that's enough for today, it's getting late now, you'd best be getting home, dear,' said Nanna. Cradlick slung his leather jacket over his shoulder and picked his helmet up.

'What am I supposed to do now? Can I help? I can't just forget that,' said Cradlick.

'Of course you can't, dear. I don't want to drag you into a battle that's not yours, but at the same time the eyes of the night will have found you now, it's best we keep you close. This chapter needs nipping in the bud, sooner rather than later,' replied Nanna.

'Eyes of the night!?' said Cradlick unnervingly.

'Oh don't worry about that too much,' puffed Nanna, waving a tea towel around. I loved how Nanna dropped bombshells then painted over them with her trademark tea and toast attitude. I suddenly had a lightbulb moment.

'Couldn't… Couldn't Shaun watch Ill Newley for us?' I asked.

'Ill Newley? PC Newley?' quizzed Cradlick. 'What's he done?' he added.

'More like what he's going to do,' I replied.

'Hhmmmm, yes, yes. You could, dear… Keep an eye on him, see what he's up to, tomorrow is the village fete and Newley is up to no good!' informed Nanna.

'PC Newley!? He's PC Perfect, in't he?' asked Cradlick.

'Not anymore, it's a long story, but he's on their side now,' replied Nanna.

'Wow… oh OK, so I'll tail him, report any news?' replied Cradlick. Nanna gave him her number. She didn't have one of those new mobile phones; she was still on the old wired ones, with the rotating dial. I did question her need for such an old, outdated device when surely she had the power of dimensions at her fingertips.

'Well we have to keep up appearances, don't we dear?' she said, giving me a sideways glance, answering my questionable thoughts again.

'What about my walkie-talkies?' I suggested. Nanna and Cradlick gave me a less than enthusiastic look.

'Oh, OK… I was just thinking,' I said disappointedly.

'No, no… actually, that might work… go get them,' said Nanna, catching her give Cradlick a discreet wink as if humouring me.

'They're good ones, you know, Dad got me them, they're not toys,' I added, defending my suggestion.

'Yes, yes dear, I'm sure they will help,' replied Nanna.

I hurriedly rummaged through my bedroom, taking care not to

wake the Major, and quickly found them. I checked they both worked and were on the right channel then returned to the kitchen and handed Cradlick one.

'Cheers,' he replied with a broad smile. 'Right, I will be in touch, eyes on Newley... or Ill Newley,' he said, signalling his exit.

We watched him off, his metal steed illuminating the dark and waking the dead from their slumber. I loved his 'don't care' attitude. For me he had the balance of responsibility and not giving a damn down to a tee. Nanna put her arm around my shoulder as the sound of Cradlick's scrambler faded into the night.

'You like him, don't you?' she said. I nodded.

'I do too,' she said, smiling. We headed back in, and I got ready for bed. Nanna had set me up a cosy spot on the sofa in the front room. She tucked me in and crouched so her head was close to mine.

'So what's the plan tomorrow?' I asked.

She paused. 'Hmmm, well, not letting Ill Newley do anything dastardly for a start. Everything will be OK, dear, just you wait and see. No matter how scary things may get remember who you are, what you are, keep a grip on your thoughts, and you will be fine,' she said, stroking my head.

'And we've got Cradlick now too, I think he will help,' I said.

'Yes dear, I'm sure he will,' replied Nanna, and with that, she bade me goodnight.

I settled down after a while. I was getting better at controlling my thoughts; they swirled around in the blackness of shut-eye. Tiny pinpricks of light merged together, forming images that tried again and again to break me, but I stopped the gargoyle faces from taking shape. I batted them away one after the other, changing them into amusements of my mind until I was no longer burdened by their presence; slipping away out of their sight into a protective dream space where I bounded across the surreal landscape of the Veil, playing with my powers, controlling my environment, feeling it running through my very being.

The following morning I was woken by the distinct sound of a bell ringer telephone echoing through the silent hall. I heard Nanna stir and pick up the receiver. I pushed off my cover and shook my sleepy head, making my way into the hall.

'Oh, PC Newley,' said Nanna, looking over her spectacles quizzically. I could hear his voice on the other end.

'Oh right, so you have my number,' said Nanna, her eyes widening with interest. 'Well, PC Newley, let me tell you this, we have yours too,' and with that Nanna put the phone down, hearing the maddening voice of Ill Newley before the receiver cut him off. Nanna removed her spectacles and pondered over the call. 'I think we've rattled them. He will find it difficult to hide his true intentions... People will notice... Tea... Toast?' said Nanna, showing no concern to the nuisance phone call.

'How's the Major?' I asked.

'Bob... Bob,' called Nanna through the cottage. Mr Milly didn't wait for an invitation; she just nudged the door ajar and headed straight for the Major's pale face. He lay with Maggot motionless until Mr Milly's abrasive tongue licked him awake. He spluttered and coughed, woken abruptly from a presumably canine-themed dream.

'Hounds of the Baskervilles!! Go on! Get off, you silly mutt,' he spluttered, the colour flushing back to his cheeks. Maggot woke with a celebratory yap and joined in the licking.

'Morning Bob... you ready for a cuppa?' asked Nanna. He

coughed hard, still showing the faint signs of last night's altercation with ShawlInka. 'I'll bring it in, best you stay where you are today,' said Nanna.

'Nonsense. I'm fine, lass… I'll be up in a jiffy,' he replied. Nanna tutted and shook her head at her stubborn friend. We had just sat around the kitchen table ready for our morning sustenance when the phone rang again. Nanna rolled her eyes, not amused by the interruption. My mind was buzzing with multiple timelines. How was today going to play out? Who was on the phone now?

'Hello… Oh, hello love… Oh… Yes… Right… Well then… Distract him if you can, till we get down,' laughed Nanna, and put the receiver down. She returned to the table and carried on buttering her toast then chomped down, tearing a large piece off.

'Well! Who was that?' I asked, enthused.

'Oh… Shaun,' she said, speaking through a full mouth. She chewed it down and continued, 'Sorry dear, yes, it was Shaun. He's been watching Ill Newley's house, it's out on Coalman's Road, he says he has left early, carrying a crate of beers out to the van. He says he was pale and sweating, and chuntering to himself,' informed Nanna.

'Beers!' I mused.

'I bet it's homebrew for the village fete, it'll be Gunwin's way of making a bob or two,' said the Major, entering the room.

'But I saw him doing something! It could have been the bottles!?' I added.

'What did you see, dear?' asked Nanna.

'Through the watch, I saw him, he was using the influence of the Veil and the watch Dier gave him. He repeated this action over and over,' I said, mimicking the motion I'd seen Ill Newley do.

'As if making a batch?' said Nanna, chewing on her spectacle arm.

'Beer! And bombs! How can that work?' I asked.

'Oh… dear, if he has fused the creative influence of the Veil, he could have taken the properties of the dynamite and cast them in an unsuspecting form… The worst part is that the destructive power will be different, the explosion will cause physical damage like any, but it will also create a rip, a tear linking to lower dimensions, where the resonance of trauma and shock will manifest easily. If these rips aren't closed darkness will spread and we could end up with another Blackend!' said Nanna sternly.

'Bloody hell! That's some potent brew,' said the Major, not quite getting the seriousness of the situation.

'Hhhmmmm…. Yes, could it be the cap? Or the crate? Or the beer itself? What's the trigger? That's the question,' mused Nanna.

'You mean what's going to set the bleeders off?' said the Major in a gruff military tone.

'Yes… we need those bottles!' instructed Nanna.

Nanna proceeded to inform me of the plan of action. 'So, basically, you snatch them,' she said bluntly.

'And then what?' I asked.

'Take the sealing stones; make a small portal; use your imagination, make it one way, it must be one way! Make it to the realm that matches its vibration, a lower realm, just think of sending it home, dear! And then… Chuck them in,' puffed Nanna, waving her tea towel round.

'Tally ho,' clapped the Major, captivated by Nanna's covert plans to vanquish a multidimensional weapon.

'On my own!' I objected, slightly overwhelmed by the task in hand.

'No, no, dear, many hands make light work,' she said.

'Well, let's get down there before the boozing starts,' suggested the Major.

'You shouldn't be going anywhere,' snapped Nanna with half a smile. 'But yes, you're right, let's get a move on,' said Nanna as she opened the paper and began to cast her eye over the village news.

'Nanna!' I shouted.

'Oh yes, of course, let's be getting on then,' she said, a playful smirk rising over her face. I think she was just trying to relieve the potentially weighty situation.

Despite Nanna's nagging the Major insisted on coming. He nipped home and freshened up first; myself and Mr Milly accompanied him. I was still wary of the cottage; there was a residual memory of last night's events. The light and the dark had both made their mark, leaving the atmosphere somewhat changed. It had for the moment lost its comfort and cosiness; the frequency that hung in the air was a stark one, there was nothing soft about it. I'm sure though, with time it would return, and once again I could sink happily into his high-back chair. Nanna poked her head around the front door.

'We ready then! Chattersley will be thirsty,' she said.

We made our way down the lane and onto the main road. A car approached from behind and let out a friendly toot; I turned to see the Smythes' car. Mrs Smythe gave us a lovely smile and wave, while Ronnie and Buster's beaming faces were both fighting for space, trying to impress their most grotesque look upon the glass. They broke into a squabble, their flaying arms and legs visible through the fogged glass. Mrs Smythe's smile turned into a grimace, shouting into the rear-view mirror at the bothersome brothers.

'It'll be busy,' said the Major, waving at the car.

'Good, plenty of cover to get those bottles,' replied Nanna, pausing, watching them pass. I carried on walking, Mr Milly eagerly pulling me on.

'Come on,' nipped the Major as Nanna was still stood fixed in thought.

'Err, Bob... Why don't you go and fetch Dolly? Save our legs later. Don't worry, I'll drive back,' she said. The Major look perplexed.

'Well... If that's what you want,' he replied. Nanna passed him the keys to Ivy Gate. 'See you in a bit then,' said the Major. He didn't complain, for he knew there was more to it.

CHAPTER 15

Chattersley Beers

It was just before eleven when we reached the village. The sun was beating down, and already the aroma of barbequed food drifted our way on the slightest of summer breezes. Various stalls were set out on the village green, with a large marquee pegged down in the centre backing onto the duck pond. I could see a few familiar faces; Mr Vanishall was manning a coconut shy. I wondered if he'd done the old trick of nailing them down.

'Ooh, there's Maggie,' said Nanna, making a beeline for her stall. 'Have a snoop, keep it low key,' she said then wandered off. Sometimes I was lost for words with just how blasé she was about the whole thing. I mean, wasn't this an epic battle of light and dark, wasn't Chattersley and humanity itself in the grips of a corrupt, distorted mechanism that only ever wanted to see us suffer, keeping this whole existence in a cycle of pain. Didn't she realise that these beer bombs could go off at any moment, opening a rip for all manner of evil entity to pour through? Didn't she? Why did I feel the weight of responsibility was ever-increasing on me, while Nanna buggered off for a natter? I had to believe it was because she wasn't subscribing to the drama, thus not giving it energy. She remained detached, but above all, I trusted her absolutely.

I sighed, letting out my frustration, when a familiar voice pricked my ears.

'It's not that bad, is it?' asked a sweet feminine tone, as a fragrance of fresh meadows preceded her. Rosy Saddler rounded my field of view, blotting out the streaking sun that filled my squinting eyes. She sucked on a cherry-coloured boiled sweet lolly. 'Is it then?' she asked again, somehow having an effect on my body's temperature and my ability to think and speak rationally.

'Is what?' I replied, confused by her questioning.

'Is it that bad?' she said playfully, always keeping her smile from just rising. I puffed out, exhausted by the enormity of a possible explanation.

'Nar, it's all right really… just boys' stuff.' She paused, the lolly encased between her lips.

'Boys stuff? Like in the video with Shaun? Or the mirror in the shop? Or the big! Black! Cat on the moor! I will find out, I know you know…' She poked; at that moment a buzzing came from my backpack. *Cradlick,* I thought, quickly removing the bag from my shoulders. I knelt down and located my walkie-talkie.

'Pete… Pete… it's me, Shaun… Can you hear me?' Cradlick's voice was hushed but clear.

'Is that Shaun! Where is he!' she snapped. Rosy didn't wait for an answer, she grabbed the device from my hands and shouted at it. 'Where are you! You were supposed to come over last night! Where were you? You better not be messing with that cheap ride Tina

Gunwin!' Rosy, clearly not one to mess with, fumed at the walkie-talkie, glaring sternly upon it waiting for her boyfriend's pitiful excuse.

'Pete… Pete… can you hear me…?' Came Shaun's meek covert voice.

'Didn't he hear a flaming word!' she snapped.

'You have to press the speak button, the green one, on the bottom,' I replied hesitantly, afraid I may be next to suffer her wrath. She then proceeded to fiddle with the device, pressing the button then releasing with Cradlick, only getting drips of drabs of an angry ranting girlfriend. In the end, Rosy's frustration won over as she slapped the walkie-talkie back into my hand.

'Boys stuff!' she said with a vicious edge, her serenity all but evaporated now. She turned and stomped off towards Maggie's stall. *Phew,* I thought for a moment she'd joined team dark.

Back to the matter in hand, I pressed the talk button. 'Shaun… Shaun, where are you, over?' there was a slight pause then he replied.

'Bloody hell! Was that Rosy!'

'Yes, she isn't best pleased… over,' I said.

'I'm round the back of the beer tent, Newley's chatting to Pat Gunwin,' replied Cradlick.

'Does he have the beer bottles with him…? Over,' I asked.

'Yeah, yeah, he brought a case in… Plo… dd… ers… pun… ch,' he replied, reading the bottles' aptly named labels.

'Plodders Punch!' I said out loud. Ill Newley's sarcastic quip made me wonder if he even knew what they would do. I didn't associate humour with the dark I'd encountered so far, that was my optimistic side speaking. In reality, I bet he laughed when branding them, thinking of the terror it would strike in the very heart of Chattersley's sleepy bubble. There is one thing for certain, cruel souls have taken the world by siege throughout history, and now one of those twisted callous beings was in charge of law and order in our own back yard.

The walkie-talkie crackled as Cradlick opened the channel. 'What's with the beers?' he asked.

'They're explosives… over,' I replied.

'Explosives? Like they're too fizzy?' he asked.

'No! No! …Oh err… just wait, I will be round in a minute… over,' I replied, slightly frustrated at trying to explain the details of a multidimensional weapon, that I had no clue about. I realised how silly it sounded, but as stupid as it may be, I was now more than confident in the dark's ability to spawn some nightmarish terror right into our reality, right under our noses. Without the night as a projector, or an ominous spine-chilling scene, it would strike Chattersley at its most vibrant and loving. When everyone had come together to celebrate their wonderful piece of English countryside. Spirits were high; people laughing and chatting, completely unaware of what could be just around the corner.

I made my move across the green, keeping low, staying on the perimeter, rounding the back of the fete's many stalls. I didn't want Ill Newley clocking me; the longer our intentions stayed hidden, the better. I was almost home and dry, seeing Cradlick behind the side of the marquee. His face looked alarmed as he beckoned me to come quickly.

'Come on! He's coming!' he said in hushed panic. Mr Milly lurched forward, compromising my footing. I cleared the front of the tent just as Ill Newley strode out, my left foot catching one of the tent pegs, sending me flying into Cradlick. We rolled in a bundle, coming to a stop just feet from the duck pond, where the resident flock freaked out and took to the sky in a fluster. 'Bloody hell! Watch it!' moaned Cradlick.

'Sorry... sorry,' I said, apologising for my clumsiness. Cradlick paused, listening, his senses attuned to the locality of the local constabulary. The thud of a purposeful stride came our way.

'Move it,' panicked Cradlick, pushing me towards the tent flap. Luck was on our side; Pat Gunwin was busying himself by the entrance. We quickly crawled towards the long serving table draped with a catering cloth.

I could see Ill Newley's black polished boots through the gap; he rocked back and forth, then bent down to examine the unsecured flap.

'Quick, get under now!' I said, pushing Cradlick as he lifted the table cloth; to our uttermost surprise our soon to be hideaway was already occupied.

'Buster! Ronnie!' I gasped.

'Quick, in! In!' nudged Cradlick. We all shoved into the narrow space. I pulled in Mr Milly's tail just as Cradlick dropped the cloth in the nick of time.

'Shush, shush!' I said. Buster's face was all lit up but soon sensed the severity of the situation.

'Oh... trouble...' he whispered as he tossed the beer bottle in his hand to Ronnie.

'You open it, I can't,' he whispered. They'd only got one of Ill Newley's special brew.

'No! No! Don't,' I said through clenched teeth.

'Bloody hell! Boring. It's only the copper's brew… bet it's like a shandy,' said Ronnie.

'Give it here!' I snatched the bottle from Ronnie, who curled his face at my uncharacteristic action.

'All right, calm down,' he sneered. I could see the assumption gathering in his mind; he glared at Cradlick, seemingly blaming him for my behaviour.

'Hey kid, it's nowt to do wi' me!' explained Cradlick, bearing his open palms.

'Sorry,' I said sheepishly. 'It's hard to explain, but this is bad!' I said, pointing at the bottle.

'It's only beer,' giggled Buster.

I hadn't got the faintest where to begin. *Do I start at the beginning?* We simply didn't have time for a trip down the memory lane of a newly awoken, dimensional-shifting, reality-crafting ten-year-old boy.

'Look, it's just bad, it's not what it seems! Ill Newley is bad! He is going to use these to do something terrible,' I exclaimed.

'What? Give them the squits! Or is it really strong stuff?' asked Ronnie genuinely.

'No! No! Kill them, he is going to kill people,' I said, wishing now I'd kept the brothers in the loop. I looked at Cradlick for help; he acknowledged my silent request and pitched in.

'Look, summat's up. I've seen things, weird things, bad stuff that don't belong in this world. I believe Pete… you should too,' said Cradlick sternly. The Smythe brothers paused, sharing a look. 'Show them,' said Cradlick, pointing at the bottle.

I didn't know what to do. As Nanna had said, 'What's the trigger?'

Could it go off at any moment? I thought quickly and rummaged through my backpack, pulling out the pouch of sealing stones, and tipped them out on the grass floor, arranging them in a small circle.

'What's he doing?' asked Buster. Cradlick just shook his head and watched intently as I went about my preparation. I zoned out for a minute, bringing the power of Mother Earth up and the energy of our source down. A familiar tingle surged and pulsed through my energy centres, dropping the Veil. I opened my eyes to see my companions glowing gloriously, each surrounded in a living painting depicting their every emotion. I clasped the amulet round my neck and focused, feeling it hum with energy. When I thought it was fully charged, I let it flow to the other stones. They all glowed with a soft peaceful light.

'Right,' I said.

'What's the plan?' asked Cradlick.

'If I create a portal to send it back… if I hold it in and open the cap, it will explode in that dimension, right?' I suggested, none too confident in my untested procedure for safely disarming a multidimensional beer bomb.

Cradlick shrugged his shoulders. 'Sounds good,' he said, wide-eyed, taking it all in.

'OK, here goes nothing.' I held the bottle which was now emitting a velvety purple mist; the liquid inside was luminous green. Looking closer at the bottle, I saw a gateway to another world. Inside was a fog illuminated by a raging storm, cages swung high in the clouds, rising from a dark landscape, their hosts lifeless and forgotten. The presence within this lower dimension sensed me, hurtling my attention through a battle-torn sky. Faster and faster, my consciousness travelled until a pyramid rose on the horizon. Dust kicked up from marauding twisters, smothered the megalithic structure. The presence took me down two rows of menacing gargoyles; crows flocked in to see my arrival and settled on their stone flesh. Finally, the motion rolled to a stop. Stood in front of the towering pyramid was a great winged creature, hunched over, its eyes piercing through the murk staring straight into my soul, its grey skin wings entombing the rest of its grotesque form. This is what waited, this is what was behind it all, the control, the game of reincarnation, this is the power holding life on earth by the balls. It lurked in the background, a nameless threat that haunted humanity's existence.

I felt its coldness and utter contempt for mankind. We were mere fodder, it relished our deaths and suffering. For thousands of years the blood of war had been its elixir. Slowly the ancient creature opened its giant skin sails, revealing a silhouetted human figure. The figure paced forward into the bronze light; its face began twitching and snapping back and forth, flicking through a who's who of history's worst warlords, villains, killers and corrupt rulers. As it cycled through them, I felt its lurking presence masquerading in all of their rotten deeds. They did its bidding on our earthly plane, mostly unaware of the ancient puppeteer that manipulated them. Buried deep in Ikron's essence, a far-flung memory crawled forward. I knew this place, it was a terrible merciless realm that I had once battled my way out of.

I'd seen what I needed to, and it had seen me. I pulled back, breaking my connection with the lower dimension. The bottle fizzed and started to vibrate in my hand. Buster tucked in behind Cradlick. I thought of the stones and sending the bottle home; instantly a small portal opened, the size of a dressing table mirror. I held the bottle over the shimmering gateway, but it repulsed the bottle just as opposed magnets would do, pulling this way and that, any way but in.

278

'Come on! Come on!' I said, panicked.

I called on Ikron, and he soon roared forward, encasing my arm in the familiar silver-blue glass armour, giving me the power to push the bottle through. It was half in when the cap popped off and exploded. A tremendous blast blew us back with a piercing bang; the table cloth flew into the air, scattering its tasty spread everywhere. The arms of the dark dimension surged out, grabbing at anything they could, but it lasted seconds as it was sucked back into the gateway. I quickly cut the power to the stones and gathered them up.

'Bloody hell!' cried Buster, his eyes filling up. 'What was that!?' he continued.

'Move! Move! They're coming,' shouted Cradlick, as the sound of concerned voices approached the tent.

We all scrambled out of the flap that Ill Newley had incompetently secured; running for cover, we settled behind an unmanned Hook a Duck. Everyone was gathered around the tent, not suspecting our involvement at all.

'Phew! How close,' I panted.

'Best not look suss; mingle, and they won't suspect owt,' said Cradlick, sharing his pearls of wisdom from a misspent adolescence. We all nodded, catching our breath, lost more to the shock of the situation than physical exertion. Cradlick nodded towards the crowd of Chatterslians gathered at the marquee entrance. 'Come on then. Remember, spread out.'

We followed his instructions and tried to look as innocent as we could; the crowd was distracted, and we managed to filter into the back rows unnoticed, sharing glances between each other for none of us knew how this would play out.

Cradlick was the calmest, looking like a proper little tinker mooching within the gossiping villagers, making his way to the front. What he didn't see was his rather disgruntled girlfriend approach from behind. When in range she punched him on the arm. Cradlick's face was a picture; he spun round, his heart almost visible in his mouth. 'Bloody 'ell, Rosy!' he said, sinking into an anxious relief.

'Where you been!!?' she snarled.

'Look, Rose, not now. Honestly, I will tell you later. There's some heavy shit going down.' His face said it all. We shared a glance as Rosy followed Cradlick's eyes highlighting the Smythe boys and me; our collective expressions of controlled fear and panic tamed her agitated reaction. She placed her hand on Cradlick's shoulder and squeezed gently. Her eyes softened, letting him off the hook till later. Cradlick winked and kissed her cheek, whispering in her ear. She hugged him tight, and all was forgiven, their trust in each other made obvious.

The voices from inside the tent grew more intense, pulling Cradlick's attention back to the mission in hand. He broke their embrace, and we all moved forward towards the marquee's entrance. I poked my head through a small gap between two old dears trying to get a better look. Pat Gunwin was stood in the centre of the mess surrounded by sandwiches and sausage rolls, his hand placed across his brow. He puffed and sighed. Old Mrs Flowers was flapping with another equally distressed apron-clad lady over a decimated cake that lay on the floor. Ill Newley was searching for his prize home brew, rummaging under the table. He pulled the crate out intact.

'It's OK!! It's OK! I've got them! All's not lost,' announced Ill Newley, loud and clear as he hoisted the crate onto the tabletop; turning to the gathered Chattersley populous, his face ashen, sweat visible upon his forehead.

The crowd hushed at the officer's misplaced statement; all eyes were on him. The cogs began to turn through the group; ripples of questions surfaced.

'Bully for you!' snapped Mr Vanishall, looking despondently at the colourful collage his savoury selection had made upon the inside of the marquee.

'What about my cake! I spent hours on it!' barked Mrs Flowers, her angry, pointy figure aimed at Ill Newley's apparent disregard for the rest of the villagers' misfortune.

The grumbles spread; the gathering now arguing with each other over nothing. I could feel the vibration change. Maggie and Nanna were inside the tent at the side observing the pantomime as it infolded. Nanna clocked me and beckoned me over; I pushed my way through the rabble.

'You?' she said.

'It was going to go off!' I exclaimed.

'You sent it back?' she asked.

'Yes, yes, it went, but it didn't want to. I saw it, I saw the place!' I said, the distress clear in my strained, hushed voice.

Nanna nodded and pulled me in. 'Good lad. Now we've just got to get the rest,' she said, looking at Ill Newley just as he prepared himself for another announcement.

The sickened officer leant back upon the table; looking increasingly pale and weary, he gathered himself.

'Quiet! Stop it... Quiet!' he snapped, but the ramble didn't respond. His patience broke, and the negative beast surfaced within him. 'Oyh! Shut your moaning, whingeing racket! You're all nothing but a collection of old fossils and farts!!' Ill Newley's outcry was tipped with cruelty and venom as his contempt for the sleepy village crowd poured out.

He swayed, looking like he'd had one too many. Chattersley's disgruntled mob began to hush until silence fell, everyone's attention now focused on their beloved officer of justice who looked increasingly dishevelled. He pulled at his collar in an attempt to ease his discomfort. I didn't know quite what was happening, but it appeared that Ill Newley's disguise was unravelling.

The distorted soul inhabiting his mortal body was unable to hide anymore. Nanna and Maggie held a focus upon him, as my amulet pulsed in sequence with pressure upon my brow. I yielded to the energies, and my vision slipped into the Veil, providing a filtered perspective of this and that reality. The auras of the crowd were visibly bubbling with oranges and flecks of red. Sparks floated in the air; a diminishing residue left from the arguing.

I was drawn to their feet and the thick smoky carpet that wrapped its way around them; it came from Ill Newley, he was engulfed in a burgundy and black mist, his eyes burning as if they were two red-hot pieces of coal. Nanna was pushing a sphere towards him; it was her usual brand of magnificent bliss. Although she was subtly exercising her multidimensional mastery, it was oblivious that Ill Newley couldn't take the influx of light and his cruel animator was bursting to get out.

A whirring started in his stomach, growing denser and darker until a black pillar shot out extending from his head and feet which were now embedded in a pool of tar. The whirring spun faster and faster as his breath increased. He stopped suddenly and inhaled, shooting a droning cloud of sooty negativity from his mouth.

'Nothing to say! Nothing!' he raged, snapping me back to the physical realm. Ill Newley turned to the crate of beer and rested his head upon it while chatting nonsense under his breath. Mr Vanishall stepped forward and tentatively began to speak.

'You OK, son? Do you need some air…? Why don't you take a seat… and I'll… I'll get you a drink?' Ill Newley remained in his strange adopted position, not answering immediately, but soon began to chuckle, his laugh mixed with coughs increasing to a manic state until he spun round.

'A drink…! A drink…! What an excellent idea, baldy!' scolded Newley. Mr Vanishall touched his smooth, shiny head; his face looked hurt by the cruel officer's words. 'Let's all have a drink… Here!' he said, picking a bottle from the crate and throwing to Mr Vanishall. 'It's on me!' snarled Ill Newley as he swayed over to the nervous-looking shop keeper. His persona shrouded Mr Vanishall in anguish and threat.

The burly villager shrivelled, looking weak and frightened, engulfed by the officer's negativity. Ill Newley pushed his sweaty ashen face into Mr Vanishall's space. 'Open it…' he said, rounding on him. 'Opennn… it,' he repeated with a lower tone. Ill Newley's confidence had found a new lease of life; his state had quickly transitioned from a drunken boxer on the ropes, to a mastermind villain, feeling his evil mission was nearing a grand finale. He played with poor Mr Vanishall as he fumbled for his key chain.

I looked at Nanna. 'Do something!' I said.

Nanna took her gaze from Ill Newley and nodded. Mr Vanishall lifted the bottle and placed his key chain opener round the pressed metal cap; he was about to pull when a small girl appeared at the front of the crowd.

'Daddy… Daddy,' she said, her voice unsure and frightened. Ill

Newley stopped and glared at the girl. 'Why are you mad, Daddy?' she questioned, to which he poked his neck forward, pulling a contorted face.

'Because I am, you stupid brat!' The girl buried her head into her hands, crying, just as the safety of her mother's voice called.

'Alice… Alice!' yelled Ill Newley's wife, pushing her way to the front, crouching and cradling her daughter. She then turned to her compromised husband, 'Kevin! Really! What the hell has gotten into you…? Just look at you… Come, come home now, let's sort you out,' she said, angry but sympathetic to her partner's obvious change in character. The corrupt copper strode over in a disjointed walk, as if his bones didn't fit his body anymore.

'No! No, I'm fine,' he said, crouching to his daughter's height and stroking her hair. 'Sorry dear, it's the stress you know,' his voice softening, sounding like the Newley we all knew. Alice turned and placed her arms around her beloved father's neck.

'It's OK,' she whispered through her tears.

'I'm sorry… I'm sorry you've had such a wet, boring, sad excuse for a dad! I'm sorry, but it's… it's my turn now!' he said with cruelty flooding back into his tones. Alice pulled her head back and released her grip, but Ill Newley quickly whisked her up into the air in a firm hold and returned to his place beside the anxious shopkeeper. 'Now you drink it! Or she will!' he shouted, snarling at Mr Vanishall.

'Leave her alone, Kevin!' shouted Newley's wife as she broke rank, attempting to retrieve her daughter, but Nanna held her arm out, stopping her.

'Enough now! Enough!' she scolded.

The marquee stood still as if time had frozen; the onlookers captivated by the goings-on, not realising they were bait upon a poisoned hook. Nanna stepped forward.

'Jim… don't listen to him, go on about your business now.' Mr Vanishall turned to Nanna with a look of dread. We knew a sickness churned deep in his stomach, screaming to him that this whole situation was seriously wrong. He was stuck between the light and the dark. 'Nothing to see now, leave us to sort this out,' called Nanna while signalling Maggie to usher the villagers out.

'Oh no! No! Look, I've plenty for all you miserable beggars!' spat Ill Newley who was greeted by a sea of confused, worried looks, all too eager to get out of the marquee now. Maggie got the last ones out with old Mrs Flowers bringing up the rear. 'Well, I quite fancied a tipple,' she griped.

Ronnie and Buster stood in the entrance, not knowing their place in this drama. I felt their internal struggle, between duty as friends and overwhelming fear of this absurdly bizarre story they had opened the door to. Their faces mirrored the day in the den when the Hound was close. I didn't know what to say. Thankfully Mrs Smythe resolved the situation, pulling them away as Maggie closed the marquee entrance leaving Mrs Newley with Cradlick, myself, Nanna and Mr Milly.

'You! You're always there, aren't you! A pain in the back of my head, with your ivory tower ruining everything!' barked Ill Newley, his attention switching to Nanna. 'You think you've got it covered… don't you! Well, you don't know everything! Who am I! Who am I!' he asked. There was a pause, a silence that Mr Vanishall, sweating and shaking, felt the need to fill.

'You're… PC Newley?' said Mr Vanishall, who cowered and shielded his face awaiting the answer to the seemingly obvious question. Ill Newley reared back, letting out a chilling hollow cackle. He laughed and laughed then surged forward right into his face.

'I'm a killer, that's what I am... Mr Dier gave me one last opportunity to take my fill of horror,' he said through gritted teeth, spitting in the shop keeper's face. 'Now drink so we can get this party started... I will be most! Offended! If you don't,' he snarled. Mr Vanishall's will was withering.

'It's only a beer?' he said, turning to Nanna whose lips moved, but the words were beaten by the fizz of the escaping air. Mr Vanishall had cracked the cap and opened the bottle, the gas flowed from the opening down onto the floor; a noxious smell of rotten meat and eggs weaved its way into our world laying a sick carpet for its honorary guests. The glass container lit up, and the storm within filled the marquee's ceiling with menacing clouds.

Ill Newley didn't wait; he pushed the bottle up to Mr Vanishall lips and made him chug the luminous green liquid down. Mr Vanishall stepped back and burped, dropping the bottle by his side.

'This should be interesting,' said Ill Newley while releasing his captive daughter then callously rubbing his hands together. Alice ran to the security of her mother; both exiting the marquee with haste.

'Pete! The stones, quick!' shouted Nanna. I pulled the velvet pouch from my pocket and tossed them to her. Nanna quickly emptied its contents on the floor behind Mr Vanishall, roughly making a circle by pushing the stones with her feet. He stumbled back and made a horrid whining noise. Ill Newley's face was full of expectant pleasure. Mr Vanishall dropped to his knees, clutching his stomach. This was accompanied by a low rumbling sound as a guttural scream came from within him. I winced, feeling the dread surrounding the shop keeper's fate.

Mr Milly pulled on her lead, desperately wanting to intervene. Cradlick looked at me, waiting for a cue, and we both then looked at Nanna who was bringing the portal online. Seconds felt like minutes. Mr Vanishall let out another cry as he was lit up from the inside in a yellow-green burst. Cradlick couldn't wait, and his instinct took over. He ran at Ill Newley side-on, catching him off guard. The scrappy youth shoulder barged him into the buffet tables, breaking them like a scene from a wrestling match. The enraged bent copper scrambled, ranting insults about Cradlick and his wayward family. He struggled to his feet trying to cohere his human doll into action as the light seemed to have compromised the effectiveness of the evil host upon its flesh-and-bone vehicle.

Cradlick gathered himself and quickly attended to Mr Vanishall, his lower half shrouded in a foot of noxious mist. He covered his mouth and nose and leant forward, placing his hand under the shop keeper's chin.

'Jim! Jim, come on!' called Cradlick, tilting his head towards him. Mr Vanishall's eyes were shut, but a snotty liquid seeped from their corners. He shivered and mumbled then another explosion sounded from inside, his gut lighting him up like a Christmas tree. His moans grew louder and louder until his eyes burst open; a blaze of molten goo flushed from them.

'Rrrruuuunnnnnn!!!!' screamed Mr Vanishall. Ill Newley was on his feet and almost upon my brave ally.

'Cradlick!' I shouted, quickly gaining his attention. He responded with swiftness, jumping and rolling to one side.

'Do something!' pleaded Cradlick.

The possessed copper paused as Mr Vanishall rose to his feet, seemingly hoisted by an invisible force. He grew and stretched far beyond his actual physical form. The brown shop smock that he religiously wore ripped down the middle as a row of dark brown spines pierced through it.

Ill Newley's face was one of wonder; of an expectant father awaiting the arrival of his pride and joy to be. It was at that point I saw him go; poor Mr Vanishall's soul left his Halloween costume of a body. I saw his energy, he didn't know where to go, or what to do as he was trapped right in the middle of a dark vortex.

'Go! Go! Get away from here!' I shouted. He must have watched his body being cast aside like a tattered old rag by a presence that didn't belong on earth. We all looked on as the lower-dimensional being exposed itself from Vanishall's remains. It was like the gargoyles I'd seen in the bottle; stony, ash flesh and piercing red eyes, its arms were long and sinewy, hanging almost to the floor. The winged horror stretched out, filling its macabre form with energy, its bony fingers tipped with barbed, serrated nails clicked together as if tasting the atmosphere. With only a few seconds to take it in, I realised this was a fallen angel, a harbinger of death sent by the ones who came to enslave us. I sensed its intelligence; it wasn't just a horrid killing machine, it was smart, smarter than us or so it thought. Every negative quality poured out of its vibration. Cruelty and arrogance seemed top of the tree; it didn't know empathy or kindness, it was void of them, it was made without them. I saw in my mind's eye galaxies far and wide. I saw a powerful force ruling them in pain, taking and destroying anything good; beneath the ghastly Halloween gargoyle stood evil in its purest form.

'Vileoment,' I muttered, seeing the word pass over my internal storyboard.

'A death angel,' commented Cradlick, making his own assumptions.

'Worse,' I replied.

'Boys!' shouted Nanna, nodding towards the glimmering portal behind the beast.

'Bring him, Pete! Bring him now!' she commanded.

I did think, *Bloody hell! Can't you step in for once?* but with a big gulp, I quickly did my preparation.

'Bring who?' said Cradlick. I just looked and shrugged my shoulders, returning quickly to my focus. Light flooded the marquee. Nanna was on full bore – a torrent of diamond white light poured through her, anchoring into the ground.

'Come on, come now,' I murmured as the ancient creature began to adjust to our reality. Between squeezing my eyes shut and focusing I could see the beast glitch. Part of it disappeared; clearly it was a multi-dimensional being and would be hard to track once loose.

'I'd do it now, Pete!' said Cradlick. The familiar rushing of air surfaced and the ringing in my ear grew. 'Here he comes!' I thought and *bang,* just like that Ikron charged from the back of my subconscious, across time and space into our reality. My connection grew stronger every time. I felt more and more present within him and him within me. Cradlick stood open-mouthed as I towered above him. Ill Newley looked like a cockroach, and the death angel looked like it had seen a ghost. It let out a defiant roar exposing its needle-like teeth.

'Push it in, send it back!' shouted Nanna. She had cast a net of light around the creature and was pulling it back into the portal. It shrieked and writhed, fighting to free itself.

Ill Newley backed off, his gleeful face washed with cowardly fright. He made for the remaining bottles while our struggle continued. Cradlick and Mr Milly clocked the fleeing copper and cut him off before he could reach the stash. Mr Milly showed her true colours; Ill Newley now showed his, a coward and a bully, weak and sly. He looked for an escape, lunging for a bottle which he tossed into the air, creating a distraction. Cradlick dived backwards and caught it just before it hit the floor as the dodgy copper disappeared through the tent entrance.

Ikron strode over to the creature; the power gathered within was immense. I felt it outweighed the foe before me tenfold. Clutching its scaly neck, I pushed as Nanna pulled it back. I saw the wars within its blood-red eyes, millennia of distortion snuffing out light by force.

They reigned over space and time, there was so much we didn't know, but Earth was different, Earth was its jewel, its stronghold where it had perfected and implemented intricate layers of corruptions, creating a constant recycling system of pain and fear, for this is what they ultimately lusted for.

Earth was a prototype, for this is what awaited all inhabited planets. They had learnt over time that the vibration of fear was lost with the annihilation of a species. These ancient beings now played a long, dark game. A game where control would never be questioned. The victim planet would just take it for granted that evil and cruelty, death and wars were just part of their existence. I felt the anger rising; Ikron burst alight in a plume of violet ivory fire as I pushed the horrid excuse of life back into the mirrored portal. Ikron's plate glass gauntlet sparked as if held against a grinding wheel as it crossed into the shadow realm. The dark entity lashed out and struggled but was no contest for Ikron's divine power. Goodness was fighting back through the echoes of time; bravery and hope, love and light were back, and I was blessed enough to wield them.

'Release it now! Now, Pete! Now!' shouted Nanna as she was about to cut the power to the portal. I had half of Ikron's arm in the other dimensions. I felt powerful, I felt untouchable, I felt like I wanted to obliterate this horrid being in my hands. I wanted it to suffer, to feel the pain it had cast upon the innocent souls trapped in Earth's life-and-death cycle. I wanted to tread upon its very essence and grind it into nothing. I felt, I felt… cruelty creeping in. 'Let go now!' shouted Nanna again. But my hand was stuck, I was trapped in this feeling, transfixed in the suffering I was capable of creating. The shadow realm bore its magnetic influence upon me. I realised what was happening, I was being drawn into the portal as the dark angel had compromised Ikron's defences in the subtlest of ways.

I looked to Nanna for help, and without a second thought, she cut the power, redirecting the energy into her hands which she then blasted at me. 'Let go now!' she called out, discharging a beam of focused light which hit my arm just as I released the enemy. Ikron was knocked back and shrunk back into his waiting place. The portal shrunk in front of me and to my horror had trapped Mr Vanishall's confused soul into its negative pull.

'No! No!' I screamed, watching his ethereal form disappear into the shadow realm. Nanna ran over and checked I was OK.

'Poor Jim,' she said, cradling my head.

'He's gone there, with those awful things!' I cried.

'There's always a way back home, a way back to where we all came from,' sighed Nanna, attempting to comfort me. 'It's not over, dear, we still need to get rid of those bottles… or?' mused Nanna stroking her chin. 'Quick, bring the crate over here,' she said, pointing at the floor. Cradlick placed the crate down gingerly as instructed.

Nanna gathered the stones, placing them around Ill Newley's

homebrew. She lit them up and brought the light down. Cradlick's face was a picture; his mouth was constantly open in awe at the secrets this world had hidden from us.

'Defusing them?' he asked.

'Oh, I think we can do better than that, let's say a slight modification, shall we?' she said, winking.

The crate was engulfed in a sparkling white sphere; the negative grasp on the multi-dimensional beer bombs struggled to hold on, lightning flickered within the glowing dome as it expanded in a final flourish then sucked back with a bang into the rattling bottles. Now the glowing green mist was replaced with glittering particles and shimmering clouds. 'Oh yes, I think that will do!' said Nanna, quite pleased with the results.

'What's in them? What will they do?' quizzed Cradlick.

'Not sure,' puffed Nanna, 'but it will most certainly be more hospitable than its previous form,' she added with a smile.

'Ill Newley?!' I shouted, remembering our mission.

'He got away!' replied Cradlick.

'Come on, this is far from over, boys,' commanded Nanna, gesturing us to get up.

'What about Mr Vanishall? What will they say? What will we say?' I said, looking back at his tattered smock. Nanna paused, the possible consequences visibly flickering across her mind. She then strode over and gathered his remaining clothes, bundling them up in his old smock. 'I suppose a disappearance is easier to explain than what really happened. Well, for now. It will work itself out, dear,' she said, gazing longingly at the place where he fell. 'Come on! And bring those bottles,' instructed Nanna. Cradlick picked the crate up. I patted my leg, and Mr Milly fell in close.

We all emerged from the marquee; the crowd hadn't gone far and were most likely treated to an epic light and sound show. I imagined the marquee was lit up with booms and bangs, and the soundtrack must have been very disturbing, the horrid screams of Mr Vanishall then the roar of Ikron finishing with Nanna shouting, 'Let go!' followed by her blast of dazzling light. It didn't take long before they swamped us with a torrent of questions.

'What's going on? When's the bar open?!' asked old Mrs Flowers.

'Where's Jim?' asked Pat Gunwin.

Then Maggie rushed forward. 'Liz! Liz! He took her... He's got Rosy!' she said, panicked.

'Rosy! Where?!' barked Cradlick.

'I saw him come out of the tent, he stumbled into her, then took her...' said Maggie.

'We thought she must have been involved in wrecking the fete,' said Mrs Smythe.

'He put her in his van and drove off out toward the moor,' added Maggie.

'Right! Come on, boys... and girl,' said Nanna, looking down at Mr Milly. We pushed our way through the rattled mob. Nanna had spotted Dolly parked up; the Major was leant up her having a puff on his pipe, minding his own business. 'Come on, Bob! Business to do!' she called over as we approached.

'Business...? Funny business?' he quizzed, opening the door, spying the clinking crate of bottles. 'Oooh, nice road beers,' he joked.

'Yes to the funny business and no to the beers,' answered Nanna sternly. The Major rolled his eyes as we all piled in; he got behind the wheel and looked for instruction from his aged companion.

'The moor,' she said.

'By Foxes Den?' he asked to which Nanna nodded. He sparked the little car into life and we set off up the road.

'Looks like we've got company,' said the Major, glancing into the rear-view mirror. I looked back to see the Smythes' car pull out, seemingly follow us.

'They could just be going home?' I said.

'Hhmmm, we could do without anyone else getting involved,' replied Nanna. As we approached the turning for Ivy Gate she stared long and hard, holding her beloved sanctuary in her field of vision for as long as she could. I felt her focus casting out an energetic line to those who may be listening.

'Look up there! That's his van!' exclaimed Cradlick, pointing in the distance to the fluorescent chevron vehicle.

'Good, he hasn't got far!' replied Nanna.

'Where's he going?' asked Cradlick.

'I don't think he knows, he's panicked!' I said.

'Oh, I think he knows whether he realises or not,' answered Nanna.

'What the dickens has gone on anyway!' asked the Major. I found his delayed interest amusing considering the disarray he'd observed at the fete. Surely this was the biggest news to hit Chattersley since 'Pork's', the prize-winning pig, escaped from the Smythes' farm. 'Pork's' was hit by several cars, causing significant damage to the vehicles before waddling home without a scratch. Ronnie and Buster labelled him 'Super Pork's' after that; funny how my mind wanders at the most inappropriate times.

The police van was around a mile in front; it carried straight on at the crossroads without stopping, narrowly missing a cyclist, who swerved, losing control, bailing off into the thick heather verge.

'Holme Road… You're right then,' said the Major.

'I gathered his compass would be pointing to a strong negative vibration,' said Nanna.

'Is he going to Blackend then?' I asked.

'More than likely, he will feel stronger there, he will be more of a handful,' replied Nanna.

'Great!' I replied sarcastically.

'Come on, Bob, make her hum,' said Nanna, egging on the old Major to push her little Dolly faster. The engine buzzed as he shifted it down and pushed the throttle to the floor. We bounced our way over the potholed road, arriving at the gravel parking area in no time, the scene of where it all seemed to go very wrong, where Newley was lost to this world.

The van was left abandoned by the cattle gate with its door wide open; the Major pulled up next to it. There was no sign of Rosy or Ill Newley.

'They can't have gone far,' said the Major. Nanna looked back at the crate of bottles and bit her lip.

'We can't drag that around with us. Chuck a couple in your bag, dear,' she said.

I did as she asked, shoving them in, using Blue as cushioning. Something caught my eye at in the bottom of my rucksack; I pushed the contents to one side so I could identify the object. *The light shedder key?* I thought, knowing I didn't put it there.

'Everything all right?' said Nanna, half turning her face, giving me a knowing wink to which I nodded in return.

'Teddies bit old for you, hey kid,' smiled Cradlick. We all piled out and headed off toward the gate. Nanna stopped, having a second thought.

'Bob? Eeerrr… be a love, watch the car will you…? Just in case anyone follows,' asked Nanna persuasively, nodding at the empty road that carried the faint hum of an approaching vehicle. I sensed she didn't want her dear friend being dragged into any more battles.

'You could have left me at the Den then!' he griped.

'Come on, Bob, be a love…' said Nanna, appealing to the Major's better side.

'Oh all right then, of course,' he said, sounding a little dejected. She smiled and touched his hand fondly before we carried on our way. When we were out of earshot, she replied to my unvoiced musing.

'Yes, dear, he has fought enough for one lifetime,' she said as we jogged down the tree-lined path.

CHAPTER 16

In the Pines

The air was thick with the smell of fresh pine; clean as washing, but it also carried a summer chill with it: or was it the prospect of what awaited us on the moor that pricked my hair on end? My stomach was heavy with apprehension and my mouth bone dry. I gulped, but my arid throat made swallowing laboured. *Were we off to our doom?* I mused.

'Enough, that's quite enough! Not here, not now, watch those thoughts!' barked Nanna.

'Sorry,' I replied meekly.

The track led off down into a fir tree plantation; we bore left. I glanced back to the car park where the Smythes' car had just pulled up. The Major would have his hands full explaining this little lot. On either side the wood became dense; thankfully the much-used gravel path made our progress swift, well, as swift as a masquerading dimension-shifting OAP could go. She still looked burdened by the rules of this reality; her body was her shell, and it wasn't as sprightly as it had been. Age and gravity bore its weight upon Nanna like us all; it was her mind that was free, it could run like wild horses and soar as eagles do. High into the heavens, that's where you'd find Nanna or Shelaya in the freedom of her thoughts. That's when I realised that our attachment to the physical form was our anchor in this life of deceptions.

Cradlick bounced along with ease, his leather jacket flapping open. He certainly wasn't the usual type to be traversing this landscape. With his heavy boots thumping along like a deep barrel kick drum, his grungy dissident look was more at home at a grimy backstreet gig than the wilds of the Yorkshire Moors. Mr Milly was ahead by ten to twenty feet when she suddenly stopped and whined into the blanket of thick pine trees.

'What is it, dear?' asked Nanna, coming to a halt. She squatted down to Mr Milly's view line and stroked the back of her head.

'In there!?' I panted, catching my breath.

'The heather looks trampled, and that branch has been snapped,' added Cradlick.

'Hmm… predictable, very predictable?' mused Nanna.

'Where does it go?' I asked.

'Well, it would bring you out on the edge of Sackhole Moor… but…?' said Nanna, deep in thought.

'Come on then! He will be getting further ahead!' insisted Cradlick, his eagerness to rescue Rosy overflowing. Our attention was drawn to the pine tree nearest, from which a familiar angelic sound tweeted.

'Wit!' I exclaimed with delight. The little rosewood bird fluttered over and landed on my shoulder, her language embroidered with chimes and bells was as magical as ever.

Cradlick's face displayed his distinct brand of disbelief as Wit buzzed around expelling gold glitter every time she got excited. 'How did you know, Wit?' I asked. Nanna winked as Wit flew over to her. 'When you looked at Ivy Gate… you called her,' I added.

'Just throwing thoughts about, better than using those silly telephones, hey Wit?' smirked Nanna. Wit's excitement grew; her innocent notes began to bear some subtle signs of darker chords. 'Come on then, show, before it chars your wings,' said Nanna. With that Wit burst into a sphere of sunlight illuminating Nanna's aura as they both connected.

I could see the images like before; Nanna had her eyes closed, concentrating on the incoming feed. I saw Ill Newley dive off the path pulling a bedraggled Rosy into the blanket of pine trees. He pushed them aside and disappeared from view. Wit continued showing Ill Newley trampling through the wood, its floor thick with dried needles, his prisoner pulling, tugging and dragging her feet, trying to stall her kidnapper, but he was too strong, possessed by the villainess soul and driven by a dark power that called him on, deeper and deeper into its clutches, doing its bidding, corrupting the already lost spirit, making it eternally harder for it to ever return to the light.

They approached a low fog bank that swallowed the wood in front of them. Rosy cried out and fell to her knees. Ill Newley wouldn't stop, he grabbed her arm with both hands and dragged her into the fog. We watched as her feet disappeared. The images were now of swirling mist, lost in the confusions of the blinding fog. There was no focus, nothing to pick out until an object appeared just before Wit's feed finished. We saw a stone building nestled in the fog blanket, its weathered door swung ominously back and forth. On the floor, two channels ran clear through the pine needles; they led into the darkness within.

'What! What is it!?' snapped Cradlick.

'Did you see?' I asked.

'What! See what?! What's happening to Rosy!?' said our agitated companion. I was kind of relieved Cradlick wasn't fully linked to the Veil, if he had seen Wit's feed I fear he would have mindlessly charged off into the twisted grip of the dark. Nanna waved her hand in a calming motion.

'OK, let's follow their trail, but stick together,' she said sternly. I had the suspicion we wouldn't be coming out on the edge of Sackhole Moor. I figured Nanna knew this too. We had been coerced into playing a role in a horror story, and at this moment it wasn't our story, we weren't the authors, we were the dispensable characters used to add shades of light to the shadowed pages it was written on. 'Pete! Don't let them in!' said Nanna sharply, sensing my thoughts.

'Sorry!' I replied as we pushed aside the branches and entered the pine wood.

Cradlick easily picked out the footprints on the needled floor; he jogged off a little in front.

'Not too far,' called Nanna. Cradlick nodded but didn't take heed, maybe he might have if he had seen Wit's images. Our progress was slower; the wood floor was full of raised knotted roots hidden under a blanket of nature's toothpicks. I'd already tripped, twisting my ankle, and Nanna wasn't too steady on her feet either. 'Shaun, wait!' shouted Nanna as he bounded ahead, his feet not faltering, adrenaline heightening his senses and dexterity. He was nimble and eager to find Rosy. After seeing the cowardliness in Ill Newley's face, exposing the corrupt souls' weakness, Cradlick had sized his opponent and was on the hunt. He reached a ridge and stood still for a moment.

'Rosy! Rose!' he cried out into the darkened wood. We all heard what came next: a woman's wail echoed in the distance, it was a one of helplessness and terror. Cradlick called back, 'Rose!' He gave us a look knowing he should wait, but he didn't.

'Stop, Shaun! Stop, wait!' shouted Nanna. Mr Milly barked and set off after him but he turned and disappeared down the embankment. Mr Milly quickly reached his last position and stopped, looking out over the gloomy vista. She didn't proceed, just panted and looked back awaiting our arrival. We ran, disregarding our footing; the three of us stood silently on the ridge overlooking a large hollowed area of the wood. A thick carpet of fog sat at the bottom and engulfed all within it – nothing below its surface was visible. Wit buzzed onto my shoulder tinkling with solemn tones.

'Where is he, girl?' I said, stroking Mr Milly. She whined in response, uneasy at the prospect of what lay ahead.

'Shaun!' called Nanna.

'Cradlick!' I cried, but nothing came back. The fog swirled gently on top with a creeping satisfaction; it had concealed its secrets well, its whispering threats radiated into the scented air chilling my bones. 'What now!' I exclaimed, pacing back and forth in frustration. 'We can't leave him!' I snapped, not at Nanna, more at the manipulated situation we appeared to have been led into.

'Calm down, it's OK dear, remember your thoughts are energy… Control them… be their master, don't let them be the ruler of you,' she said in her usual serene way. The fog was a screen for which ill intentions hid behind. I gulped and reached for Nanna's outstretched hand, knowing we must dive into the unknown. She half-smiled and sighed, but her expression suddenly turned steely as we caught Cradlick's voice screech out, bursting free from the fog's concealment. He was in trouble. We shared a look for a split second, then turned and ran hand in hand into the murkiness.

'AAAAAHHHHHH! …Cradlick!!' I cried, a ferocious howl, a warning to those that lay within that hope and bravery were coming. The fog bank quickly consumed us; visibility was down to four or five feet.

'Stay close,' said Nanna. Cradlick's voice cried out again, as did Rosy's.

We went this and that way trying to home in on the source, but the sounds seemed to be swirling and confusing us. Everything looked the same; we had no idea where we were or where they were. Nanna stopped. 'Wait! Wait, a minute,' she commanded. 'As above…' she said, winking, starting the procedure for entering the Veil. I closed my eyes and imagined the light flooding up from the centre of the earth and shooting down from the source of all into my head. The light felt heavier here, taking more concentration to bring it down. A pulse rippled through my body and when the two met a sensation of bliss ran over my being. For a second I opened my eyes hesitantly, for we were in hostile territory; this wasn't the training grounds nestled in the safety of Ivy Gate. The fog was tinged purple, I could see it more as a physical entity now, the wisps and swirls sinisterly moulded and formed fingers and arms. Faces appeared and disappeared, trying to pull and twist us, but it was clear the light that encased our forms was painful for the mist to touch, for it nipped and reeled back as if touching a red-hot fire. All the same, it endeavoured to trip us, to mislead and split us up for together our light was stronger.

My companions' auras were still a sight to behold; the gloominess of the creeping fog made the light shine brighter, contrasting starkly against the filthy backdrop. Golds and yellows, baby blues and emerald greens, electric flecks of ice diamonds streaked through our living vibrations. The edges of our energetic painting weren't soft though, as I'd observed before, they were sharp and bold as our alertness shone through.

'Look... residual energy!' said Nanna, pointing at a faint trail of yellow and red particles floating in the air.

'Is that Cradlick's?' I asked.

'Hmm red... hothead... anger, temper... yellow can be mental energy... sounds like him,' mused Nanna.

'Come on! That way!' I said, pulling at Nanna who was now looking at another path; this one was different, smudges of brown and black, dark purple and blood reds floated above a trail of violet, pinks and yellows that were torn and melted. 'Rosy?!' I asked. Nanna nodded, pausing, deliberating over which path to follow, but her decision was made when we heard Cradlick call out again. This time there was a fight in his cry.

We set off in haste following the red particles, pushing the fingers of the fog back as they pinched and pulled at our limbs, the ghostly faces materialising right in front of us hissing and moaning. Nanna expanded her light sphere out further, and I followed suit; this made it harder for the crooked smog to reach us. The energetic trail led us farther into the woods. The Veil offered us little signs of our position; the purple blanket looked as if it went on and on. Cradlick's red and yellow streaks were getting more vibrant, though, and I could distinguish words in his voice now.

'He's close!' said Nanna. She looked at Wit and nodded. 'Up, girl, give us a better view if you can,' she said, instructing the oracle bird. With that, Wit buzzed off leaving a streaking golden trail as she pierced through the blanket. After a few seconds a broken image came into Nanna's aura; it flickered and glitched, but we got the gist. Wit was above the fog blanket relaying what she could see. We could see the white glow of our position and a faint red trail leading to Cradlick; he looked to be around a hundred yards or so away, and was heading towards a structure, its peaked roof breaching the fog's skin. Then we noticed other trails seemingly circling our position.

'That doesn't look good!' I said.

'Hush, dear,' replied Nanna, placing her finger up to her lips, not wanting to give the situation a victim's energy. The trails, four in total, glowed burgundy red and sharp black. They pierced through Wit's filter and were coming in from all sides. My unvoiced questions paused in anticipation now answered as the ghostly smog parted, letting the unseen foes approach.

'What are they?!' I exclaimed.

'Agents of ill, I'd say. Our presence has been noted,' tutted Nanna. I heard a familiar sound behind us, a sound that had turned my stomach when it first entered into my world. The roar, the howl, the grinding pounding sense of doom.

'Sulphur Hound,' I whispered.

'Hmm, multiple,' added Nanna.

'Come on! Before they get here!' I pleaded. Nanna nodded, and we raced off again into the unknown. She pulled me away from Cradlick's trail.

'He's that way!' I said.

'Trust me,' she replied, breathing heavier now as we covered the uneven ground more quickly. The Sulphur Hounds' cover was blown. I gathered they wanted to take us by surprise bursting from the concealment of their allied smoke screen; teeth and gore would have been on us before I had a chance to call Ikron. 'It's not worth thinking about! Remember the Slaughter Hand and Moggins,' puffed Nanna, answering my worried thoughts.

The howls and grinding roars filled the air, replacing the hisses and moans of the malevolent fog. Mr Milly was glistening looking this and that way, protecting our space. The ground shook, pounded by the dreaded Sulphur Hounds, their howls rumbling through the air, surrounding us, sounding ever closer. Mr Milly flickered, as her alter self-rose from its resting place. The callous faces sneered as we pushed past them; visibility was bad, and we looked to be running into nothing.

'How long!' I panted.

'Not far!' said Nanna, turning her head as we ran. Her expression changed suddenly as shock spread over her face. Wide-eyed, she shouted, 'Pete! Duck!' pulling me to the ground quickly as the fog parted to reveal its accomplices.

A Sulphur Hound in all its devilish glory leapt out without a moment's warning, its eyes electric red flickered with hate and desire to kill, its carbon black teeth and claws shimmered against our light as the beast sailed over our heads.

Mr Milly reacted quickly, launching herself into the air, bursting with power and fearless bravery. She hit the Hound side-on with the power of a charging rhino, her open jaw striking a ferocious bite, sinking her diamond-white fangs deep into the Hound's neck.

The beast screeched uncharacteristically in panic as light poured into its forever-damned carcass. They both hit the floor in a bundle of rolling, snarling fury, each trying to get the upper hand. Mr Milly released her grip momentarily, then diving in again she pushed hard with her hind legs, gaining the advantage. Bowling the Hound over, she bit down hard. Oily blood spilt out of the gargling foe. In one final move Mr Milly pulled the Hound's neck up off the ground while pushing down on its body and rotated her lock hard; a loud crack sounded the defeat of the beast. The wounds made by Mr Milly filled with light, eating its way through the limp body, dissolving and transmuting the cruel killing machine.

'Phew!' I said. Mr Milly whined and licked her lips with disgust, as she attempted to clear the foul, oily liquid from her now tainted snow-white fur. Nanna pulled me up, as the others howled ready to take their revenge.

'Come quick!' she said, driving me on. I sensed an urgency that I hadn't sensed before in her tone; this wasn't the training grounds, we were in ShawlInka's back yard now, and I gathered Nanna didn't want any unnecessary altercations. Even though I knew Ikron and Shelaya could despatch the Hounds and worse if it came to it. 'Come! We've enough on our plates,' she said. We gathered ourselves and made ready to run when the deceitful purple mist paused its cruel whispers, and emitted an unsettling laugh, exposing three passageways. At the end of each, a snarling Sulphur Hound fixated on taking us out. Mr Milly spun and turned to face the middle passage, hunkering down, showing no fear. 'Now, Pete! Run!' commanded Nanna under her breath. I looked at her in disarray.

'But Mr Milly… we can't leave her!' I said.

'It will be all right!' said Nanna, tugging my sleeve. Mr Milly looked back towards me; she howled and threw her head back in a 'get going' gesture. Then her focus returned to the approaching enemies.

'Come on... don't look back... trust me!' Nanna said, pulling me forward. I broke into a trot with one eye fixed on the scene behind me.

'We can take them! We can! We can't leave her!' I cried, pleading with Nanna to go back as the three terrors of the Veil circled my beloved companion.

'Don't look, it will give it energy!' she said, then the tension broke, and I knew they were on her, the roars of the Hounds filling the air. I feared the worst as my stomach hit a sickly rock bottom. I could hear her battling, Mr Milly's howls and yelps engulfed my senses. Nanna looked at my grief-stricken face, tears rolling down my cheeks. She squeezed my hand. 'It's all in hand, trust me!' she said sternly, now requesting I stop with the negative thoughts, and if I knew one thing from all this it was to trust Nanna even if I didn't have the foggiest why or how.

We broke into a full sprint, the battle still blazing behind us. The fog cleared a little, and the stone building I'd seen in Wit's feed became visible. We were around a hundred feet away when Nanna shouted, 'Now, girl! Come! Come!' she whistled an ear-piercing call out to our friend as we raced towards the eerie building. When we were about forty feet away I heard the thumping feet of the cavalry bearing down on us. I turned to get a glimpse; Mr Milly had two Sulphur Hounds in pursuit; she must have dispatched the other but not without cost as I noticed she carried a dark lesion down her front leg, but this wasn't holding her back as she covered the ground faster than the heavier built Hounds. A few seconds later and she was alongside me just as we entered the building's clearing.

'Light! It! Up!' shouted Nanna, her intention echoing deep into the dark wood, and with that command rays of laser light pure and white shot up from the ground in a circular pattern, encompassing the strange forlorn building. They joined at the top and filled out, making a dome. We crashed through the doorway unable to stop our momentum; I fell head first, Nanna only just managed to hold her footing while Mr Milly bowled in knocking an unsuspecting Ill Newley off his feet, releasing Cradlick from his vicious chokehold. The possessed copper scuttled back against the wall.

'Oh! Not you! Not him, not her,' he snivelled, his face feebly repulsed by our arrival.

'Him's a her!' I said. Ill Newley's face looked pathetically puzzled; he stared at Mr Milly and Nanna and back to me, his lip curling anxiously.

'The dog, not me!' snapped Nanna.

Cradlick, free from Ill Newley's grip, pulled himself up and planted his heavy boot firmly in the bent copper's crotch, at which he reeled with the obligatory, 'Oooowweeee!' He then proceeded to curl up like a baby, whimpering to himself.

Rosy was slumped up against the cold stone wall; her eyes were closed as she rocked, murmuring incoherently. Cradlick tried to rouse her, gently cradling her face as if a precious vase.

'Rose... Rosy...' he whispered softly. She stirred; her eyes flickered open, leaving the safety of her internal walls, to the scene of the nightmare she had been dragged into. Upon realising this she pushed back against the wall trying to get away, her pupils shrunk to a pinprick, and the whites took centre stage as we all peered at her.

'What's happening? Why...? What?' she said, confused, rubbing her head. 'Your dog? What's happened to your dog?' she stuttered. We all turned to see Mr Milly was still puffed up in her magnificent alter form.

'Ah, that's just Mr Milly… she's been working out!' joked Nanna, letting out a small self-indulgent laugh.

'It's OK, Rose, it all sounds crazy, but it's alright,' comforted Cradlick.

'Yes dear, all's in hand, all will be explained, well, as much as we can, but for now I'd ask you to just keep an open mind… OK… Trust me, dear, all's in hand,' said Nanna, her words soothing the traumatised girl's concerns.

Rosy nodded in answer, as Mr Milly approached bearing the cutest face she could muster in her battle mode. She lifted one paw into the air offering her protection and friendship. Rosy reached forward and accepted her offer, giving a pat to the first multidimensional dog she'd ever met.

Our attention was soon drawn back to the immediate danger we had fled. The Hounds roared with frustration outside the protection of the dome. Rosy's head spun around and fear spread across her face. Mr Milly turned towards the open door and let out a low growl, her fur spiking up in irritation. The fog rolled up against the light sphere, pushing its twisted faces and smoky ethereal limbs against its surface. The Hounds lurked within its cover, pacing back and forth, waiting for our exit.

'What about those? How we going to get out of here now!?' asked Cradlick. Nanna strolled over to the door opening.

'Oh don't worry about those, dear,' she said, unconcerned, closing out the lurking threat. The room plummeted into darkness as both windows were boarded. Nanna's aura pulsed and a soft glow much like her kitchen filled the room. Rosy's eyes still wide had now softened as she gazed over the beauty of her essence.

'I know…' said Cradlick, sharing the moment with her.

'Now back to you!' said Nanna sternly, her focus back on the whimpering Ill Newley.

'What! What you going to do with me?' he whined. 'Let me go, I'll take my chances outside, just let me go, you won't see me again,' he pleaded.

'Oh! No!' chuckled Nanna. 'Not now! You're just where I wanted you!' she said, pulling a piece of cord from her coat pocket. Ill Newley looked puzzled and scared; he flinched as Nanna placed the cord around his ankles. 'Hands!' she barked. The snivelling copper spat at Nanna which she reflected back upon his sorry face. She tilted her head and glared commandingly. 'Hands, now!' she shouted. He held his hands out reluctantly, realising the power of the old lady in front of him.

Nanna tied the cord loosely, much to Ill Newley's delight; his arrogance and sense of superiority got the better of him, and not being able to help himself, he sneered, 'You stupid old bat,' amused by the seemingly poor attempt to restrain him.

Nanna replied sharply, 'Oh be quiet, you horrible little man.' She looked over and nodded. 'Pete, be a dear, tighten those will you?' she said, pointing at the cords.

I knew what she meant; without hesitating I focused upon the thin, loosely tied restraints. Bringing the creative power of light forth, I pictured a suitable solution in my mind's eye, then placed my hand on the whimpering copper. Pushing the energy into my arm and out through my fingers, the manifestation instantly occurred. The glint of my new creation brought illumination through my closed eyelids. 'That will do just lovely, dear,' said Nanna as I peeked to see a heavy platinum chain glinting with etheric power round Ill Newley's ankles and wrists. I was linked to my creation, just like Ikron and the staff

310

he threw on the training grounds. The shackles responded to my thoughts, tightening at my will, much to the disapproval of the corrupted officer. The words flowed over my mind's movie screen, played by my higher knowledge.

'Flesh and spirit under lock and key.' I repeated it, sending the intention to the shackles.

'Perfect, yes, all of you must stay here… if we are to rectify this mess!' said Nanna, looking at Ill Newley.

'Here? Why here?' said Cradlick.

'No, dear, no… sorry, all of him,' she replied, pointing again at the confused captive.

'His body and soul,' I added.

'Yes, yes dear, we don't want his nasty little soul slipping out into someone else. Newley's body must remain alive if we are to swap him back,' said Nanna, tapping her head.

'We aren't here by accident, are we? The fog, this building? That night you went to the village and left me with the Major, I saw you turn towards the moor. You came here, didn't you? You planted those sealing stones in preparation,' I said, starting to piece the events together.

'Ah very perceptive, dear. I have, let's say a higher view. Like I've said before I can see a little further down the road. I can't see the exact detail of the vista, but if I squint I can get a good idea of the landscape ahead,' explained Nanna in her usual abstract way. 'Of course Wit helps, she gathers information too, it's like casting a line out into the future and pulling in a chunk of information; you never know quite what you'll get, or be given, or how far they are willing to let you see,' she said cryptically.

'You mean them... the control?' I asked.

'Yes, dear, rules! Rules! Rules! We are just bending them a bit, slipping between the lines on the pages they a written on, or not written on,' she replied, puffing her cheeks and swaying her arms, caught up in her explanation.

'Err, sounds way too deep,' said Cradlick, looking like his brain was hurting.

'So, what now?' I asked.

'Oh, I don't know, dear, it all got a bit murky after we got here,' she replied, seemingly without a care in the world.

'But you must have a plan,' I asked. Nanna walked over to Mr Milly and stroked her head bending down, looking into her piercing blue eyes.

'We have a plan, haven't we Mills? Of course we have, just don't remember it yet!' she mused. I didn't know what to say in response. I was mentally and physically exhausted and sat for a moment, giving my mind a rest from the speculation of our situation. I rummaged through my bag, seeing Blue at the bottom. I so wanted to be home tucked up with him, I was weary of these games.

I rested my head upon the wall and closed my eyes for a moment. The woods were quiet now; the Hounds had either given up or adopted a new stealthier tactic. The creak of the trees could be heard but nothing else, no wildlife, no birds. *No birds,* I thought, again picking a faint tinkling in the air outside.

'Wit,' I said.

Nanna looked up at the roof, homing in on the angelic tones. 'Come on, girl,' she said. The bells and chimes increased, filling the building's chimney stack with golden light. She burst into the room like Santa on Christmas Day, bringing such delight, taking our worries away if only for a moment. She buzzed around scattering golden dust and glitter over the earthy floor. 'Oh, isn't this cosy now,' said Nanna, commenting on the comforting glow her rosewood bird had brought.

Wit's state soon changed as she had news to tell and started to feed the images into Nanna's aura. The view was above the fog bank, but below the tops of the pine trees, we could see the light dome looking like a snow globe, only the snowy mist was on the outside, the fog bank spread wide and far.

She showed two auras deep in the thick mist, with as far to go back as to get to us. My stomach sank again as I had a horrible hunch I'd seen these auras before, like when I found the tractor keys.

'It's Buster and Ronnie, I tell you it's them!' I said sternly. One was green and the other more turquoise, but I just knew their inquisitive, mischievous ways had landed them here. I bet they'd given Mrs Smythe the slip.

'Oh… oh… Hmm, well I didn't see that coming, hmm,' said Nanna. That's when we heard them again, the Sulphur Hounds rose from the depth of the dark crevices they'd laid in and ruptured the silence once again.

The machines of doom made their presence known to all that may wander into their domain. We turned to the door, our senses aligning with the call of the stalking beasts. Ronnie and Buster didn't have a chance. I looked at Nanna, and she returned my feelings; the situation now required action that Nanna hadn't planned upon. She threw the door open, and hastily paced toward the edge of the dome, searching for a sign of the boys. Mr Milly, Cradlick and I followed, Wit buzzed around, and Nanna nodded to her astral insider, signalling her to go high for a better vantage point.

Wit streamed into Nanna's aura, albeit a broken signal, for some of the transmission was lost between the dome's interior and the cloak of the dark's fog bank. I could see the pictures in her energy; they flashed like old lightbox picture cards. Ronnie and Buster's auras were coming towards us but still too far away. The presence of the Hounds was shielded by their creator blending seamlessly into a canvas of dread. Only when they howled did it give their position away as a pulse of terror rippled out across the Veil. They were either side of the Smythe boys and moving in quick.

I looked at Nanna and gulped.

'Well you said we could take them!' she said strongly, giving me her trademark glinting wink then grabbing my hand. 'Bring him!' she said, closing her eyes while focusing on her own energy. I did the same, and the now-familiar rush of power whooshed through my core, igniting all my energy centres. He turned from the loneliness of eternity and came for me again, storming down the corridors of lives lived and lost. Ikron burst into our reality stronger than ever, his lake-blue glass armour glimmering with divinity. Nanna had shed her earthly form, and Shelaya stood in her place, strong and silent. Mr Milly was back to her majestic self. We were all ready to extinguish the Sulphur Hounds and bring the boys to safety. Shelaya looked up to the towering Ikron and then looked out into the fog. 'Come,' she said with a soft but stern tone.

We paced forward just a bit to break through the safety of the light dome's sanctuary. Shelaya held her hand out. 'Wait!' she commanded. We paused, focusing our senses upon the unseen and unheard. Something brewed; I could feel its energy. Ikron was impatient and I could feel his urge to get on with the job. I held him for a moment as my intuition won true. First came a flicker of yellow pastel lightning, sparkling through the thick layers of whispering deceitful fog, then a red one, then green, blue, orange and purple, the whole gloomy cloak of ill was alight with colour. Then came the cries and whistles.

'Wwwweeeeeoooowwwww!' rang out through the trees sounding like a tube being whipped around, as a child would do, finding amusement in its wind-like tones.

'The Rag Tree Boys,' said Shelaya.

'Moggins,' I said in Ikron's metallic tones, as I saw my beloved pirate cat burst through the grounded cloud. He hovered, the golden wings of his mechanical bat-like suit suspending him in the air for a second before he unleashed an array of impressive weaponry back into the murk. The terror in the Hounds' howls weakened as an unseen assault had opened itself upon them.

The light show intensified; bangs and booms, swooshes and ferocious fearless war cries rang out. I thought the lads had the upper hand when I picked out little Choc's voice.

'I'm on it! I'm on it! Ha-ha-ha-ha!' The thumping sound of the powerful Hound came towards us. I summoned an iron and glass hammer into my hand and took a stance ready to send this thing back into its last life. Nanna brought a ball of flickering licking light into her hands, and Mr Milly was ready to shred the sorry excuse of a mutt into pieces.

Then our stances softened slightly in surprise as the Hound appeared through the fog. It bore down on the dome with thunderous speed, only it wasn't alone. Choc was astride with a beaming smile. Behind him were Ronnie and Buster clinging onto the matted, bloody fur of the beast. They were struggling to hold on as the Hound desperately bucked and twisted, trying its best to eject its unwanted passengers. We stood back and made way for the dark emissary. In a last-ditch effort the Hound leapt through the dome, legs outstretched, claws spread wide, searching for contact. But it fell short, as the light shield stripped its shadowy dark essence, killing its momentum.

The beast plummeted to the floor its venom depleted. The boys barrel-rolled like little stuntmen and came to a halt. I walked over to the sad creature and placed my glass boot on its head. It whimpered as the cruel soul accepted its fate, transmuting into particles of ash and light. Dust blew out of the bone and skin carcass, its threat and expelled in one last breath. Choc jumped up ready to finish the beast off with his stubby orange glowing sword. 'Ooowwweee,' he said, disappointedly kicking the remains of the Sulphur Hound. 'I was gunna have him. Pow! Whoosh!' he said, spinning around, demonstrating his finishing moves. Ronnie and Buster stared up at Ikron, their jaws wide open and eyes full of wonder.

'Mr Milly?' stuttered Ronnie. Mr Milly licked her lips and let out a friendly whine.

Another howl soared with contempt for its fallen comrade, and our attention was once again cast out into the fog. We looked and waited; the lights flickered and died. Wit's feed showed the coloured auras approaching, and soon the rest of the gang came into sight, looking battle-weary but all intact; they were chatting and re-enacting their best moves.

Moggins swooped in, folding his wings as he landed and brushed up against Ikron's leg making a chinking, scratching sound.

'Watch the paintwork, old friend,' I said, bending down, getting closer, allowing our energies to blend.

'The rest fled! Something called them back,' said Ikol.

'Nar, no way, they just papped themselves,' said Okol, puffing his chest out. The others laughed and carried on playfighting.

'The ghost boys?!' said Buster.

'Are we? Are we dead?' asked Ronnie hesitantly.

Shelaya laughed. 'No, no, my dears. Well, not yet,' she said with a smile that belittled the end of one's existence. The boys both laughed uncomfortably. Ikron subsided, and I fell back into my ten-year-old form while Shelaya seamlessly faded into the folds between the two realities. The Smythe boys' relief was evident as they both sprang to their feet.

'Pete… Nanna Nuts!' they said, running over and diving into a circular embrace.

'What the dickens are you two rascals doing in the woods? Did you smell a juicy expedition!?' said Nanna. The boys nodded solemnly, truly sorry for their misadventuring. 'Well you very nearly got more than you bargained for, didn't you!' added Nanna.

Ronnie looked up from underneath Nanna's arms. 'Are they real?' he said sheepishly, looking over at the frolicking Rag Tree mob. Nanna sighed and laughed, pulling him in.

'Oh, my dear! Yes they are, these are the Rag Tree Boys. They live in Snickets, but they are hidden from human eyes most of the time,' explained Nanna.

'Like ghosts?' chipped in Buster.

'Yes and no. Do they look like ghosts now!' she said, giving a nod to Choc who came over and tapped Buster on the shoulder, winking as he verified his solidity.

'Like living dreams,' I said, trying to explain what would have seemed unexplainable in several lifetimes, let alone five minutes.

'But I have bad dreams sometimes!' said Ronnie concernedly.

'And good ones! In fact, great big fansquidlytastic ones,' beamed Nanna. The boys both chuckled as Nanna worked her magic.

'Pete, you were…? You were…?' questioned Ronnie, his words eluding him.

'The awesome! Glass knight of light!! IKRON!!! You should have seen him the field; he threw a spear through twenty trees… wwwoooshhhh!!' said Choc enthusiastically, sounding like a fight night announcer.

'Ikon?' asked Ronnie, confused.

'Yes… let's say… he's a new side of me,' I replied.

'Could you do that at… school?' quizzed Buster. I paused and looked at Nanna, not really knowing myself, and I have to say the thought of blitzing into Ikron and scaring the pants off the school's knuckleheads interested me greatly.

'Err… No! He wouldn't come for such squabbles or to massage your ego!' said Nanna, tutting at my train of thought.

'Oowweee…! That would have been great… wouldn't it? Can you imagine?' said Buster to Ronnie, setting them off into their own little conversation, fantasising about bringing Ikron to school.

The Rag Tree Boys gathered around the Smythe brothers, gleefully welcoming their new playmates into the fold. For a moment the situation was forgotten. I seemed to be constantly shifting from slightly understanding the what, where and when, to being thrust blindly into the next set of challenges. I was left feeling like a rabbit in the headlights most of the time, only settling and briefly operating in the now for small fragments of time. Wit buzzed back to the gang, her trail of glitter falling gently upon the ground like the residue of a miniature shooting star. She caught the Smythe boys' eyes, their heads drawn to the fluttering wooden bird following her flight path as she settled on Nanna's shoulder.

'Wit! You did exceptional! My friend!' said Nanna. She then leant in and whispered, 'What the dickens are we to do now!' Wit buzzed and tinkled and then suddenly stopped as the wood's ears were captivated by a new sound. A feminine, anxious call came over the airwaves for all to hear. It pierced through the blinding fog with loving serenity, and above all worry.

'Boys... boys...' came the call. I dare say on a brighter more light-hearted day it would have been a call more suited to an enthusiastic school teacher, summoning her flock back from play, but today it was fear that wove its way through the words. 'Boys... Ronnie... Buster... Boys,' it came again. The Smythe brothers' heads spun around and looked out into the thick fog bank.

'Mum... MUM!!!' they shouted, clambering to their feet. Nanna caught them and pulled them back.

'Wait... wait a moment.' Then a second voice boomed out, gravelly and rough.

'Come on, lads... let's be having you!'

I looked at Nanna, and our eyes sighed once again.

'The Major.'

'Bob.'

We spoke in unison.

Nanna shook her head, loosening her light-heartedness. I knew she sensed something else; my intuition said she had seen this outcome, and it didn't play out well.

'Well I don't have all the cards,' she said, letting out a long, deep exhale. Despite all her strengths, the frailty of humanity and its extinguishable inevitability had a measure on her thoughts.

'Those things aren't still out there? Are they?' questioned Ronnie, his eyes heavy with concern.

'Oh, my dear… all's in hand,' said Nanna, her words offering little believable comfort. She scanned the deeply layered blanket. It whispered among itself, muttering and sniggering, giving me the feeling it hadn't played all its cards.

'Eyes of the night, fingers of fear,' they said, starting an eerie chant. Nanna looked worried, pacing back and forth, then she called out uncharacteristically, 'Bob! …Mrs Smythe!' her voice casting out a line into the blanketed pine wood.

We waited for a second until the echo of Nanna's voice lost its last reflections. Silence fell briefly until they answered. 'Liz! …Nanna!' they called back.

'Follow my voice, you're not far,' replied Nanna.

'Mum… Mum!!' called the brothers.

'Oh, thank God!' cried Mrs Smythe. We wailed out into the wood, giving them a lifeline to latch onto. I sensed an urgency in Nanna's voice, a stern look took root upon her face, then finally we caught a glimpse of them.

The fog seemed to part and appeared to be letting them through. We cried out louder, beckoning them to run towards us. The Major mustered a trot. Both looked relieved and confused with what awaited them. I wouldn't be happy until they were in the light dome with us; they looked to be home and dry when Nanna uttered sombrely, 'Oh no…' My head spun, looking at her and then looking back at the approaching lost wanderers. The fog swirled and shifted behind them; it parted, exposing a channel. A lone figure stood behind them; two Hounds came in at its side.

'ShawlInka,' I gasped.

A chalky white face gazed back across the wood, devoid of empathy. ShawlInka's features were hideously exaggerated, jaggedly carved out, forming a deep dark crevasse that you would surely lose your mind in. She wasn't cloaked or disguised as an old witch this time. *Is this her chosen form?* I mused. She was at the same time more human and less earthly. Her dark skin carried an ashen smudge, jet-black hair interweaved with Scraggen feathers dotted with white and red eyes crowned her pumpkin-sized face. Finally, her cracked, crooked mouth turned a sarcastic smile. Filled with callous abandonment for all things light, I felt her energy much more than before. She oozed detachment from the life-death scenario, above all pain and suffering were the frequencies she resonated with.

The Major and Mrs Smythe sensed her presence quickly as our gathered allies fell quiet upon her exposure. The Major cricked his neck, slowly glancing behind.

'Bloody hell!' he cursed, grabbing Mrs Smythes' hand, pulling her forward. We all started shouting; with the panic escalating, Ikron flooded back.

'Go, Ikron, go!!' cheered Choc as he swung the Earth Cracker into life. The boys flared up into action, Mr Milly and Nanna shedding their heavy shells too. I sprinted out of the dome. The Major, bewildered, tripped over a raised root and they both tumbled. ShawlInka called out in a witching tongue and the fog showed its vicious teeth, snaking, swirling and twisting around the fallen. They were quickly engulfed.

When I reached their last position they were gone.

I swung at the fog as it jeered, laughing at its successful deception. An anger rose in me, and Ikron's frustration bubbled to the surface, climaxing in a mighty roar, bringing the blade's tip down with godly power upon the wood's floor, shaking the ground beneath our feet. A low boom released a wave of energy, disintegrating the fog's nameless personas. It screeched and hissed as the wave reached its full travel, creating a clear area, but this was short-lived as the dark's deceptive shroud slowly skulked back in.

'Where are they…? Mum! Mum!' shouted Buster. Ronnie tugged at Shelaya's arm.

'Please… Miss… Nanna? Find them… please!' he begged.

Shelaya turned and crouched. 'I will… We will!' she said, looking deep into his eyes and then turning to Ikron with a fierceness now present within her light.

'What now?' I asked in Ikron's metallic tones.

'Blackend… ShawlInka played a stacked hand… I don't have all the cards… but neither does she,' replied Shelaya as her hair turned a shade darker, curling back into Nanna's normal cut. Her velvet embroidered cloak slid off her shoulders and vanished back into its native dimension before hitting the floor. The years and weight of this earthly reality brought back her well-earned laughter lines. I followed suit, thanking Ikron for his help, and shrunk back in a bright blue glow. Mr Milly sighed and sat on the pine-needled floor, licking the wound the Hound had inflicted. The Rag Tree Boys extinguished their multitude of fabulously outrageous weapons and armour.

'She was the witch at the Major's… wasn't she?' asked Cradlick.

'Hmm… Yes dear, that is the regional sales representative of the north.' She winked at me, lifting the tone. I could see what she was trying to do; she was taking the energy out of the situation, as we were all buying into it, well, all but the Rag Tree Boys who continued to lark around with their wooden weapons.

'Sales rep for what?' asked Cradlick.

'Fear… horror… nightmarish stuff… you know, that sort of thing,' puffed Nanna, swinging her arms around playfully. Cradlick sniggered. Buster and Ronnie both looked confused; Nanna bent down to the two brothers and pinched their cheeks. 'Don't you worry, we will have them back safe and sound.' They both nodded, their eyes full of emotion. Ikol and Okol came over, embracing the two brothers.

'Don't worry, lads, we will wipe that stupid smile off her face,' said Okol.

'Yeah, look at us!' shouted Choc while struggling to see straight through his crooked anti-Lurker helmet. His arms were wide apart, proud and brave. 'I mean just look at us!' he said, circling, encompassing the gathered motley crew. 'She doesn't stand a chance… Wwoooshhhh, wallop!' he shouted, swiping and swinging the now normal-looking conker.

'He's right, boys,' said Nanna, casting a flickering projection of all our alter selves. She painted a picture of great warriors, full of light, full of heart and bravery, a force that would drive the ill and cruel back until it had nowhere to go, no crevices to skulk in, until it had no other option but to turn to the light. She patted them on the back, and the imagery stopped. 'Right, where were we before it went so royally tits up?' She sighed and chuckled, and made her way back towards the stone building.

I could hear Ill Newley sniggering to himself. 'Shut your rattling,' nipped Nanna upon entering the room. The possessed copper snivelled and cowered as Nanna cast her glare over him, but the rat in him couldn't keep quiet. He jeered again from behind his raised hands, shielding the coward that had now taken full manifestation, in ironically society's pinnacle idea of just and true.

'Didn't expect that... Did you!' he said slyly, poking at the loss of Mrs Smythe and the Major.

'Oh what joy I will have, seeing your horrid little soul sucked into the back end of Blackend,' replied Nanna. 'Back end of Blackend,' she repeated with melody, then chuckled to herself. 'Everyone in here!' she called out. The Rag Tree Boys obeyed as much as they could, but couldn't resist tumbling and clambering over each other. A thirty-foot walk had never looked so difficult, as they created boy-sized obstacles out of each other. Mr Milly pulled herself up, looking a little weary and Moggins rather affectionately pounced upon her back and rode his canine companion in. I placed my arms around Buster and Ronnie, offering support to my old pals. Their minds must have been spinning with emotion.

'What's going on, Pete...? I mean... really going on?' asked Buster, his voice lacking the bullish enthusiasm he usually displayed for mysteries, quandaries and general adventuring. I didn't know what to say, being mindful of creating more fear, so I tried with a few ums and arrs, 'Well... It's unbelievable really... I know you've been chucked in at the deep end but well... it's real... really real!' I exclaimed.

Buster and Ronnie's faces both exhibited the same look of, 'Well that doesn't really help us!' so I stumbled my way into explaining further.

'It's the piece of the puzzle between life and death, the piece that's always been hidden from us. I'm only just starting to understand bits of it… Err… put it this way, if it were a sweet, it would be like a rhubarb and custard, only the flavours would be gloriously frightening and heavenly delightful… Both very different, opposites but wrapped together,' I said, quite pleased with my sweet analogy.

'Aaahh,' said Buster while Ronnie stroked his chin and nodded in agreement. Both allowed a short smile to form before the weight of the situation resurfaced and dragged them down again.

'Come on… let's see what Nanna wants,' I said, leading the boys to the building entrance.

We all gathered in the cold room, its stone walls harbouring the chill of the malevolent presence that had spread its intent over the pinewood.

'Wit, do the honours,' said Nanna, nodding at the fireplace. 'Pete, dear, shut the door, will you?' she asked, swiping her hand across. I nodded and did as she asked while Wit danced over the empty hearth which looked like it had forgotten what warmth was. She sprinkled golden dust upon the unloved hearth which suddenly birthed an etheric flame; warm and inviting. 'That's better!' chirped Nanna, rubbing her hands together. She turned her attention to Rosy who through the commotion had remained slumped against the wall in a half-comatose state. 'You OK, dear? What a lot of fuss, eh!' said Nanna. Rosy stirred back into herself, blinking back her focus.

'Yeah… Yeah… I'm fine, I think?' she stuttered, her frailty showing through. Cradlick perched beside Rosy and rubbed her arm reassuringly.

'Rosy!' exclaimed Buster upon seeing his secret crush.

'Oooowwwwee!' jibbed Ronnie to which Buster returned a scowl. Ronnie dipped his head, embarrassed by forgetting himself, Buster's eye also catching the restrained officer cowering in the corner.

'Newley! PC Newley!' he sighed.

'Blimey,' added Ronnie.

'Yes! Yes! It's all got rather complicated!' said Nanna, hands on hips, puffing over the bothersome predicament.

'What now, what about him!?' barked Cradlick, pointing at Ill Newley.

'What about the Nighlight? And the Major and Mrs Smythe…' I said, pausing, waiting for Nanna's pearls of wisdom. 'And her!! …What about her?!' My words tumbled out, clearly expressing my frustration and confusion. Nanna waved her hand, dampening my elevated concerns.

'We do what we were going to do… and what we will always do and what we've done before,' she announced, making little sense to the gathered. 'For the path may twist and turn, dip and dive but is true… give or take a few snags? We're not here by mistake, in this gloomy wood surrounded by a malicious deceitful fog. It's all as it should be… Give or take a little,' replied Nanna.

'So… what do we do?' I asked, my frustrations tamed as I meekly sought a rational answer from Nanna's multidimensional reasoning.

'We open the door to the next chapter!' she replied.

'OK!' I said, impatiently striding over to the closed door.

'No! No! Dear, not that door!' she said, halting my actions. 'The one you're going to make… With the key in your bag,' she said, looking over to my rucksack.

'The light shedder key? You put it there?' I asked.

'It's not only for the light shedder, dear,' replied Nanna. 'Well come on, chop-chop!' she said, clapping her hands.

I picked my rucksack up and rummaged past the glistening bottles of brew and the walkie-talkies, pushing Blue to one side. I felt a magnetic pull as the key snapped to my hand, its copper spiral emitting a high vibrational frequency as if charged by an unseen force. The key permeated my whole being with a sense of certainty, a sureness that the action it was about to create was the right one, the only one. It spoke to me in a coded message; no words or pictures needed, it was a knowing that it passed to me. I was supposed to be here just as Nanna said, right here, right now, this was the only path to take, which looking around the room at the assembled menagerie of beings was hard to believe, but as Nanna would say, 'As it should be.' I felt the spiral key was a marker on a twisted journey I had unknowingly taken. I held it out in my open hand, the gems and copper winding glowing orange and red.

'Where…? What do I…?' I asked, unsure on how to use it. Nanna looked over the stone walls.

'Over there, dear… opposite the door,' she said, pointing. Following Nanna's instruction I approached the chosen surface with all eyes upon me. 'Go on, dear. You know how,' encouraged Nanna. I placed my hand on the stone, feeling its physical attributes, how it was real and tangible. My senses reacted to its texture, its temperature, even the faint earthy, mossy smell it emitted. Now I held something completely different up to its surface, a device that could change all its physicalities, peeling one reality's realism away and exposing another. The key pulsed in my hand and so it started; a tiny flame ignited from the wall's surface as if a welder's flame was bursting through from the other side. The flame trailed round, drawing a keyhole shape; once the form was completed the spark extinguished leaving a solid opening.

I looked over at Nanna for reassurance; she nodded and smiled, gently mouthing, 'It's OK, dear.' I gulped and sunk the key into its keeper, making a heavy clunk that echoed from beyond. I turned the key anticlockwise a quarter turn, after which another loud clank came. I stepped back from the wall as it vibrated. A crack formed in a rectangular shape, expelling a blast of dust which filled the room. We all wafted and coughed, clearing the mucky air away. When the dust did settle it exposed a heavy, solid door with chunky, dark wood panels clasped together with robust brass braces, its riveted hinges the barrier between one reality and the next. Everyone looked at the door silently for we knew it would not lead us out into the pinewood. I'd rather hoped a blissful meadow basked in sunshine lay beyond, where we could play and forget this shadowy business, but I seriously doubted it. 'No, we have a bit further to go before that, but rest assured we will be there soon, my dear,' said Nanna, again answering my musing.

Mr Milly let out that whine again; even the Rag Tree Boys fell silent as a shuffling could be heard behind the door. We homed in on the mysterious sound as it came closer until it was right outside, then came three loud long knocks made with purpose. We all turned our eyes on Nanna, at which she shrugged her shoulders. 'Well, get the door then, dear,' she chirped in her carefree manner, not surprised or worried; detached from the drama. She nodded. 'Go on then, dear!' said Nanna, puffing and swaying her hands eagerly.

I placed my hand on the brass handle and slowly began to turn it.

To Be Continued…

ABOUT THE AUTHOR

Writing has threaded its way through Scott's life, surfacing over the years in different formats, from creating fantasy scenarios for his younger brother to play with, to spending twenty years writing, recording and performing music. Heavily influenced by the nineties Seattle music scene, Scott's writing is embroiled with grungy streaks from that era. Now Scott's creative outlet has surfaced in the form of his first novel, *The Veil Trap*. Set in his childhood home of the Yorkshire countryside, Scott takes us back to his youth, and tells a story of awakening, played out in the setting of his grandmother's home and surrounding rugged countryside.

Scott's passion of the metaphysical and spiritual field started at a young age. With an overzealous imagination, company was difficult to find that could match his enthusiasm for tales of UFOs, aliens, life on far-off planets or mysteries of the paranormal. These interests resurfaced again in adulthood, bringing Scott to a deeper understanding of life events and experiences, entwining his beliefs with his writing, albeit now dressed up in theatrical attire.

Scott lives in Warwickshire and enjoys family life. He has worked as an engineer since leaving school which always provided a stable platform from which to explore his passions.

AFTERWORD

Dear reader, thank you for joining me on this journey. I hope it has kept your interest, and that you will continue to follow Pete and his companions, as they adventure further into the Veil.

For news on upcoming releases. Sign up at:

www.theveiltrap.com

Any reviews would be most helpful in getting the book noticed. Please leave these at:

Amazon.com

Thanks for your time.

Now… *"Tea? Toast?"*

Printed in Great Britain
by Amazon

40861012R00193